## PRAISE FOR OTHER NOVELS BY STANLEY GORDON WEST

### Blind Your Ponies

"Stanley West writes novels that transform the world. In this tender story of love and courage and grit, he gives each reader a vision and a dream. This is the best reading you will find."
  Richard Wheeler, award-winning author of *The Fields of Eden*

"Stanley Gordon West, one of my favorite authors, has done it again. *Blind Your Ponies* is the kind of novel that takes years to write . . . but well worth the wait. A wonderfully haunting book . . . where every character has a ghost, and every ghost has a great story to tell."
  Steve Thayer, author of *The Weatherman* and *Silent Snow*

### Amos: To Ride A Dead Horse

"West's first novel is powerful and moving . . . a celebration of the human spirit . . . a heart-stopper, a strong, unblinking deeply human tale." *Publishers Weekly*

"West has penned an unusual, well-written novel . . . The book features some marvelous descriptive passages that will be remembered long after the last page has been turned. The skillful plotting and the warm human relationships make it exciting, first-rate reading." Judy Schuster, *Minneapolis Star Tribune*

"I have just finished *Amos*—an extraordinary book. I read it straight through—literally unable to put it down . . . it is a celebration of the capacity of the human spirit for compassion and sacrifice and courage . . ." Millicent Fenwick

## *Until They Bring the Streetcars Back*

"It's great storytelling. Reminded me of *The Last Picture Show*. A wonderful way of life was dying, and nobody could stop it."
   Steve Thayer, author of *Weatherman* and *Silent Snow*

"Stanley West, an extraordinary novelist and storyteller who writes with searing beauty and truth, has written a lyrical and moving novel . . . a story that pierces to the core of life . . . compelling reading for people of all times and places . . ."
   Richard Wheeler, Golden Spur Award, author of some fifty novels

"One of the most gripping books I read all year."
   Marjorie Smith, *Bozeman Daily Chronicle*

## *Finding Laura Buggs*

"A story that reaffirms the miracle and wonder of life, and ultimately its preciousness . . . a terrific, uplifting read, written with great insight and compassion."
   Harvey Mackay, New York *Times* best-selling author of *How To Swim With the Sharks*

## *Growing an Inch*

"This third volume in [West's] St. Paul trilogy is a charm—"
   Mary Ann Grossmann, St. Paul Pioneer Press

"A young boy takes you on an emotional journey as he faces life at its most unbearable and its most sublime. Just when you think everything is fine, he gets slugged in the guts. A feel good story you can't put down. "
   Bill Neff, PhD, Professor of Film and Video, Montana State University

STANLEY GORDON WEST was born in Saint Paul and grew up during the Great Depression and the World War II years. He graduated from Central High School in 1950 and attended Macalester College and the University of Minnesota, earning a degree in history and geology in 1955. He moved from the Midwest to Montana in 1964 where he raised a large family. He now resides in Minnesota. His novel *Amos: To Ride A Dead Horse* was produced as a CBS Movie of the Week starring Kirk Douglas, Elizabeth Montgomery, and Dorothy McGuire and was nominated for four Emmys.

# YOU ARE
# MY SUNSHINE

*A Novel by*

# Stanley Gordon West

LM

Lexington-Marshall Publishing
Shakopee, Minnesota

Published in the United States by Lexington-Marshall Publishing
P.O. Box 388, Shakopee, Minnesota 55379

ISBN 978-0-9656247-3-2

Book design and production by Judy Gilats
Printed in the United States by McNaughton & Gunn, Inc.

1 3 5 7 9 10 8 6 4 2

First edition: October 2013

# PROLOGUE

WHEN ABRAHAM WAS A BOY he didn't dream of going west to make a fortune in the fur trade. Abraham didn't dream of going west to strike it rich prospecting for gold or silver and he didn't dream of going west to fight the Indians. Neither did he dream of going west to follow the railroad and speculate in land grants. Abraham dreamed of going west to build a ranch and raise cattle, a novel—and somewhat strange—idea to all those with whom Abraham shared his dream. Living on a farm in Ohio with his family he knew that dream was his destiny when he was only nine years old. Little Abraham announced this dream to his parents one day and they nodded indifferently, sure that next year he'd want to be a sailor and next a carpenter and eventually settle on the family farm and work side by side with his father, only occasionally glancing to the west.

"Don't you want to run the farm some day, son?" his stoic father would ask.

As the years passed Abraham herded their few hapless Guernsey cows around the farm riding an old mule. He sneaked up on rustlers and Indians and hanged desperadoes and horse thieves and he lassoed anything that wasn't moving, including his two sisters and little brother. He loved books and read everything he could lay his hands on about the West. He went to work after eighth grade but kept reading with an insatiable curiosity.

Besides growing up with animals and planting and harvesting crops, Abraham had worked with a carpenter for several years and could build a house from the ground up with his own hands. He learned from a blacksmith how to shape metal and

1

shoe horses. Not to overlook the danger he would face, Abraham practiced religiously with the muzzle-loader until he was an excellent shot and could reload three times in a minute, even impressing his father who wasn't easily impressed.

When he was twenty, he'd grown into a thick-set, powerful young man with iron-like determination and an unflagging vision. He told his wife Kathryn that he'd send for her when he built a cabin and got established. When folks realized Abraham was really going to go, there were those who thought he was crazy giving up the good life in Ohio. Others figured he was stupid to venture out into that wild and untamed land. Some of the more tenderhearted couldn't understand him leaving Kathryn behind shortly after their marriage. But a few applauded his fortitude and bravery to meet his destiny in the West.

People gathered early one morning when word spread that Abraham Rockhammer was leaving. Family and neighbors and the inquisitive strangers gathered as he finished loading his sturdy wagon and hitched up his two pair of Belgian horses. He trailed Poke, his large saddle horse, behind the wagon and said his goodbyes. When he was about to climb onto the wagon, Betty Barlow, a short, chubby neighbor, came puffing up the road in a genuine state of panic, calling for Abraham to stop. With the instinct of a mother bear, she climbed into the back of the wagon and, after digging around in Abraham's stores and equipment, she came out tugging Tommy, her eight-year-old boy.

"See what you've done, Abraham," she said, "put all these foolish notions in a young boy's head."

Not out of the yard and Abraham had a stowaway.

"That'll burn the beans," Abraham said and let out a belly laugh. Tommy screamed and cried as his mother took him by the ear and marched him home. Abraham figured there were others in the small crowd who were silently itching to join with him on the adventure of their lives. With the large-grub stake he'd started to frugally save when he was twelve, he swung his strong, husky body up onto the wagon seat. His parents were against it up to the very end, kept saying it was too dangerous to go out to that wilderness, where he'd most likely get scalped or worse.

But as Abraham settled in the wagon and took up the reins, his father handed him a leather purse stuffed with two hundred and sixty-five dollars to add to his grub stake, enough to stay afloat an additional year and perhaps a token of his father's quiet support. With a smile on his face and joy in his heart, Abraham started his horses. A bunch of chickens blustered out of the way, protesting, and a handful of children and dogs ran alongside for a stretch and then gave up.

At eighteen, Kathryn displayed a wise understanding, knowing Abraham had to take a run at his boyhood dream. She and her little sister Martha waved enthusiastically as the teams hauled the heavy wagon down the road. She was hoping to hear from Abraham by the end of the summer to follow him west. It was as if she sensed she would be the first of many Rockhammers to follow him into this grand adventure to become actors in this push westward.

A few dubious neighbors shouted their good wishes and then he was on his way, with a lump in his throat and, for Kathryn, an ache in his heart.

The first time he laid eyes on the valley, Abraham was certain God had led him to the Promised Land. He believed without a doubt that God created these magnificent meadows of sweet native grass, watered by this clear rushing river, for the sole purpose of raising cattle. He knew it first belonged to the buffalo, and he wished they were still abundant like so many other animals, but on his journey across the high plains, he could see, and he heard from others, that the buffalo were being driven out and killed off, in some cases slaughtered.

He heard tell there were still Indians here—Blackfeet mostly—and that they occasionally harmed white settlers but he had faith that he would befriend any Indian he met and they would in turn offer him friendship. In that way he moved steadfastly forward with his plans.

# ONE

HE WAS MAKING GOOD TIME in early afternoon, the horses steady, the harness holding true. The Belgians strode as though they knew where they were going. In a way he couldn't believe how smoothly it was going, across this great grass sea.

He'd had some normal trouble and minor breakdowns but mostly he enjoyed jawing with other settlers about things like the time a porcupine wouldn't let him back into his wagon or the day a large cow moose ran off with his red long johns he was hanging out to dry. An old timer told him: If he ever found himself nose to nose with a coiled rattler, piss on it! That would drive it away instantly. Abraham heard this advice in the presence of several women and wondered how they would accommodate this advice. He didn't know if he should laugh or blush. Some of the niceties from Ohio hadn't followed them out here.

They had seen no Indians.

Urging his teams, he was surprised by a single wagon pulled off the trail a ways into a dry-grass meadow. He reined his four Belgian drafts and slowed. He couldn't see any people and immediately sensed danger. Someone had turned off the trail in a failed attempt at staying out of sight. Abraham scanned the wild landscape that was scattered with large glacial boulders and sagebrush. After what he'd heard about the Blackfeet, he felt forewarned. He hesitated and attempted to go quietly up the trail.

But as he picked up the reins and started to prod the horses he saw children playing in the woods, could hear their high-pitched voices and Abraham relaxed.

This was no Indian trick.

"Hello," he shouted and stopped his horses off a bit. Several faces peered from the wagon like little raccoons while he jumped down and shook off the trail dust.

"Hello," a handsome middled-aged woman said as she gracefully climbed down from their outfit as though she'd done that a thousand times. A flock of children came from all directions and Abraham thought that was what he wanted, a flock of children. Two of the boys looked to be in their teens, old enough to help with the adult work, and a man sat in a homemade chair in the shade with a blanket over his lap.

"You got trouble?" Abraham asked as the family unconsciously drifted closer.

"Yes, we have trouble," she said and she stood beside the man in the chair with a hand on his shoulder.

"If I can be of any help I'd be obliged. I'm Abraham Rockhammer, coming from Ohio, on my way to stake a claim."

"Good to meet you, Abraham," she said, "we're the Olson family, coming from Indiana. I'm Helen."

"Horseflies, we've come a long way, haven't we?"

"Your wife with you?" Helen asked.

"No. I'm alone."

Abraham thought somehow she didn't fit out here and it seemed strange that Olson didn't stand, didn't shake hands, which was the custom here in the West, but the man didn't look well, kind of pale. Abraham noticed the family grew tense and a few of them backed away a step or two as if something was about to happen and the playing stopped.

"Yes, we have trouble," Helen said, with anger in her voice and Abraham thought they were acting suspiciously, like they were hiding something.

"You been held up long?" Abraham asked.

"Long enough to turn around," the sullen man said.

"Oh, gosh no, you don't want to give up so soon. There's a whole new world out there just waitin' for us."

"It isn't giving up too soon," Olson said, "it's giving up too late."

"Can I help get you rolling again? Your outfit looks shipshape."

Abraham went down on one knee and checked the wagon's rear wheels. Their horses were hobbled a short way into the aspen woods.

"Thank you, but this outfit isn't going to roll again anywhere," Olson said, as he followed his wife with his eyes. She moved around behind him and took hold of the wood chair. Abraham quickly surmised that she was at the end of her rope. She sighed deeply. The sorrow in her face called for mercy.

"We've had some bad luck," Helen said as Abraham scanned their camp and still came up with nothing amiss, nothing out of line.

The children had melted into the woods as if they were expecting something at any moment and an unspoken tension had settled over the family like storm clouds.

"Your horses are in good shape," Abraham said.

"I tell ya the horses aren't the problem," Olson said.

He became agitated and she patted him on the back and steadied the crude chair. It was only then that Olson jerked the blanket from his lap. His left foot. It was gone.

The shock from what he saw nearly knocked Abraham down. "Holy Jesus! God almighty, Oh Lord, Oh Lord!"

Abraham couldn't breathe, all air sucked from his chest, his legs started to buckle, and he had to grasp one of the wagon wheels. Olson's wound was heavily wrapped, blood seeped from the bundled atrocity. The family stood silently, helplessly. Abraham looked into Olson's eyes for a heartbeat and then had to look away from the soul of God.

"Is there anything I can do?" Abraham asked with choking voice.

"Can you get me another foot?"

Abraham winced at the man's brave sense of humor.

"God almighty, what happened, a wagon wheel nail you?"

"It was no wagon wheel," Helen said, "no wagon wheel."

Abraham couldn't comprehend the horror, the brutality. All of them stood paralyzed, staring at the ground like earthen statues unable to answer the question. Abraham had a powerful urge to hug the man and woman and all the children who hungered for mercy but he couldn't make his body move.

"Who would do this?" Abraham asked as he caught himself stealing a glance at the bloody stump.

"Four rogue Indians," Olson told him. "I was helpless, they had a knife at my son's throat."

"I'll bet they had alcohol as well," Helen said.

"What are rogue Indians?" Abraham asked.

"They are rebels, usually young, who have broken away from the tribe," Olson said. "They accept no authority, no allegiance to chief or tribe. They honor no agreements with the Army, obey no local laws or government, and feel free to raid and kill as they choose."

"These are my bloody words to them: 'Go to hell,'" Helen growled.

Abraham stayed two days, doing what he could to help care for the man but Olson seemed to be failing. Word had been passed up that an oncoming wagon string had a doctor in tow and hope or miracles in his medicine bag. Abraham grew attached to the family, especially the kids he played with in the woods the way he planned to play with his own kids on their ranch. When they said good-bye, Abraham found it hard to meet Helen's eyes when she looked into his and he saw there a quiet desperation. This isn't the way he expected it to be, all that he'd read. They hugged each other with a surprising intensity and both found it hard to let go.

Then, with a new and brutal education under his belt, he drove his pairs into the foothills, alone and singing a popular tune of the day, "You are my sunshine, my only sunshine."

Abraham knew after circling and backtracking and sitting on a smooth boulder for hours and listening, meditating, and contemplating, that this was *the* valley, *his* valley, the valley that he'd known when he was nine years old.

Could that be, a bald-faced miracle? Did he come all this way overland believing the valley was there? And even more incredulous, that with a few tattered maps he'd find it! Well he'd found it and he'd never be able to erase it from his mind and heart. Far better than his wildest dream, feeling guided to this place, he drove slowly through a narrow gorge, afraid he'd break an axle or wheel on the rock-strewn passageway, guessing this was the first wagon that ever dared pass through this partly hidden passage.

Then, like a huge curtain on a gigantic stage, the country opened, spreading out before him a vast valley cradled in snow-crested mountains. He would gladly give up his claim to this land and move on except for the reality that, if he did, other pale faces would come and stake their claim, and others behind them, and others behind them. . . .

The Blackfeet reputation kept most settlers at bay but even with the gruesome evidences of rogue Indians, Abraham harbored hope that they could live peaceably with such a vast expanse of country. He even thought, naively, that he could go his whole life without running into any of them.

There his long journey from Ohio came to its end with a prayerful thanksgiving and a shout of joy that echoed its welcome off the bedrock and steep canyon walls. It seemed that the wagon sagged and the horses shook off the trail dust as though they knew they were home. From a modest farm in Ohio, with a young boy's dream, he'd come across a continent, but not easily. All the broken wheels and a lame horse; he outlasted countless storms: hail, sleet, lightning, and snow; he tried to outrun swarms of insects, mud, rattlers, needle-sharp prickly-pear cactus, more mud; he crossed swollen, angry rivers, avoided grizzly mothers and all manner of sickness or broken bones.

The unyielding, uncompromising encounter with the West could not quench his enthusiasm. He marveled at the tremendous mass and towering height of this awesome display of the naked earth. The mountains marched toward him each day on the far horizon, coming slowly like a frozen avalanche. The overwhelming shock of their vast, looming presence, was grander than any image his mind could have conceived.

He had left a large train of wagons and turned north into uncharted land with a handful of other daring settlers until one by one they turned off in search of their private dreams. Then he was alone.

A great silence hung over the earth, embracing him with its unseen presence, as if he were Adam, the only person on the paths of the earth. He slowly surveyed his camp, nestled in the pines and aspen, his wagon and tent, horses feeding and swishing their tails, the sun about to set in the West in a nearly cloudless sky. The heart of the little boy from Ohio nearly burst with joy. He was home.

He had been gone more than a year and though he mailed letters, Kathryn couldn't answer until he had an address. The only thing he hadn't prepared for was the solitary existence.

He would learn the Blackfeet called it *The River That Rolls Rocks* and in spring, it could become like a buffalo stampede, as melting snow frantically rode the beast of gravity in its desperate search for the soft ocean blue. He slept in the wagon and every morning when he woke he felt like a young boy on his birthday who couldn't wait to open his presents. At times he'd find it hard to believe he was "there." He'd catch himself, standing, gazing out over the land, hypnotized by his childhood dream. Sometimes it scared him, out there utterly alone and he'd talk aloud, first to Kathryn and then, after awhile, aloud to himself, a bit worried that he was losing his marbles.

There was so much to do and so much to see and he had to keep reminding himself that the cabin had to come first. The only higher priority, by necessity, was a sturdy corral to pen the five horses at night with the many flesh-eaters roaming around the camp.

He began building with great enthusiasm, wanting the tightest cabin possible. It was hard work and he was tempted to start on other things but he knew he had to keep the cabin at the top of the list. He told himself old jokes and laughed out loud; some jokes he remembered the beginnings but couldn't come up with the punchlines.

He was at peace being there, finally reaching his true home. Knowing he was utterly alone did not deter him, though occasionally he felt something dark and unnamed. He well understood that if he fell and broke a leg or became incapacitated in any way, he would probably die alone and unfound for days or weeks or forever. He wondered if that would be a final punch line.

# TWO

ON RARE OCCASIONS Abraham solicited help from travelers who had wandered aimlessly until by accident they found his camp. He welcomed them—mountain men, trappers, prospectors, and the like—who helped him set a heavy log or some difficult task in return for several meals, news of the world, and protection during the night. They would awaken his deep longing for Kathryn and he would lull them to sleep reminiscing about her.

One day a tall seasoned man with a large pack and a fur-lined hat spotted Abraham's camp and hiked in.

"Boy am I glad to see you," Abraham called as the man approached. "You're like answered prayer."

The man slipped off his bulky pack and extended his hand.

"Name's Sparks."

"Well then you shouldn't have any trouble starting a fire," Abraham said with a laugh.

They shook hands, each trying to out-muscle the other as young bucks tend to do. Abraham was impressed with Sparks's strength and Sparks by this young man's iron.

"I am Abraham Rockhammer. Welcome to Rockhammer Ranch. You're just in time for supper."

"Thank yah. I could smell your beans a mile downwind."

Abraham wiped a tin plate on his pants leg and guided Sparks to the bench beside the stove. This was exactly the kind of man Abraham hoped to meet. Sparks was well-worn and half his clothes were animal fur, his hat beaver.

"Where are you headed, where have you been?"

"Been in Canada, heading for Hitching Post. Heard there was a big strike around Hitching Post. You hear any word about it?"

"No, no, I don't get much word about anything up here, but I think you're too far east if you're going to Hitching Post."

"Yah, well, I think I'm temporarily lost."

Sparks laughed from deep in his chest and held out his plate. Abraham dumped another spoonful of beans and oatmeal and took more himself. He hoped Sparks would stay but the daylight was fading fast. Abraham kept him talking and drinking coffee but he could tell the man was anxious to be on his way.

Sparks wanted to reciprocate after such hospitality but he was planning to hike out of this valley before dark.

"I s'pose," Sparks said as he stood and walked over to his hefty pack. "I sure thank yah, it was good having someone to talk to."

"Yeah, I don't have many conversations out here except with the moose and ravens and a whole bunch of other critters."

He helped the prospector sling the pack on his back.

"It feels like you have about fifty pounds of gold in here," Abraham laughed lightly.

"Oh, the gold ain't in here."

"Well, pardon me for asking, but where is it?"

"Down the trail a spot. You don't expect me to go hiking into some unknown camp with gold in my pocket, do yah?"

"Well, by golly, I wondered about that, how you'd get around with gold in your pocket."

Abraham held out his hand and they shook. He was the tough rugged man that Abraham looked so forward to meeting.

Sparks felt something unfinished and caught Abraham's eye as they parted.

"Don't forget your gold," Abraham said.

Sparks turned after a few steps. "What did you mean about answered prayer?"

"Don't want to hold you up," Abraham said.

Sparks turned back to Abraham. He took hold of Abraham's shoulder with one hand and looked into his eyes.

"My good friend, there is something I can do for you."

"What about the strike?"

"I can let them do all the heavy digging and then I come in and do my panning. Can I help you with the cabin, with a heavy log or two?"

"You'll lose the last of daylight if you don't go now," Abraham countered.

"I am tired. I can stay the night." Sparks slipped off the pack once again and set it down. "There, now, what are we going to do?"

Abraham smiled. "Come with me."

He led Sparks toward the river, through the aspen and sage, out onto the grassy slope above the cabin site Abraham had chosen. With excitement in his voice he outlined his plans for the ranch and, as always, filled his dream with lots of children. Sparks picked up on Abraham's enthusiasm.

Abraham told him: "I bought an old church bell from a man in the wagon train, the bell was too heavy for his outfit. I want to hang it near the cabin as a way to signal to the family. When they are all here, we can ring it to celebrate the important events in my family's lives. Right, they aren't born yet!"

Sparks didn't speak for a moment, Abraham held his breath. Did his guest think he was a little cuckoo?

Sparks could sense that the bell had come to represent a spiritual quest to this young man and he wanted to be a part of it. He walked down to the bell and studied the crossbar Abraham had fashioned. The mountain man hadn't said a word. He gazed out over the valley, as daylight slid away.

"I think it's the best damn thing you could do," Sparks said, fingering his bearded chin, "right here, in this place, where it was cast to belong, and I'd be honored to do it with you."

Sparks slapped his hands together.

"Lets hang the bell!"

"All right, by golly, first thing in the morning."

They sat around a small fire as darkness came on. They talked quietly into the night. Abraham kept building up the small fire; for some reason, Sparks kept holding it down. The fire crackled with its own language.

"You all right?" Sparks asked.

"What do you mean?"

"Out here alone."

"Oh yeah, it's beautiful, waited my whole life for this."

Abraham hoped there was no doubt in his voice.

"You see any injuns?" Sparks asked quietly.

"Yeah, a while ago. Didn't see them. Saw their handiwork, a poor fellow lost a foot. Didn't know if we should talk about it, you know, stirring the pot. Don't think there are any around here."

"Oh they is around," Sparks said as he stared off into the night. "They is plenty around, you just don't see 'em."

Abraham felt a shiver slide down his back.

"Have you seen any lately?"

"Don't see 'em, I feel 'em. Sometimes it's better you see 'em out in the open, then you know they ain't comin' after yah."

"Have you actually seen some?"

"Seen signs . . . their signs, they been here, in this valley."

Though he didn't realize it, Abraham scanned the darkness behind them with a new vigilance. The night seemed cooler, he traced shadows from the dancing fire and heard sounds he hadn't noticed before.

Sparks pulled out a harmonica and began to play as if he knew it was Abraham's favorite song.

*You are my sunshine, my only sunshine, you make me happy. . . .*

"You got family?" Abraham asked, changing the subject to something more pleasant.

"Got seven youngsters."

"Seven children! My God, man, what'er you doing out here?"

"I'm finding gold for my little darlings so we can buy a ranch, so we can have a nice place. I been working at it several years."

"When were you last home?"

"Oh," Sparks tossed a chunk of wood on the waning fire. "Oh 'bout a year or so, when the last one was born. It was a girl. We named her Lily."

"Your wife raises the bunch?"

"Yep. They all raise each other. Gert's a tough gal, my wife, I send them gold, I sure do. When it calms down out here I'll bring a few of them older ones with me; I already showed 'em how to pan."

Abraham knew it wasn't his business to stick his nose in but he figured Gert would rather see Sparks coming down the road than all the gold in the territory. Still, she must welcome him when he does appear. Maybe she's happy. Abraham could imagine those kids, gazing to the horizon, watching for their father, lonely, hopeful. He promised himself it would never be like that at the Rockhammer ranch. No prodigal father he.

It was a safe bet that night that Sparks fell asleep first and they both woke with their scalps intact.

In the morning they hung the bell, though it took the best of them. Abraham, his shirt dripping with sweat, and Sparks, puffing like a man dragging a dead horse uphill, was catching his breath.

"She was tougher than I thought," Sparks said.

They paused and regarded the old bell that had hung in a church back in the eastern states somewhere.

"This is where she belongs," Sparks said.

Abraham handed the clapper rope to him to do the honors.

But sensing how important this was for Abraham, the prospector deferred. Abraham took hold of the rope and called out across the valley.

"May this valley be henceforth known as Rockhammer Valley with a welcome and shelter to all those who travel this way."

Abraham pulled the rope and the clapper slammed against the heavy brass and the bell peeled majestically out across the land and up through the foothills to the peaks. He rang it over and over, dancing a little jig under the bell. It was a christening, a baptism, a crowning, a celebration, as if the Rockhammer Ranch now had its official beginnings.

When Sparks left that morning, Abraham picked him off the ground with a powerful bear hug, the only way Abraham could think of to express the affection he felt for the man.

"If you're ever in the neighborhood, be sure and drop in with your wonderful wife and children."

As Sparks started down the path, he shouted back over his shoulder.

"God bless ye, Abraham Rockhammer, take care, good friend." But he couldn't leave it at that. He turned and called. "Abraham, I got something to tell you."

"You forget something?"

"The truth, I forget the truth."

"What are you talking about?" Abraham asked.

"I have no family, I'm not married, made it all up."

"You mean there's no Gert, no kids, no Lily?"

"I don't send gold to anyone, made it all up," Sparks said. "They're my make-believe family, I'm alone. I'm sorry for lying, it just come out the way I thought it should, hoped it would. For a while last night it came true. It *was* true. I had a wife and family, and people who cared about me. I felt good inside and I wanted to feel that way with the next folks I meet. I'm shamed for giving you such a story."

Abraham stood numbly, knowing exactly how Sparks felt. Sparks turned and hurried down trail without a word.

"You are real for me," Abraham called. "And you're my friend and I hope to see you again."

Sparks walked away but he felt a strong emotion to turn around, to stay, to belong.

Besides building a sturdy horse corral, Abraham worked on the cabin from dawn to dusk through a mild winter. Each morning he'd open the flap on the wagon and hoot with excitement when he'd see the cabin, a sturdy naturally built home, rising up magically in that glorious setting, his and Kathryn's dream coming true.

He was nearly finished when the Blackfeet burned it. He couldn't believe it though he feared it daily. He rushed through the camp shouting, taking inventory, what they had taken, what they had destroyed.

"Come back you sneaking skunks. Fight me even," Abraham shouted in desperation.

He had taken the trip to the closest settlement for supplies and to send Kathryn a joyful letter, telling her to come to Buffalo Jump, his new address.

Wasn't much of a town, Buffalo Jump, still as much a trading post as when it had its beginnings years earlier. A dozen scattered buildings in various stages of construction and twenty or thirty folks you'd never know if they'd be there come morning. Indians would show up from time to time to trade; word was that the little settlement had survived because Julian Black, the young owner and proprietor of the only store, had traded with the Indians to their mutual satisfaction when that wasn't a popular thing to be doing in the eyes of the scattered settlers.

The trip took a long two days with the wagon and two of his faithful Belgians who had recovered from their long, cross-country trek and were getting lazy and fat. He trailed his saddle horse, Poke, feeling that leaving him four days unattended was too much of a temptation for anyone. Abraham restocked with essentials and Julian had some fresh eggs and milk.

Abraham had been wise enough to stash everything of value in a cave behind the camp in a thick lodgepole grove. He left such furniture he had carried west to whomever might have the wherewithal to haul it off. His camp sat so far into the trees and sage he figured the Indians would likely be the only ones who would find it. But he was relieved to discover upon his return that nothing had been disturbed.

Abraham enjoyed getting to know Julian, who he guessed was about his age and who carried his sense of adventure into this raw outpost. Julian Black's mustache didn't hide his buck teeth and the large man wore a beaver pelt hat that appeared to be sewn on his scalp. Abraham didn't have the gumption to ask him if he'd been scalped, but he liked him right off and found him to be an affable young man, enterprising. Julian was already a town booster, believing that one day Buffalo Jump would be a thriving town with a railroad spur. Both of them had a bride-in-waiting in some far-off civilized world, so they would compare their experiences with nods and understanding. Julian helped Abraham load the wagon and was happy to get good hard cash and coin.

Abraham found the cabin all but burned down. He never saw the Blackfeet but he could taste the bitter disappointment of their calling card.

"God Almighty, come and fight like a man, you son of a bitch," he shouted out across the foothills. "You sneaky, slimy snakes."

Surveying the damage, he figured he could use a few of the better logs that hadn't caught fire, that it was part of getting established here, a test of endurance, a neighborly warning. But he felt a deep, frozen fear as he looked at the wounded building that represented his bright future.

What if he'd been there? Would he shoot at them? Could he kill a man with his powerful rifle? Should he stay in this valley or find a place closer to Buffalo Jump? One voice said move on.

He listened to the other voice.

Abraham got to work keeping an eye to his back. The weeks marched by and he worked hard into early spring, taking advantage of the lengthening daylight, the warming weather, and expecting the Blackfeet any moment. A few weeks, and he'd be done.

In the excitement of the moment, he wanted to know if Kathryn had received his letter. He buttoned down his camp, penned the horses, and rode to town on Poke, sure he could make it in one day. And he did, urging Poke on a wild ride that took shortcuts he couldn't travel with a wagon. And yes, he had a letter from Kathryn. Abraham read it quickly and started jumping around the store.

"She's coming! She's on her way! Hallelujah!"

Julian clapped his hands and shouted along with Abraham. He was the only person who knew a little of what was going on in the rest of the world, on occasion even having a newspaper that was only six weeks old. He let Abraham sleep in the store and Abraham read Kathryn's letter many times by lamplight. He dashed back the following day, worried sick for his horses. He pictured them cut down and butchered in the shallow snow. When he raced through the gap and galloped to the cabin, he found the horses safe and well.

He settled in, chinking walls and splitting shingles and setting some of his furniture into the little dirt-floor cabin. He could visualize Kathryn making her home here and he stared into the mirror as he cut back his beard, afraid he'd scare her with his woolly black nest.

A month later, when he went to town to resupply, they burned his cabin again.

"If you don't get out of there, if you don't leave," Julian said, "the next time they'll chop off a hand or just kill you. They killed two prospectors up a gulch a few miles west of here a couple weeks ago."

Julian worried about Abraham, didn't want him to get himself killed by being brave, but he also wanted him to stay, one of his only friends in this wilderness.

"Why don't you stay here in town for awhile," Julian said, with his own feelings muddled, and tasting fear in his own mouth.

"The horses," Abraham said and shrugged.

"Oh great, they'll say he went down with his horses."

Abraham took the warning to heart—he couldn't imagine fighting the Indians. He'd heard tell about the bloody fighting that had gone on between the Blackfeet and the Crow. He realized this was dangerous country, but he'd fallen in love with the valley and he didn't know if he could just walk away, like Sparks. He'd sent the letter to tell Kathryn the cabin was finished, to come, and he didn't know how he could reach her to tell her it was gone, again. Then something happened between Abraham and the Blackfeet that changed everything.

After several hours of indecision, Abraham headed home, back to his wounded cabin with a growing, naked fear in his saddle bags. When Abraham left, Julian couldn't decide if he should cheer or cry. At the camp, Abraham went right to work and he caught himself scanning the horizon for any human sign. He wanted to show them that he was a mule-headed, stubborn man, and he was prepared to keep building his cabin as long as they kept burning it down.

Hard at work, Abraham urged one of the Belgians to drag burnt logs away from the cabin. He was watching his back when he heard a strange cry coming from the river. He couldn't immediately tell if it was animal or human. The warm, sparkling spring day had The River That Rolls Rocks roaring with melting snow, yet over that upheaval he could hear the mysterious shrieking. Were they about to trick him? He dropped the rope he'd been using to guide Samson and hurried to the river. There, on a small island of uprooted trees, jammed brush, and rock, was a young boy, waving frantically, pleading with terror in his eyes.

An Indian boy.

# THREE

THE INDIAN BOY clung desperately to a large tangle of driftwood at the edge of a raging current, being pounded by the hammer of spring run-off. The river roared as though it were trying to swallow the boy and carry him off to the ocean's deep. Baffled by the shaver's appearance, Abraham acknowledged the boy with a wave and signaled him to stay put. The native boy looked to be nine or ten. Abraham scrambled up the bank and ran for the horse. He knew he'd never be strong enough to drag the boy through that current, and he knew, when he pulled the boy into the river, the boy would never have the strength to hold onto the rope.

He hurried Samson to the river. Tying a loop at the end of the rope and sliding it over his head and under one arm, he demonstrated for the boy what he'd have to do. The kid nodded and waved, appearing to be losing his battle with the sucking river. Abraham slipped out of the rope, coiled it, and threw it upstream from the boy. As it rushed by the boy missed it. Abraham reeled in the empty rope and repeated the toss several times, while an inner voice warned him that he might unwittingly exhaust and drown the boy.

After many frustrating throws, the boy snagged it. Even with the rope empty it was difficult for the boy to hang on to it and he fought the unrelenting current with his thin little arms and a visible courage. Abraham swallowed his fear. The river raged, out for a kill. If the boy slipped free of the rope, he'd be quickly swept away and surely die. Abraham went through the motions again, showing the boy how to get the rope over his head and under his armpit. When the boy had the rope secure, Abraham spurred Samson away from the river, jerking the boy into the swollen white water and tugging Abraham's heart into his throat.

Halfway across the boy disappeared. Abraham leaped off the horse and was about to jump into the raging water when the boy surfaced, hurled by the current up onto the shore as if a great monster trout had a taste of the little Indian and spit him out. The boy scrambled onto the rocky shore where the powerful horse had dragged him through the roiling river and up onto dry ground.

Abraham helped the boy stand and get untangled. He had banged his head on something and thankfully Abraham could see it wasn't serious. The boy shivered violently and Abraham didn't know if it was from his experience in the river and the icy water or his fear of this white man. He figured on both.

Abraham got the boy into the wagon and helped him strip away his clothes, dressed him in dirty long underwear and a wool shirt, and wrapped him in a blanket. He checked the wound on the boy's forehead and saw that it was minor. Then Abraham sat him by the small cook stove and served him a plate of warm beans and some potato soup. The boy ate halfheartedly, nervously, always keeping a worried eye on Abraham as if he was ready to bolt at the first chance.

Abraham attempted to calm the boy's fear, speaking gently and smiling a lot through his bushy black beard. He wanted to ask him how he ended up in the river but the boy spoke little, only single Indian words and gestures. Abraham did manage to find out, he thought, that the boy had been separated from his people for two days, two moons. When Abraham helped the boy climb into the wagon and crawl under a large quilt, the boy, obviously worn out, fell quickly to sleep. Abraham turned the boy's buckskin clothes inside out to better dry and hung them on a small pine. He went back to work, keeping an eye on the wagon and hoping someone would show up searching for the boy. He figured the lad was no more than eight and he hoped he'd have a son like him.

With the din of the river he never heard them. A small band of Indians—Blackfeet he guessed—quickly surrounded the camp. Two of them grabbed Abraham and held him at knife point. His immediate response was to fight the two as he was much bigger and clearly stronger. Another pointed out the boy's clothing, strung out on the small pine. Abraham noticed blood on the boy's cape for the first time. The intruders spoke excitedly, words Abraham didn't recognize. So these were the cabin burners, showing their faces, the chicken-shits. He tightened his powerful body as another Indian moved quickly to help the two. One of them found his rifle standing uselessly against a corral rail.

Some were still mounted, their horses prancing around the campsite. Abraham had never seen the Blackfeet but these warriors fit their reputation splendidly. Dressed in buckskin with a variety of white men's clothing, shirts, and a few hats, they appeared to belong to the country. Some with paint on their faces or horses, and a mixture of animal fur on their clothing or weapons. Some of them had rifles, some bows and arrows, and they looked like they could fight at the drop of a hat.

Abraham thought he'd pressed his luck too far, that he should have listened to Julian Black and taken the burned cabins as serious and final warning from those whose land he was squatting on no matter how the government of the United States saw the matter. He tried to stifle his full bore panic and keep a great big smile on his face but there were too many. Even if he shook off these two, the gun would be useless. Abraham shouted.

"The boy! The boy!"

He held his hand about the height of the boy and pointed at the wagon.

"In the wagon! In the wagon!"

One of them climbed into the wagon and to Abraham's shock, came out empty-handed. It was easy to recognize their leader, a hardened, fierce-looking man who slid off his horse and shouted instructions. They quickly lashed Abraham to a log on the ground, his arms spread eagle. He strained against the leather ties. He couldn't breath. One of them grabbed the axe stuck in a chopping block and handed it to the leader. He looked like a no-nonsense character. He stepped to the log, placed one foot on Abraham's arm and raised the axe overhead.

"No! No! The wagon! Boy in wagon!"

Abraham shouted, instantly covered with sweat, baffled as to

the whereabouts of the boy. The eyes of the one with the axe narrowed. He raised the axe. About to lose his right hand, Abraham
hollered frantically while nodding toward the wagon.

"Boy! Wagon! Boy! Wagon!"

Then, one of the braves shouted excitedly and all eyes turned
to him. Their leader lowered the axe, a bit reluctantly Abraham
thought. Like a small rodent, the boy crawled out from under
the wagon seat, calling, jabbering like a chipmunk. The Indians
quickly pulled him free and began shouting and cheering and
dancing. Abraham figured the boy had hidden for fear of punishment, that he'd disobeyed his parents and ended up in the river.

The celebration calmed and the leader turned to Abraham.
He still held the axe. He barked instructions and two men hastily
cut Abraham loose. They helped him to his feet and brushed him
off. The leader walked to the chopping block and with obvious
power sunk the axe blade where it had been. Abraham flinched.
He thought the man looked disappointed, that he had been looking forward to the amputation. This boy from Ohio had seen all
he wanted of Indian hardware. Abraham couldn't help wondering if he could take this young brave one on one, Abraham certainly outweighed him by twenty pounds or more. If he wasn't
careful he might end up in Helen Olson's home for the crippled
back in Ohio, and then he told himself this wasn't funny. The
Indian spoke what Abraham guessed were words of apology or
thanks or both.

They gathered the boy's clothing, now dry, got him dressed, and
led him to his horse they'd found grazing nearby. The young native
stole a glance into Abraham's eyes in a plea for understanding.
They moved away quickly, shouting and yipping, and Abraham
began breathing again, feeling chilled and shaky, realizing how
close he came to losing a hand or much worse. Something in his
gut shouted at him to run back to that safe and happy Ohio barnyard and Kathryn's love.

Six days later the Blackfeet were back. They came into the
campsite slowly and Abraham waved a welcome. It wasn't the
same bunch, though the boy was with them. There were ten
of them. One wore a brilliant eagle-feathered bonnet. He dis-

mounted and the rest followed. They stood in a ring and then sat. Abraham sat beside the man with the bonnet. They lit a pipe and passed it around. Abraham took his turn instinctively, inhaling and puffing.

Abraham figured the man in the bonnet was some kind of a chief and he conversed with Abraham with the few words in English he knew. He used a great many gestures with his hands in a kind of sign language. He told Abraham that they would never burn his cabin again, that he wouldn't be bothered living in that valley, that the mountain had a spirit, a soul, and if Abraham treated it with respect, it would always provide him with water, good grass and timber, and game and fish. But if he dug up the iron and carved up the mountain, the valley would no longer bless him and provide him with all good things. That day Abraham promised the Blackfeet chief that he would never scar or abuse the valley as the white face had done in other places.

When they finished they mounted their horses and quickly disappeared into the great towering silence. Abraham felt overwhelmed and he was sure he understood correctly that they would no longer burn his cabin. He worked the rest of the daylight somewhat numb and that night he kept feeling for his limbs, amazed at this reprieve.

Early the next morning six young Indian men walked into his camp and, with gestures and single words, demonstrated that they were his work crew to rebuild the cabin. Abraham couldn't believe the miracle the Indian boy had brought him. He was awed and grateful. With this much help, he would surely have the cabin finished before Kathryn arrived.

They worked hard. Abraham showed them how to use some of the tools, how to notch a window and chink the space between the logs. They were impressed with how accurately Abraham measured the logs so that when they hefted them in place they fit like they had grown there. With this much manpower he built the cabin twice its planned size.

It took them most of four weeks. At first they worked with somber faces but day by day smiles grew with their enthusiasm for the cabin. They often laughed and poked fun at each other as they worked. They shouted at each other when they strained to move a heavy piece and they were often playful as they worked. Abraham felt a sadness coming on when the cabin neared completion and his six friends would vanish into the great wide land. He felt close to them, he knew their personalities, and he looked forward to working with them. He knew that loneliness was his most dangerous enemy but he figured from the letter he sent months ago, that Kathryn was long on her way. They finished a fine, sturdy weather-tight cabin that the Indians took great pride in. They laughed together when they realized that now they'd all have to protect the cabin from whoever would want to burn it, White Face or Blackfoot.

Though he heard stories of killing and scalping and burning in their name, he'd seen both sides of the fence now. Fate decreed that the Blackfoot never bothered Abraham Rockhammer again, nor did they bother his family who settled there and flourished for generations.

Abraham's far-flung neighbors were impressed with his imposing stature. Though he didn't know it, the Blackfeet, too, were struck by Abraham's physical power and gentle nature. He appeared as immovable as a granite tombstone, well over six foot, as though determined to live up to his name. No longer the small boy from Ohio, the Blackfoot called him Stone Face and his stubbornness was legendary. It was told that one autumn he stared down a grizzly in a narrow mountain pass when they each wanted to go where the other was standing. Some thought he looked like a bear with hair protruding from the long johns he wore year 'round.

Though his bullheadedness never allowed him to admit he was wrong, it fortified him to face the harsh weather, the unending work and the unforgiving land he chose to settle. He thought if he ever admitted he was wrong he would start questioning himself and waver while making decisions, something he could ill afford in this raw and primitive land.

Abraham, with a renewed excitement, began work on the gate that would span the rocky gap at the valley's entrance and prevent his cattle from straying. It took him nearly three weeks to construct and secure a strong gate to do the Rockhammers proud, a gateway that would announce to the country that a thriving ranch existed here, a gate that, if his father saw it, would nod his head in approval.

When he was done with the rough entrance to Rockhammer Ranch, his excitement knew no bounds. The time had come to start the herd.

After talking with Julian Black and reading a few hand bills, he found Clay Spoon, an experienced, knotty farmer who had a small place south of Buffalo Jump. People called him "Cowboy." Abraham never heard that nickname used with a farmer before but Spoon agreed to ride with him to buy the beginning of a herd. They rode halfway to Cheyenne to find good cattle and Clay rode a lot easier in the saddle than Abraham. They found a ranch with several hundred Longhorns that had been driven up from Texas. They took all day carefully selecting the best of the lot and they drove five pairs, cow and calf, and a fine bull, back to Rockhammer Ranch.

The first day was more like a roundup and they nearly put Poke and Clay's horse in the grave chasing the eleven animals in every direction. He and Poke would push them north and the cattle would veer to the east. Sometimes in circles, sometimes into the pines. It reminded him that this ranching business was a task for three or four or more. He needed children! Grown up children. Family. He thought of Sparks.

The riders finally settled them down at nightfall because they were run-into-the-ground exhausted. Clay roped the young bull and tied him, hoping that would hold the pairs, but they were so worn out they were contented to feed and rest and Abraham slept on the ground in his bedroll near his herd. He was a cattleman, a rancher, and he couldn't wait to get them home to the valley. He couldn't wait to show them to Kathryn. He couldn't wait to get her in his arms.

# FOUR

KATHRYN HAD MET THE WAGON TRAIN in Waterloo, Iowa, finally on her way to join her husband and begin their life together on the ranch he was building in the Rocky Mountains. They'd been apart for nearly two years while he carved a home out of the wilderness she'd heard so much about. Her patience had dried up long ago and she decided to go "home," whether Abraham was ready for her or not. Their letters must have crossed; hers saying she was waiting no longer, his telling her to come with all speed.

Her friends and family back in Ohio were starting to believe her absent husband was a figment of her imagination. Of course some of them had been at their simple wedding, but that seemed so long ago. Her younger sister Martha had been ring-bearer, a cute little girl who had since transformed herself into a young woman during Kathryn's long wait. Sometimes Kathryn thought she was going crazy. She'd abruptly start walking west as if in a daze, several miles before she'd realize what she was doing. Once she walked long into the night. Her loneliness gripped her at times and she couldn't sleep or eat and a black cloud of depression stalked her. She longed for Abraham so desperately that it hurt, physically, in her chest, her stomach, a large stone of despair. She wished he'd left her with a baby, someone to lavish her love on, who was part of him. He insisted they wait until they were together in the West before starting a family, something that added to her despondency in Ohio.

But now Kathryn was on the way, oh the joy! Weeks across the country with a wagon train of settlers all looking westward for their destiny. She paid her way with a family from Pennsylvania—Ruth and Joel Davis and their two daughters. They were happy to have Kathryn join them, helping with the expense and sharing their large wagon. Much of the journey had been trouble-free in the July weather as they gradually climbed onto the high northern plains through the tall prairie grass and often treeless horizons. The daily discomforts of blazing heat, rough river crossings, grasshoppers, mosquitoes and other insects were endured. Fearful rumors of hostile Indians kept them vigilant. The wagon master always had scouts out ahead of them and several times he had them circle their wagons for the night and keep their animals within the enclosure or close at hand. Kathryn counted thirty-eight wagons.

Sometimes, when the weather permitted and the country they were in seemed safe, they'd build a large bonfire and dance in the cool of the evening. They had banjos and fiddles and guitars and even a small piano. Two brothers from Illinois competed with each other trying to impress Kathryn even though she made it very clear that she was on her way to join her husband. The brothers were quite shy and she laughed at their attentiveness, watching them working up their nerve to beat the other to ask her to dance or fetch her a pail of water. Whatever they did for her she always responded the same with a chuckle.

"My husband Abraham and I thank you."

Kathryn grew more anxious with each passing day, achingly eager to see Abraham again, to touch him and hold him and open herself to him. Anxious to get reacquainted after what seemed a lifetime apart, anxious to see the home he had built for her, seeing at last the valley and mountains he'd written about with such joy.

They were fording a river in what had come to be called the Badlands. It was a hard crossing with steep gravel banks on both sides and large rocks to negotiate. Everyone pitched in and helped each wagon across. Kathryn and Ruth waded right in and pushed at the back of a wagon that was having trouble. The two woman chattered as they pushed, laughing.

"Have you ever had so much fun in your life?" Kathryn asked.

"No," Ruth said with a hoot in her voice, "they wouldn't allow us."

Kathryn enjoyed the cool water and the seeming recklessness of this romantic adventure. Things she'd never dreamed of doing back in Ohio. They were like a big family, facing the unknown with courage and no little trepidation.

Kathryn and Ruth leaned into it with their hands flat against the wagon box, grunting, their arms extended, their bodies bent. The wagon hesitated climbing the bank. Its four horses couldn't quite yank it over the top. The wagon master called for more help and several more men and women waded into the slow current and added their muscle to the task. Everyone pushed and tugged on the ropes tied to the front of the wagon. The wagon crawled slowly up the bank, the horses straining, farting, and grunting. But nearly at the top, the horses began losing ground, sliding back, their hooves pounding and digging into the crumbling gravel and rock.

The wagon creaked and all at once it lurched back down the bank into the river. With her hands still on the wagon box, Kathryn stepped backward quickly, dragging her long water-logged dress with her. Not quickly enough. Under water, the right rear wheel rolled over the hem of her heavy dress and in a heartbeat jerked her under.

She screamed but her mouth filled instantly. Under the water the heavy wheel rolled along her dress like a sewing machine doing a hem and it came to rest on her right arm. She struggled to pull free, kicking and paddling with her left arm, able to see the watery sky above her. The river was not much more than three feet deep but she was pinned on the gravel bottom.

Ruth heard Kathryn's scream and she turned quickly toward the oncoming wagons, thinking Kathryn was warning them. Unaware of what had happened, Ruth also shouted and waved her arms and signaled the oncoming wagons to stop. A man in the next wagon, about twenty yards back, jumped out of the seat and came running frantically, shouting. Ruth didn't understand what he was doing. She waved him back as he leaped into the river.

"Stay there! Wait! We're stuck here!" Ruth shouted.

"There's a woman under the water!" the man shouted, but it didn't register with Ruth.

He stumbled and fell, assaulted the river like a man gone insane. It was then that Ruth sensed something wrong, terribly wrong. She looked back at the wagon and saw a single hand flopping above the water like a hooked fish. She shrieked and grabbed the solitary hand, trying to lift it, pulling with all her strength. She could see Kathryn so close under the clear killing water. In seconds they swarmed around the wagon, trying to lift it, trying to roll it forward or back, trying to pull her free.

One man knelt beside Kathryn and plunged his head under the water and blew into Kathryn's mouth. Like a kid bobbing for apples he gulped large mouth fulls of air and plunged headfirst back into the river. Finally, after what seemed like eternity, several men managed to lift the right side of the wagon a few inches and they pulled Kathryn free.

Frantically they carried her up the bank and laid her in the prairie grass. They tried everything the gathering people suggested. It had only been minutes. They laid her on her back and pressed hard on her chest and stomach. They folded her into a sitting position with her head almost to her knees and then back again like a pocket knife. They laid her on her side but nothing revived her. Ruth, becoming hysterical, kept blowing into Kathryn's mouth, faster and faster, until her husband had to drag her away.

Kathryn was dead.

She died with her eyes wide open, watching the people who were trying so desperately to save her and failed.

Word went through the wagon train that after everyone had crossed the river they would camp there for the night even though they'd have another three hours of good traveling light. They had a short Christian service for Kathryn Rockhammer that many of the company attended. They buried her on a little knoll beside the river. They didn't know the name of the river that drowned her. They didn't know the name of the beautiful river that stole her dream. They didn't know the name of the river that carried away her life with her husband in the Rocky Mountains. But in the calm of that evening beside a campfire, Ruth remembered what it was that Kathryn had called in that last instant before she was pulled to her death.

She had called "Abraham."

\* \* \*

Abraham took the trip to town before he would have had to, hoping there would be fresh news from Kathryn or, glory be! Kathryn herself. He did need a half dozen sacks of grain for the horses and salt for his herd. He enjoyed calling his eleven Longhorns his "herd" and he laughed at himself because in the expansive valley meadows, the foothills, and the forest he seldom saw hide nor hair of his "herd." He worked continuously building fences from around the cabin site going outward in all directions, not fences to keep the cattle in but fences to control them when the time came to work with them up close. For now let the animals assume they're wild.

When Abraham was tying the team to a hitching post Julian Black called from the boardwalk in front of his store.

"Your wife's trunk's here!"

All Abraham heard was "wife's here."

Abraham rushed across the road and leaped up onto the boardwalk, hooting and laughing.

"Where? Where?"

"In the back," Julian said as he waved a hand toward the back of the store.

"Kathryn! Kathryn!" Abraham shouted as he scrambled through the store like a headless chicken. "Kathryn!"

"Not your wife, not your wife, you crazy man, your wife's trunk."

Abraham stopped dead in his tracks and looked back at Julian, all the air pumped out of him.

"Trunk? Her trunk? You said my wife was here."

"You better get the beans out of your ears. I said your wife's trunk's here."

Abraham caught himself before the words slipped out but what came to mind was "if you'd pull those damn buck teeth people could understand you." Julian tended to spit a little when he spoke.

"There's the trunk," Julian said, nodding at the large steamer trunk lashed together with leather straps. "It must weigh seventy pounds or more."

"But where is Kathryn? Why isn't she here?" Abraham said.

"Mail and freight don't never go together. Can be weeks between things sent by freight and letters. But it must mean that she's getting close."

Abraham brightened. Julian was right, it was a good sign, a wonderful promise that she would soon be here.

Abraham hung around town another day, helping Julian shingling a new lean-to at the back of the store and hoping Kathryn would arrive at any minute. When he finally loaded the trunk and rode home, he wrestled the heavy trunk into the cabin and couldn't wait to open it. But an inner voice told him no, to wait and let Kathryn open it, all of her personal things as well as the things she'd made sewing and recipes she'd learned. He'd wait and they'd open it together, celebrating her arrival at Rockhammer Ranch.

When a short letter arrived from the wagonmaster that Kathryn had died on the journey, Abraham rode north to where the valley becomes a high narrowing canyon with steep sides. He dismounted, removed the saddle and bridal from Polk, and climbed for hours, country that only mountain goats and sheep could negotiate. He found a rock ledge high above a lake, wrapped himself in a blanket, and sat there for hours, deciding if he would jump. Guilt had the upper hand, drawing him closer to the edge.

Kathryn's loving smile and sweet voice did battle with the darkness in his soul and wouldn't relent, waging war against cold despair with the warmth and power of forgiveness. He remembered how deeply she had touched him that day in school, the very day Kathryn stole his heart.

The first day of school in that Ohio autumn and the kids had gathered in the schoolyard, buzzing with the excitement of new students who hadn't been there before. Abraham was in his final year and Kathryn had two more to go. Miss Hester could recognize some students by last year's clothes, which had been worn by an older brother and sister. But Bess, a classmate of Abraham's, looked different on this morning. She was wearing a new dress, and beside that, a dress her mother made. Her fellow classmates gave it a once-over to be polite and then got to work. The dress was soon to cause a ruckus. It was a busy day, everyone getting reacquainted after a long summer. There were side glances and quiet snickers behind large books, and two of the older boys were feeling their oats and broke out laughing behind their hands. Miss Hester gave them a withering look and shooed them outside, as if everyone didn't know what the boys were laughing about. With twenty-six students enrolled at all levels the teacher often had her hands full. Bess was husky, plain, a little unsure of herself, a girl who liked school but didn't always feel comfortable there. In the afternoon, Abraham found Bess in the woodshed when all the other kids were out playing.

"What's the matter?" Abraham asked.

"Nothing," she said and scurried out behind the latrine.

The dress was coming a little unraveled and everyone saw Miss Hester pinning the material together. No one could any longer pretend they hadn't recognized it for what it was: a long potato sack that Bess had difficulty getting into.

Bess's mother had done some innovative things with what she had but the snickers spread like the pox and a potato sack is what it is. Miss Hester kept most of it under the rug and ran a tight ship. A few of the mean found ways to quietly fan the flame and the day found the kids heading for home with the same question in their craw. Would Bess wear the potato sack again tomorrow?

In the morning they didn't have to wait long. In fact a bunch were early. After greeting a few of the classmates as usual, Bess drifted off by herself along the back of the wooded schoolyard. No one paid any attention. The students played tag and kick the can and shouted in the crispy fall morning.

Then, one by one, the kids stopped dead in their tracks as Kathryn Gables came walking as normal as pie. Only one thing. She was wearing the potato-sack dress. Nobody moved except Kathryn. She sauntered across the playground, smiling to all and Bess came right behind her, appearing confused. They must of traded clothing in the latrine. Kathryn wore the dress all the rest of the day and not a word, not a gesture, not a smirking face showed up at school for a long time.

And that's how Abraham fell in love with Kathryn.

\*    \*    \*

Finally, in a standoff, his hunger and thirst won out and drove him off the mountain. He found Polk grazing halfway home and he rode him bareback to the cabin. Before anything else he rang the bell over and over and over again, mourning the courageous woman who would have been the loving heart of Rockhammer Valley. He would stay, he would go on in this harsh land alone and carry out their dream, Kathryn's and his.

Inside the cabin Kathryn's trunk sat silently beside the bed. He couldn't bare opening it, not then, maybe never. Each item would be a piece of his broken heart. He went through the agony of informing Kathryn's family back in Ohio, and his own, and he could hear his father's "I told you so."

He only went to town when he had need of something necessary to do his work. He buried himself with the work. He hoped his bull had done his job and he'd have ten calves in the coming spring, heifer calves. As the summer wore on his pain shadowed him and he caught himself thinking what Kathryn would think of this or laugh at that.

He worked until he knew he would fall quickly to sleep each night to escape her voice and face in his dreams. The summer months bloomed and faded and Abraham had taken the wagon to town. He wondered if some day he'd be able to be there without the sadness. Julian could see the damage in Abraham's face, a young powerful man so wounded, and each time he saw him he hoped it would have healed. One day there was a letter for Abraham.

It was a letter from Martha, Kathryn's little sister. Martha was proposing marriage. She said she was all grown up since he'd last seen her, that she'd learned to be a good cook, a gardener, a seamstress, and a strong housekeeper. Besides all that, she had studied and was now teaching school. She said she'd always admired him and still had strong feelings for him that she was sure would grow. In other words, she was more than willing to come west and become his wife.

Abraham read the letter every day for three weeks. Then he rode Poke into town to send a letter. It was addressed to Martha Gables. All it said was "Come."

# FIVE

MARTHA MADE IT TO BUFFALO JUMP unannounced. Amazed at this plucky, becoming young woman in a sun-bleached blue dress and frayed blue bonnet, Julian Black put her up for the night, something that didn't sit well with his wife. By the next morning everyone was getting along just fine, and Eugenie Black drummed up a hearty breakfast for the three of them. Julian found Martha and her modest belongings a ride on an oxen-powered freighter's train going past the Rockhammer Ranch turnoff. The teams of oxen plodded so slowly Martha strolled part of the way as if that would lighten their load and get her to the ranch faster.

The scruffy-looking freighters scrutinized her out of the corners of their eyes but she carried on a lively conversation with them about her adventures crossing the continent. They hated to see her go when they dropped her off at the Y in the road, the trace to the ranch hardly visible. One of them wanted to marry her and promised he'd settle down. The others roared their disapproval assuring Martha that he wasn't a good bet anyway.

When they plodded off to the northeast with their creaking oxcarts overburdened with goods, she stashed her small trunk and stuffed valise in a snarl of sagebrush, took her bedroll with her, and followed the faint wagon road into the immense unknown.

She'd come over two thousand miles, carried by all manner of transports: stagecoaches, buggies, wagons pulled by mules, horses, oxen, cows, and some of that distance she walked, exhausting three pairs of shoes.

When daylight faded into darkness she picked out an enormous, sprawling spruce with its lower branches sweeping around its massive trunk and a bed of dry needles to cushion her sleep. She crawled in almost to the trunk and ate some hardtack and dried prunes. Only a few miles from Abraham, she rolled up in her blanket and listened to the nocturnal sounds of the forest, barking and hooting and chattering that could have been human, that would have frightened her miles ago but now only made her feel as if she were one of the forest's night creatures.

She fell asleep with a calm confidence. Tomorrow she would begin her life on the Rockhammer Ranch. She had finished the journey that Kathryn had started with Abraham years ago and she wanted to carry on with her sister's courage and in her sister's memory.

On a clear fall day, Abraham cut lodgepole pine and led Samson to drag them into the meadow where he built a zigzag cross fence. These fences had an important purpose—moving his cattle from meadow to meadow after they'd eaten down the grass. With the present size of the herd, this was unnecessary, the grass outgrowing the cattle, but with the numbers he planned, it would be crucial. And he would build large corrals for the time when he would have to work the cattle, round up the spring calves and wean them in the fall. From time to time he would scan the horizon as he worked. He could see it all in his mind, visualize a hundred cows and calves grazing contentedly as far as he could see.

Then he spotted something, or was it someone? He squinted into the sunlight and held a hand to shade his eyes. It was a mile away to the southeast and it was difficult telling if it was moving. There. A traveler, prospector, homesteader, they came this way now and then, lost, looking for passes through the mountains, looking to find a place to settle. Abraham enjoyed their company and usually talked them into staying a spell to catch up on what was going on in the world.

He went back to work, occasionally glancing at the tiny object coming his way. It would take the vagabond a half hour or more to reach him. He had strung out a good distance of fence that day and he always felt a surge of pride when another meadow was encompassed in the scheme of his plan. The secret was keeping a very sharp axe, among other things, and he enjoyed the sweet sound of its music, the cold, sharp, steel biting into the clean, white lodgepole.

Then suddenly, out of the sky, it hit him, sucked his breath away. That tiny figure growing larger in this vast mountain land-scape was *Martha.* She came alone, she had no horse! She had no baggage. She was on foot.

*My God, she was here!*

Abraham pulled the harness off the horse, tied the halter for a bridal, and leaped onto his back. He turned the horse and headed for the river, as fast as old Samson could run. Abraham rode to a large pool the river had carved out of a bedrock cliff. He leaped off the horse, pulled off his boots, and peeled away his clothes, every stitch. He plunged into The River That Rolls Rocks and scrubbed himself from top to bottom. He washed his hair, the best he could without soap, and scrubbed at his full-grown beard. Time was running out. That little girl came on relentlessly.

He scrambled out of the river and onto Samson, grabbing only his boots from the pile of dirty clothes. Without a stitch, he rode pell-mell across an open meadow and up a slight draw where he figured she couldn't see his approach. He bounced bare-bottom, clinging to his boots and halter rope with one hand and Sam-son's mane with the other, nearly sliding off one side and then the other, the broad draft horse untrained for a rider.

Abraham came to the cabin from the back, working his way through the Aspen grove where he could arrive unseen. He leaped off Samson and ran in a crouch through the trees and across the open ground behind the cabin. He thought he'd won the race as he scampered around the side of the cabin to slip quickly inside through the front door, the only door.

Too late!

Martha stood beside the cabin, wide-eyed, staring, one hand over her open mouth, speechless, while Abraham was so unset-tled he stood there buck naked and made no attempt to cover up. They stared at each other, frozen in what seemed like a lifetime. Finally, Martha broke the ice.

"Abraham?"

*Was this the way they worked out here, naked? Had he worn out his clothes?*

Abraham gathered himself enough to hold his boots over his crotch.

"Martha?"

He held up one finger, signaling a plea for a few minutes alone, then disappeared into the cabin. Inside, he rummaged through piles of bedding and furs and coats until he found the clothes he'd set aside for this occasion. Damnation! He'd gone over it in his head a hundred times, how he would show her the valley and welcome her to the ranch after he met her in Buffalo Jump. Flowers in the cabin and a special meal he'd cook for her, the cabin swept clean. And instead he comes running bare-assed naked like a crazy man who'd gone insane in the wilderness.

Stumbling, he pulled on his clean overalls and slipped on the buckskin shirt he'd purchased for this occasion, cussing himself for being so stupid. With the door ajar he could see her standing several strides in front of the cabin, waiting with a puzzled expression on her girlish face, as if she didn't know if she should stand pat or run.

*My God, he'd stood there naked in front of her. What does she think?*

He pulled on his boots, found a comb and ran it through his snarled hair, took a swipe at his beard, and looked around the cabin for some hidden store of courage. Trembling, he swung the door open and sheepishly stepped out. Neither spoke for a moment. They met eye to eye. Then Martha broke out in a large smile.

"Abraham?"

Hesitantly, he followed her lead, finding a smile behind his unabashed chagrin. He smiled and nodded.

"Abraham, is it you?" she asked with merriment in her voice, "It seems you've been expecting me."

They stood for a moment, digesting her humor. He saw that, despite her shredded and cumbersome dress, she had certainly grown up since he last laid eyes on her. The girlish manner he remembered had been transformed into the sensual curves of an earthy woman. She had lost her baby fat and her high cheekbones framed her lovely face.

"You look so . . . different from how I remember you," he said.

"Is that good?" She frowned and he remembered she had dimples.

"Yes, that's good, that's very, very, good."

Then, like planets too close to the sun, they were drawn together in a great rush and buried themselves in the other's smothering embrace. This wasn't Kathryn but Martha was the next best thing. And here she was in his arms. She had come all this way for him. He started laughing and crying at the same time. It was contagious. Martha started in to crying and giggling. They laughed in the face of the death they had stared down and, in the end, found each other somewhere along the road to eternity, two tiny figures, swallowed up in the vast overwhelming landscape of life.

That night, with the cabin shut against the dark, they kept bumping into each other in an awkward dance. The cabin suddenly seemed small to Abraham and they both talked incessantly, as if allowing the silence to come in through the chinks, they would suffocate. Abraham lit several oil lamps and kept busy not knowing what to do. Martha sat on the edge of the bed and pulled off her ragged socks. With the hem of her dress she began to wipe her feet gingerly, as if they were weary and sore. In the lamplight Abraham saw the callouses and the blisters and the scars from her journey.

"Guess I'll have to darn some socks." She laughed lightly, holding the ragged socks head high.

"Did you have to walk a lot?"

"Some."

There was something about her weary feet. Abraham felt his throat constricting and his eyes welling. He went to the stove and poured hot water in a dishpan. With a bar of soap and washcloth, he knelt in front of her, surprising her. He took her right foot and set it in the water. Without a word he began to tenderly bathe her wounded feet.

He washed her feet and massaged each of them, carefully, affectionately. She regarded him on his knees and hid her own tears. She couldn't look into his eyes for the joy she felt, seeing that this man, this large, strong man, was ultimately compassionate. That had been her greatest misgiving throughout her journey. Would he be the kind and tender man she remembered?

When he'd finished he pulled a large, wooly pair of stockings out of a drawer and slipped them on her feet. They went up to her knees, now bare. She leaned back and waved her legs in the air. They both laughed and Abraham caught the smell of lust stealing into the cabin.

They retrieved Martha's baggage the following day. She dismissed her own awkwardness and started in on her new life. Martha proved to be a formidable partner. She took over the cabin, cooking and executing daily chores in short order. To see them together you'd guess them father and daughter, Martha five-foot-two with a girlish smile and laughter, he with his husky, bearlike body and voice. After putting the cabin to her liking she was soon sketching the next addition to the building with the talk of using sawed lumber instead of logs and getting another window. And soon after that, she had a list for their next trip to town.

By unspoken word they seemed to agree to put off any lovemaking until they became better acquainted. They planned to marry the first time they ran across a minister. When she rearranged the contents of the cabin she discovered that the large bed was made up of several inches of young, soft willow branches, then covered by a large canvas. Spread over it all, there were four soft buffalo robes. One could decide how warm the bed would be by varying the number of buffalo robes under which one slept. If he slept under two, she could choose to sleep under three. When she blew out the lantern and slipped under the buffalo robes they exchanged stories, she of her journey there, he with the Indians, and they'd weave plans in the cool night air, plans of a large, happy family, growing up in the valley, plans of a large, happy herd, grazing in the meadows, and the elegant house in the foothills overlooking the valley. Abraham usually fell into sleep first and she would drift off memorizing his profile.

He was pleased how Martha took over the cooking and splitting wood for the stove and how she managed the horses, hobbling them so they were usually on fresh grass, relieving him of a variety of chores. One evening, when they were walking in the sunset's afterglow, she asked Abraham about the big brass bell hanging there so prominently. He explained how he traded for some tools with a family in the wagon train who intended it for a church but it proved to be too much weight for their outfit. Abraham wanted it to be a milestone, a historic landmark for this land and ranch.

He told Martha it would be their way to signal each other when they were spread near and far in the valley. Mainly for emergency, a way to call the other to come with all speed. He wanted it to be a landmark. He wanted to tell her that she could ring it whenever she was aching to sneak into the bed with him, but he didn't. They eventually developed their intimate humor about the bell with phrases like "You want to ring the bell?" or "You really rang my bell last night!"

Martha understood about Kathryn's trunk that stood in a corner unopened. It served as a shelf with much bedding and clothes piled on it in an attempt to hide it from memory. He asked her if she'd like to open it, that it probably had many things she could wear or use, but she said she couldn't bear to, not yet. Often, after she'd done what needed doing in and around the cabin, she came out in the fields and helped with the work. She was strong and cheerful and her enthusiasm was enormously uplifting. Daily she was overwhelmed by the valley and thanked God for her life there.

Even after her heroic journey, Martha didn't understand distance. She wanted to invite neighbors to parties and go to town for a dance, as though she wouldn't give in to the isolation. But it was time to start raising that big family. On the thirtieth night after her arrival she blew out the lantern and lifted her long flannel nightie. With some trepidation she slipped under the second layer of the buffalo robes where Abraham was lying naked, waiting, hoping.

Hesitantly, they found their way in the dark, found themselves under the buffalo robes in the way the Indians had for hundreds of uncounted years, and became one more in a long procession of lovers. This small woman surprised him with the intensity of her passion and he was overwhelmed by the power of their sexual hunger. They had been so lonely and so patient. So now they rushed ahead eagerly, without speaking. When they were finished and she lay in his arms, he whispered in her ear.

"We are now married in God's sight. You are Mrs. Abraham Rockhammer."

She cried softly.

"Why are you crying, did I hurt you?" he asked.

"No, no, it's just that I'm so happy."

# SIX

ABRAHAM AND MARTHA MARRIED in Julian Black's store with the ceremony done by an itinerate Presbyterian minister who provided them with an official document and preached for thirty some minutes to the seven people who were present. Abraham gave him two dollars and told Martha he'd have given more if the young minister hadn't been so longwinded. Martha slipped the preacher another dollar when Abraham was preoccupied loading the wagon.

Martha held her own in disagreements with Abraham and laughed loudly when he chased her. They had breeding in mind in earnest, both working with the cattle and building a family. And Abraham wasn't one who believed to be proper you must have relations in the cabin, in the bed, half clothed. And in the manner of their precious bull, he would surprise her, at any time of day, in any place he found her. She would run, giggling, thinking it was scandalous, but in the end, though she could outrun him, she would be caught in a place of her choosing. Once, when they were on the ground under the bell, no children in sight, she had a hold of the clapper rope and, when he cried out like a great, wild bull, she rang the bell.

With Lizzie Calendar's help, a midwife who lived near Buffalo Jump, Alfred came first—a big, healthy, solidly built boy, who was an agony for Martha to deliver. But he soon became a joy to their hearts. A little more than a year later, Jeremiah was born with the help of young Doc Simpson, who was starting a practice in and around Buffalo Jump. They waited in the doctor's log house for Jeremiah, a boy clearly created in his father's image. The pregnancy was another strain on Martha.

They skipped a beat when Martha miscarried the following year but then Nellie restored their hope by joining the family in the coming spring. After that, the two of them could no longer conceive. Abraham believed there weren't enough Rockhammers to sustain the family ranch in this land. Still, he kept chasing Martha with an undying hope.

The herd grew gradually, as did the children, and the family caught the glory and the wonder of their calling, the extraordinary, singular attempt to follow a dream west into the unknown wild and battle there against all odds. First Abraham, years ago as a boy in Ohio, then Kathryn, undaunted to carry her vow west. Martha, to follow Kathryn's promise and build on it, and finally, Alfred, Jeremiah, and Nellie, the youngsters, who would someday carry on.

Coming to believe in the dream that Abraham spoke of often, the younger ones would try to keep up with the older, the smaller with the bigger, each working up to his or her capabilities and often beyond, challenging each other and the raw-boned wilderness around them. Each felt a personal pride in the part they were playing. Sometimes Abraham found doubt lurking in the shadows of his heart but he kept it secret and deeply hidden, refusing to confess it to anyone for fear that it would become contagious.

Sometimes Abraham was overcome when witnessing their undaunted efforts and a bittersweet sadness would grip him: Alfred, lifting into place a measured log that outweighed him; Nellie, wading waist deep in the frigid river to repair a washed out head gate; Jeremiah, exhausted from a long day's work yet refusing to give up wrestling a tough, wild spring calf until he had the critter subdued. He fell asleep in his bed with his clothes still on.

Martha taught the children at home, the distance to school prohibitive, and until a school was organized much closer. They would learn reading, writing, and arithmetic with the kindness and warmth of their fun-loving mother. Books became treasures and Abraham would bring a new book home whenever he could lay hands on one. Jeremiah loved reading whatever was available, except the Bible, though he knew the Holy Book was supposed to be good for him in some incomprehensible way. Abraham accepted God's law as simple and clear, something no man should break at risk of burning in hell. The children rarely had other playmates and they were encouraged to create their own games and to act out plays and skits and to recite poetry in made-up costumes. Martha and Abraham would applaud loudly and heap upon them their encouragement, afraid their children would grow up shy and withdrawn from this life of isolation, where a trip to town came about once a month at best. When the weather was congenial they would camp overnight in Buffalo Jump in hopes the children might make friends.

Alfred, Jeremiah, and Nellie worked like adults carving the ranch out of the rugged land. The three of them learned how to survive. They grew up fast because they had no other choice. They became seasoned riders and they spent hours in the saddle working the steadily growing herd of Longhorn cattle. Nellie had an ongoing battle with Martha to allow her to wear men's britches when she worked at home, claiming the dress was an unnecessary burden. She pointed out that her brothers didn't have to drag one around as she did. Martha caught her, from time to time, wearing one of the boy's pairs of pants and all she could do was roll her eyes and look the other way.

The family worked from dawn until sunset when the fall calves needed to be gathered and the oats and hay were ready to harvest. Though many open range cattlemen were doing it, Abraham felt no hurry to brand his cattle since no other cattle could mingle with his unless they could fly.

The family scrambled on horseback to chase, rope, and catch the calves who had run wild until then. By the way they fled and bucked they seemed to know that some of them were destined to become steers. Abraham had little trouble selling cattle and his reputation slowly grew among like-minded, far-flung cattlemen.

One fall, Abraham had carefully selected three pairs that looked like they'd make good mothers and with Jeremiah's help was driving them to town. Jeremiah sat on the boardwalk porch in front of Julian's store, sucking a peppermint stick and observing the traffic, which seemed to increase every time they came to town. Abraham had his horse tied to the hitching post and was stuffing goods into his saddlebags when a rough-cut man crossed the wide muddy road and hailed him.

"Hello, sir, are you Abraham Rockhammer?"

Abraham paused, as if he were contemplating his answer, and sized up the man. About twenty, dirty overalls, worn-down boots, rawhide vest and he topped it all with a cock-eyed, black stove-pipe hat.

"Yes, sir, and who might you be?"

"Name's Henry Weebow. Been trying to catch up with you for a spell."

The men shook hands and Abraham smelled alcohol.

"Well, you caught up all right. What can I do for you?"

"I've got a place around the back of your mountain, only a few miles as the crow flies. I'm homesteading it. Been prospecting some and I hit a limestone thrust, must be a hundred feet straight up and down."

"Well," Abraham said, "you surely know you won't find much in the limestone."

Abraham buckled the flap on the saddlebag and hung a sack of flour over the pummel of his saddle.

"Yes, sir, I know. I just want to get around that outcrop and work uphill, but to get around it I have to cross your land, if the surveyed stakes are right."

"Oh," Abraham said, "the stakes are right, you can count on that. I spent several weeks up there working with the government surveyor."

"If I can't cross up there I have to come all the way around the backside which'd be several miles."

Henry pushed his hat back and put one foot up on the porch.

"That's it, all you want is to cross my ground?"

"Yep, tha's all. Jes' trail across yer land fer a few hundred yards."

"Have you found any sign?" Abraham asked.

"No, no . . . but where I'm scratchin' looks good. Ya never know."

"You planning on farming your place?" Abraham asked and glanced at Jeremiah.

"Yeah, prove it up, grow some potato and corn."

"Well, Henry, you can cross my land any time you want on foot or on horseback or mule, but, if you ever hit some color, there'll be no wagon road switchbacking across the face of the mountain. Understood?"

"I sure do, I sure do. Thanks Abraham. Thanks a lot."

"Do you know that the mountain has a soul?" Abraham asked.

"No . . . don't think I know what ya mean." He scratched his head.

"It means that the mountain is a living thing, it has a spirit, like people do," Abraham said.

"Yessir, if you say so, by golly, I never thought about it like that, it's jes a big pile of rock."

Abraham stepped up on the boardwalk about to go into the store.

"Do you s'pos we could put it in writin', permission fer me ta cross your land?" Henry asked.

"No need for paper. My word is good." He looked into Henry's eyes. "Is your word good, Henry?"

"Yessir, it surely is."

Abraham held out his hand and the men shook.

As they rode out of town, Abraham said, "He's already found some color."

"How do you know, Father?" Jeremiah asked.

"He wouldn't be wanting permission if he hadn't found anything. He's already found color. Remember this day, Son. The mountain has a soul."

One winter day Alfred and Jeremiah were on horseback, checking the herd with their father, Abraham. Nearly two feet of snow covered the valley floor and a cutting north wind came at them over the ridges and peaks. They checked along The River That Rolls Rocks and in the willow brush along it where the cattle turn their backs to the storm and hunker down. They figured the herd wouldn't stray too far from the river.

Alfred was already an excellent horseman and young Jeremiah wasn't far behind. By swapping and selling and breeding, Abraham had worked his way up in the quality of saddle horses they owned. At that time they had seven, plus a proven brood mare.

He loved watching his boys work with the cattle as if it came to them naturally, hollering and whistling, racing to designated landmarks on the ranch. They'd be moving along at a leisurely pace when one of them would whoop it up and shout "Last one to ring the bell has to fill the woodbox!" and an explosion of hooves and gravel and snorting animals would burst over the ground and they'd be galloping pell-mell for home.

They spread out that day, searching places where they'd found bunches of cattle before. Abraham and Jeremiah were on the east side of the river and Alfred on the west. Except for the wind, the country was silent and serene, fresh snow painting the landscape quietly white.

"Over here!" Alfred called and waved. "Over here!"

Jeremiah and Abraham forded the shallow river on a gravel bar and trotted to where Alfred waited on his horse. As Abraham and Jeremiah reached the spot they saw the dead cow, what was left of it. The Longhorn had been killed and butchered, leaving very little of the carcass. There were tracks all around the area, some horse, some human.

"The Blackfeet!" Alfred said.

Rarely did they see tracks or signs of the Indians, who still inhabited the valley on occasion, but this was the first time they'd bothered the cattle or taken anything. When they made a count in early summer they'd always be a few short, figuring wild animals picked off a few yearlings and realizing that maybe the Indians had done the same.

Abraham slid off his horse and studied the kill.

"They killed our cow," Jeremiah said.

Abraham circled the carcass and studied the prints in the snow.

"She was pregnant," Abraham said.

"That's like they killed two," Alfred said.

"The poor cow," Jeremiah said.

"Well, Alfred, what should we do?" Abraham asked, without looking up, always making use of a situation for Alfred's education as the oldest son.

"Let's go after 'em," Alfred said.

"Very well, and what if we catch up to them?" Abraham asked, "and they shoot at us?"

"Shoot back," Alfred said. "They're the cattle thieves, we can hang 'em."

"Should we hang them?" Abraham asked.

"Make 'em pay for the cow," Jeremiah said.

"Make 'em give the meat back," Alfred said.

"What if we can't find who did this?" Abraham asked.

"We can track 'em," Alfred said with excitement in his voice.

Abraham knelt in the snow and examined the Longhorn's head, the color of its face, its particular markings.

"I know this cow," he said. "She was a good mother."

Abraham tipped his hat to the carcass and then swung up on his horse. Several ravens and a magpie waited impatiently for the feast to continue. Abraham turned and rode away. The boys looked at each other somewhat baffled. Then, shrugging, they followed their father back across the river and headed home.

"Mother! Mother! Some Indians killed one of our cows," Alfred shouted as he burst into the kitchen.

"Yeah," Jeremiah said on Alfred's heels, "and they butchered her and she was pregnant."

"Oh, that poor mother," Martha said. "What's your father going to do about it?"

"We don't know, he didn't say," Alfred said, pulling off his heavy winter coat.

"We should go after them," Nellie said, "and get the marshal after them."

"The marshal can't be chasing all over this country," Martha said, "for every missing critter."

For a time a small uproar of blustery threats and bravado blew through the Rockhammer kitchen. It seemed unlikely that they would be threatened in any way in their safe and quiet valley, even with the stories they'd hear in town or on the road.

Then Abraham sent everyone to do their chores before supper: wood, water, livestock, stove, fireplace. When Martha called them to the table murmuring among the troops continued. The aroma of frying bacon wafted through the house. They filed to the table, set simply with dishes, silverware, and water glasses. Abraham came in and settled at the head of the table.

He glanced around at his family and, as usual, bowed his head. They all followed suit and Abraham prayed.

"Lord, we thank you for the food you provide for us and for all your blessings. May we receive them with a thankful heart, may we remember those who are hungry and be willing to share. In the name of Jesus, Amen."

Everyone looked up and regarded Martha, who seemed perplexed. She didn't move. Glances shot back and forth. No one moved.

"Would you like me to help, Mother?" Nellie asked.

"No, thank you, I don't need any."

Then Abraham glanced around the table into his children's eyes.

"We will go hungry tonight. There will be no eating in this home until breakfast. This is my doing so don't look at your mother. I asked her to fry bacon to help us remember the aroma of hunger. It seems we've all forgotten what it feels like to be hungry. We must never forget that, how it feels to be hungry."

No one spoke for several minutes. All kinds of expressions crossed Rockhammer faces, unspoken words hung in the air. Then, Alfred picked up his knife and fork and acted as if he were cutting meat on his plate. Everyone watched, somewhat spellbound. He cut an imaginary piece and with his fork he put it in his mouth and chewed vigorously.

"Jeremiah, would you please pass the mashed potatoes," Alfred said, and Jeremiah passed him an empty bowl. Alfred dished up a whooping spoonful and passed the bowl to Nellie. Giggling slightly, she set it down and scooped a spoonful on her empty plate and soon the family began laughing as they ate an imaginary meal.

"This is delicious beef, Mother," Alfred said and he passed the platter to Abraham. "It must come from the Rockhammer herd."

"I'm having two pieces of the pumpkin pie," Martha said.

Abraham didn't know if his family had found its footing, if they personally identified with the Blackfeet, Piegan, or Blood, and their hunger, their deadly, stalking hunger. But Abraham, laughing with their antics while eating the invisible meal, found tears in his eyes.

# SEVEN

IN STEP WITH THE SEASONS, the days marched swiftly through the valley, relentless, often bringing with them joy and laughter, sometimes breaking their hearts. Blessed with good weather and a growing herd, they prospered on the land, perpetually upgrading the house, outbuildings, and fencing. And almost unnoticed, the drumbeat of time counted faithfully.

When he was nine, Jeremiah saw his brother killed instantly by the kick of a horse. The horse wasn't after Alfred; it was horseflies. Their father was teaching Alfred how to shoe his horse, a normally gentle well-mannered gelding. His brother's head snapped back like he'd been shot with a buffalo gun. He dropped at Jeremiah's feet, twitching in the straw and dry manure, his head a slightly misshaped pumpkin with blood crawling out an ear like a red worm, dead as a doornail.

All of them took Alfred's death in different ways, but for each, it was a devastating blow that staggered them and brought a veil of gloom over the valley. They buried him on a small hill near the aspen grove, up behind the house, and Martha sang the hymn *Rock of Ages*, which echoed in their minds forever. A week later Abraham went berserk. With inhuman strength and power, he picked up the large, round boulders they had stockpiled to build the new fireplace and hurled them, overhead, down the bank with an unearthly howl. Some of the thirty or more stones rolled all the way back into the river. The family stood silently and embraced the temper storm wishing they could explode with him. He never hurt anyone in his outbursts, never hurt an animal. Like a wounded bear he wandered in the timber and across snow-covered meadows until Martha found him and led him home.

From then on, every time Jeremiah worked around a horse, a primitive fear showed up under his rib cage, the hairs on the back of his neck stood on end, and he would think of Alfred. They had been constant companions, roaming the valley and surrounding mountains when they finished the day's work. It was like a part of Jeremiah was missing and he caught himself talking to Alfred as if he'd forgotten his brother was gone. Alfred haunted his dreams and Jeremiah, working harder than ever, never got to finish his childhood.

The following winter, Nellie came down with pneumonia or something much like it. She took to her bed with a rattling cough, congested chest, and sore throat. They did all they knew to do but she grew steadily worse. Hardly able to breathe, burning with fever, headache, coughing up thick phlem. Abraham paced, beside himself, praying to God for the wisdom of what to do.

"How are you doing?" Abraham asked as he stood at the foot of her bed.

"I'll get better, Father, I will," she said with a tremor of fear in her voice.

Abraham glanced at Martha who sat in a chair at the head of the bed. Martha slowly shook her head.

"Of course you will, of course you will," Abraham said with his own tremor of fear. "Who are you?"

"I'm Nellie Rockhammer," she said softly, "a Rockhammer girl."

"That's my daughter, by gum. I'll be right back. I got to check the horses."

He nodded at Martha and ducked out the door. If he raced to town through the nasty winter ice and cold, it would take him more than three days to get there and bring Doc Simpson back, much of it slogging through the night. If he chose to take Nellie to town, it would be at best more than a day with her bundled in the wagon and that could kill her.

Abraham realized it had fallen to him to make the decision as Nellie's life hung in the balance. Maybe the doctor wouldn't have anything more up his sleeve to heal her than they did and she could die on the treacherous ride to town. He had never prepared to make these heartrending decisions when he'd taken his family into the valley, into the wilderness, to leave them vulnerable to the dangers they faced every day. He saw clearly that it was up to him. He had to choose. He went back, still undecided to Nellie's bedside.

"Father."

"Yes, Nellie."

"I get a vote, Father."

"Yes, Nellie."

"I vote we go," Nellie said.

Abraham held his breath.

"She decided," Jeremiah nodded.

"That's my girl, by God almighty, we'll run for it," Abraham declared. Quickly, Martha outfitted the spring wagon with many blankets and pillows while Jeremiah and Abraham harnessed and saddled the horses. They wrapped Nellie with layers of blankets and finally a canvas tarp. Martha, bundled like a snowman, sat behind Nellie with Nellie's head in her lap. There she'd try to absorb and cushion the bumps and lurches of the dirt road. Besides the team Jeremiah rode his saddle horse so that half way there he could charge off toward town to find Doc Simpson. They rumbled through the gorge and out onto the sagebrush foothills, wondering if Nellie would ever see the valley again.

It was a race for Nellie's life! A race between God and the Devil! In their hearts the Rockhammers raced, urged the horses to fly like Pegasus, to outrun the filthy beast that stalked Nellie with bared teeth and sharpened claws. Abraham knew the road well, where he could run the horses over solid ground and where he had to guide them slowly over icy and frozen stretches. Martha kept a running conversation with Nellie to keep track of her condition in the dark. Abraham attempted to encourage Nellie by calling out to her often, telling her how well they were doing.

"You're doing great, little lady," he shouted. He knew he couldn't fool her that easily and he wanted to encourage them all as the night seemed to be growing darker, the world turning colder.

Nellie was dear to Abraham's heart in a different way than Jeremiah and Alfred. Though she was the youngest, Nellie would often confound the boys with her humor and wit. She was intelligent beyond her years, mentally tough and could outduel her big brothers with words, which exasperated them often.

"You need to rest the horses, Father," Nellie commanded softly from under her blankets.

"Just a little further, Nell, just a little further."

"You'll have to carry me if you kill the horses."

At times they broke through snowdrifts, at times they slid on ice, and dawn found them a little more than half way. The closer they got to town the more the snow on the road had been knocked down by wagons or horseback. They stopped at times so that Nellie, as well as the rest of them, could relieve herself. She seemed weaker, her fever raging.

Abraham sent Jeremiah.

"Ride, boy! Don't let Star touch ground!"

"Good-bye, Nellie," Jeremiah called. "See you at Doc Simpson's."

Jeremiah charged down the road, snow and ice flying behind his horse.

"How is she doing?" Abraham asked Martha as he checked the harness.

"I can't keep her head still, we're banging around back here badly."

Abraham climbed in the wagon. "How's her fever?"

"Feels about the same. I'm giving her water. Can't you find a smoother road?"

"You know the answer to that."

He shouted at the horses and slapped the reins. Martha tried to cushion Nellie's head in her lap and one moment she wanted Abraham to go faster, and the next, beg him to slow down. The sun broke out from the billowing clouds and Martha pointed them out to Nellie, surely a sign from God that Nellie would be all right.

Abraham fought the darkness gathering in his mind. He thought of Alfred. He couldn't bare to lose Nellie, but something in his soul told him it was too late.

Just a mile from town, Jeremiah came galloping through the snow, shouting.

"The doctor's here! I found him, he's in town, how is Nellie?"

They slid and skidded into town, almost hitting a stage-coach and buggy, scattering dogs and magpies. Martha helped pass Nellie into Abraham's arms and he shuffled carefully to the house. Doc Simpson had them sit Nellie on the high table in the small infirmary. He pulled the wool scarf from Nellie's face.

"Well, well, young lady, how are you?"

"I'm not going to die," Nellie said.

"No, no, you're a Rockhammer. You're not going to die."

"Alfred died," she said.

"Yes, that was an accident."

Martha caught a glance from Abraham.

The doctor felt the pulse in her wrist. He paused. Abraham and Jeremiah held their breath. Slowly he lifted his eyes to Martha.

"You say this girl has a high fever?"

"Yes, she's burning up," Abraham said.

The doctor had her open her mouth. He compressed her tongue with a swab and searched in her mouth as if seeking the hunter who was coming to kill her. He didn't say anything. No one spoke.

"Is your throat sore?"

"Yes . . . No . . . it was."

"Does it hurt now?" the doctor asked.

Nellie swallowed. She cleared her throat. She looked at Abraham with a bewildered expression and shrugged.

"No."

"Can you cough for me?" the doctor asked.

She coughed thinly, nothing like she had a few hours before, nothing heaved up from her small frame. He put his hand on her forehead.

The Rockhammers stood with their mouths hanging open.

"I've never seen anything like it," Abraham said. "I'd a bet she'd die. She was a goner."

"She was a very sick girl, Doc," Martha said. "How can you account for that?"

Dr. Simpson shrugged. "Maybe it was the rough ride, jerking her around, clearing her congestion. Maybe it was the bitter cold in her lungs."

"I figured she'd cough up a lung," Abraham said.

"Oh, Mother," Nellie said, and Martha hugged her.

"If you folks will wait in the other room," the Doctor said and pointed to a door, "Nellie and I won't be long. You folks must be worn out."

In another room, the three flopped on chairs, totally baffled and confused. Had they all been under some hallucination? Were they victims of exhaustion? Had they allowed panic to blow a head cold all out of proportion? All three of them?

"It comes down to this," Abraham said to Martha and Jeremiah. "Nellie was deathly ill. We thought she'd die. So, how did she heal on the road to town? Is this a miracle or a strange accident of nature? Perhaps Doc Simpson is correct. Whatever she needed was there on the road. The rough ride and the ice and the bitter cold air routed the sickness and gave Nellie back her health. This is for sure: we have been spared."

After his sister Nellie nearly died of pneumonia, or whatever it was, Jeremiah became very protective of her. At first she thought it was nice, even fun, but soon she tired of his attention. Eventually the family had tucked away the pneumonia incident like something in Kathryn's steamer trunk. Jeremiah didn't understand it; he just kept on being overprotective of his perfectly healthy sister. When an invitation was extended to Nellie to travel to Ohio and meet the rest of her family, she jumped at the chance. It was a long journey and she was so young—just over seventeen—but she was determined, just as Abraham had been when he left Ohio to come west. Letters crisscrossed the nation and plans were made. As the day came closer, Jeremiah wanted to call the whole thing off; he couldn't protect his little sister out in the big unknown world. Abraham felt strongly that Nellie should grow up more and she belonged at home at the ranch, keeping the family together. Martha would miss her terribly but quietly thought it would be good for her to get out in the world.

Almost as if they were sleepwalking, they put Nellie on the spur line with Mrs. Campbell, a women who would ride to St. Paul with Nellie and turn her over to a Rockhammer. They all waved and everyone cried except Abraham and they all felt duly apprehensive. As fate would have it, Nellie only returned once—on the occasion of Martha's death—though she led a good life in Ohio, marrying a college teacher, and raising a brood of children. She could draw beautifully and she sent drawings of the children so Martha knew exactly what they looked like.

Jeremiah was cut from the same block of granite as his father, and though he was leaner than his father, he inherited Abraham's large bear-paw hands and forearms that appeared as though they could rip tree stumps out of the ground with ease.

Working beside his father over the years, among many other things, Jeremiah inherited his father's respect for the land. He remembered the Blackfoot he used to see occasionally when he was a child. He seldom saw them anymore. But he knew in his heart they were right; that the mountain had a soul. It seemed that Jeremiah hadn't inherited his father's temper or at least he'd found other ways to deal with the anger, disappointment, and hardships that ranch life constantly hurled at them.

Though the Rockhammers were outmanned, the ranch continued to prosper. They hired help to work the cattle and to harvest hay and oats as other settlers were showing up along the road to Buffalo Jump, almost close enough to be called neighbors. At times it seemed that Martha was wearing down, carrying a certain melancholy for her lost child, assuming it was her fault that they couldn't conceive and build their family large enough to withstand the attrition this life demanded. She damaged a knee in a wagon accident, chopped off a toe splitting firewood and her voice had an edge to it when she'd give Abraham or Jeremiah orders about the work that needed doing. But if she'd become bossy along the way she always held up her end of the ranch life, did more than her share, and loved the man and the valley where she'd chosen to make her stand.

# EIGHT

THEN THE WINTER FROM HELL came to call. It began as a picturesque snowfall, large lovely flakes drifting and dancing in the soft southwesterly wind on their way to the ground. Abraham and Jeremiah were in the upper meadows checking the herd and they paid little attention when the wind stopped and the valley hushed in a snowy silence. A half hour later, under a brooding, darkening sky, the wind returned. But this time it blew out of the northeast, a different storm, roaring across the mountains and over the land, an animal-killing, man-eating inferno, hurling ice-laden sleet and snow.

Martha was the first to accurately identify the monster and, on foot, bundled in her winter coat, she charged into the teeth of it to the Rockhammer Ranch bell. She attacked the bell again and again, harder, louder. It pealed, muffled, into the driving snow as if the snow were attempting to smother its warning. It was an incongruous sight and sounded as if she were calling the congregation to gather and worship one last time. Jeremiah, mounted, came through the swirling cold first.

"Where's Father?" he shouted.

He had to lean down from the horse and put his mouth on Martha's ear for her to hear.

"Was he near you?" she shouted.

"I hadn't seen him for a while, he was above me! Should I go back?"

Martha kept pulling the rope.

"No, no, that's the last thing to do. Then you'd both be lost."

Jeremiah slid off his horse and took the rope from Martha. Like a bellringer gone insane he banged the clapper, slamming it against the brass bell with all his strength. Martha leaned in close to him.

"We may have to go for the house," she shouted. "He may have holed up in the line shack!"

"Just a little longer!" Jeremiah yelled, attacking the bell as if his father's life depended on it. He thought of Alfred and in his heart of hearts he drew a line on the ground. By God! He wasn't giving up one more Rockhammer to the stalking beast of death.

Then suddenly, like a frosted ghost, Abraham materialized out of the blizzard. For the moment their fear of the storm gave way to relief. Abraham slid off Charger and they huddled together.

"How did you find us?" Martha shouted.

"I just gave Charger his head and then, after a while, I heard the bell," Abraham shouted. "I thought I was hearing things. I thought the cursed wind was playing tricks on me."

Then quickly, single file, they headed for the buildings. Abraham first, on foot, like a family struck blind. They felt their way the short distance and came upon a corral where there wasn't supposed to be one. In no more than ten yards they almost missed the house and corrals. Abraham guided them sharply to the left, into the teeth of the northern tempest, and they found the horse barn. Except for Paint, the other horses were accounted for. Jeremiah tied a rope to the barn door and the three held on to the rope and strung it to the kitchen door. The family quickly went to work, doing what they could against the night to come. It would have been better if they didn't understand what was coming down on them but they had heard from old timers about the winters from hell. They came once in a hundred years, without warning, drastically thinning the population of both beasts and human beings.

The blizzard shrieked through the night, sounding as if it increased in velocity hour by hour and anything made of wood was methodically being consumed to feed the iron stove in the kitchen. Furniture. Books. Bed frames. Inside doors. Anything they could pry off the wall or floor. With clawing icy fingers the storm searched out every crack and corner of the house, howled down the chimney and made prey out of anything not firmly nailed. In a large kettle on the stove they melted snow for water, water that quickly refroze when only a few feet from the fire. Everything inside the house was dusted with snow. By morning they could only see outside from the kitchen window. Inside it was as dark as night with mountainous drifts covering the other windows and threatening to bury the house. It was as if a horde of termites had invaded their home and were methodically eating it.

The three of them embraced this battle for survival as the storm intensified all through the day. When the wood box was empty, burn the wood box. Throughout the day they stripped the interior of the house. Then they began prying and chopping wood off the inside of the horse barn which they could reach by holding onto the rope that Abraham had tied from the horse corral to the the kitchen door. Their visibility was ten feet.

Beside their own survival, their great concern was for the herd. Their beloved cattle were out there in this godforsaken weather completely helpless. As the storm descended, Martha, thank God, had stabled the horses. But there would be freezing and starving cattle out there, wandering in the deepening snow like ghosts from a lost ship. Abraham paced in the dark hollow house agonizing about Boss, his prize bull, who he'd paid a fortune for last fall. Where would he find shelter and water? Where would any of them? Fortunately he'd sold forty steers just before winter. But the others out there, their butts to the wind, their faces caked in ice, bawling for someone to feed them, would be wondering what had happened to their world.

The Rockhammers also wondered what had happened to their world, to their serene and glorious valley. Who had brewed up this cruel joke? Where did nature create this raging monster, swooping down from Canada with arctic teeth to chew and kill everything in its path? Martha could no longer avoid the question growing in her heart. Was God a lunatic? She could see that question on the faces of her men.

Hour by hour, they'd cock their ears in hopes that the blizzard was letting up, going to the kitchen window a hundred times to peer out at that world of huge white waves on a frozen endless sea.

They limited themselves to light meals: beans, oatmeal, cheese, hardtack, bacon, beef, dehydrated apples, and coffee.

The unexpected disaster taxed them to their limits, challenged their endurance, and threatened to shipwreck Abraham's dream for the Rockhammer Ranch. Without saying the words they each understood that their herd, cared for and nurtured with affection these many years, could be wiped out. The animals they'd grown to know and appreciate, gone! And added to that growing present heartache the howling insufferable never-ending wind threatened their sanity.

On the third day, when it seemed to be letting up, Abraham decided he'd go out and see what he could do. Martha protested vehemently to no avail. Abraham dressed himself in layers while Martha tongue-lashed him in a way Jeremiah had never heard.

"You've always been a stubborn fool, won't listen to anyone, haven't got the common sense you were born with, trying to get yourself killed for a cow or calf or that blasted bull!"

Like some heroic soldier, going into battle, Abraham forced his way out the clogged kitchen door and disappeared into the shrieking white jaws of death. Martha pushed Jeremiah, who was already tying down his hat, to go after his father, to stop him from leaving the house. Jeremiah followed him out, grasping the rope that led from the kitchen door to the horse barn. The horses stirred excitedly, nickered loudly as if understanding. They nuzzled the men eagerly, expecting food. Abraham picked up his saddle.

"Don't go out there, Father, there's nothing you can do, it's twenty below, the wind will get you!"

"I'll stay close to the buildings," Abraham shouted. "See if there are animals I can help."

For a fleeting moment Jeremiah thought of stopping his father, physically, wrestling him to the floor, but Abraham still carried the size and strength of a powerful man and Jeremiah, still young and growing, doubted he could prevent him from going. Neither did he want to do anything that would drain his father's stamina against the storm.

"Then take Star, he'll buck the snow the best!" he shouted.

They saddled the stallion and Abraham pulled on a long canvas duster. He tied his hat on with his red bandanna and he was ready. He swung up onto the horse, ducking the low ceiling.

"Stay in sight of the buildings!" Jeremiah shouted into the shrieking wind. "Stay in sight of the buildings!"

Abraham nodded.

With all his strength, Jeremiah shoved the door open far enough for Abraham on Star to squeeze clear and climb through the drift that nearly covered the other end of the building. His father fought his way out into the wind-raked yard with his horse jumping and trying to find footing in the deep snow. And then Jeremiah lost sight of him in the enveloping white wind.

When he didn't come home that night, Jeremiah and Martha set several oil lamps ablaze in the kitchen window, the only window that wasn't drifted over. They had hopes that Abraham would see that feeble little light in the teeth of nature's brutality.

"Maybe he's holed up some place," Martha kept repeating. "Maybe he's holed up."

Jeremiah would nod and repeat the liturgical prayer. Every twenty minutes or so he wrenched the kitchen window open and fired a round from the buffalo gun until early in the morning when he ran out of ammunition. But the usually earthshaking blast was muffled into impotency in the roar of the storm.

Jeremiah went out the following day and tried to track him, but the wind had completely erased any sign of the horse or man. Jeremiah stayed in sight of buildings and fences, no more than about thirty feet, and he stumbled on Star, the stallion's face caked with ice and snow, his butt to the wind, standing patiently along the lee side of the corral with the reins tied loosely around the pummel. Jeremiah led him around the maze of drifts and got him into the horse barn. Star nickered to the other horses and Jeremiah wished he could translate, wished the horse could talk.

"Where is he, boy?" Jeremiah asked, "show me."

Day after day Jeremiah and Martha nurtured the hope that Abraham was in one of the outbuildings only a short distance from them, had been unable to see the lamps or hear the rifle. They continued burning wood pried and chopped off the horse barn, to keep from freezing, after they had broken up and burned all the pine and cedar furniture, consuming everything within reach. Now and then they'd hear a large thump or bang above the shrieking wind and they'd hurry to investigate through the pitch dark house in hopes it was Abraham trying to get in. Martha knew Abraham was incredibly strong, and she knew how many times he'd withstood danger and catastrophe, but the horror that was going on just outside those log and sawed lumber walls was the devil's treachery and she didn't understand why God didn't intervene.

# NINE

WHEN THE BLIZZARD BLEW ITSELF OUT, an overpowering calm
came over the country with a deafening silence. Martha cracked
the kitchen window and surveyed what she could of the valley,
now one great white canvas. A magpie skipped across an open
patch of yard as if nothing had happened. They saddled horses
and spread out from the buildings and yard, weaving around monstrous drifts and riding across large open spaces of bare ground
where the ferocious winds had swept the land clean. Bundled with
dread, they searched, terribly afraid of what they would find.

Little by little, they found cattle, some dead, some alive, hunkered down in willow thickets and aspen groves, backed under
cut banks and huddled in ravines, two here, one over there, a
bunch up in the cottonwoods. The sad truth of it was that these
tough animals who had survived the uncounted days and nights
of winter's hell would now probably starve with the winter grass
buried in snow below them.

So deeply engrossed in the search, Jeremiah hadn't noticed
until Martha came galloping around drifts and shouting.

"Chinook! Chinook!"

Jeremiah paused and looked into the wind. It had come back,
only now it was from the southwest, mild and downright warm,
and it was cranking up a blow.

"Chinook!" she shouted like a condemned prisoner just set
free.

"Chinook!" Could he still be alive? Dare they hope?

Martha reined in her horse. Now the remaining cattle might
not starve, the Chinook winds would quickly melt away some of
the snow and uncover some of the winter grass. But what else

would it uncover? That day the temperature went from fifteen below zero in the morning to fifty-six degrees by sunset.

After so many days there was no longer any urgency. They went out each day knowing the balmy temperatures would one day reveal Abraham's body and they hoped they'd get to him before the scavengers. They even took an urgent wagon trip to town to resupply some essentials. Julian Black, devastated by Abraham's death, found it hard to believe, said he'd heard of others lost in the blizzard, told of a woman who lived in town who went to the outhouse in her backyard, got turned around, walked off and froze to death.

Eleven days after the storm moved on, under a brilliant blue sky, Jeremiah searched northeast of the house. They had divided up the land and systematically covered the ground from the ranch buildings out, knowing he couldn't have made it far from the house. With his horse at a walk, Jeremiah glanced across a wide snow slide and something caught his eye. In the middle of the bright gleaming snow he saw red. He paused, staring at the distant, small red object, partially blinded by the reflecting sun. He turned his horse and shielded his eyes with his hand and gazed at this mysterious thing. It wasn't natural, it didn't belong there.

He rode to where the snow got deep and slid off his horse. Nearly up to his thighs he trudged uphill through the melting slushy snow, realizing he was in the fanned out bottom of a monstrous avalanche. The few aspens here in the meadow were bent downhill or snapped off. He then hurried, winded, drawn toward the strange red curiosity like a magnet to iron. He crawled the last few yards. As he stared it didn't register immediately and then, like the blare of a trumpet waking him from the grave, he recognized the twisted, red bandanna tied over his father's hat.

He held his breath and touched the bandanna as though to see if it was real. Then he knelt in the slush and dug with both hands until he'd uncovered Abraham's face. His father's eyes were closed and there was a quiet serenity on his face. How could this powerful, vigorous man be dead? He had beaten back everything thrown at him, had stood against it all. Jeremiah gazed out across the valley. Then he cried out like a wild animal. It carried across the sunlit land Abraham loved so dearly. Slowly, Jeremiah knelt forward beside his father and kissed him on the forehead. He was ice cold.

Jeremiah slid and stumbled down to his horse and galloped to the house. He stopped in the front yard and rang the bell, the clapper banging out the word that Abraham was dead. Martha heard it from south of the buildings and she knew immediately what it meant. Jeremiah had the buckboard hitched by the time she got there and with shovel and canvas they headed out. Martha insisted on climbing over the snow up to where Abraham lay. By the time she made it to the site, Jeremiah had him mostly uncovered. Martha sat beside the body and talked to him as if he heard every word.

"What were you doing way over here? No, you wouldn't listen to me. Stupid, stubborn, pig-headed man. I told you not to go out there, I told you but you never would listen to anyone, just do as you please. Well, look where it got you!"

When Jeremiah had the body free he started to slide it downhill. Martha helped by scooting on her bottom alongside. They hadn't gotten far when Abraham's body stretched tight and wouldn't move. His right arm reached above him as if he were waving to them, waving goodbye. On inspection, Jeremiah saw the end of a lariat wrapped around Abraham's right gloved hand. He pulled on the rope and felt dead weight at the other end.

Jeremiah followed the lasso, yanking it up out of the slush. When it would no longer budge he started digging. After sinking the shovel several times, he hit something that made the shovel clank. He dug again, again, and then found the head of a Longhorn. He dug far enough to identify the animal at the other end of the lasso. It was Boss, their prize bull. They went together.

Martha sat beside Abraham's body and allowed the floodgate to open, wailing loudly under the sad blue sky. Jeremiah sat in the melting snow and tried to understand. His father died trying to free a bull from a snowdrift when the deadly avalanche came down and swallowed them both. Abraham wasn't a tenth of a mile from the house. His father died doing what he had dreamed of and loved since he was a boy in Ohio—protecting his cattle on the Rocky Mountain frontier.

They loaded the body on the buckboard and drove to the small graveyard on the hill east of the house. Jeremiah dug the grave, finding only a few inches of frost, thanks to the chinook. With a feed bag needle and twine Martha sewed Abraham's body in a canvas shroud. When they'd topped off the grave with a layer of rock, Martha read words from the Bible. They said their good-byes and rode the buckboard back to the house. Jeremiah thought how much he hated good-byes. Anymore good-byes and he planned to duck out, to avoid them at all costs.

When they got to the house, he rang the bell, over and over, peeling out across the valley, not a final farewell to Abraham but a recognition that his spirit would always dwell here amid all that he loved. And somewhere in this country or on the road to Buffalo Jump or at Julian Black's General Store, quietly, within earshot, one might hear the story of Abraham Rockhammer who died in the blizzard trying to lead his bull to cover.

The shock of nature's sledgehammer had subsided. As best they could tell, they had lost more than half the herd with cattle starving to death daily. Martha and Jeremiah, mother and son, were exhausted physically and emotionally. They talked about picking up the pieces and carrying on or giving it up and going back to Ohio, selling what was left and pulling up stakes as so many were doing.

In a shocked stupor, they gathered the cattle that had survived. They ate beef, while the carcasses remained frozen in drifts, and talked late into the night. The unresolved question hung over the ranch like a shroud. They swayed back and forth, quit or stay. Stay or quit. Would they be able, could they bear the sorrow and memories that dwelt there? What emerged from all their procrastination was the image of Abraham and his deep powerful voice, as if he were there with them, giving them his strength and passion. In the end, it was Abraham who kept them from giving up and going home. He convinced them that they were home. Jeremiah agreed.

It would be starting over but he believed it was his God-given duty to carry on, to pick up Abraham's dream and brush it off, to relight the torch the blizzard blew out, to bring the Rockhammer back to what it had been, to follow in his father's footsteps and raise cattle in this extraordinary valley. Jeremiah and Martha saw misgiving in each other's eyes, but they could find their own dreams as well.

There would be two new commandments in the Rockhammer Bible. One: The supply of cut-and-split firewood always stacked a year's worth in advance! Two: To harvest hay during the summer and stake it where it was protected and readily available to feed cattle during the winter!

Jeremiah realized to do this they would have to build a family. He was barely nineteen.

# TEN

THE NEXT CHRISTMAS Jeremiah met Elizabeth at the fledgling Methodist church in Buffalo Jump and he knew immediately he wanted to make a life with this attractive young woman. After looking over some cattle to buy, he had been passing through Buffalo Jump in a hurry to get home to his mother with no intention of spending any time in town. When he heard about the worship service about to begin, he decided to take advantage of the opportunity to worship. His father would have approved— Abraham always welcomed becoming acquainted with his far-flung neighbors. When needed, Jeremiah was able to hire help from time to time to keep the ranch going. At times, they might have four or five riders keeping up on the land and the herd.

Sitting at the back among some four dozen souls, he noticed Elizabeth. During the service he stole hidden glances like a star-struck school boy. He remained afterward to share in the festive holiday and the abundance of Christmas food, but he really wanted to meet this bright, willowy female who appeared as if in a fairy tale coming out of nowhere on Christmas morning. He discovered that she, too, had been passing through Buffalo Jump with a large family in an elegant six-horse stagecoach.

Jeremiah buttonholed Julian Black and found out that it was some wealthy lumber baron who was scouting out the local forests and taking his family along for the sightseeing and adventure. Jeremiah began to breathe again when he found out that the becoming girl with the family was their governess and he immediately asked Julian to introduce him.

Waiting for the appropriate moment in the busy store, Julian brought Jeremiah face to face with Elizabeth. While the storekeeper went on and on about the magnificent Rockhammer Ranch that Jeremiah owned she gazed from Julian's face to Jeremiah's with a devastating smile. His duty done, Julian turned and scooted away, leaving Jeremiah like a lost puppy with no place to hide.

With his self-confidence melting in the warmth of her sky-blue eyes he caught himself and remembered who he was. He was the son of Abraham Rockhammer with whom he'd faced all that life had thrown against them, worked like a man when still a boy, carved Rockhammer Ranch out of wilderness, and stood against sickness and weather and disaster and death, stood against years of hard work, against trials and losses, pulled calves from their mothers' bellies into the world, pulled floundering cattle from the icy river, alive and kicking, and buried his brother and father along the way. Jeremiah stretched taller and returned her inviting gaze with his own, knowing that he was a man a woman would be fortunate to marry.

Elizabeth Downing had come to the northern Rocky Mountains as an adventure; actually, an only child, it was to get away from her domineering parents. She searched the Boston newspapers and found a position as a governess with a wealthy family in the new Montana Territory. While applying for the job, exchanging credentials both ways, Montana sounded quite primitive to her parents who were balking at every turn, informing their independent daughter of murdered settlers and brutal scalping and Indian massacres and finally outright forbidding her to go. But Elizabeth, now nineteen, had persevered and couldn't be turned.

She had read about the West and heard stories from those who had been there and with great excitement her heart was made up. It seemed she didn't take the danger seriously and they parted with animosity, her parents speaking as though they would never see her again. Neither parent came to the station to sanction her farewell. With a song in her heart and butterflies in her stomach, she rode the train westward to work for the Carleton J. Shepherd family, father and mother and four young children, a prominent family who had become wealthy in the lumber business in Michigan and Wisconsin, and who had built a home in Helena with one eye cocked on the virgin forests in the Rocky Mountains.

When the Shepherds discovered that Elizabeth was trained as a teacher, they added tutor to her list of responsibilities and increased her salary for her teaching experience. She got Sundays off to do with as she pleased. The other days she often walked or drove the buggy around the burgeoning town with the children in tow. Mr. Shepherd said he would provide a driver for her but she persuaded him to teach her to drive the buggy. And to ride horses. She was a natural and soon became tired of riding side-saddle. Convincing Mr. Shepherd to let her use a western saddle with pommel and wide stirrups on each side of the horse, she wore a split skirt while riding for pleasure and for teaching the children. Only the youngest, the three-year-old boy, couldn't ride by himself.

In her new and adventurous life, Elizabeth kept crossing the path of Grace Overby who lived in Helena with her class-conscious family. The same age, nineteen, they became close friends and managed to spend time together most days, whether it was a picnic with the kids, helping with their schooling at home, or teaching them how to make cinnamon rolls.

When Jeremiah came courting Elizabeth, Grace did everything in her power to dissuade Elizabeth from seeing the tall, handsome rough-cut rancher who always appeared to be walking into a stiff wind and who came from an obscure, godforsaken town named Buffalo Jump. Grace wanted Elizabeth to wait for a man who could offer more, keep her in the proper social stream, provide her with a life of culture and respect. Grace warned her that if she went off with that unpolished cowman, she'd end up doing the work of a man while missing the finer things in life. And though the man had been schooled in the country, Grace had to admit, in all fairness, that he was surprisingly well-read and quietly intelligent. So, despite all the warnings and sabotage, Jeremiah's persistence and his strong masculine manner won Elizabeth's heart.

It took him most of a year, and many days and miles on horseback, to convince Elizabeth, but they were wed the following Christmas so that beautiful day would be the anniversary of their meeting and marriage. When he was courting, he would be gone for over a week, riding to Helena to be with her for a brief time.

When he was in Helena, he'd worry about his mother alone at the ranch, and when he was at the ranch, he'd be longing to be with Elizabeth in Helena.

The couple didn't wait till the wedding to consummate their union. One fall day, when Jeremiah arrived at the Shepherd's place to see Elizabeth, the Shepherds were out of town—the whole kit and kaboodle—back east to visit. Maids and cooks were gone for the duration and Elizabeth had the place to herself. She prepared an elaborate dinner for Jeremiah, who was weary from his travels, thus beginning her reputation for being an excellent cook.

Young Jeremiah and Elizabeth could not restrain themselves and, with some giggling and trepidation, gave up their virginity in Carleton Shepherd's bed, irrationally fearing Mr. Shepherd would walk in the front door any moment.

After the Christmas Day wedding, which they held in the little Methodist Church in Buffalo Jump, Elizabeth moved into the home that the Rockhammers had been expanding and improving for these twenty-five years. It had doubled in size more than once and had been Martha's house most of those years. She and Elizabeth took awhile to stake out their personal territory, though they soon realized they had to pull together to help Jeremiah keep the ranch afloat.

Elizabeth proved to be capable of keeping a grand, orderly house. She worked on the land when needed, while splendidly maintaining her wit and earthy femininity. She was confident in her stature as a woman and wife but she could get her back up and stand her ground when she didn't see eye to eye with Jeremiah. She knew when to let him have his way and when to let him think he had his way.

Jeremiah had seen what happened when a family got whittled down by attrition in this harsh land and he planned on having a flock of children. Elizabeth had no idea that Jeremiah possessed any rage until the day he caught her five months pregnant on horseback. She was sneaking into the horse barn, mounted, when she thought Jeremiah was far up the valley.

"I forbid you to be around the horses in your condition," he shouted. "Didn't I? Didn't I?"

"Yes . . . but. . . ."

"I watched Alfred's brains color the straw! It can happen in a heartbeat. You fall off that animal and our child's brains could be coloring the straw!"

His face reddened, the veins in his forehead bulged.

"I only walked Daisy, you know how tame he is—"

"It can happen to any animal, any time, Daisy could be spooked, stung by a wasp, step in a gopher hole. Martha's horse was spooked by a bear, that's why her right knee doesn't work. I forbid you. Didn't you understand?"

Elizabeth shook her head. Jeremiah helped her slide off the horse and set her down gently.

"I'm sorry . . . I didn't think. . . ."

He took the horses and she quietly retreated to the house, feeling like a disciplined child who knew the parent was right. Jeremiah never mentioned it again and Elizabeth stayed clear of horseback riding whenever she was pregnant, knowing that other women rode right up until they were about to deliver and that the buggy or wagon bumped her around much worse than horseback. But she was wise enough to recognize this terrible wound that Jeremiah bore and she respected it.

Daniel was the first born, a treasure to Jeremiah's eye, a healthy, sturdy baby who one day would surely be the master of Rockhammer. During those early months of marriage and welcoming their firstborn, Jeremiah struggled to bring the ranch back to what it had been. Slowly the herd grew. Jeremiah rode all the way to Cheyenne to drive back a Hereford bull and three cows. The Hereford was a new breed to the land with a growing reputation of wintering well. White-faced cattle, squarely built, with delicious marbled meat, the animals stood up well on the open ground.

Jeremiah admitted to a deep paranoia when it came to harvesting hay. He could never have enough stored for the coming winter. The winter from hell had left an indelible imprint on his memory and soul. He built stacks in areas best protected from the wind, built high lodgepole fences around the stacks to prevent the cattle from eating it in the fall. They disagreed when it came to hiring available help for the harvest. Martha felt they should do it themselves, save their money the way they always did, though she was no longer capable to do much herself. Jeremiah thought it was sensible, with so much to do and given they had the money, to hire a few men at critical times. Elizabeth flip-flopped and each time the topic came up she'd have a different opinion. Jeremiah looked at Daniel with longing, visualizing him as a husky grown hand, urgently stacking hay with great purpose.

Then Elizabeth added to Jeremiah's dream when she informed them that she was pregnant again. Her close friend Grace found refuge from Bozeman and spent the long winter months with Elizabeth on the still-isolated ranch to help with little Daniel and the deliverance of the baby. Martha welcomed Grace who would seem like a special guest during the bleak months of winter, and who helped brighten the house with good conversation and laughter. Martha could do less and less with her bum knee and, because of her past history, she'd been banned from splitting firewood, wanting to spare her nine remaining toes.

Grace was betrothed to a major in the Army who was assigned elsewhere until the middle of July. He met Grace's well-thought-out requirements in that he came from a wealthy family of culture and breeding and was very influential socially. And besides that he was handsome and charming. Governor material. Grace was not only a good sport about her first opinion of Jeremiah but had come full circle and viewed Jeremiah as family, a brother-in-law.

With Grace at her side, Elizabeth gave birth on January twenty-fifth. They were fortunate that Doc Simpson was in the area and made it to the ranch in time to deliver two girls. The first born they named Gabrielle. Maddy came along about twenty minutes later. Jeremiah was ecstatic—two at one time—he was building the family he'd dreamed of. Elizabeth recuperated for a couple days and then was up and running the ship again. Grace remained for nearly three weeks and then Elizabeth convinced her that the ranch was under control and she could go home and prepare for her major's return.

Gabrielle and Maddy were not identical, and as they grew they became as different as sun and rain. Elizabeth said more than once that she'd dressed them alike too much when they were young. Now they do everything they can to be different: Maddy, the proper young lady, and Gabrielle, the ranch hand in britches. Elizabeth worried that Maddy would flirt her way to premature marriage to a local cowboy or worse, and planned to ship her off to live with Grace for a while at first chance. Growing up, Maddy helped on the ranch, as they all did, but she never took to it like Gabrielle and her brothers. She could ride and harness a team and pitch hay, but her eyes were always turned downriver toward civilization and the lure of the world beyond the valley.

Gabrielle was trim, athletic, rough and tumble without the facial beauty of her sister. In fact, she didn't look much like her siblings, though she had her mother's eyes. From early on she rode a horse as though the two were one. She roped, broke, and trained them, and got them to do whatever she wanted. She constantly challenged her older brother at whatever they were doing. When she'd outshoot Daniel or outride him, he'd always turn it into a contest of strength and he'd pick her up in one arm and carry her as though she were a shock of oats.

Gabrielle would rather be a ranch hand than a student and she languished in school, longing for the summer when she'd be set free to spend all of her time, after chores and work were done, on a horse or fishing or exploring the mountains. When Maddy would go to town with their parents on shopping excursions, she'd try to talk Gabrielle into going along, but usually her twin would prefer tagging along with Daniel to explore an eagle's nest or climb to an unscaled ridge or search for a wolf den.

When their second boy came along a year and a half after the twins, they named him Zechariah and Elizabeth informed Jeremiah that Zack would be her last born child. From then on she was like a young heifer, as Martha once had been, ducking and dodging Jeremiah who never gave up on the idea of more children. He was like a bull with one thing on his mind. The children grew up witnessing their father's constant pursuit of their mother and thought nothing of their father's lusty nature.

Jeremiah remembered the long sessions with the Bible that Abraham used to visit on him and he decided he wouldn't put his children through that, though he did read to them some of the more entertaining stories. He made it clear that God's law was their guide to life. If they broke it, and repented, God would forgive them. But there was the unforgivable sin that caused you to be damned. Jeremiah never said what it was so they guessed it had something to do with sex. Growing up in the midst of the cows in heat and the thrusting bulls, Jeremiah and Elizabeth both figured they didn't have much explaining to do on that score.

Jeremiah also remembered how he had to work long hours like a man while he was still a boy, and though each of the children grew up with work as a major part of their daily life, he'd regularly send them off to play. They made up games, in and out of doors. They put on plays, composing the story and fashioning their costume from whatever they could scrounge. They had wild contests and they read every book Jeremiah brought from town.

Their black Labrador, Bandit III, grew up with them and they learned to walk hanging onto her tail or ear. When they were at one of their favorite haunts, the deep swimming hole beneath the bedrock cliffs where Grandpa Abraham bathed in his birth-day suit to welcome Grandma Martha, the dog would leap from the ledges into the pool with the children. By blowing through her teeth, Gabrielle had learned to mimic the red-tailed hawk's high-pitched screech so perfectly that ground squirrels and mar-mots would duck for cover when she'd whistle. Gabrielle would leap from a ledge high above the river, whistling like the hawk, plummeting feet first through the air into the water, and Bandit would come flying behind her like an abandoned child.

Some years when they could not get a teacher in that part of the territory, Elizabeth and Martha schooled the children at home. Most years, the small school was their ongoing opportu-nity to interact with kids their ages. Still, with great distances between them and their closest neighbors, the four children grew up inventing creative ways to entertain themselves, side by side, and were encouraged to explore the humor and drama of the mi-raculous life bursting all around them.

# ELEVEN

JEREMIAH RODE THE ROCKING, overloaded wagon along the empty road home.

"What a day!" he shouted.

On this pleasant fall afternoon his heart sang with joy, traveling through a wild and handsome land that was continually turning up surprises. Around mid-afternoon he could see someone walking ahead of him about half a mile, appearing and disappearing with the curves and humps of the road. As he slowly gained, he expected the figure to grow larger but it didn't. It must have been a child, or maybe a small person, and when Jeremiah got close, the stranger paused and turned to wait for the rumbling, creaking wagon.

Jeremiah stopped the mules and gazed down on a strange diminutive creature that for the moment startled him. The little person had a swollen face as if he'd been bitten by a bumble bee or hornet, but Jeremiah could tell that the puffed nose, chin and forehead were permanent. The fellow wore a derby, had no facial hair, and carried an ample-sized rucksack on his back.

"Hello," Jeremiah said, as he gathered himself.

"And a fine day to you," the little man said with a low, throaty voice, obviously impressed with this large, over-bearing man.

"Where are you headed?" Jeremiah asked.

"Wherever the road takes me."

With one stubby hand he shielded his eyes from the sun, looking up into Jeremiah's bearded face.

"I live down the road a spell. Actually it's *up* the road, a long grade to my ranch. Have you a place to stay out this way?"

"Are there many settlers hereabouts?"

"No, aren't many folks out our way. There's our ranch, and then the Coopers and Weebows and a new family settling across Obsidian Creek."

"Have you a barn or hay mow?" the curious fellow asked as he gazed up the road.

"Better, a good soft bed in the bunkhouse just going to waste."

Jeremiah couldn't say for sure if the stranger was ten years old or forty. He felt sure he was male, but not completely sure.

"Well . . ." The little fellow hesitated. "It sounds right friendly and I'll surely consider the invitation."

"Climb up here."

He handed Jeremiah his pack sack and then scampered up the wagon wheel like a chipmunk and sat beside Jeremiah. His feet didn't reach the floorboards. Jeremiah had never seen anyone so extraordinary, a small, solid boy with a man's weathered face and voice. Jeremiah snapped the reins.

"Ha-yah! Ha-yah!"

The mules stepped out and leaned into the harness.

"I'm Jeremiah, Jeremiah Rockhammer. Have a ranch with my family about twenty miles up the road."

"Looks like you're building."

"Yes. Elizabeth, my wife, wants to make the house bigger. This is the third time we've added on. But she's fussy, doesn't want a lean-to tacked on the side. It has to look like all one piece, one plan. She was raised back east, finds pictures in books or sketches in a catalog."

"Are there many people living at your ranch?"

"No, just my family, have four kids growing like weeds."

"Do you get many travelers out this way?"

"No . . . we're pretty much the end of the line."

Jeremiah tried to keep from gawking, but he couldn't help noticing his strange features: large hands, stumpy arms and legs, quite bowlegged, a coarse, toughened face with the derby on top. Not more than three foot six, Jeremiah wondered if the fellow'd had some terrible disease and he wondered where he'd get his disproportionate clothing if not in a children's catalogue.

Jeremiah flicked the reins and encouraged the mules.

"Hey, Dolly, hey, Jeb, hey-ya, hey-ya."

The little traveler bounced half out of the bench seat at times and his rucksack had several books protruding from its stuffed top as if they were being swallowed by a large fish.

"You like books I see," Jeremiah said.

"If you have a book you're never alone," the man said.

"You'll be welcomed by the kids like wealthy relatives. We've accumulated a small library over the years," Jeremiah said, "Maybe we can do some swapping."

"Sounds good. I've worn out a few hauling 'em around. Can't ever work up to leavin' one behind."

"See there?" Jeremiah pointed ahead as a bunch of cow elk ran across the road into a cluster of Douglas fir. "We spooked 'em." Jeremiah said.

"You have them on your land?"

"Yeah, it's a tradeoff. Come winter they like our haystacks and we enjoy elk roast."

"Haystacks?"

"Oh, yeah. Many haystacks. Many, many, haystacks. We all but lost the ranch some years ago; my father, killed in the blizzard from hell, nearly eighty percent of our herd destroyed, family whittled down to two. We came very close to giving up and going back to Ohio."

"You lost your father?"

"Yes. He tried to save our best bull. We can talk about it now, some. We try to laugh at our pain. My mother and wife and I boast that we're the ranch raising the best sweetgrass hay this side of the mountains and the cleanest, slow burning oak that will burn well overnight."

"I enjoy seeing the wild things in this country," the little man said. "Saw a mountain lion a few weeks back, at least that's what folks told me."

"What's your name?" Jeremiah asked.

"When I was born they told me my mother took one gander at me and screamed, 'Mercy! Mercy!' When the priest baptized me they told me he prayed 'God, have Mercy!' as if he were asking God to take me back. One day the dean of boys at the orphanage told me, in front of all the boys, that I was a wart on the ass of God. By the time I ran away from the orphanage 'Wart' had stuck. I tell anyone who asks that my name is Wart, but I know in God's great book it's really Mercy, Mercy Possible."

"Is Possible your family name?"

"Got no real family."

"You don't know your father or mother?"

"Don't remember. I'm lucky they didn't drown me once they saw me. Folks do that with us sometimes, embarrassed and ashamed, they don't want people seeing us as if something is wrong with *them*—the mother and father. People think they did something bad or sinful and we're their fault, we're the punishment God gave them."

Awestruck, Jeremiah could find no words in the moment. This abandoned little man, who had been deserted by his mother and father, dealt a cruel, even tragic, hand, summed up his destiny with a spit-in-your-eye attitude without a hint of whine or complaint. In a dozen words he had peeled back the fiber of the human heart and touched it. He had even kept the name given him in derision and carried it proudly. And he glowed with something bright, something happy. Jeremiah gathered himself and hoped he could persuade Wart to stay at the ranch for a day or two, trusting that the children would find him fascinating and welcome him with warmth and respect.

"Well, where are you headed now, Mer, er, Wart?"

"Oh, I don't know, I like this country a lot, never seen the likes of these mountains."

"Well, you can sure stay with us a spell if you've a mind to. We've got lots of room, and I warn you we may put you to work."

"Many thanks, Mr. Rockhammer, but I've found it best if I don't start growin' any moss."

"You have some destination in mind, someone expecting you?"

"No, not really. They were looking for me for a while when I ran away from the orphanage, though they probably didn't care a whole lot. Then I lived in the streets for a while in Philadelphia and I got roped into an outfit that placed homeless kids out in the country to give them jobs and a decent home and family. They thought I was a kid. I got sent to a farm family in Dakota Territory. Good folks, they tried, but it were too much for them. I'm a dwarf."

Jeremiah glanced at the strange character riding beside him and he realized he liked the little fella.

"I've never seen a dwarf. I've read about them somewhere, I think, a book or magazine."

"Not too many of us around." Wart laughed.

"How long ago did you run from the farm family?"

"Oh . . . six months or so. They probably give up on me as a lost cause long ago."

Wart didn't want to bring down any trouble on this kind man and his nice family but he had a hunch that he would be safe here in this isolated outpost. He damn well knew he wasn't a runaway orphan the law was nonchalantly, half-heartedly searching for. He was a freakish-looking little man wanted for serious implications in the murder of a circus ringmaster.

Would this family be held accountable if Wart stayed here for a time, even though they had no idea of what he had done? He felt weary, worn down, always moving as far into the wild country as he could, avoiding people. Avoiding people—something he grew up doing; he didn't hate people—he knew they were uncomfortable with his being a dwarf. He knew the crushing weight of loneliness and Jeremiah's offer felt warm and safe and somewhat permanent. He had done what he could to protect Stella, to throw them off her scent and draw them onto his. With the evidence he carefully left behind they couldn't possibly convict her unless she'd grown a thumb.

He missed her and was surprised at how much he could come to love an animal. He remembered, with some emotion, the crazy days they experienced, desperately searching for a place where he could leave her in safety and love. He had asked some of the locals about the land to the west and was assured it was rocky, barren desert, unoccupied save for rattlers and vultures.

He still found it hard to believe that the two of them waited quietly in the damp shadows of that old fruit cellar while the circus gang and the townspeople carried out a spirited search for almost two days and a night. Wart could hear them shouting at times, far out from the train where an elephant could run free or where an elephant could be found and shot to death in a local contest.

Finally, the locomotive built up steam and the circus left town with Bixbee's body and with Wart shaken to the core. He never planned to hurt Bixbee, let alone kill him, and now the law would be after them like hornets. The circus had set up along a railroad spur, the last human endeavor at the edge of a raw western expanse and all they had to do was wait patiently until dark and then walk away. It was nothing short of miraculous and Wart began believing in the weight of God's grace.

As Jeremiah and Wart followed the rutted road, something inside Jeremiah wanted to laugh, though he didn't know why. This surprising, mysterious dwarf, who appeared out of the foothills like magic, could just as well have stepped out of a fairy tale. They bumped and bounced along the rocky road, the mules pulled together, the sun slipped quietly to the west.

"How have you been keeping alive? Doesn't look like you have much gear for this country."

"I make do. People are kind, most of 'em. I work for a meal. Like to keep movin' when I can."

"Some people give you a hard time?"

"Some." Wart glanced at Jeremiah.

They both rode silently for several minutes as if neither wanted to open that wound. Jeremiah dared first.

"Like . . ."

"Like sicking a vicious dog after you, tree you like a coon and then have a good laugh. Like pissing on your pack and then showing their dog how to do the same."

They bumped along the little-used road.

"I fought 'em sometimes, tried to, but it only riled 'em more, made a sport of it, stirred 'em up, entertained 'em. Sometimes they refused to serve me in a store or inn. Once they spiked the outhouse door shut when I was in it and let me out the next day."

"Didn't anyone help you? Where were the people?"

"Often they were there, some, and the ruffians knew when

they couldn't get away with it. But sometimes the 'good people' were afraid to get involved. They'd turn and walk away."

"I'd never guessed, not out here. These folks are decent down-to-earth neighbors, trying to build a life. We'll have none of that around Buffalo Jump, we won't tolerate it."

"I'd stay out of sight most of the time. Once, when they were threatening me with bodily harm, an older woman came roaring out of her house with a sawed off shotgun and started blazing away. You shoulda seen those polecats scatter."

"Well, by God, I'd kick a few into the outhouse they try something like that out our way."

Wart looked into Jeremiah's face and smiled.

"I believe you would, I surely do. The strange thing," Wart said, "I came to realize they were afraid of me. I was a threat to them, a plague, something they couldn't understand. Maybe I'd contaminate their children or spread some ghastly sickness on them."

The men traded stories and soon Jeremiah pulled off the road and stopped the team on a grassy bank beside a rushing creek.

"Obsidian Creek. We'll camp here for the night."

While Jeremiah watered and hobbled the mules, Wart quickly gathered firewood and hauled water from the creek. Before long Jeremiah had coffee brewing and a hearty meal of beans and bacon sizzling over the fire. When they'd eaten, Jeremiah laid out his bed roll under the wagon and Wart rolled out a light canvas next to his. A night chill encompassed them and they sat near the fire talking, with the sound of Obsidian Creek soothing them.

Jeremiah realized that Wart was reluctant about revealing his history so he began to tell Wart the story of the Rockhammers, how Abraham came out to this country and started all alone, the confrontation and friendship with the Indians, the winter from hell that took Abraham's life, filling in the saga of the ranch with all its drama and loss and triumph.

After listening to Jeremiah's epic story of the ranch, Wart had a strong feeling of trust and affection for this man he had only just met. Without knowing how this kind man might react he decided to unburden himself and tell Jeremiah his story. He started by admitting that he had most recently been with the circus. He told Jeremiah about the ringmaster, a cruel, arrogant man named Bixbee, who mistreated the animals, especially a gentle elephant named Stella.

"Only reason I stayed was to save Stella and I had no idea how I could do that."

"How long did you stay with the circus?"

"Oh, a couple months. I enjoyed the animals, especially the elephant. I didn't like the way Bixbee—he owned the circus too—treated the one elephant they had. For whatever reason Bixbee was downright mean. I tried to keep her out of his way. Stella helped raise the big tents but the ringmaster would jab her and hit her with his cane and curse her. When I witnessed the ringmaster treating Stella cruelly I began to hate him. When she was in the big top with an audience he'd kick her or punch her to show off, like she was a bad animal and he could make her behave. The crowd loved it, thinking it was part of the act. I knew Stella enough that I could tell when she'd cry.

"Bixbee would talk about how he would soon have to butcher Stella since she wasn't performing well anymore and they couldn't afford to feed her. I could see a growing desperation in the elephant's eyes, could tell that she wanted to run away, but where could an elephant run? She acted like she'd given up. Bixbee got angrier and she'd perform listlessly. The only reason I stayed was to save Stella from capture and butchering. We didn't mean to kill him, it was an accident. But who would believe that? If you're still willing to let me stay with you for a spell, we better not let your family know about Stella and why I'm hiding."

Jeremiah held his breath. He knew where the story was leading. Wart had tears in his eyes as he continued to detail the accidental killing of the vicious ringmaster. He told Jeremiah that Stella had stomped on him, simple as that. That he was on the run. That he, against all odds, had found a safe place for Stella. And now it looked as though Wart had done it.

# TWELVE

JEREMIAH WAS UP EARLY and making coffee over a small fire when Wart crawled out from under the wagon. After a breakfast of oatmeal, bread, and cheese, they broke camp and harnessed the mules. After traveling a mile or more, Jeremiah noticed Wart looking over his shoulder as if he were being followed.

Wart did feel as though he were being followed, as if someone had recognized him from that last town he'd come across, a rough, muddy place trying to get started. It reminded him of the small town in Dakota where the ringmaster had been tormenting Stella. Jeremiah urged the mules along and slowly shook his head. "Ye Gads!"

He was riding home with a dwarf who didn't know where he was going or when he arrived. Jeremiah and Wart knew he hadn't killed anyone though the men who pursued him believed he had. He had saved Stella from the man who would hunt her down and, with hatred, slaughter her. Now he wanted to disappear in the wilderness.

Jeremiah was a man who accepted things at face value and had no cravings to know somebody else's business. But he was more than a bit curious how Wart found a safe place for Stella. Where in the world one finds a good home for an elephant in the American West was a tough nut to crack for Jeremiah. But because he was a respectful man first and foremost he was going to let Wart hold on to his story forever or let Wart tell it when he was good and ready.

As they made their way to the ranch, Jeremiah traded stories with Wart, wanting to fill him in on the family so he might feel more comfortable with them, if he chose to stay. Jeremiah wondered what the consequences would be if authorities came for Wart. Would the family be arrested, jailed, could they be harmed? What did harboring a fugitive mean? Is the law still hunting Wart somewhere out there? Jeremiah decided to put these thoughts in the hands of God. He had already envisioned Wart at the ranch as if Wart had been there all along.

One of the stories Jeremiah told Wart was a family favorite and, as Wart bounced on the wagon bench and hung on for dear life, Jeremiah commenced. It always started the same way. One spring day the Rockhammer children finally came to blows with Henry Weebow's boys, Ben and Rufus, on the play area around the small country school. Jeremiah remembered that spring day vividly, when Daniel was in sixth grade. Zack found him in the Douglas firs beside the schoolyard during lunch break, stalking marmots with Bandit, their faithful dog. Zack knew where to look because he knew Daniel hated to use the stinking outhouse and was probably peeing in the woods. Zack informed Daniel with stuttering emotion that Ben was hurting Maddy, bringing Daniel in a headlong sprint for the schoolyard. Ben Weebow was almost two years older than Daniel, outweighed him by twenty-five pounds, and was by nature a bully. He had tried to bait Daniel into a fight more than once over the years but Daniel would always regard it as good-natured fun and with a calm openness defuse the challenge.

Somehow every kid in the school, all fifteen of them, including Ben, knew that it wasn't fear that made Daniel avoid a fight, but rather his generous and happy spirit. But when Gabrielle asked him once why he wouldn't fight when Ben had insulted him and made fun of him in front of others, Daniel told her, "If I fight him I just might kill him." She never forgot what he said and it confused her since Ben was much bigger than Daniel.

When he rounded the schoolhouse he saw that Ben had a hold of Maddy's pigtails in one of his fists, which he held at arm's length. She struggled to sock him or kick him in the shins. No longer kid's play, she was crying as he tormented her, while his younger brother Rufus laughed and cheered.

"Just say you love me," Ben said, "and I'll let you go."

Daniel never broke stride, hitting Ben waist high with a flying tackle. Both of them sprawled on the dusty playground. When they sprang to their feet, Daniel came up with clenched fists ready to fight. Rufus quickly crouched on the ground behind Daniel and before Daniel could be warned, Ben shoved him and he flipped backward over Rufus. Before Daniel could get up, Ben was on his back, his arms under Daniel's armpits with his fingers locked behind Daniel's neck. Daniel was extremely strong for his age and size, but he was helpless in Ben's hold.

They struggled to their feet, and Ben shoved Daniel forward until his face was mashed against the gnarly trunk of a spruce at the edge of the playground. Ben was grinding Daniel's face against the tree and as he struggled, Daniel refused to let out a sound.

Gabrielle, a fourth-grader, picked up a broken broom handle and shouted, "Fight him fair, fight him fair!"

Then she caught Ben across the kidneys with a haymaker. Ben immediately lost his grip and dropped to his knees with a howl. Gabrielle held off Rufus with the crude weapon and allowed Daniel to gather himself. Daniel ran at Ben like a goat in rut and rammed his head into Ben's chest, driving him back against the wooden well with such force that Ben flipped over the well wall and hung precariously for a moment with his fingertips and toes. Then, with a great frightened howl, Ben Weebow dropped into the large well like a stone.

Everyone laughed, even Rufus. They couldn't contain their exhilaration. Then all the gathered classmates rushed to the well and gaped. There, at the bottom, ten feet below, Ben stood waist deep in the water looking like anything but a bully. His pants caught on a nail head halfway down and what was left of them hung there on the wooden wall without Ben in them. Their howling laughter brought Mrs. Holland out of the schoolhouse. With the girls banished to the schoolhouse and all the boys pulling on the rope, they rescued Ben, bare-assed, from the drinking supply. The bully spent the afternoon sitting in one of Mrs. Holland's skirts, learning long division. She said it was what he deserved for starting fights. Snickers could be heard most of the afternoon, and for the rest of the school term, the Rockhammers brought water in jars, figuring any water Ben Weebow had been standing in wasn't fit for drinking.

When Jeremiah heard about the incident—all four versions—he paid a visit to Henry Weebow, though he had important work to do at home. He had learned a lot about Henry Weebow since that day in town when Henry asked Abraham for permission to cross Rockhammer land. Henry, a drinking man a little older than Jeremiah, whose much-younger wife had left him some time back, lived in a ramshackle house two hours down the road on a hundred sixty acres he'd homesteaded. There he ran herd on his two boys and managed to scrape up a living and keep himself in liquor.

Also, Henry had a mining claim on the backside of the mountain at the edge of the Rockhammer stake. Gold, in a quartz vein that Henry felt sure would widen and make him rich if he just dug long enough and far enough. And laid off the booze. Nothing had come of the gold strike. Jeremiah remembered and treasured the promise Abraham had given to the Blackfeet and he had seen what the miners had done to other parts of this country and it wasn't going to happen in his valley, gold or no gold.

When Jeremiah arrived at the Weebow's at eleven that next morning, he rousted Henry from a nap and told him that his son was being rude and disrespectful of his daughter and he wouldn't tolerate it. If Henry couldn't raise his boys proper, Jeremiah told him, he would take an interest in their upbringing. He had Henry repeat the threat out loud to be sure he wasn't in a whiskey swoon. Henry Weebow took a willow switch to his boys and for the rest of the spring not one of the Weebows spoke a word to a Rockhammer unless it was required by a teacher in the pursuit of higher learning.

Ten days later, on the way home from school, the children found Bandit beside the road, dead, her back broken under a deadfall. The kids mourned the death of their beloved and loyal pet. Daniel carefully tied the dog across his horse to carry her home. Then something made him go back and examine the lodgepole she had been pinned under. To his shock and disbelief,

he discovered that the snag had fallen sometime last fall or summer; he could tell where it touched the ground, where the bark
had begun to rot, where the ground under it showed its imprint
from the past growing season.

Someone had killed Bandit and wedged her under the log, and
the Rockhammers damn well knew who. On the sad trip home,
with the girls weeping and Zack trying to be brave, they tried to
comprehend how anyone could be that mean. Bandit made no
distinctions, she loved all the kids at school, even the Weebows.

It was so horrible that someone would deliberately kill Bandit
that Daniel could never utter a word about it. All of the adults
thought it sounded mighty suspicious when they heard about it
that night at supper, and when they looked at Daniel's trembling
chin, he figured he'd say no more. Jeremiah knew the chances
of a deadfall hitting a dog was about as likely as one of his bulls
playing the fiddle. But he figured his young son had grown up
some and he had caught a glimpse into the wicked side of men.

"There," Jeremiah pointed through the gap. "There she be,
we're almost home."

Wart gazed at the immensity of it all. "Is this the
Rockhammer?"

"Home sweet home," Jeremiah was nodding. "Home sweet
home."

Jeremiah could see the gorge and the ranch gate. Boy, did
he have a surprise for them. Wart scrambled off the wagon and
swung open the gate.

"So this the Rockhammer."

He gazed through the rocky gap at the ring of mountains ahead
and he thought this might be a good place to hole up.

# THIRTEEN

JEREMIAH DROVE THE OUTFIT around behind the horse barn and wondered who'd notice first. Elizabeth called from a kitchen window when he passed.

"Welcome home! Looks like a heavy load."

"The kids all home from school?" Jeremiah called.

"Yes!"

"Whoa, Dolly, whoa, Jeb."

The mules stopped and shook their harness and gave a weary blow. They knew they were home.

"That was your missus?" Wart asked.

Jeremiah climbed down and started to help Wart get down when he sensed Wart didn't want his help.

"Yes, Elizabeth, best cook from here to Helena." He winked at Wart.

Wart scrambled down easily and surveyed the ranch, the several buildings and corrals, the cattle and the river to the west below the house, snaking its way brightly through the valley.

"Your place is much larger than I figured," Wart said.

At that moment Gabrielle came running from behind the house. "Father, did you get any new booo . . ."

When she saw Wart, like no one she'd ever seen before, she stopped dead in her tracks and almost fell down.

"Gabrielle, this is Wart. He's going to stay with us a spell. We'll unhitch the mules and then we'll be in to say hello."

Gabrielle hadn't moved an inch. Her mouth slowly opened.

"Hello," Wart said in his froggy voice. "I'm a dwarf."

Gabrielle recovered. "I know, one of my favorite books is about dwarves."

"Do you like books?" Wart asked.

"Yes, I love them."

"I have several in my pack you can read if you'd like."

Wart climbed up into the wagon and grabbed his rucksack. He handed it down to Gabrielle.

"Oh, look at this one, and that one," Gabrielle said as she walked slowly toward the house with Wart and some of his books in tow.

Jeremiah realized he'd get no help from that pair and he felt a rush of joy that his daughter would accept this strange little man as if he were as normal as apple pie. He hoped the rest of them would do the same.

Wart felt uneasy as he scrutinized the house and met the rest of the family, expecting more than the seven to materialize out of this solidly built ranch and magnificent valley. There was a part of him that wanted to stop, to dare to stay here, if they invited him for a time. It was off the beaten path; who would ever find him tucked back into the shoulders of these mountains on a road that dead-ended? He could have hidden Stella here. Then there was the voice in him that warned against trusting this place long enough to stay and rest. He'd take a day or two and see how it felt.

They gathered around the large supper table and Jeremiah made a temporary seat for Wart with several books piled on a chair. Wart was impressed with the plates and silverware as if the meal were a special formal gathering of this family instead of an everyday occurrence. An unfamiliar awkwardness settled quietly as they found their places. When they had started eating the family was a little shy at first but questions were burning holes in their pockets like unspent coins. Daniel broke the ice.

"Where do you live?" Daniel asked.

"Where are you going?" Maddy asked.

"How old are you?" Gabrielle asked.

"I don't know," Wart said, and that stopped the questions for the moment.

Martha, who was advancing in years, told the children to pipe down and give the visitor a chance to eat and catch his breath. But then she turned to him and asked about his Christian name.

At that point the barrage of questions started all over again. Wart told them he'd stay another few days, that he'd need that to rest from all the activity, and then he laughed, which sounded more like he gargled. With some drama he asked them in a throaty whisper to promise not to tell any of their friends or neighbors that he was there, a dwarf.

"Why don't you want them to know you're here?" Daniel asked.

"Some people might not treat him kindly," Jeremiah said. "He'd just like to rest for awhile, he's all worn out."

Wart decided he'd lay low at the ranch for some time and then leave this family before he was discovered and they'd be held accountable for sheltering a fugitive. Jeremiah and Elizabeth fixed up a room in the bunkhouse for Wart with its own pot-bellied stove.

In the coming days Gabrielle hounded him as if he were a living, breathing book. Daniel adopted him as a new companion to run with apart from the younger children. Only Zack was a touch standoffish with the newcomer. Elizabeth figured it was a little jealousy. Wart was replacing Zack as the favored youngster of the family.

Wart settled in but it wasn't always smooth-going with him and the family, they adjusting to living with a dwarf and Wart adjusting to living with them. From time to time they'd treat him as if he were a child.

"But he's so small," Maddy said, "like a little kid." Even Elizabeth would catch herself thinking of him as a child, talking to him, scolding him as if he were a little kid. Sometimes Wart would laugh and answer, "Yes, Mommy." At other times he'd pause and shake his head as if acknowledging they'd lost their perspective.

One of Wart's strange behaviors baffled the family. All of a sudden, as if he'd been hit by lightning, Wart would explode after a chicken, racing across the barnyard with his stubby bowlegs, zigzagging through corrals, trying to wear the poor bird down, until finally diving headlong with an attempted flying tackle, only to come up with a mouthful of dirt and straw and chicken feathers. Using a stalking mode, he tried in dead earnest but could never catch a chicken and he'd brush himself off and curse under his breath and hope no one was watching, especially the kids who could run a chicken down and catch it with ease. When the children asked him why he did it he'd tell them it was a long story.

For the time being the whole family thought it was the best entertainment they had and felt disappointed when they heard they'd missed the spectacle that occurred every ten days or so, as if Wart were storing up speed. Since Wart arrived, the Rockhammer chickens led a wary existence.

And then there were the influences from the little man that Elizabeth tried to keep from the children. Now and then a new cuss word would surface at a time of anger or injury. Sometimes there'd be a small-stakes poker game in the bunkhouse, where Wart would demonstrate how he could deal from the bottom of the deck and the kids could never catch him at it. Gambling of any kind was outlawed, a vice Elizabeth strongly forbid. If she approached the bunkhouse unexpectedly the game would magically become Go Fish.

With Jeremiah's help and Wart's cooperation, the kids were only partially tainted by their relationship with the fun-loving dwarf who often acted more like a mischievous little boy. One evening Jeremiah gathered the family in front of the house by the bell. He announced that they were going to adopt Wart and make him part of the family, to recognize what had already been taking place. Jeremiah spoke the words and read something from the Bible and then Daniel, who was gaining a big brother, rang the bell a dozen times, proclaiming to their world that Mercy Possible had become a Rockhammer. Mercy Possible Rockhammer had found his home, his family. Elizabeth and Martha cried.

# FOURTEEN

"IT'S LETTING UP COWBOYS! Let's hit the ground, there's cows out there getting in trouble!" Jeremiah yelled. Jeremiah rounded up Daniel, Gabrielle, and Zack and they bolted into action, pulling on their warm clothes and saddling horses. This was the most dangerous time for cattle who were trying to find water along the icy banks of the freezing river. Some of the ice would be strong enough to bear the weight of the cows if they didn't bunch up too badly. The ice varied in thickness depending on the current running below it; calm water, thick ice, strong current, thin ice. And the fresh snow covered the ice making it difficult if not impossible to judge.

They were spread out on horseback scanning the river for cattle that may be in trouble and finding animals that were reaching water safely along the shallow stretches and gravel bars. Martha, Elizabeth, Maddy, and Wart remained at the ranch doing the outside chores as the weather abated. Those on horseback spread out along both sides of the river, riding north into the valley. They called back and forth, whistling and shouting to each other, facing a cutting wind that found its way through the face into the bones. After almost an hour, Zack came galloping through the snow, shouting.

"Father! Father! Napoleon fell in the swimming hole."

Their worst nightmare. Their prize bull in the river. Jeremiah turned quickly as he pulled his rifle from its scabbard and fired three shots into the frosty air.

They came at a gallop from all directions. Jeremiah shouted instructions as they reined up at the swimming hole. Thirty feet from shore the bull had broken through the ice over one of the deepest spots on the river. The animal stood on his hind legs in about six feet of water, trying to climb out with his front legs and head up on the ice. With only his head and shoulders above water he thrashed and drummed on the edge of the ice with his front legs. He'd struggle for a moment and then fall back and go under, only to come up snorting and gasping. They couldn't tell how long the bull had been stranded but he would shortly drown without help. The bull's prehistoric scream was something the four would never forget.

"We have to hurry! We don't have much time here!" he shouted as he grabbed his coiled lariat. Immediately they all had their lassoes out and whistling in the air to make a loop. With their horses as close to the edge as they dared, they reined rope loops out on the head of the bull but only one caught. Jeremiah had a rope around the bull's muzzle. Gabrielle and Daniel recoiled while Zack put a loop over the bull's head and snagged it taut. Other loops were landing true and their trained cutting horses backed away, straining the lariats against the weight of the bull.

"He's getting close to the hole!" Gabrielle shouted. "We'll lose him in there!"

"Pull, Rockhammers, pull!" Jeremiah shouted. "Pull, dammit!"

In the excitement and terror of the moment, Zack had wrapped his rope around the saddle horn once and it snagged taut while his horse backed up. Reacting in that moment, Zack wrapped the slack in the rope around his wrist. When the bull slipped off the edge of the ice and rolled over in the water, Zack's lasso rolled up around Napoleon's neck and front leg as if on a reel. It jerked Zack off his horse and out onto the snow-covered ice, snagged so tightly he couldn't pull his rope free.

"Zack's out on the ice!" Daniel shouted, "Zack's on the ice."

"Pull!" Jeremiah shouted, "I'll get Zack!"

The bull slipped off the edge of the ice again and went under, rolling one full turn and coming up gagging and coughing, pulling Zack under water and then onto its back, snarled in rope. Zack choked and gagged and tried to pull himself free.

Jeremiah leaped from his horse, pulled out his knife, and started out onto the ice.

"Hey! Hey!" Gabrielle shouted as she turned her horse, Ramrod, out onto the ice. The horse took short chopped steps as Gabrielle urged it toward the stricken bull and Zack.

"What are you doin'?" Jeremiah shouted as he stood at the edge of the ice, "get that horse off the ice!"

"Let her be! Let her be!" Daniel yelled.

Out on the ice Gabrielle urged the horse to within four or five feet of the bull and Zack. Then she pulled back on the reins and Ramrod momentarily rose up on his hind legs. At her command the horse brought his front hooves down with a crashing blow. Nothing happened. Ramrod rose up again and came down with a thudding blow. The ice cracked, then broke. The edge in front of the bull broke away three or four feet.

Jeremiah looked at Daniel with his mouth hung open. Daniel smiled at his father. They both didn't believe what they were witnessing.

*The horse knew what it was doing!*

Gabrielle backed Ramrod, rising and pounding and with great power breaking a path to the shore. Soon the bull walked on the rocky bottom out of the river. Napoleon stood quietly, wheezing, knock-kneed, exhausted, while they unsnarled the ropes and set Zack free.

Jeremiah rode over to where Gabrielle sat on her horse just shaking his head.

"I figured there could be rattlesnakes in the river," she said and then smiled.

"I thought I was a goner," Zack said, already shaking from the wet cold. "I thought Ramrod was going to flatten me like a pancake. Wait till I tell Mother and Wart."

They bundled Zack and got him on his horse. Jeremiah would gallop home with him while Daniel and Gabrielle would watch Napoleon for an hour or so and see if he was all right, fearing the worst, pneumonia. They all realized they'd seen something that day that they might never tell about. Who would believe?

# FIFTEEN

THOSE WHO KNEW THEM would say the Rockhammers were a normal, God-fearing, American frontier family. The third generation, growing up and continuing to carve out a livelihood on their isolated ranch in that rugged mountain valley of Montana Territory.

In Daniel's twentieth summer the hay grew tall and lush, some of it blessed by irrigation and the rest nurtured by ample summer rain. In mid-August the family worked on the lower meadow, harvesting hay they'd cut the day before. This day they used wagons and teams, pitchforks and strong backs, to store the feed that would hopefully prevent their cattle from starving in winter's killing grip. They stacked it in the ninety degree waves of heat and would most likely feed it in January's frozen world.

Elizabeth had been trying all summer to convince Gabrielle to go off to college in the fall with Maddy but Gabrielle fought off every argument, determined to stay and help run the ranch, knowing that Daniel could be off any day at his age. And with Maddy gone it would be just Zack and Wart and her parents and though she didn't want to recognize it, they were slowing down. Jeremiah had some dread under his sweat-soaked shirt as his daughters were about to go off into the world to find their lives, but he countered that sadness with the joy that Daniel gave every indication he'd be happy as a prairie dog in the oat bin to stay on and find his life there in the valley. With Elizabeth's untiring prompting for higher education the whole time the children were growing up, Jeremiah figured he'd lose one or two to her efforts and hoped no more than that. And he hoped they'd return to the ranch after they'd earned their sheepskins and a husband or wife.

When the sun was far to the west and about to slide behind the mountains, Elizabeth drove the empty wagon away from the rising stack and Maddy prodded the other team to pull her overflowing wagon in close. Gabrielle and Zack climbed on the wagon and began slinging hay with pitchforks onto the growing stack, now about eight feet high. Jeremiah, riding on the back of the wagon he'd helped fill, began pitching large clumps onto the pile in great thrusts with the rhythm in his pitchfork of one who had done it for years, one who had fought the blizzard from hell, spreading the hay evenly on top of the stack with a learned art. He shouted down to Gabrielle.

"Why don't you get some hay on that fork, as long as you're waving it around in the air."

"I'd take more but you'd never be able to keep up," she said.

The aroma of fresh-cut hay drifted pungently across the air-still meadow; grasshoppers clacked their wings, fleeing from the winging pitchforks; honeybees darted among the sticky geraniums and mountain bluebells. Elizabeth brought a gallon crock to the wagon and passed it up to Zack, who took a long drink and then passed it to Gabrielle. Elizabeth looked at Gabrielle as she drank.

"Just try it for a semester; if you don't like it—"

"I'm tired of hearing about it," Gabrielle said, pulling the crock from her lips and spilling water down the front of her shirt. "I'm not Maddy!"

"How about water for the hand doing all the work?" Daniel asked.

"You haven't done enough to break a sweat," Zack said.

Gabrielle thumped the cork back in the jug and with a round-house swing, heaved the jug to the top of the stack where Daniel almost slid off when he snatched it.

"No wonder you got it here; it's next to empty," Daniel said.

Gabrielle began tossing hay as if the wagon were on fire. Daniel took a long swig, watched Gabrielle as he popped in the cork, and dropped the jug to his father.

"Get the ropes," Jeremiah called to Maddy.

They finished unloading and several ropes, weighted with heavy rocks at each end, were draped across the stack from side to side to prevent the wind from scattering it. Spears of sunlight angled across the meadow, illuminating butterflies and insects and thistle seeds drifting in the air. Hanging on to the front rack, Maddy drove one team and wagon with Zack at her side and she was taken by an unexpected sadness that reminded her that she wouldn't be a part of this way of life any longer. Elizabeth drove the other wagon, with Jeremiah hooting on horseback and they raced across the meadow for the barnyard, everyone glad the long day's work was done, even the horses that hurried toward their promised reward of grain.

Gabrielle and Daniel, who had their horses tied near the stack, mounted and started after the wagons, easy prey for their cow horses. But as they began to gain on the others, Gabrielle cut north and headed away from the house.

"Where are you going?" Daniel shouted, slowing his horse.

"To wash the dust out of my hair."

Daniel cut north and took off after her, knowing she was heading for the swimming hole more than a mile up river. Always amazed at how fast she could fly across the land on horseback, he knew he had no chance of catching her. When he arrived at the familiar bend in the river, she had already peeled off her boots, britches, and to his astonishment, her cotton shirt. She waded the river where it was waist deep clad only in her underpants and one of Zack's undershirts. Surprised at her brash immodesty, he tied his horse and pulled off his boots.

"Mother would tan your hide if she saw you," he called.

"Well, she isn't going to see me."

He watched her come out of the water and climb the ledges on the other side where they'd played so many times as children. She stood poised on a ledge about fifteen feet above the water.

"Are you going to tattle, big brother?"

"No," he said, as he watched her standing there following the flight of a red-tail hawk, the undershirt clinging to her breasts.

She whistled precisely the screech of the hawk and with her arms outstretched, leaped into the warm summer air, flying for that brief singular moment. When she came up, she let the lazy current take her until she stood up to her armpits. She shook her long dark hair over her shoulder with one snap of her head and smiled.

"That sure blows the hay dust away."

In his waterlogged overalls, Daniel scrambled to the other side, climbed to the ledge and jumped, falling through the August sunset, shouting as though he were dying, until he exploded like a cannonball into the pool. When he came up, he grabbed her and they laughed and splashed and ducked one another. He went under the water and came up behind her. Wrapping his arms around her, he pulled her against him. For a moment, they stood watching the sun coloring clouds, after it had ducked out of sight. He could smell her wet hair, feel the sun's warmth in her body. She tried to turn but he held her firmly against him. He trembled though the water wasn't cold, the mountain air still hot.

"What are you doing?" She laughed playfully.

"I want to kiss you."

She turned in his grip but he kept his hands firmly around her waist.

"What are you talking about?"

"I want to kiss you," he said excitedly, looking into her eyes.

"You're joking and it isn't funny."

"I'm not joking."

"Don't talk crazy," she said, with a tenuous smile.

Then she frowned and studied his face for any sign of his usual sense of humor.

"I love you," he said, with a catch in his throat.

"Stop talking like an idiot. You're my brother."

"I love you not the way a brother loves a sister, I love you the way a man loves a woman."

"Stop it! You can't! It's, it's wrong, it's terribly wrong!"

"But I do, I do. I can't think of life without you, I can't live without you," he said, breaking through the fear. "I love you. I didn't want to."

"Quit it! Just quit it!" She pushed him and turned away; he took hold of her arms and pulled her back against him.

"Cut it out, Daniel, quit it. Let go of me."

"I can't, I can't. I don't want to ever let go of you."

She broke free and plowed through the water several yards. Then she stopped, her back to him. She didn't respond for an eternity and he felt his stomach tighten, fearing her laughter, her ridicule. He couldn't see her face. He had hidden this for so long and now he was making a fool of himself, he'd never be able to face her again, a clown, an idiot. If she told Maddy? Wart? Father? He held his breath.

She turned, standing in the water waist deep, with a great sadness in her eyes.

"Oh, Daniel, what are we going to do?"

"What do you mean? What are you saying?"

She came thrashing through the water and jumped into his embrace, nearly knocking him backward into the river. She blurted words hidden for years.

"I know what you're saying. I know, I've loved you like that for as long as I can remember. I promised myself I'd never tell you, I thought you'd laugh. I figured I'd go away, I didn't know what else to do. I love you, too."

Daniel couldn't believe what he was hearing.

"Really? Really? You do, you do?" he asked as a great sense of relief overwhelmed him. "I was so afraid it was just me, that I was imagining it, that I could never tell you, or anyone. But . . . but now we can hold each other, we can love each other, we can . . ."

"No. No. We can't talk like this," she said. "We can never let on. We must bear this secret, always. We can never be together."

"Yes, we can," he said. "I've felt this way about you for more than two long years and it seems like forever. To hear you, to see you, to be close to you. I've wanted to tell you so many times but I never could. I thought you'd laugh, or shame me."

"I know, I know," she said. "I've wanted to tell you a million times, too, but I thought you'd think *I* was crazy, your dumb little sister. I thought I was crazy, I thought Mother and Father would disown me, would throw me out, I'd be banished, we'd be ostracized, we'd destroy our family, we'd be—"

"I thought the same thing," he said. "I've thought of running away without ever telling you."

"God help us."

She threw her arms around his neck and kissed him and he met her long pent-up passion with his own. He couldn't catch his breath and he felt as though he were still falling through the sun-kissed sky. She pushed him back to arm's length.

"We can't be like this, it's wrong, it's wicked, we know better, we can't talk like this, we have to stop."

"I know it's crazy but one day I just knew," Daniel said. "I didn't want to, I didn't ask to, I asked God to change me."

He kissed her again and they let the current take them, turning slowly in each other's arms as a hatch played over the water. The sun had slipped away and a fiery afterglow colored the land with indescribable colors and light, this day digging in its heels against the night. They drifted to the gravel bar and he helped her to her feet.

"C'mon." He held out his hand.

"No, we can't," she said quietly and the smile on her face was running away with the sun.

"Come on," he said and he led her out of the water and over to the horses, into the tall slew grass and cattails where they used to play.

"No, Daniel, we can't . . . we know . . ."

He kissed her fiercely, she matched his fire, they were breathing like running horses.

"How can this be, what can we do?" she asked. "I thought I was insane."

"I know, I thought the same thing."

"I'd look at you and wonder if you felt the same," she said. "Sometimes I'd cry, I'd lie awake at night and wonder how I could ever tell you, that you'd laugh."

"Yeah," he said, "and I'd lie awake night after night and know I can never let on, never tell the girl I love that she's the girl I love, the girl I love with every beat of my heart."

She took his hands in hers.

"I'd want to touch you," she said. "I'd look into your eyes and then duck away before you caught me. I almost slipped so many times. I'd get on my horse and run and run until he could run no more."

"I'd try to stay away from you but I couldn't," he said. "I'd want to grab you and hold you. I wanted to tell Father I was going to get work down in Idaho country, but every time I worked up the nerve to open my mouth my heart slammed it shut."

He took her hand and led her into the reeds and lush grass. She balked and held her ground. "No Daniel, we can't, we know we can't, we're not doing that."

"I love you," he said "When can we be together? When? When?"

"I don't know but we have to be awfully careful. We can never let them know, anyone."

"In a month, a year, never?"

"When we figure out what we can do. We need time. I don't know what to do and we have to get to dinner."

"I can't go on without you," he said.

"You'll have to, I'll have to," She turned and embraced him with tears streaming down her face. "Daniel, I don't know what to do and they're waiting on us," Gabrielle said as she collected her clothes with a slight panic.

He grabbed her and kissed her as if he'd never see her again, never hold her again, a kiss into the world of the impossible.

At the supper table, with wet hair and dry clothes, they both talked too much about how perfect the water was, never daring to make eye contact with anyone. Zack complained that they hadn't told him they were going swimming and Gabrielle told him she only thought of it on the way home. Elizabeth scolded Wart for chasing chickens and trying to get Skipper the dog to help him. Martha served her famous huckleberry pie. They jabbered about the good hay and the good haying weather with only a few more days to get it in and then Gabrielle stopped all conversation.

"I've been thinking about college, Mother, and I think you're right. I've decided I'll go, just for one semester, and see if I like it."

"Oh, that's wonderful, Gabrielle," Elizabeth said with surprise in her face, "I know you'll like it."

"That was a quick change of heart," her father said, cocking an eye at her.

"You'll last about three hours." Zack laughed.

Daniel looked at her but she wouldn't meet his eyes.

"We'll have a grand time, and you'll meet dozens of boys," Maddy said excitedly.

"And Grace will be there to help with anything you need," her mother said. "We'll have to get a letter off tomorrow to the college that you're coming."

They finished the meal discussing all the advantages of attending the fledgling college at Bozeman. Daniel, trying to find his balance, didn't take part in the conversation.

"Don't you think it's the sensible thing to do?" Elizabeth asked Daniel, "to see if the shoe fits?"

"Ah . . . yeah, for a while," Daniel said with a notable lack of enthusiasm. "With both of them leaving who's going to do all the chores?"

"Who do you think is doing them now?" Wart asked.

It was much worse now that Gabrielle and Daniel knew of the other's love, a bonfire they couldn't quench, an ocean's tide they couldn't avoid. For the next ten days the two squirmed uneasily around the ranch. They'd agree to rendezvous at some distant place on the ranch and then one of them would back out or both would back out or one of the family would unexpectedly show up. When they were around each other they tried to act natural but often overdid it, too much or too little, too sweet or too sour. What was easiest was not to be around the other but that also was the hardest.

In three days, they finished putting up the hay and then worked at whatever attention the ranch needed the most. Though days flew by as swiftly as a mother swallow, those ten days stretched endlessly.

At the spur railroad station at Chimney Falls, the family and a few friends had ridden east for several hours to send Maddy and Gabrielle off to college. It was a rare thing in that neck of the woods for a son to go off to college but especially for a daughter. Jeremiah, with mixed emotions, puffed out his chest and Elizabeth dabbed at her eyes and Zack loaded the luggage. Wart stayed out of sight in the buggy and Gabrielle watched the horizon for any sign of Daniel, who had disappeared early that morning. Just as the train was ready to pull out, Daniel rounded the little station house on Ramrod, Gabrielle's big gelding. It worked; she broke away from the family and scrambled off the platform to where he stood beside the horse.

"I thought you'd want to say good-bye to Ramrod," he said.

She stroked the horse's neck. "Thank you."

"I'll come to see you," he said.

"No, you mustn't."

Daniel glanced at the family on the platform. "I have to see you, I can't help it, I have to."

"No, we've shamed everyone, turned our backs on God, given up on Him."

"I can't live without you."

"You must," she said, glancing at the train. "We must."

"All 'board!" a conductor shouted.

She looked over the horses withers into Daniel's eyes as their hands reached across.

"Good bye, Daniel, my love, I will love you forever."

"I will find you, wherever you are, I will find you!" he shouted, hoping the train's roar would cover his words. "Don't ever give up on us, don't ever give up on me! No one or nothing can ever tear you from my heart."

He squeezed her hand and for the moment wouldn't let go. She held his a heartbeat longer. Then she turned abruptly and hurried to the family and both girls stepped up into the train. Daniel waved but she never turned. Like some prehistoric beast, the locomotive tore out his heart as it pulled away with great billows of black smoke and erupting steam.

"See you at home," his father yelled.

"See you at home," Daniel shouted back.

Then he leaped on Ramrod and galloped pell-mell toward the mountains. His "home" was steaming away on hard iron wheels that were crushing all hope and happiness from his life.

# SIXTEEN

THE ELEGANT CARRIAGE with a white matched pair pulled up in front of one of the imposing homes on Willson Avenue. Two young men, like excited hornets, hopped out and offered hands to Gabrielle and Maddy as they stepped down. The girls thanked them profusely, at least Maddy did, and then walked eagerly toward the white two-story home with dormers and pillars and what looked like twenty rooms or more. The carriage pulled away with the boys waving and calling and Gabrielle sighed.

"We should've walked," she said.

"When we could ride in a lovely carriage with those nice guys?"

"I don't care about—"

"Glenn took a shine to you, I could tell."

"Glenn! Boys! Blah!"

"What're you going to do, marry a horse?" Maddy laughed lightly as they stepped up onto the wide porch.

"Who says I have to marry any—?"

"You'll have lots of boyfriends here if you stop being a grouch."

"Oh, stop cackling like an old crow."

The thought of herself with anyone but Daniel turned her stomach. But the terrifying thought of loving her brother also turned her stomach.

Gabrielle banged the brass knocker several times.

"What's the matter?" Maddy asked. "You homesick? You just haven't been yourself."

"Yeah, I guess so; I miss the ranch, the valley. . . ."

She tried to disguise the pain that grew each day like a stone of granite in her belly.

"I know, I'm a little homesick, too, but we've only been here three weeks; it'll get better; you have to get out and meet more people. It'll be great to see Grace."

Grace had always insisted they call her by her first name, even when they were young girls chasing around at the ranch. And Grace had always been loads of fun, always seemed to be on the children's side of things. She was in cahoots with Wart and kept things stirred up with games and books and adventures around the ranch. When they were little Grace's favorite game was Follow the Leader and she'd always come up with some wild places to lead them. The kids also liked Grace's husband, Randall. Like Grace he was full of the dickens. He had been a major and then went into politics. Eventually he became governor of the territory. Currently he ran a few businesses in town. They were well-off and Randall took Grace on his frequent travels.

The door swung wide and Grace Armstrong stood there in a long flowered dress and open arms.

"Maddy, Gabrielle, so good to see you, come in, come in."

Gabrielle's mind wandered through much of the visit, though she enjoyed seeing Grace more than she thought she would, mainly because the only place she used to see her was in the valley, at home. They had tea and crumpets on fine china and Maddy and Grace did most of the talking. Aunt Grace asked after Martha, who had seemed unsteady the last time she had visited the ranch. The twins assured Grace that Martha seemed to be in decent health and good spirits.

"Well, look at you girls, you've still got those beautiful, blue eyes you had as little girls," Grace said. "You were different in other ways but you sure had the same eyes. Your mother's eyes."

"Daniel's, too," Maddy said.

Gabrielle winced.

"Why I remember when you two were little tadpoles," Grace went on, "swimming in the river until your mother had to drag you out, and your dog, what was its name?"

"Bandit," Gabrielle said, "but he was killed and now its Skipper."

"Oh, yes, I've met Skipper, he's the one without a tail."

"He chased off a grizzly, saved our lives," Maddy said, with a stoic tone.

"And you, Maddy, you wanted to be a dancer, a ballerina; why you'd dance around the house with your mother's scarves and point your toes, and here you are, going to college in Bozeman. The years go so swiftly." She looked at Gabrielle. "What is it you want to be?"

"I'm hoping to be a veterinarian."

"My, I've never heard of such a thing for a girl."

"It isn't decent," Maddy said. "She isn't serious."

"I am so . . . if they'll let me."

"Well, I suppose there's nothing that says you can't," Grace said. "You always had a mind of your own."

"I'm just trying this out. I plan to go back to the ranch and help Father run things."

"Gabrielle isn't sure yet just what she'll study," Maddy said, "but we'd better be getting back."

"Oh, yes," Grace said, "I'm sure you have a lot of studying to do. Please come often, and if you ever need anything, anything at all, please let me help you. I promised your mother."

The three got up and chatted on their way to the front door.

"You know, I probably shouldn't tell you this," Grace said, "but I did everything in my power to persuade your mother not to marry your father. Of course that was before I knew what a fine man your father is. I think the world of Jeremiah."

She paused in front of the door with one hand on the knob.

"I was a rascal. I wanted your mother to wait for someone who could give her more of a social life, more opportunities for culture and the arts and educated friends. With her elegant looks and manner I could see her on the arm of a general or governor, still can, but land sakes, I'm glad she didn't pay any mind to my meddling. I don't know of a happier woman than your mother, and look at your lovely family."

"Well, Father is a little rough around the edges," laughed Maddy.

The twins left with Grace waving and they hiked uphill through sparsely settled country toward the campus.

"Did you know that Grace tried to talk Mother out of marrying Father?" Maddy asked.

"No, Mother never said anything."

"I guess Mr. Armstrong is an important man around here, being a major in the army and all," Maddy said. "Owns a hardware store and lumberyard and he's a legislator up at the capitol in Helena."

"Would Mother have been happier on the arm of a governor?"

"They squabble a lot," Maddy said as she waved at a buggy full of boys coming down Willson. The boys waved and they exchanged raucous banter with Maddy as she giggled.

"That's mainly over us and what we should do with our lives," Gabrielle said. "They still love each other, you can see it in their eyes and how they still hug and such." Gabrielle looked at her sister. "Mother couldn't be happier than she is."

"Maybe. Do you think Grace is as happy as Mother, by waiting for the correct man?"

"I don't know, but she's a stitch," Gabrielle said. "I'd like to stop and see her again."

Gabrielle carried a saddle through the campus barn, looking forward to a long ride. Before she reached the stall where she'd tied the black gelding, Daniel reached out from an empty stall and pulled her into its shadows.

"Daniel!"

He kissed her and she dropped the saddle and kissed him back, her heart in her throat.

"What are you doing here?"

He muffled her questions by kissing her, and they slowly backed into the darkest corner of the stall.

"I knew you'd come and I prayed you wouldn't," she said in his arms.

"I'm going crazy at home without you, it's so different, so empty, so bleak."

"I've missed you terribly," she said, "can't eat, can't study, can't sleep."

She kissed him. Then she held him by the shoulders and looked into his face.

"How did you get here? Where do they think you are?"

"Rode three days and some nights, just about killed Buck, said I was going hunting, been hanging around here for hours, the only place on the campus I knew I could find you without Maddy."

"Oh, God, I'm so glad to see you, hold me, crush me."

"I have a room at the Bozeman Hotel on Main Street. Can you get away tonight?"

"I don't know. . . . Daniel, we shouldn't. We have to talk about this."

"Yeah, third floor; room 312, please come, I'll wait for you."

"Yes, I will, I'll come. See you tonight. Oh, God, you are my life."

She kissed him for a moment, then, picked up the saddle and hurried down the row of stalls.

He could faintly hear her knock as if she hoped no one would answer and would have died if nobody had. It was eight-forty and he was suffocating in the fear that she might not come, minutes grinding him like a millstone as he paced around the large bed in candlelight. Daniel opened the door and she was there. He swept her into the small room and locked the door behind her. As if they'd agreed ahead of time they hardly said a word. Slowly they crawled onto the wide feathered bed and curled together like children who no longer had a family. Gabrielle spoke first in a whisper.

"I'm going with you no matter where you go so don't try to talk me out of it. If I don't go with you I'll have no life at all."

She spoke with her face snuggled against his neck and she clung to him as if she were drowning beside him.

"Yes, I know. We can go where no one knows us and I can find work," he said. "We can go west, Oregon Territory, Canada, we can build a new life."

"I can find work too," she said.

The cozy candlelit room went slowly quiet. The terrible question hung in the silence and neither could quench it. Gabrielle noticed first, as if a warm, calm ocean quit lapping the shore. Who would tell Father! Who would tell anyone?

"If you loved me, you'd leave me," Daniel said.

"Stop it, don't talk like that, you promised."

They fought off the words that tried to corrupt their world. *Sinful. Wicked.* Brother and sister, large happy family, they were drowning in the sea of their love, turned to ashes in the bonfire of their desire.

"Do you have to go?" he asked.

"No, I told Maddy I was staying with a girlfriend I've made who lives here in town. I can stay the night with you."

"Gabrielle, what do you think? We need to leave soon. We need to be together."

"We're damned, Daniel, we're damned! We could never have a normal life . . . family, children. They'd be inbred, half-wits, or worse. It's wrong, you can't love me."

"But I do! What do I do about that? How can this good, beautiful feeling for you be wrong?"

"It's forbidden; it's a sin; it's unnatural."

"No, never. The way I feel for you is the best part of me. It can't be evil or dirty. It's the most wonderful and natural thing I've ever felt."

He sat up in the bed beside her.

"Who made that law? Who says a brother can't love a sister that way?

"God!"

"God? I know my heart; I love you, I didn't want to love you, I didn't ask to love you, I didn't plan to love you. God gave me this heart. Is my heart evil and bad?"

"No, it can't be," she said.

She leaned back into his arms and whispered in his ear.

"I pray to God over and over that one day there will be a world where it will be all right for us to love each other. Do you ever think that, Daniel?"

"Every day, every minute. I thought you'd always be in my life, I can't think of living without you, come away with me, please say you will."

"Oh, God, forgive me, I will, we'll find a place like that and be together for the rest of our lives."

"I've got it all planned." He kneeled beside her on the bed

with his hands animated in the air. "I'll go back to the ranch and get all the money I can raise. I'll come back and get you and we can take the train. We can find work; and after a while we'll get our own place and build it up and—"

"I don't care what we do if we're together."

"Get into cattle out there, or maybe salmon fishing, or something on the ocean."

"We've never seen the ocean; oh, there'll be lots of things we can do."

"Could always work horses, breed horses," he said. "You can make a horse stand up and whistle 'Yankee Doodle Dandy'."

"What will we tell Mother and Father?" she asked. "What will we tell Zack and Maddy? What will we tell Wart?"

Daniel didn't speak. The air stood still. The rotation of the earth stopped. Sorrow filled the room and they clung to each other as though they would drown in it, neither able to speak the answer they both knew.

God would judge them. God would judge them indeed. And harshly. No, they both knew that, though their love was real, it was not something they would ever be able to wear on their sleeves. God had kidnapped their love and was holding it for ransom. They didn't know the cost. They already felt damned. At the beginning of the evening Daniel and Gabrielle thought they would finally succumb to desire, but desire was replaced with futility and Daniel simply held Gabrielle in his arms in the long hours. They barely slept.

In the morning she fled. "I have to be in class or Maddy will wonder where I am."

When she was ready, he kissed her at the door.

"I'll be back as soon as I can," he said, "maybe a week, two at the most, be ready."

"All right, be careful, until then, my love."

He embraced her for a moment, afraid to let go.

"You must let me go."

"I can't."

Another minute and he released her. She slipped out the door and down the hallway and was gone.

When Daniel checked out a half hour later there was a note left for him, hurriedly scribbled on hotel stationery.

> *My dear heart, I cannot go away with you. I love you too much and I know what it would cost you and how wrong it would be and what it would do to you and our family. I do not understand it. I will love you until I die. Why would God do this to us, Daniel? Is there something wrong with us, are we rotten at the core? Be happy, my love, live your life and try to forget us. I know how impossible that will be. I will hold you in my heart as long as I am alive.*
>
> *Good bye, Daniel, my love.*

With the note in hand, Daniel rushed out into the street. She was gone.

# SEVENTEEN

"I'M SORRY TO BOTHER YOU so early," Gabrielle said as she sat in a stiff embroidered chair in Grace's parlor, "but I really need help."

"Oh, fiddlesticks, you're not bothering me," Grace said, in a long frilly house coat and her hair up in a scarf, "now tell me what I can do." She sat facing Gabrielle in a velvet love seat.

"I have to go away, far away, *today.*"

*"Today!* That sounds so desperate. Are you sure that's necessary?"

"Yes, I have to, can you help me?"

"What about the university, your studies?"

"They'll have to wait."

"Can you tell me why?" Grace asked. "Maybe there's something else we can do."

"No . . . I can't tell you, I'm sorry."

"Are you in trouble with a man?"

"Kind of."

"Are you in love?" Grace's voice softened.

"Yes . . . and it's impossible." Gabrielle began to cry.

"Is he married?"

"I can't tell you."

"I'm sorry." Grace handed her a hanky and Gabrielle wiped her cheeks. "I was in love like that once. There's nothing worse than not being with the person you love."

"Can you help me? I can't tell mother or father, it would kill them."

"Kill them?"

"Yes, *kill* them."

"Oh, sweetheart, sometimes things seem worse than they are; people, even parents, often understand when we're sure they won't. Why don't you—"

"They wouldn't understand *this*; *I* can't understand it. I know you and mother are close, but you have to promise you won't tell her where I am."

"You don't want them to know I helped you?" Grace asked, raising her eyebrows.

"No . . . can you do that?"

"Yes . . . I suppose so but I'm probably crazy for it."

"I'll never tell anyone you helped, I promise, ever."

"Are you pregnant?"

"No! For heaven's sake!" Gabrielle blew her nose.

"That's good. It only makes it so much worse. Tell me what I can do."

"I need to borrow some money; I'll pay you back, every cent, I promise."

"Hush, hush, don't worry about that, I'll be glad to help."

"I want to catch the train today for Saint Paul."

"Are you sure there's no other way? That's so rash. Sometimes in our panic we—"

"There's no other way, I wish there were," Gabrielle was frantic. "I'll get my things at school while Maddy's in class. I'll write to my folks and try to explain, but I don't want them to know where I am for a while, just a little while. I'll send the letter to you, in another envelope. Will you mail it for me from Bozeman?"

"Yes, I will," Grace said, resigned. "Will you stay in touch with me?"

"If you don't mind. You'll be the only one who can tell me what's happening to . . . all of them."

"What will you do?" Grace asked with a worried frown. "You're still so young to go off like this."

"I'll get a job. I'll find work." The words stabbed Gabrielle and fear rose in her throat. "I'll be all right."

"I'll have John, my handyman, drive you up to the campus to get your things and then take you to the station." Grace looked at a small watch pinned on her dress. "You have just three hours."

She stood. "You'll need enough money to tide you over for a few months."

She scooted out of the room, her frills trailing behind her, and Gabrielle stood and retreated toward the front door. Grace was back before the fear could melt Gabrielle's resolve, before her ache for Daniel could send her fleeing from the house to find him. Grace handed her a brown envelope.

"Keep this somewhere safe, my dear, there's three hundred dollars there. If you need more, write to me and—"

"Oh, no, that's much too much. I can't—"

"Hush, now, it's a hard world out there. You can pay me back some day when three hundred dollars won't seem so much to you. Don't let anyone know how much you have. Be very cautious; don't trust strangers and divide your money and store it in several places."

Grace hugged her; she'd never done that before. When she stepped back, tears washed over Grace's face.

"Go quickly, now, John is out front. God go with you, Gabrielle."

"Thank you. I won't ever forget you for this."

Gabrielle slipped out the door and scrambled down the steps of the grand mansion on Willson Avenue. She clutched the envelope and stepped into the fancy black buggy.

After huddling in a corner of the little brick railroad station, Gabrielle smuggled herself onto the train when it arrived. The car was half full of salesmen and lumberjacks and miners; mothers with small children and an old woman with a picnic basket. The aromas of fresh bread and wool clothing and sweat filled her nostrils. When the train pulled out of Bozeman and started the climb over the pass, a terrible dread showed up in her throat. When would she ever see Daniel? Something could happen to him, to her, and they'd never be together again.

She pressed her forehead against the window and watched Montana slipping away as though it were her life, the mountains fading on the horizon. Right and wrong blurred in the landscapes, brother and sister fell away into the sage-covered hills and panic clogged the voice of reason with the thought that she'd lost the love of her life. She could hardly breathe. By the time they were out of the mountains, following the Yellowstone east, she stopped a conductor passing in the aisle.

"How far is the next stop?"

"That'd be Billings, ma'am, about an hour."

"When will the next train go back to Bozeman?"

"In the morning; nine-thirty-three; get you there 'fore noon." He chuckled under his beard. "Change yer mind?"

"Yes." She felt a smile spread over her face. "Yes, I did."

Emotion filled her eyes and she began to weep. She turned to the window. This was her *life*. She would return to Bozeman and find Daniel. She would go with him to Oregon or wherever. He was the only man she would ever love and she belonged with him. Somehow, some way, they would overcome the terrible stigma. Somehow it would be possible.

She found a room only three blocks from the depot in Billings and slept in her clothes so she'd not miss the morning train. She was at the station by six and rolling west by nine-forty, praying constantly that Daniel would still be in Bozeman, searching for her, when she arrived. She felt a great relief come over her; she wanted to screech like the red-tail hawk; she jabbered with the people around her and sang inwardly when the Rockies rose out of the plains. She was going back to her heart, to her life, and she would never leave Daniel again.

After searching through town for most of the afternoon, with her heart in her throat, she was informed by the livery stable owner that Daniel had collected his horses and left mid-morning; she'd missed him by two hours. The despair took her breath away. She didn't know where to turn. She spent the night in their room in the hotel; tried to find the scent of his skin in the newly laundered sheets. She burned a candle and cried until exhaustion put her to sleep.

The morning Gabrielle ran away from him, Daniel had searched all day and into the night. He stayed in the same hotel room in a desperate hope that she might return. It wasn't until the next day, after a sleepless night, that he thought of the train. The station master remembered a girl who fit Gabrielle's description, told Daniel he thought the young woman took the train east. She was gone!

Daniel rode north for the ranch. Winter was coming and he was sure his heart would freeze to death. He shot an elk when he was near the ranch and dressed it out and tied it on the pack horse. They welcomed him home from the successful hunt but he knew he was no longer home. His home was somewhere on a train racing east and the world was turning cold around him.

When Gabrielle's letter arrived several weeks later, her running away left her family shocked, then baffled, all except Daniel.

"You know anything about this?" Jeremiah asked Daniel.

"No, nothing," Daniel said, but Jeremiah noticed something in Daniel's voice.

It was so unlike her, so rash, so irresponsible. They followed the usual heartbeat of ranch life without speaking of it, as though it were a blemish on the family's face, a secret to keep. Maddy knew there was something different with Gabrielle. She had become dour and secretive in Bozeman, no longer sharing her innermost thoughts and feelings, but Maddy thought Gabrielle was just off balance with their starting college.

Elizabeth blamed herself for pushing Gabrielle to go off to college, fearing it was too overwhelming for her and she couldn't face coming home in failure. Maddy wrote and told them that Gabrielle had given no sign, no hint of her strange disappearance. Jeremiah feared for her safety, off in some big city alone. His anger at Elizabeth for persuading her to go erupted with one loud shouting outburst followed by several days of slamming doors and finally the cold silent treatment.

One day, while working on the latest addition to the house, Jeremiah stood halfway up the ladder, handing Daniel and Wart, who were on the roof, another bundle of cedar shingles. Zack, on the ground, held another bundle ready. Jeremiah paused where he stood and shook his head slowly, breaking his silence.

"I just can't figure what made her run off like that," he said. "What got into that girl, where did we do wrong? What on earth did we do wrong?"

"You didn't do anything wrong," Zack said quickly, trying to smooth the waters. "She's just restless; she'll be back, Father, wait and see."

Jeremiah hoisted the bundle to Daniel.

"Did she ever say anything to you about leaving?" Jeremiah asked Daniel. "Anything?"

"No, never did." Daniel took the bundle and wrestled it onto the roof. Daniel avoided his father's eyes.

"She could have talked it over with us," Jeremiah said. "We always let you talk things over. What will people think?"

"It's none of their business," Wart said.

"Comin' up," Zack said and held the bundle up to Jeremiah.

Jeremiah, leaning against the ladder, lifted the shingles and cradled them to his chest.

"Doesn't she know how much this hurt us?" Jeremiah asked.

Daniel took the load from Jeremiah and said,

"She knows."

The work went on in silence, each with his private thoughts, their deepest feelings, nailed to the roof with the cedar shingles.

Everything on the ranch reminded Daniel of her; he became surly and moody, unable to tell any of them the truth. Her memory stalked him. He'd hear the call of a red-tailed hawk and catch himself expecting to see her. Winter came. They fed hay that Gabrielle had helped stack and Daniel could hear echoes of her laughter as he pitched it to the Herefords, see the glisten of sweat and hay dust on her lovely face, smell the river in her hair.

Winter passed and spring came, the snow melted, the calves dropped, and every day Daniel caught himself glancing to the horizon to catch a glimpse of her on horseback. Word from Maddy and Grace indicated there was no sign of her in Bozeman and everyone conceded that she'd left Montana. A few letters had come from different cities—St. Louis, Saint Paul, Chicago—telling them she was fine and that she missed them very much, that she hoped to see them before long. The urge to go and search for her plagued Daniel like gravity and only reason, armed with the impossibility of it, prevented him from trying, but just barely.

The summer turned mellow in June and the men had their draft horses, Romeo and Juliet, rigged to pull a slip. They were cutting an irrigation ditch on an upper hay meadow. It took a strong man to work the slip. It looked like an upside down wheelbarrow with no wheel. If you hit a rock it could be dangerous with the horses pulling and the slip cutting through the soil, sometimes bouncing out of the ground. But Wart insisted he be given a shot at it. They shook their heads and gave in.

Daniel walked in the freshly cut ditch, steering the slip. Jeremiah went ahead of the horses with the measuring board and Zack drove the team with the reins while walking beside them. Wart followed on foot, tossing uncovered rocks back onto the bank of the newborn ditch.

They had been watching three horseman coming toward them for nearly an hour. Wart slipped away into a thick aspen grove and disappeared. When the horsemen got close enough they recognized Henry Weebow on his big gray mule and his sons Ben and Rufus on gnarly swaybacked horses that looked like they had already gone through the glue factory.

"Morning, Jeremiah!" Henry called as they halted their horses a few yards from the team and slip. "Looks like you're hard at it."

"Morning, Henry," Jeremiah said, "We haven't any fresh coffee but we've got good water. Get down, all of you."

The Weebows slid off their animals and the men exchanged acknowledgments. Henry walked up to Jeremiah and the two of them shook hands.

"I should be home doin' what you're doin'," Henry said. "All this land needs is water and it'll grow gold."

"You're right about that. We try to add a mile or so of ditch every year," Jeremiah said, "and then there's maintaining the ditches we already have. Just one more ranching chore that's never done."

Ben and Daniel eyeballed each other, remaining several yards apart as if to allow their fathers to parlay uninterrupted. Rufus and Zack got to talking fishing, telling stories, boasting and comparing lies.

"Well, Henry, what brings you way out here today?" Jeremiah asked.

"I figured I'd let you know how my scratchin's doin' since my cattle ain't amountin' to anything. But I'd ask you and your boys," he said as he waved his hand at the Rockhammers, "to keep it under their hats that my luck has changed. We don't want a rush of prospectors climbing all over our land, if you see what I mean. They'd be crawlin' all over yours as well as mine."

"I see what you mean, Henry. What've you found?" Jeremiah asked.

Henry dropped the reins and let his mule graze.

"I've tunneled more than forty feet, Rockhammer," Henry said with more enthusiasm than Jeremiah had ever seen, "and the vein is gettin' bigger, just like I figured. There's going to be some real gold in that quartz, enough to hire some boys and go after it."

"I've heard your dynamite from time to time, kind of sounds like low thunder in the valley. I wondered how you were doing."

"That's why I wanted to talk to you, let you know about it."

"Well, good for you, Henry, I'm happy for you." Jeremiah said. "You sure been picking at it long enough. Guess your hunch was right."

"Yessir, and we need to talk about a road up there, haulin' equipment in, haulin' ore down where we can crush it and smelt it."

"Henry, I hope you pick a million dollars out of that hole, but you know our agreement from the first. What you agreed with Abraham and what you agreed with me."

"I know, I know, but this is different now. Who could have guessed how big it would be. This has to do with lots of other people, jobs for some of the boys in town, Buffalo Jump growing like a weed, a spur off the railroad, some money around for a change."

"That's all well and good, but a man's word is his word."

"Rockhammer, I'm askin' you a big favor, a neighbor to neighbor."

Ben looked Daniel in the eye and didn't blink. Daniel swished flies away from Romeo's head and eyeballed him back. He never liked Ben Weebow much, still believing Ben had killed Bandit, their black Labrador. Ben had grown into a solid man who looked like he could throw an anvil over a church, his eyes meaner than his bullying days at school. Daniel had grown as well but Ben still outweighed him by thirty or forty pounds.

"Henry, our agreement stands," Jeremiah said. "I gave my word to Abraham as he'd given it to the Blackfeet."

Henry's mood soured.

"Hell, Rockhammer, you care more about your goddamned word to some crazy injun, who's probably long dead, than you do for your flesh and blood next-door neighbor! What kind of man are you?"

"A man whose word is good. I'd like to help you but you agreed to it, Henry. You can haul anything you want in and out of that claim twenty-four hours a day, by horse or mule across Rockhammer land. But there isn't going to be any switch-backing road carved in the face of that mountain, scarring up the valley, and that's that."

"That ain't right, Rockhammer," Ben said, moving up alongside his father with his horse.

"You keep your nose out of it, son," Jeremiah said evenly, without looking over at Ben.

Though he showed his aging, Jeremiah was still more than a match for Ben Weebow.

"I'm sorry, Henry, but if the vein is as good as you say, you can become a rich man just hauling it out on that animal you're setting on. Or, if it turns out to be as rich as you think, you can afford to carve your road up and around the other side of that rock face. Now that's the end of it. I don't want to hear any more about it."

Jeremiah turned and waved at the boys.

"Let's get to work."

Henry climbed on his mule and rode off without a word. Ben swung up on his horse and sat there a moment.

"That *ain't* the end of it, Rockhammer."

Daniel moved in front of his father. "You better ride that bucket of bones off this ranch while you still can."

"No, no," Jeremiah said. "None of that, none of that. We'll talk with them like gentlemen, like neighbors."

Ben spit a string of tobacco off to the side of his horse, stared at Daniel for a moment, and spurred the nag away.

"That ain't the end of it, injun lover!" he shouted. "That ain't the end of it!"

After the death of Abraham, when Jeremiah was running Rock-hammer Ranch, he had always hired a man to shoe the horses, too unnerved to do it himself though he could have from watching the process over the years. He'd helped at times, shaping the hot shoe on the anvil, but he'd only watch the skilled shoer hold up the horse's leg and nail the shoe in place. Jeremiah had found a man halfway to Buffalo Jump who hired out, from time to time, to shoe horses and such. But Daniel had also learned while growing up, and one hot day in July, several horses were tied in the shade by the work shed waiting to be shoed. Wart worked the bellows on the forge to heat the shoes.

Daniel worked on Romeo first, one of their large powerful draft horses. Bent at the waist and backed up against the rear end of the horse, Daniel had its right rear hoof up on his thigh as he measured the fit of the new shoe. He dropped the hoof and went to the forge, heating the shoe for a minute longer. Wart pumped the bellows. When the shoe was hot enough, Daniel held it with the tongs in his left hand and laid it on the anvil. With the hammer in his right hand he began tapping the shoe, conforming it to the curve on the end of the anvil. When it looked good, he laid it on the anvil and began hammering it lightly, to flatten it.

He tapped it rhythmically again and again as though in a trance and then suddenly broke the rhythm with a crushing blow, flattening the shoe into a misshapen piece of iron; again and again he pounded it as though he were killing a rattler. Half of the shoe was severed and fell to the dirt floor but he kept hammering the top of the anvil, berserk. He flung the tongs away and then the hammer. Wart ducked behind the work bench. Daniel picked up a ten-pound maul and with all his strength pounded the top of the anvil, iron against iron, faster and faster, harder and harder, driving spikes on some unseen railroad. Wart made a beeline out the back door.

Sweat ran down Daniel's face, his shirt soaked, the force of the concussions reverberated up the oak handle and into his arms and hands. He staggered back, turned, and assaulted the tack room wall, splintering a board halfway up; he withdrew the maul like a broad sword and swung again; it bounced back; he battered it again and again and again. Boards cracked and split. He swung viciously and the heavy maul head snapped from the handle, going through the wall.

At that moment he noticed his father standing at the shed door, watching him with a great sadness in his eyes. Daniel dropped the splintered handle and looked away; his chest heaved and he fought to catch his breath.

"I always thought that wall was in the wrong place," Jeremiah said, "but we don't have to move it right now."

Totally spent, Daniel sat on a nail keg and dropped his head into his hands. "I'm sorry."

Jeremiah sat on the anvil. "I think I know what's bothering you, but I've been known to be wrong about such things."

Daniel looked up at his father, startled for a moment but then realizing he couldn't possibly know.

"I figure it's seeing your sisters going off into the world and you're left behind, wondering if you're missing your life by staying home. Sometimes we don't appreciate what we've got until we get far enough away to look back. Maybe you should go off somewhere and give something else a try. Zack and Wart and I can manage for a while, we can hire help when we need it."

Daniel looked at his father.

"I thought you'd—"

"Never mind what you thought," Jeremiah said. "I was young once, never took my chance to leave, got kinda trapped here, never did find out what it would be like . . ."

Jeremiah gazed out the door at the valley.

Daniel had pondered it through sleepless nights and tormenting days since Gabrielle ran off. If God had damned him because of his love for her then by God he'd go Him one better with his damnation. Daniel would punish himself in a way not even God himself could think of. He would demonstrate how deep and strong and everlasting his love for Gabrielle was if it took him a lifetime.

"I'm going to Butte, work in the mines," Daniel said without looking up.

"Butte! Good God, boy, that's a pitiful place to go; underground in that suffocating heat and foul air; you'd be better off in hell."

"Yes, sir."

Daniel regarded his father, sitting across the dirt floor from him with eyes that were struggling to understand.

"I don't know where I belong," Daniel said.

"Well it sure isn't Butte. You forget you can't stand being closed in? You can't even go into a cave. You're not a mole, you're a cowman," his father said, shaking his head slowly.

"Sometimes I feel lost," Daniel said.

"Lost? *Lost?* You're my son, Daniel Rockhammer. You're home, this is the Rockhammer Ranch, your home. This is where you belong."

Jeremiah stood slowly as if he had a great weight on his back and stood in the wide doorway while gazing out over the valley.

"I thought I knew my own pups and then they grow up and turn into strangers."

"I'm sorry, Father."

"It's like we were snake bit, like we were damned. Life was good, and then, suddenly . . . like a lightning bolt from God. . . . Wart is always saying he's living under some kind of jinx, some kind of curse. Who knows, maybe it's rubbed off on the Rockhammers."

Jeremiah paused and glanced around the work shed.

"Where is he?" Jeremiah asked.

"He barreled out of here when I went nuts."

"Well," he pulled his hat snug as if he expected wind, "your mother will never understand, but give it a try if you must. You'll always be expected here, coming down the road, and there'll always be a place for you."

"I'm sorry, I just can't stay any longer."

Daniel turned his blurring eyes to the ground, wishing he could somehow explain to his father. It wasn't the Rockhammer that was damned. Only he and Gabrielle.

# EIGHTEEN

GABRIELLE LEANED AGAINST the cool brick wall in the alley, shaded from the rising August sun, glad to get away from the bakery ovens for a moment as downtown St. Paul came alive. Another muggy day, something she couldn't get used to, remembering well the crisp invigorating mountain air. A train whistled off toward the Northern Pacific depot and she thought of her journey here, almost a month ago. She had pressed her face against the tear-smeared window as if to see better, trying to savor every view, every Montana horizon. Each time the train stopped she had all she could do to keep from getting off. Big Timber, Billings, Miles City, Glendive, all of them tests of her determination to do what was right. She watched the land sliding away like an emigrant seeing her homeland for the last time.

Though there had been a sleeping berth available, she took a coach seat, unwilling to spend the extra money. She had pinned the brown envelope Grace had given her inside her underwear and she could feel it against her belly.

When the train crossed into North Dakota she felt something deep inside go off kilter, the needle come off her compass. She turned rootless, lost, with no home in the world, roaming the country, belonging nowhere. She had explored St. Paul for a while and then rode the train to Chicago. She walked the streets, gaping at the size and number of so many things. The cities surprised her with their vitality and energy, the diversity of people, and buildings and industry, but she missed the Rockhammer so deeply that she felt numb, no longer belonging to the human race, a misplaced corpse searching for its grave. Unable to make up her mind to stay, she took a train to St. Louis, not knowing for sure what she was looking for or what she would do if she found it. With summer coming on, she traveled back to St. Paul where she felt closer to Montana and Daniel and the ranch.

She rented a one-room apartment with a small kitchen and a bathroom down the hall. She found temporary work at a bakery and delicatessen on East Seventh Street in lower downtown. Carla and Otto Schultz ran the small delicatessen and catered to the working people who came for their pastry and coffee early and for their sandwiches and soup at lunch. A bald barrel of a man, Otto looked as if he'd been born to his profession with a walrus mustache and a twinkle in his eye. Like salt and pepper shakers, Carla stood as rotund as Otto and looked like Mother Earth herself. They took Gabrielle under their wing and she worked out so well they wanted her to stay on permanent; she was quick and strong and tireless and Otto asked if all the girls from Montana were like that.

An ice wagon creaked down the alley, pulled by a black, sway-backed horse, snatching Gabrielle from her reverie. When it stopped she sidled up to the horse and rubbed its neck. The driver jumped from his perch and scrambled around to the back. He wore rubber boots, a vest, and a beanie cap.

"Mornin'. Ol' Whiskey's been lookin' for you for two blocks or more."

"He knows I like him."

"Never seen him take to anyone like he does you."

"How old is he?"

"Don't rightly know; old enough to be retired," the man yelled from inside the wagon, "but every time I think of going without him I just can't do it."

He came around the wagon with a large block of ice over his back, held with tongs against the rubber cape he wore. His short muscular frame bulged with strength.

"He's more like a friend than anything. He wakes me up in the morning if I'm slow getting up, makes enough racket to wake the dead."

"I'm glad you're kind to him," she said, "I look forward to seeing him. He reminds me of a horse I had on the ranch when I was a girl."

"You miss your ranch and Montana?"

"Yes . . . every day, every night."

"Your family?"

"My family, especially, my sister and my mother and father and my brother . . . I miss my brother, Daniel."

The man ducked in the back door of a saloon across from the bakery, and Gabrielle took several sugar lumps from her apron pocket. She offered them to Whiskey and the old critter slopped them up with his lips and tongue.

Carla, in her white apron and dress came to the delivery door. Her hair was in a bun and she wore a white cap.

"You done feeding the horse?" she asked and shook her head slightly.

"Yes, are they ready?"

"First oven is, second soon."

Carla stepped back into the brick building. Gabrielle hugged the horse.

"Good-bye, Daniel," she said and then followed Carla into the rest of her life.

Gabrielle untied her apron and hung it on the back of the door. It was nearly two o'clock and their day was about done, although Otto and Carla would work another hour or two cleaning up and getting ready for tomorrow. Gabrielle came to work at four in the morning and she'd put in her ten hours.

"When are you going to find yourself a nice young man?" Carla asked as Gabrielle came through the front of the shop.

"I have one. Back in Montana. We're going to get married someday."

"Not much good to you back there," Otto said.

Gabrielle liked his brown puppy-dog eyes and his jolly nature and how when he laughed his large firm belly bounced.

"A bird in the hand is worth two in the bush," he said.

"Take this out to the young man at the table on your way; the one with the books," Carla said and she handed Gabrielle a plate with a corned beef sandwich, dill pickle, and a little bowl of slaw.

"See you in the morning," Gabrielle said.

A man sat hunched over his work at a table in the shade along the sidewalk; his brown hair was parted neatly and he wore a shirt and tie despite the humid afternoon. When she came around where she could see his face she thought he had not yet been damaged.

"Here's your sandwich, sir," she said and she set it on the edge of the small cluttered table.

"Oh," he said, pushing books aside, "thank you."

He looked up at her and smiled. She saw that one of the open books was a Bible and she hesitated.

"Sure a hot one," he said, his light blue eyes reaching out to her.

"Yes, so muggy."

She wanted to walk away but something held her.

"My name's Paul."

He waited, never taking his eyes off her face.

"I'm Gabrielle. Do you study the Bible a lot?"

"Yes, I'm a seminary student, studying for the ministry. I had to come to school this summer to finish some classes. I'd rather be fishing."

He laughed easily and she felt comfortable with him.

"Do you know the Bible?" he asked.

"Only some. My father and mother used to read it to us a lot when we were kids, the Old Testament stories and the parables Jesus told, but I haven't read it much for a while. Are you from around here?"

"No, I'm from a small town in Iowa. Clear Lake. I'm just a farm boy at heart I guess. Maybe, if you'd like, we could talk sometime, when you're done working."

"I'm done now, but I can see you're busy and I should—"

"No, no." He stood and pulled out a chair for her. "Plenty of time; I'm tired of studying anyway, maybe we could walk or just sit here in the shade. Would you like something cold to drink?"

Gabrielle sat in the chair and he almost fell down getting back in his. She watched the traffic steaming by through the August humidity, sweating horses pulling buggies and wagons, and people mounted and on foot, dragging through the heat. She didn't look at him when she spoke.

"Have you thought a lot about God?" she asked.

Paul shrugged. She turned and glanced into his boyish blue eyes.

"Is there an unforgivable sin, something so terrible that God can never forgive it?"

"Well, there's the sin against the Holy Ghost, refusing to believe." He paused. "But God can forgive anything we're truly sorry for and when we ask for forgiveness."

"But what if it's something you're *not* sorry for?"

He seemed puzzled. "You wouldn't want to be forgiven for something if you weren't sorry for it, would you?"

"Oh, yes, that's what I mean. What if someone did something that was the most wonderful thing that ever happened to them in their whole life and they wouldn't change it if they could and they could never say they were sorry it happened but it's wrong, a terrible sin? Would God forgive them if they asked, or would they be damned to hell?"

She watched his eyes closely, his expression, for an answer, for the answer she had longed for since she first knew she loved Daniel.

"Golly, I don't know," he said, studying her face with confusion on his. "If someone committed a grievous sin, broke God's law, and they wanted to be forgiven for it but felt no sorrow or remorse for doing it, that it was a wonderful thing in their life?"

"Yes, yes! If they don't feel sorry for it can they be forgiven or are they damned?"

"Boy, you don't beat around the bush. I don't know. . . . I guess I'd say that they probably wouldn't want forgiveness, ask for forgiveness, if they weren't sorry."

"Oh but I . . ."

Gabrielle caught herself and tried to keep the disappointment off her face.

"Well thanks. I'd better get going," she said and moved to the edge of her chair.

"I don't know if I can answer your questions but I'd like to try. Where'd you come up with that one?"

"Oh, I was just thinking one day. It's not important."

"Well, I sure hope it doesn't turn up on one of our exams at the seminary, I hope you won't pass that on to one of our teachers."

They laughed. She hoped her laughter sounded genuine when it felt so hollow.

Carla stood in the doorway of the shop, fanning herself with her apron and watching the two youngsters sitting at the table talking. She called Otto and nodded. "I think your corned beef found Gabrielle a gentleman friend."

They say that when Gabrielle one day realized Paul was more interested in her than in discussing theology it was as if she jumped back from a hot stove. She felt an immediate panic that broke out in a cold sweat and lined her stomach with lead. She could only think of Daniel in a romantic way and found no such attraction in Paul. He showed up as regular as daylight and she began a strategy like a cunning fox of now-you-see-me-now-you-don't.

She had to wait on customers while he was there, usually a little after noon, and they exchanged normal pleasantries. But when she was done working she pulled her disappearing act. Paul often asked Carla where Gabrielle was, peering back into the kitchen, and Carla reluctantly told him she had gone home. Sometimes Gabrielle used the alley to get away, coming out a block away. Other times she sneaked around the corner and up the stairs to the second floor. There she hurried down the long hall and climbed down the iron stairs that were meant to be a fire escape. On the few occasions he caught her when her work was finished, he insisted on walking her home or asking if she'd like to go for a walk. She used every excuse she could conjure, but he wouldn't give up and his tenacity seemed to grow.

Then he didn't show up for more than a week and she sighed with relief. She had outlasted him, like breaking a horse. But he hadn't been broke. One day there he sat at his usual table and when she said hello and wanted to take his order she couldn't help noticing his collar. There sat a minister with that familiar face who had gone to Chicago to get ordained and whatever else. He was assigned to the church in Saint Paul where he'd been serving the past year and therefore he could go on eating lunch at Schultz's Delicatessen for all eternity.

Gabrielle began to disappear again, only now she was hiding from a man of God. Was that like hiding from God? He didn't always eat there when his obligations with his ministry took him elsewhere but sometimes it seemed as though he grew in that chair, lived on Otto's sandwiches, and found a way to invite her for a walk or a ride in the buggy the congregation provided. One day, when things were slow, she asked him again, now that he was an official minister.

"If you asked Him would God forgive you for something you weren't sorry for?"

He smiled and said, "I don't know, but if we went for a walk maybe I'd come up with an answer."

She said there was something she had to do after work and later sneaked down the alley.

They say this went on for many months until one day, out of the blue, she sat at his table and accepted a date to go for a walk in the evening. An epiphany! She had been awakened in the middle of the night by a vivid and gripping dream. In the dream she was married, not to Daniel but to another man and they had children, a family. Was this like in the Bible where God spoke to people in a dream? Was God answering her question, her prayer? She had the dream three nights in a row. She ached to tell someone but had no one to confide in. The dream was so clear, so powerful. No matter how hard she tried, she couldn't see the face of the man in the dream but it was the same man in all three and she woke abruptly from each of them.

And then on the third night when she woke from the dream she realized something, something she'd missed. The man in the dream wore a clerical collar, he was a minister! She got out of bed and walked to the window, gazing out at the vast display of stars. At that moment, from some small doorway in her soul, she could see that the only circumstance capable of preventing her from running off with Daniel into a life of the damned would be if she married another man and raised a family. And greater still, if she married a minister, a man of God who could vouch for them in the anterooms of heaven. If she did marry a minister and dedicated her life to God's calling, would they no longer be damned, neither Daniel or her? Was this their one chance for redemption, their offering at the altar? How could God refuse to

forgive her if she married a minister and dedicated her life doing
God's work?

The following days she wrestled with the dream and its meaning. It was crazy, insane, she couldn't marry another man. It
would shatter Daniel. How could he possibly go on, knowing she
was married to another man, how could he bear up under that
kind of pain. How could she explain? She had sent letters to the
family now with a general delivery address in Saint Paul, no longer going through Grace, but she had no address for Daniel in
Butte. She knew the minister in the dream was Paul. If by marrying Paul she would save Daniel she would, but she felt she was
drowning in the utter confusion.

Though busy with his flock, Paul courted her for another three
months. He made time for them to spend together; he was a good
man, kind, honest, with a wonderful laugh and sense of humor.
Down to earth and without pious airs it wasn't hard for her to
be with him. They walked to the East Side to see the Indian
mounds, they took a buggy ride out to Mahtomedi, and went to
the carnival at Wildwood. They toured to Minneapolis and all
the way to Excelsior to picnic on the shore and ride the paddlewheel boat on Lake Minnetonka.

They explored the caves along the river bluff and he held her
hand for the first time when he claimed they were lost. Down
on one knee, he asked for her hand in marriage when they were
sitting on a bench in Rice Park near midnight. When she accepted and shook with emotions and tears, Paul thought it was
for them, he and Gabrielle, when the emotions and tears were
for Daniel. How would he ever understand? How could she ever
explain?

She wanted the wedding to take place on the ranch in Montana. Letters flew back and forth. Elizabeth and Grace and the
family in Montana would take care of most of the arrangements.
Gabrielle wanted to keep it simple and Paul's small immediate
family wouldn't be able to travel that far, taking so much time.
They would have a small reception in St. Paul upon their return.
Paul got two weeks off and he looked forward to seeing the Montana Gabrielle had described to him so passionately.

Jeremiah and Zack were waiting on the platform when the train made its turnaround stop at the spur eleven miles northeast of Buffalo Jump. They loaded the luggage into the wagon and buggy, Zack driving the team on the wagon, Jeremiah driving the buggy for the long trip to the ranch.

"Where's Maddy and Daniel?" Gabrielle asked as they bounced and swayed along the gravel road.

"Maddy's at the ranch, got here Monday," Jeremiah said. "Haven't seen hide nor hair of Daniel yet, coming from Butte. Said he'd be here."

Just speaking his name brought a rush into her heart and a flush to her face she hoped wasn't visible.

Paul and Jeremiah visited most of the four-hour trip and Paul was overcome with the grandeur of it. Gabrielle cherished the memories that came to her at every turn, at every view, all of it saturated with Daniel. When they reached the Y in the road and turned for the ranch, the good life they'd shared there assailed her like the turning pages from a book—the hundreds of journeys to school and to town, driving a bunch of cattle to buy or sell, racing the horses across the summer meadows and swimming in The River That Rolls Rocks.

At the ranch Martha, Elizabeth, Aunt Grace, Maddy, and Wart had been at work preparing the house for the wedding guests and keeping one eye on the horizon, south toward the gorge. When the bridal party came into view Wart rang the bell over and over, coming off the ground with each swing of the clapper. Those at the house welcomed them with shouts and cheers when they pulled up the road into the yard. The bride and groom had arrived all the way from Saint Paul. The ranch hummed with people, the house bloomed with wildflowers. For several hours they all pitched in and helped with the work and chores, getting better acquainted. When Elizabeth had everyone settled with sleeping arrangements and Wart had sneaked away with Paul to catch some trout, time stood still. They were all holding their breath until Daniel came riding home.

Daniel was sure that Buck knew he was going home. He kept forging ahead, hurrying, urging Daniel to turn him loose, following horse trails north, through meadows and foothills, flowing across the landscape like music.

"Going home."

His emotions, as fickle as the wind, overwhelmed him. He was going home to the place where he was born, where he grew up, to his family, to all the unforgettable and indelible memories. But "home" was Gabrielle now, to be in her arms, to be with her and nowhere else could be home to him again.

But he'd been in shock ever since he'd gotten word that she was coming back to the ranch with a minister she intended to marry. On the one hand, he wondered why she would do that. This was crazy! Had she changed? Didn't she mean she would love me "forever"? On the other hand she had left Montana convinced that they were sinful and wrong to think they could be together. She was following through on her word. Tormented with these conflicting thoughts and stalking doubts, he nudged Buck and let him run. Windstorms of the heart.

Late in the afternoon, when the others were preoccupied, Gabrielle saw him coming, fast, on Buck, oh the joy! Daniel. She leaped from the porch and ran to the bell. With both hands around the heavy weathered rope she rang the bell loudly, with all her strength, proclaiming to the valley her love for Daniel. She knew only the two of them would hear what the bell was proclaiming. She would certainly not have them ring the bell at the wedding.

He slid off his horse and came for the porch where she stood, breathless. Oh, Lord, she'd grown up, bloomed, more beautiful than ever, her eyes, face, her shoulders, and he rushed toward her. But the bell brought folks from all corners of the yard and buildings and they intercepted him before he reached her. When the family had surrounded him and welcomed him with hoots and hollers and hugs, he turned to her.

"And my little sister, Gabrielle." He gave her a brotherly hug that she thought was too nonchalant if anyone in the family was paying attention. Normally, before they fell in love, he would have lifted her off the floor and smothered her with a bear hug. When he stepped back politely she turned to Paul who was beside her.

"Daniel, this is Paul, Reverend Douglas."

The men shook hands.

"Good to meet you, Reverend," Daniel said, "welcome to Montana."

"Very nice to meet you," Paul said, "but please, 'Paul' is enough."

"Golly," Maddy said, "I never thought of it but you could marry yourself."

They all laughed.

"What do you think about our country?" Daniel asked Paul.

"It's so *big*, so overwhelming. I never could have imagined it."

On the wave of conversation they all moved inside. All except Daniel who found it hard to breathe. Here she was, Gabrielle, more beautiful than he remembered, standing only a few paces away, the woman he was born to love, and they had to act as if they were estranged brother and sister, playing their parts with shattered hearts.

*Pick her up in your arms, onto Buck, and gallop away.*

He sucked in a breath and joined the celebration. Both of them avoided eye contact though the short distance between them felt stronger than gravity. He didn't hear a word of the conversation until the unexpected blow. They wanted him to be best man since Paul's best friend couldn't make the trip. He talked fast, convincing them that Zack was the rightful candidate, the son who stayed home. With Gabrielle's nod and Paul's approval, Zack would be best man, hamming it up, and never knowing the anguish he lifted from his big brother's heart.

The following afternoon Daniel jockeyed for an opportunity to be with Gabrielle. He had been stuck with the men playing horseshoes, riding into the foothills, and fishing. Finally he found her in the horse barn. As she walked through, Daniel grabbed her arm and pulled her into an empty high-walled stall. They embraced fiercely, fellow travelers who had been separated and lost. He nearly crushed the breath out of her.

"Oh, God, you feel so good," he said.

"Daniel, Daniel," she whispered, "my love, my poor sweet Daniel."

"I'm dying," he said.

"I know, I know."

He took her by the shoulders and looked into her eyes.

"Why are you doing this? For God's sake why!"

"To make us right with God."

"That's crazy, it makes no sense, it only drives us further apart."

"No, it will make up for our sin, I had a dream—"

"Don't do this. Tell them you've changed your mind, tell them you're sick, anything, but don't do this to us."

"I have to. . . . It's too late now, I have to."

"It'll only make it worse. Don't do it, please, please," Daniel said.

"I must, can't you see, if I marry a minister, a man of God, and help him with his Christian work, I'll do penance for both of us, I won't be damned, we won't be damned."

"We're not damned!" He shook her by the shoulders. "You're not damned or God has no compassion, no love, no forgiveness."

A voice called at the other end of the barn.

"Gabrielle!"

"I have to go," Gabrielle whispered, "it's Maddy. She's been sticking to me like oatmeal."

He held her by the arm as she turned.

"Meet me tonight, please, please," he said.

"I can't with all of them here."

He kissed her ferociously until she pulled away and hurried through the barn.


The night before the wedding, Daniel stole out of the house past midnight when all the family and guests were settled and asleep. Under the brilliant stars he carried a large quilt he'd pilfered from the bunkhouse where it wouldn't be missed. He hurried to their favorite place on the ranch, the swimming hole in the River That Rolls Rocks, hoping he wasn't keeping her waiting.

When he arrived he laid in the sweet grass and wildflowers alongside the swimming hole, remembering. He knew she would come. The sounds of the river calmed him, a hoot owl called from a nearby tree. Small creatures busied themselves along the bank. He laid back with his hands under his head and regarded the starlit sky. It was warm, a perfect summer night, just cool enough to keep the insects grounded. He feared that she wouldn't come. Her "forever" seemed to be no longer forever. He listened. His anxiety grew. He couldn't bear being this close to her and not loving her. Tomorrow she would marry another man. He would return to Butte and bury himself three hundred feet below ground, his chosen tomb. The night was evaporating. What if she doesn't come? Had he lost her?

Daniel held his breath as he heard a rustling in the grass. Suddenly Skipper rushed from the willows and jumped on him, wagging his stumpy tail. Then she came out of the darkness, in her long Canada robe. He leaped up to take her in his arms. Oh, God the unimaginable wonder of her. He held her tightly, without speaking, and they clung to each other as though they'd never let go. They kissed passionately, then softly, again and again. When they settled on the quilt they jabbered like chipmunks telling each other of the long months and the enduring ache in their hearts. Daniel tried to persuade her, tried to understand, begged her to give up the marriage. When he couldn't, she allowed one last hour of him holding her in his arms.

"You know what I pray every night?" she asked. "Every night before I sleep I pray that God will make it right, that God will change it, that you won't be my brother. God can do anything can't he? That's what we were taught. There's nothing impossible for Him. If there is then he's not God. Every night I pray that he'll change it, that I was adopted or you were adopted and mother and father didn't want us to know. But as I pray I hear old Doc Simpson telling how much trouble he had delivering you, how big you were, and I hear him tell how I came out first and Maddy twenty minutes later, a surprise. We were smaller, barely seven pounds and I want to plug my ears and scream."

She paused.

"Don't do it tomorrow, please, don't do it," he said. "Let's run away, come with me, we can start over, tell him you've changed your mind."

She sat up with the quilt around her shoulders.

"I can't, we'll be damned forever."

"Maybe not, maybe God forgives us, we don't know."

"Yes, I know, and you know too, Daniel. Don't you see, if I marry a minister and do God's work I won't be damned, we won't be damned."

"No, you don't have to do this, God will forgive us," he said.

"If there's a God we're damned. If there is no God we're lost."

"I'll walk with you a ways," he said, as they forced themselves to head for home.

"No, no, we can never be seen like this. You wait here for a while until I'm almost home. I'll come around from the other side where the outhouse is, in case anyone is awake."

"When will I see you?" he asked. "I can come to Saint Paul."

"Oh no, no, don't do that, it'll ruin our settling with God, promise me, promise me."

"I have to see you, please, I have to see you."

She took his head in her hands and kissed him frantically.

"No matter what," she spoke rapidly, "don't ever give up, don't ever give in to the darkness, never stop believing in us. I know how black it must look for you. Me too, me too, but don't ever give up on us, don't ever, ever, ever."

She turned and ran off across the meadow into the black night. He repeated her words with a faltering hope.

"Ever, ever, ever."


They say that the wedding went off as planned. Daniel bore up as long as he could, not hearing what people were saying, catching himself watching Gabrielle with her husband, wanting to flee. They feasted off several tables of excellent food and when all had their fill they moved the furniture from the living room and dining room and started to dance. The musicians, neighbors with banjo, guitar, and fiddle, set the tone and the joyous occasion went on. Elizabeth managed the unlikely event of getting her husband to dance with her. She had always been an accomplished dancer but Jeremiah was a reluctant dance partner. However, he did take Martha for a short spin on the dance floor. Everyone stopped for a moment to watch and clap. Aunt Grace insisted Daniel dance with her and they swung around the floor, Grace quite spry for her age. When Daniel could bear no more he found Jeremiah out on the porch and told him he was leaving, hoping to reach Taylor's way station before dark.

"I don't understand you, son, working in that hell when you could come home and help me and Zack and Wart run this place. We have to hire help at times. You belong here, this is your home, here are your roots. It's time you settle down, find your life here with a good woman. Have you found anyone in Butte?"

"No, no one. I gotta go. I'll write more often."

"It'd please your mother."

"Thanks for everything, Father, but I gotta go."

Daniel turned to leave.

"Oh no, oh no," Jeremiah said as he took a hold of Daniel's arm. "Not until you've given your little sister your blessing, not until you've danced with her on her wedding day."

Jeremiah found Gabrielle talking with Wart in the kitchen where Wart had been washing dishes and staying out of sight. Jeremiah took Gabrielle by the hand and led her into the living room to Daniel. The musicians started a slow waltz and they stepped out on the floor, dancing smoothly as they had so many winter nights, as Elizabeth had taught all her children. They smiled as they danced, played their roles perfectly. Elizabeth and Jeremiah stood watching them, proud though somewhat baffled by Gabrielle's decision to join with Paul in the work of the church. Growing up she'd been lukewarm to anything with the church and her decision to marry Paul seemed tame for the girl they'd raised.

Gabrielle and Daniel spoke into each other's ear and were careful to hold each other at a proper distance.

"Good-bye, my love," Gabrielle said. "I don't want to ruin your life too. Be happy, my love. I will hold you in my heart as long as I breathe. Know that wherever I go I will be loving you, I will be yours, forever, till the end of time."

Daniel was losing it, nearly breaking down. The music came to an end, the dance was over. He squeezed her hand, turned and worked his way out of the crowded house, turned his face toward Butte and the mines and the hell of living without her.

Maddy found Gabrielle on the porch, waving and watching Daniel ride away. Maddy came up beside her.

"Our big brother," Maddy said. "What a mystery. He's changed."

"How do you mean?" Gabrielle asked still searching the horizon for a final glimpse.

"I don't know . . . leaving so soon. I think he's in love."

"In love? Why do you think that?" Gabrielle asked, afraid to let Maddy see her tears.

"He acts as though he has someone back in Butte he'd rather be with than with us."

"I think he had to get back to his job."

"Job! Huh! He had a sadness in his eyes. He never once picked me up and swung me around, never once, like he used to."

"He didn't swing me either, we're not children anymore."

Maddy turned and gazed into the house at the celebration.

"He's lost his joy I tell you, as if he loves someone who doesn't love him."

Maddy stepped into the house and Gabrielle wanted to tell her that Daniel loved someone who loved him with every beat of her heart. He had reached the gorge and rode out of sight. Gabrielle had all she could do to keep from jumping on Ramrod and riding off with Daniel and never turning back.

# NINETEEN

WHEN DANIEL FIRST SAW BUTTE he thought the earth had fallen sick and thrown up on itself. The south face of the mountain had a jagged, gaping wound ripped open; treeless, grassless, flowerless, slag piles rose everywhere, heaps of crushed rock overflowed downhill, steam, black smoke and clouds of dust roiled in the mountain winds. It appeared as though insane armies had fought there for years with cannon, explosives, and a blind loyalty to destruction, were fighting still, frantically digging trenches in an effort to conquer every inch, to dislodge every rock. They didn't know the mountain had a soul.

It was several days before he was hired; a crew that worked on contract, and paid by how much ore they loaded each day. His physical size and obvious strength got him the job, nothing else. He thought how easily grandfather Abraham could have found work here, thankful to God that he hadn't. Daniel found a room in a boardinghouse that catered mainly to miners and he showed up for work at the Consolidated Mining office at six in the morning, aching and feeling lost.

With a bunch of seasoned miners he dropped hundreds of feet into the blackness as if someone swallowed the sun, the first trembling step into hell. His new-bought work clothes and boots gave him away and he closed his eyes and held his breath while hoping that his childhood nemesis would not follow him into the darkness like an unseen ghost. He tried to remain calm but he could feel the panic just under his skin. The lift stopped with a jolt and a man behind him pointed out one of three tunnels. A low-slung ore car sat on narrow tracks waiting to be lifted out and Daniel followed the others as they lit the oil lamp on their helmets. The dim little lights reminded him of the fireflies they used to catch in the tall grass in the meadow.

Throughout that first day it felt as though hot sulfuric hands were trying to choke him. He gasped and coughed and struggled to find his breath in the stale, sweat-soaked air, at every minute tempted to flee back along the tunnel to the lift and escape with the next ore car. Panic gathered its forces and repeatedly charged the walls of his brain but he beat it back with cannons of memories and thoughts of Gabrielle. If he did this, he told himself, if he worked the mines for a time, one day he would find Gabrielle and be able to live openly with her, somewhere, as husband and wife, and it would be all right, with his family, with God. For now, he had to completely distract his mind, stay alive, and exhaust his body to the point that he would be able to sleep without seeing her face, without losing hope, without fearing for her safety wherever she was in the world.

He loaded the fractured chunks of ore into the shallow cars, broke down the larger pieces with a sledgehammer, and in the eerie shadows of his headlamp, and those of his fellow workers, felt like a creature of the underground, a mole or shrew who would never again see sunlight. In the cramped tunnel, he wondered why the rock ceiling didn't collapse on them—hundreds of miles of honeycombed tunnels they told him—because the timbers didn't look sturdy enough to hold off millions of tons of mountain.

The sulfur burned in his throat, the acid burned his arms and clothes, and three of the six men in his crew coughed throughout the day. When he rose "above the grass" the sun was far to the west but still flying. He breathed deeply and coughed out the dust and stale air. For half of the year he wouldn't see the sun except on Sundays; he'd be in the hole through all of winter's daylight.

At supper he could barely stay awake, his body aching and sore, and he drank jug after jug of water. Eleven men ate at the long table at Etta Anderson's boardinghouse and her daughter Claire helped with the work. Arne Anderson, Etta's husband, was killed in the mine five years ago and she opened a place for miners. Claire came and went, serving the meal, and one gnarly miner kept making improper cracks about the girl, who must have been close to twenty. Daniel thought someone ought to say something about this crude disrespect but he wanted to get the lay of the land before he did; still an outsider. The food was good, served family style: meatloaf, chicken, potatoes, gravy, corn, fresh bread, and huckleberry pie.

He stayed awake long enough to get his turn in a tub and tried to scrub the day's grime from his body, tried to scrub a curse from his soul. When he fell asleep he didn't dream of Gabrielle; he fell asleep dreading the coming day and dreamed several times that the mine caved in and buried him alive.

For twenty cents extra, Widow Anderson would provide lunch to take into the mine, two pasties, a canteen of coffee, and sometimes an apple. When he stood in line to take the lifts he scanned the slopes of the distant mountains, thinking of the valley, and he watched for a red-tail hawk.

Days stretched into insufferable weeks; Daniel became adept at loading copper ore and learning how to breathe where there was little air, a test more of a man's lungs than his muscle. But he never could shake his childhood terror of being underground, catching himself believing that the tons of earth just inches above him were about to crush him like a worm. At times large chunks would calve off the wall or ceiling with a heavy thud, striking terror in him and leaving him breathing and sweating as if he'd just run a mile.

One of the men on his crew, Albert Kincaid, offered Daniel his friendship, knowing Daniel was new to this underground world and thereby taking Daniel under his wing. Albert stood over six feet but was stooped from working under the mine's low ceiling and ducking the rough timbers. He wore a short beard and his dark eyes peered out like a weary child looking for hope. Everything about him had been colored by the dull dark ore. Albert talked in a steady stream that distracted Daniel and helped pass the time. But Daniel could see that Albert was faltering, skinny, unable to keep up with his portion of the work, coughing his lungs out in the ore dust. Daniel worked close to Albert and began to cover for him by doing twice his share.

"How long have you been doing this?" Daniel asked one morning as they grubbed up the ore that had been dislodged by a dynamite crew during the night.

"Most of my life . . . since I was seventeen . . . since forever."

"Why don't you get out?"

"It tricks ya, like gamblin' and poker. It whispers, 'One more hand.'"

"You could find something else, something in the sunlight."

"I stayed too long, missed the chance when I could have learned something else, made a start."

He wrestled a heavy rock into the car and coughed against his glove.

"Sally begged me but I was stubborn; thought I'd just stay another year. That was fifteen years ago, afraid I wouldn't know what else to do."

"You can still get out," Daniel said as he loaded ore.

"Too late, got *miner's con.*"

"You got what?"

"Silicosis." He wiped his forehead with his sleeve. "I tell you, Daniel, get out now; you're young. This hell hole kills or cripples a man every day. A man can stay drunk just attending wakes in this town."

Albert dropped a huge chunk in a car.

"We call one like that 'an undertaker'."

At supper the uncouth miner chipped at Claire again, suggestive asides that made some of the men snicker. Exhaustion and a longing for Gabrielle overwhelmed Daniel as he ate, and a homesickness for the valley felt as though he was pinned under an avalanche. He would deal with the bigmouth another time.

Daniel went to a pub on a Saturday night looking for something to derail memory if nothing more than to listen to the miners tell their stories. He would not use alcohol to blur or deaden his memories of Gabrielle. He could sleep in the morning and he hoped, as usual, he could sleep part of the day.

He'd write a letter to the family and hope they would return one with news about Gabrielle's whereabouts. Elizabeth had sent news that they were all fine and that there was no new knowledge of Gabrielle. They were busy with ranch work, missing him, and Wart was still chasing chickens. She reminded Daniel that Maddy was over two passes and about ninety miles if he ever felt like taking a few days off and visiting her. Elizabeth said Maddy was taking Gabrielle's disappearance very hard and even threatened to come home.

There had been a funeral for a miner that day and at the saloon that night his comrades were slinging down boilermakers and topping each other telling what a fine fellow the dead man had been. At the busy establishment Daniel noticed the miner from the boardinghouse who made lewd and nasty remarks about Claire standing at the crowded bar. He'd found out the man's name—Ranski. Daniel sized him up: just under six foot, solid body, mid-forties with straw-colored hair and whiskers. When he laughed a mush of rotten black teeth showed themselves and under a soiled cap his ungroomed hair splayed out like a scarecrow's.

An anger arose in Daniel's bloodstream as he kept an eye on the miner who had the demeanor of a bully. When he visualized Gabrielle working some place like Claire and having some guy making those kinds of remarks to her he decided he'd put it off no longer. If he couldn't do anything for Gabrielle right then he'd do the next best thing. Daniel shoved himself up from his chair and wedged in beside the miner at the bar. He regarded the man who was well on his way to getting drunk.

"I'm Daniel Rockhammer."

"Oh, yeah . . . seen you at the house."

"I want you to remember my name, Rockhammer."

"Sounds like you work in a mine. Ha!" He displayed his black teeth.

"I don't want to embarrass you in front of the other men, but I won't tolerate you talking to that girl the way you do."

"Oh, that so? What girl we talking about?"

"Claire Anderson, the girl who serves us at the boardinghouse."

"What the hell? Who gave you the gall to stick your nose—"

"I did, and I won't tolerate it."

Ranski stood tall and stuck his face in Daniel's. His breath smelled like dead fish.

"Go away before I boil over," the miner said and flicked his right hand.

Daniel crowded him, realizing Ranski outweighed him by a good thirty or forty pounds.

"Well, I'm ahead of you, you maggot-sucking skunk," Daniel said, eyeballing him and breathing in his face, "I'm already boiled over."

The miner swung his fist at Daniel but he wasn't fast. Daniel caught the fist with his left hand, smashed it against the bar and held it there. The miner winced in pain and struggled to pull it free but Daniel's strength prevailed. With his nose in the man's gnarled face, Daniel spoke softly.

"If you talk with your filthy mind around the girl again you'll have to eat your supper with a sponge."

Daniel quickly raised Ranski's fist and smashed it against the bar again. The miner winced in pain and grabbed his hand in his other.

"Remember," Daniel said, "one more word and I'll save you a trip to the doctor."

Keeping an eye over his shoulder, Daniel shoved his way back to his chair and sat down. Noticing the brief skirmish in the noisy saloon, Kincaid, Daniel's buddy from the mine, wove his way across the room and settled beside Daniel.

"Don't rile Ranski, partner. He's a mean one."

"His mouth is so filthy, his teeth can't even stand it."

Kincaid laughed until he started to gag. He caught his breath.

"You got that right, Rock, but listen to me. He broke a man's leg last summer, put another guy in the hospital, broken ribs, you better stay clear of that one."

"Thanks for the tip, but I've got a girl at home and I started thinking that some slimy rat like Ranski could be talking like that to her or worse and I feel helpless and I get steamed and it may sound crazy but I figure that what I do with Ranski can in some small way help my girl."

"I don't think that's crazy at all, by golly, you're striking a blow for treating women with respect, like your mother or sister."

Daniel winced and ducked his eyes.

"So, you have a sweetheart, that's nice. What's her name?"

"I don't like talking about her, you know what I mean, I'll get to missing her real bad. Can I buy you a beer?"

"Don't mind if I do. Sally keeps a tight rein on the money . . ." He coughed for a minute. "And I've already spent my allowance."

Daniel glanced back to the bar. Ranski was gone.

It was several weeks later when Daniel and Kincaid were sitting at the bar of their favorite saloon. A little out of the way and a longer hike, people from all walks of life gathered there, somewhat of a relief from the horde of miners they encountered in the more popular miner bars. Many of the patrons came by horseback and buggy and carriage. Kincaid had used up his wife's allowance and Daniel was keeping them both in beer. Daniel still didn't have a taste for beer and found that one would last him most of the night.

"Is it all right to ask if you've heard from your girlfriend?"

"It's all right. Haven't heard from her lately but I'm sure I will soon. Her letters take forever."

Daniel tried to filter any information he shared with his friend and still be able to share his heartache.

"Are you courting the lass?"

"I love her, we're going to be married. We have some things to figure out."

"Does she know you're throwing your life away?"

"She's waiting for me. I'm saving my money. She'll always be waiting for me."

"You sure of that? Many a man found out she didn't wait."

"I know, I know, but our love is different, unbreakable."

"By golly, why don't you bring her here?"

"I don't want her in this hell hole."

"Then go to her, lad, don't waste another day in the mines."

"I can't."

"You can't?"

"I can't. I can't tell you why, I can't tell anyone."

Kincaid finished his beer.

"Sounds like a mighty sad story to me, by golly."

"I don't want to talk about it."

\* \* \*

They say that outside, the two men turned their collars up and hunkered into the cold and poorly lit city where ghost-like shadows lurked in the dark. After several turns they found their way through a narrow block-long alley, as they had come. Just as they turned at the corner, Ranski lunged out of the darkness swinging a long lead pipe, narrowly missing Daniel's head as it whistled by.

"Watch out!" Kincaid shouted and jumped.

Daniel ducked and swiftly stepped back several paces along a brick wall.

"Stay out of this, Kincaid," Ranski said as he squared off with the four-foot pipe in both hands. "This is between Rockhammer and me."

"Fight fair!" Kincaid shouted excitedly. "Give me the pipe! Give it to me!"

"I told him not to rattle me," Ranski said. "Now I'm going to give *him* the pipe."

Ranski hunched like a wolf stalking prey, slowly circling, tapping the pipe in his left hand while looking for an opening.

"Throw the pipe away, Ranski, or count me in," Kincaid said.

"I'll get around to you later, Kincaid," Ranski said.

"No, no . . . stay out of it, Albert," Daniel said, "this is my fight."

Daniel crouched and circled, facing Ranski, staying out of his reach.

"So ya don't like the way I talk to that built little bitch?" Ranski said and laughed. "You probably want a sweet piece of her yerself?"

In an instant he lunged, swinging his weapon. Daniel sidestepped and caught the miner in the head with a solid right. Ranski stumbled, shaken, slipped down on one knee, struggling to recover his balance. As he wobbled to his feet, Daniel drove his hardened left fist into Ranski's gut. The wolf dropped his guard and Daniel quickly hammered him with a solid right to the jaw. The pipe and Ranski hit the ground together, both of them out cold.

"Holy mother of God," Kincaid shouted. "You finished 'im off in less than a minute!"

"So . . . now he'll eat his supper with a sponge," Daniel said as he bent over the body. "Should we look to see if we've helped him with the teeth?"

"You buggered him in twenty seconds, by golly. He never knew what hit 'im."

They dragged him up on the stoop of a dreary little house, checked that he was still breathing and continued walking home.

"You put out 'is light in the blink of an eye," Kincaid said. "I never seen anything like it. You could fight Saturday nights."

"What's Saturday night?" Daniel asked.

"They have fights in the old Henderson warehouse."

"What for?"

"For the sport of it some, mine against mine, but mainly for the money. There's good money to be had. The way you took out Ranski you could win. He's a mean one."

"How do you get to fight?"

"Just show up, two-bits to get in. If you want to fight they'll match you up with someone. There's a lot of betting. You win you make four or five bucks, depending on the purse."

"And if you lose?"

"You get nothing but a headache or a bloody nose or a broken rib or two, but if you win you move up and can get a bigger fight the next week."

"I don't like fighting, I hate it," Daniel said. "Always hated it when I was a kid."

"You'd never know it the way you demolished Ranski, and he's a big powerful man."

"That was different, he was shaming that helpless girl. I won't tolerate it. That could be my girl he was picking on."

"You said you want to save up some money. I could get Sally to give me some money to bet on you. She's been squirreling away what she can for the day I can't work. Thinks I don't know about it."

"Sally sounds like quite a gal."

"I don't deserve her, she's a jewel. I always prided myself for being the breadwinner in this family. I know she's been sneaking out and working when I'm in the mine. Cleaning house, cooking, taking care of children for the wealthy on the hill. Works all day and hurries home before I come up. I never let on that I know, but it shames a man who can't support his family, shames a man."

Kincaid shook his head as they stopped, each to go his own way.

"Holy Mother of God! Never seen anything like it. One, two, howdy due, three, four, on the floor, five, six, take your licks, seven, eight, through the pearly gate. Think about Saturday night, you could win, we could win."

Daniel nodded and walked off into the dark. All he could think about was Gabrielle and what he did to Ranski made him feel a little closer to her.

# TWENTY

THE JOURNEY TO SAINT PAUL became a torture chamber for Gabrielle. A strong premonition that she'd never see Daniel again rode beside her like a traveling companion. Mile after mile the distance between them opened like a great yawning canyon. Every minute, every mile, every heartbeat she traveled further and further from his arms, from his smile, from his voice. At each stop along the way she beat back the urge to get off the train and go back, no matter what the consequences. She couldn't catch her breath, riding with a growing panic in her heart. Paul carried on with conversation as though he didn't have a care in the world but she heard little, preoccupied with her aching indecision. With a visible happiness on his face and his friendly warmth, Paul told everyone who came within shouting distance that they were newlyweds.

About the middle of the car, they settled in two seats, side by side, facing backward. The landscape she viewed from the window etched memories of where she had been, what she left behind. She couldn't see the landscape that she was steaming into, her tomorrows, her future. As with her life, Gabrielle gazed back to what was now lost, the past, racing away from her with the sagebrush and buttes and everlasting cottonwoods, all of it indifferent to the scream under her ribs.

At Forsythe she left her seat, told Paul she wanted to use the toilet at the station, that she didn't like going on the train with the tracks and ties and noise thundering from that little hole when you pulled the lever. She really didn't mind it at all but it was her excuse. With her carpet bag she got off the train and for several moments did battle with the dizzying conflictions in her soul.

"Don't stray too far," the conductor said to her outside the depot. "This engineer is very prompt."

Could this large friendly negro man read her mind? Did it show on her face?

"Thank you," Gabrielle said with a smile.

She only had to wait behind the depot until the train pulled away. By the time Paul realized, the train would be several miles east. She hesitated. If she walked off through the town until she couldn't make it back before the train left, it would be out of her hands.

*Quit thinking, just do it!*

From a small writing desk on a wall in the depot she hurriedly wrote a note to Paul. Who is she to come up with any words that would have any meaning, make any sense, soothe any wound?

She found their conductor, and looking confused, he said he'd give it to her husband.

Gabrielle hurried through the station and out into the bustling town. People filled the busy streets with horses and wagons and livestock and chatter. Some greeted her kindly and tipped their hats or nodded. Children chasing, women visiting and folks living their normal lives with those they loved. Didn't they realize she was battling with good and evil at the turning point of her life! Couldn't they see it in her face?

Numbly she pushed herself, step by step, stride after stride. She lost track of distance and time but sensed she was far enough away to ever catch the train. When she passed a livery stable Gabrielle wondered how long it would take on horseback to ride to Butte. She felt as if she were walking on thin ice over a deep, dark river that could give way at any moment, dropping her into the freezing water and below that into the fires of hell. She strained forward, forcing her legs as a cripple would.

Then, above the hum and clamor of the town, shrill and distant, the train whistled, announcing its departure east. She'd gone too far, she could never get back in time! Something fluttered in her heart. Not for Daniel, for Paul. She couldn't desert Paul like that, leave him sitting alone in the train, waiting for her, trusting her.

A short dusty cowboy came lazily along on an Appaloosa Indian pony with its hooves clapping in rhythm on the hard sun-baked street.

"Hello, hello, can you help me?" she shouted as she hurried to him.

"Ma'am?" he said as he tipped his trail-worn hat and spit a string of tobacco to the other side of the horse.

"I need to catch that train!"

He extended his arm to her. "Climb on!"

She grabbed his arm and swung up behind him. As she threw her right leg over the horse's rump and wrapped her arms around his waist, he spurred the Appaloosa. With a disciplined explosion the horse catapulted down the street, almost running out from under them with its burst of power.

"Hang on!" he shouted and she caught her breath.

Several blocks across town the train whistled again. They raced through cluttered streets, cutting and dashing around wagons and teams, scattering a small bunch of sheep, pedestrians, and chickens and narrowly missing others on horseback.

"Heah! Yaah! Heah! Yaah!" he urged speed from his pony.

The cowboy leaned forward over the Appaloosa's mane as the horse stretched out. Its hooves thudded against the ground as it reached to gobble up distance, weaving through trade goods and traffic and startled shoppers. Gabrielle had grown up with horses, some excellent breeds, but this horse, with its vision and anticipation, was a cut above any she'd seen.

In the moment, she believed in the mystery. The horse carried them as if they were weightless, flying through the town's streets as if they were expected royalty. It snorted with the joy of running and took in the world around it with flashing eyes. Some townsfolk cussed them as if they'd just robbed the local bank, others waved them on as if all of Forsythe hoped Gabrielle would reach the train in time. They jumped over a wagon tongue and ran along the boardwalk of the hotel to avoid people on foot. Two buxom women stepped back quickly and ended up sitting in a water trough. A shaggy, black mongrel ran with them, stride for stride, as if it too wanted to get out of town. Some people shouted, some waved, but for an instant it seemed that the whole town had acknowledged Gabrielle's race with her inner turmoil.

They approached the depot from the north and the train was slowly on its way.

"You want to go for it?" he shouted?

"Go! go! I have to get on that train."

The cowboy swung the horse east and it sprinted alongside the shiny Northern Pacific coach out into the open country that surrounded Forsythe. But the ends of the creosote railroad ties made it hard for the pony to get close without stumbling. It would make their stretch across the deadly gap nearly impossible.

She was losing her grip. The hard bumps and jolts were knocking her loose. The horse struggled over the ties, close to tripping. Suddenly, the passenger door on the side of the coach swung open. The conductor had followed his suspicions and threw open the coach door. He stood in the low doorway, waving, and holding out an arm to a deeply grateful Gabrielle. She sensed the moment of truth would come fast and give her only one quick chance. She well knew what the consequences would be if she fell, if the horse fell. She thought of Daniel. Oh sweet Daniel, if he could be here with her now.

The cowboy turned his head and smiled at her. She returned the smile and gathered herself. Then she slapped him on the back, shouted "Thank you," and leaped over the roaring space that was the rest of her life.

Standing in the open door, the conductor caught her as much as she caught him. Both hit by the momentum of their collision, they fell backward into the stairwell, safe and secure in the saving arms of the Northern Pacific Railroad. The two looked at each other and laughed, laughed hard.

Realizing that her husband had to be missing her, the conductor closed the bottom half door and gave her time for herself. She straightened her dress and brushed her hair and tried to catch her breath. When she got to her seat she couldn't believe what she saw. It turned out that Paul slept through the whole escapade.

The locomotive was showing off, roaring ahead with great power and speed. But, out of the steam and smoke and dust, the cowboy raced beside the train on his Indian pony, now able to stay in the chase without the weight of a passenger. He whipped the Appaloosa with his hat, keeping abreast of the train for a minute longer. Then, the young man was swallowed up in the smoke and noise, out of sight, gone! He'd be unable to name the mysterious young woman who dared to jump the terrifying gap when he'd tell his story.

They say they still tell of that Appaloosa's run in Forsythe and those who tell it say they'd never seen a horse run so swiftly, right through the clutter of town, with power and grace. But no one knew the young woman's name.

At Miles City they had a long stopover to take on water and wood. She suggested that Paul go stretch his legs and she'd keep an eye on their belongings. When Paul returned ten minutes later, she took her turn. Paul didn't seem to notice that she took her large handbag. She hurried into the depot and along the back wall found a hauntingly similar writing desk with Northern Pacific stationary. She wrote the note quickly, telling Paul she knew how it would hurt him, that she didn't want to, but she loved another man, and this marriage might damn Paul's life as it had hers, that it had no hope for happiness. She said she'd pray that he'd find a good, undamaged woman who would make him happy. She folded the note once.

Out on the platform she found their conductor helping people climb aboard. She handed him the note.

"Would you please give this to my husband?"

He hesitated. "I don't understand, ma'am."

"My husband, he's in the. . . ."

"I know where he is, but why don't you give it to him?"

"I'm not going any further, I'm leaving the train."

"What! After what you just did! Why there's nothing you can't do, you just won your battle, you can't just walk away."

He helped a bent old woman climb in and then stepped over to Gabrielle.

"You got to stay, ma'am, your husband and all."

"Please." She held out the note and he took it with his large hand.

"Lots a people get scared when they's first married. You got to give it a chance, why that man in there waiting for you is a fine man."

Gabrielle hesitated. She felt exhausted, worn down. She turned toward their seats and Paul. She stood, fighting fiercely to decide. She took one step forward. She took a step back. The train moved a foot or two with a jerk. Someone down the track shouted, "All . . . a . . . board!"

The conductor picked up the step stool and set it in the train.

"Now don't you feel better?" he asked. "You better get to that husband of yours, he'll be worried."

Gabrielle straightened her dress and ran her hand through her hair. She started through the door into their car.

"Ma'am, you forgot this." He held out the note.

She took it and tucked it into her handbag.

"Thank you. I know you were trying to help. You're a kind man."

"You gotta quit jumpin' outta trains. That's a mighty dangerous pastime. You stick out your marriage a while, give it a chance, and maybe one day you'll remember how you rode the Indian pony and almost missed the train. Maybe someday you can tell your husband."

He smiled and shut the top door. No one else was getting off.

When she got back to Paul he was about to come looking for her. She told him she was visiting with the conductor and some other people, even a cowboy. She watched Miles City and eastern Montana slip away, far into the night. They had a blanket over them as they slept side by side in their seats which were tipped back part way. Under the blanket Paul put his hand on her thigh. They had agreed not to consummate their marriage until they were back in Saint Paul in the relaxed privacy of their home.

When she woke, Paul was digging through her handbag. He saw that she was awake.

"Good morning."

"Good morning," she answered.

He pulled the folded note from her bag and glanced at the writing inside the fold.

She held her breath. "What do you need?" she asked.

Paul flattened the note blank side up on top of the Bible in his lap.

"I was thinking of the text for my sermon Sunday and I got a good idea. I want to write it down."

Gabrielle dug through her bag and found a card given to her at the wedding and signed by Daniel, though she knew Elizabeth had probably provided it. Daniel signed it With Love. She quickly reached over and retrieved the note and handed Paul the card.

"This will work better, it's blank on the back and it'll hold up better."

With what she feared was visible relief, she tucked the note into her bag.

Paul looked at the card. "Oh, honey, this is your card from your brother, I don't want to write on it. That other paper would be fine."

"That's all right," she said, "I probably wouldn't keep it anyway."

At her first chance to go to the toilet she dropped the note into that roaring hole where it quickly was sucked away. She held the lever for a moment longer, watching the creosoted ties march rapidly by in a blur, imagining her words to Paul blowing across the dry Montana plains where they would be unnoticed by the wild animals that prowled there. Could Paul ever imagine how close he was to disaster?

The train stopped at Jamestown in the middle of the night. They were sitting in their seats side by side with a blanket covering them and tucked under their chins. The negro conductor came down the aisle and paused. Paul was sleeping soundly.

"I end my shift here, ma'am. Wanted to say good-bye."

"Thank you for everything," she said.

He leaned close to her and spoke softly.

"I'm glad to see you're no longer running after Northern Pacific trains." He winked.

She nodded.

"No, I'm not."

"God bless you and your husband."

He hurried along the aisle and was gone.

"Yes," she whispered, "God bless us."

\* \* \*

They laid over in Minneapolis for half an hour and arrived in Saint Paul near noon. Paul walked over to the livery where they stabled the fine horse and buggy the congregation provided for Paul, a large black eight-year-old gelding trained to ride or pull a buggy. Back at the depot they loaded their bags, including the trunk with all the wedding gifts, and rode uphill to the manse on Summit Avenue. Paul had a multitude of things to catch up on at the church and Gabrielle unpacked and put things away, trying to ignore the fact that her stomach felt like she'd swallowed a brick. She walked to the grocery store a block away and prepared a simple meal. Paul went on and on about Montana and the ranch and all those places she tried to shut out.

When Paul got home from a council meeting he visited for a while and then kissed her lightly and went upstairs and took a bath. Gabrielle tried to keep busy downstairs. Paul filled the bedroom with candles, turned down the bed and waited patiently, sitting in the upholstered chair beside the bed reading.

Gabrielle kept busy as long as she could manage, stalling, finding it hard to breathe, not knowing which way to turn, wanting to run. What had she done, marrying Paul when she didn't love him, compounding her transgression? People say you can learn to love someone but with her heart so full of Daniel how would that be possible? Had she won God's forgiveness or had she doubled her sin. Was she double-damned for using Paul?

Gritting her teeth, she went into the spare bedroom and undressed. After lingering in the bathtub until the water turned cold she slipped into a lacy nightie her mother had given her. She looked in the floor-length mirror, held her breath, and walked softly into the master bedroom where Paul waited to consummate their marriage.

# TWENTY-ONE

THEY SAY THAT GABRIELLE was a woman on fire helping Paul with the visiting and outreach of the church, working tirelessly as if she were out to evangelize the population of Saint Paul. She did what was necessary to keep a neat house. Wishing she'd paid more attention to her mother and the kitchen growing up, her cooking improved some but she was out in the city much of the time doing what she could to be helpful. Paul seemed proud of her digging in with such enthusiasm, though he thought their love life was lacking and not meeting his needs. It seemed sometimes that all her activity and business was an excuse to avoid the marriage bed, filling her calendar until there was little time for them alone, going to bed worn out, often after Paul was asleep.

One of the causes that grabbed Gabrielle's heart was the placing-out program that many of the local churches participated in. The object of the plan was to gather the many homeless orphans that haunted the city and place them on clean family farms out in the country, mainly to the west. Even some parents, who were having a hard time supporting their many children, volunteered for this wonderful opportunity. Gabrielle was deeply involved, working with these children and preparing them for their placement in distant country homes and families. Her heart went out to them as she heard their sorrowful and incredible stories of survival.

Late one afternoon she arrived home, bustled into the house, and excitedly greeted Paul, saying she was sorry that dinner would be late. She had fallen in love with Billy Bottoms, a skinny boy who was somewhere around eight. She took Paul by his hand and led him to the secondhand sofa. She sat facing him.

159

"Paul, I've found the most wonderful boy. When he looked out of his big brown eyes, it was like looking into the soul of an angel."

"Is he homeless?"

"Yes, not only homeless, but he has no one in the world. His mother abandoned him, took up with a man who promised to take them to Duluth. Only problem was they forgot to take Billy. His last name is Bottoms. The best we can tell he's been surviving on his own for nearly a year. Imagine, a six- or seven-year-old living in the alleys and abandoned buildings and who knows only the cold and hunger with no one who wants him."

"Have they got a home to place him?" Paul asked.

"They will when they assign him. We've been cleaning him up, getting him into good clothes, getting him a haircut. You wouldn't know it was the same boy."

"You're sure excited. I'm proud of the work you're doing. I never thought—"

"Never thought what?" Gabrielle asked.

"That you'd take up this life so wholeheartedly."

"What did you expect?"

"A girl off the ranch, used to the outdoors, used to being with horses and cattle, bored silly at a Bible study, nodding off during a sermon."

"Well this ranch girl has another surprise for you. I've thought about it a lot. You're doing so well with the congregation and we have this large house and a good salary, well . . . I want to adopt Billy."

Paul pulled back on the sofa.

"Adopt?"

"Yes, adopt this small grubby urchin who is the bravest soul I've ever known."

Paul gathered himself. "Gabrielle, it's mighty generous and charitable of you to want to do this, but . . ."

"Wait till you see him, Paul, he's—"

"We need to think about this, talk about it. We just can't do it right now."

"Why, why? We have plenty of room, and—"

"A child is a big responsibility and we haven't even gotten used to living together. And besides, we can't afford a child right now, trying to make ends meet, and you're overburdened with your many groups and causes. You're just in love for the moment with this orphan boy. That's good and natural, but you can't bring them all home. Maybe in a year or so . . . and we haven't even talked about having our own children."

Gabrielle tried not to let her disappointment show up on her face. "All right, can I bring him home for dinner? Will you meet him with an open mind, with an open heart?"

"Yes, that would be good. I'd like to meet him," Paul said.

Gabrielle cooked a superb meal, as if making a delicious dinner would persuade Paul to take Billy Bottoms into their home. They sat around the dining room table and had fillets of walleye, corn on the cob, and mashed potatoes. Though still skinny, Billy looked good in his new clothes, like any normal boy in Saint Paul, though he ate like a lumberjack.

"Have you been to school, Billy?" Paul asked gently.

"No, sir, only a little, when I was little."

"Do you remember your mother?" Paul asked.

"Yes, sometimes I dream about her, She moved to Duluth."

"Do you want to be in a family?" Paul asked.

"Oh . . . yes, that would be fine. If my mother comes back. . . ."

"How did you find food on the street?" Gabrielle asked.

"Garbage cans, beg for it, steal it when I could."

"How did you steal it?" Paul asked.

"Grab it and run."

"Did you ever get caught?" Gabrielle asked.

"Yeah, lots of times."

"What happened, did they arrest you?" Paul asked.

"No . . . if they caught me they'd hit me, kick me, call for the cops. I'd usually be with two or three other boys. We'd run in different directions. I learned to run fast. One man used a belt on me, one hit me with a baseball bat, whatever they could grab."

Billy talked about it as though it happened to someone else, without attempting to enlist their sympathy or pity.

At the door Billy Bottoms said good-bye to Paul and gave him a tentative hug. While Gabrielle walked Billy to the boardinghouse where they were assembling the next batch to take the train west, she hoped Billy had touched Paul's heart.

When she got home she found out Billy hadn't. They had their first fight, first shouting match, standing across the large kitchen from each other. She reminded Paul that he always said "What would Jesus do?" That Jesus would take in the orphan boy. But Paul wouldn't give in and after several rounds of rationalizing the truth came out.

"Sometimes I think you keep so busy, filling up every minute of the day," he said, "so you don't have any time for us, together, loving time. If we had a child to care for on top of all the rest, we'd have even less time together and I'd have less affection from you."

"So it comes down to affection for you?"

"Yes! I'm a married man who is starving for affection. The marriage bed is supposed to be a thing of joy, not a lonely land of exhausted sleep! I'm talking about relations, girl, God's sweet wonderful gift to married men and women that somehow we've missed! You love those kids more than you love me."

Three days later she waved good-bye to Billy as the train pulled out of the Northern Pacific Depot, loaded with wayward children. She wanted to chase down a locomotive with the man on the Appaloosa and leap with Billy Bottoms heading west on a huge iron train, still not knowing where he was going, still not knowing who he was or where he belonged, still wondering if his mother would ever come back from Duluth.

Gabrielle continued with her personal campaign against the loneliness and homelessness of the many children wandering in the shadows of the city. She kept up with her work in the church and still managed to spend hours with the Society placing out the uncounted orphans. She impressed Paul with her energy and genuine caring for these homeless urchins but he could sense a sadness in her since Billy Bottoms rode off to the West. He didn't know if it was her attachment to the boy or her longing for her home in the mountains. Maybe both.

Then one evening she brought home a gaunt little boy for supper. They figured Dewey was about five but the Society had no information about him or his parents. He'd been found sleeping in an outhouse when someone reported him to the police. He had large dark penetrating eyes reminiscent of a barn owl and he spoke softly as if he'd been beaten for being too loud. Gabrielle had brought him home with no ulterior motives, just wanting to give the tyke a warm and happy time.

"What did you do in the winter?" Paul asked as the three of them ate around the kitchen table.

"I'd sleep by chimneys. Some horses in stables let me sleep on them. I'd sneak into carriages or buggies under the blankets. I slipped into the funeral place with dead people."

"The morgue? Good Lord," Paul said.

"Yeah, sometimes them dead people would cough or sit up."

Gabrielle, used to hearing it all, said nothing, attempted no persuasion. But she brought Dewey home several times and the quiet slender boy wore Paul's resolve away like the sun melting ice. Gabrielle worked harder at being more like the sun and Paul wondered why she wasn't pregnant. So, as though it were Paul's idea, they went through the legal steps to adopt Dewey, knowing that there was an outside chance that at least one of his parents might show up looking for him.

Gabrielle lived up to her end of their understanding. Using her mother and father as good examples, she worked at showing Paul more affection, a touch, a smile, a word. She came to bed when he did, gave him his way, and realized she was earning Dewey a new chance at life while she bargained with God, praying she and Daniel were no longer under indictment.

After several letters back and forth, Maddy arrived by train at the Northern Pacific Depot in Saint Paul where, with Dewey in tow, Gabrielle rushed to embrace her. The twin girls, now so long apart, sobbed openly. Maddy fell in love with Dewey and would hardly put him down. Gabrielle drove the buggy home, waving at people along Summit Avenue and Paul was at the house to greet Maddy. After Maddy had time to freshen up they ate a fancy meatloaf dinner in which Gabrielle was showing off.

"You made this?" Maddy asked, laughing.

"Just something I concocted."

They all laughed, including Dewey.

Relaxing around the table, Gabrielle picked Maddy's brain for every morsel of information from the ranch and especially from Butte and Daniel.

"He hasn't been back to the ranch since the wedding. He writes a little, not much really. I know it's hard on Father. He believes that Daniel will come home some day."

"How's Wart?" Paul asked.

"Oh, still a rascal. Never know what he'll do next. Told us another elephant story the other night that I'd never heard."

"He still chasing chickens?" Gabrielle asked and then turned to Dewey in his highchair. "My brother, Wart, chases chickens. Maybe when we go to the ranch you can help him catch one."

"Why does he chase them?" Dewey asked.

"No one knows," Maddy said.

"Tell us about your job," Gabrielle said, "that's so exciting."

"Well, I'm teaching higher English grammar and writing at the college in Red Pine. I'm living right on campus and there are fourteen teachers. It's kinda strange living out on the plains like that, I didn't realize how much I'd miss the mountains."

"You were always antsy to get out of them, to get to town," Gabrielle said.

"And you were always antsy to get out of dresses," Maddy said, "are you still tying them up?"

"I don't have to now that riding britches have become acceptable among society women. Paul still prefers me to wear a dress when I'm out around town."

Paul smiled and shook his head gently.

"The mountain girl in the city."

The six days went swiftly and Paul knew the twin sisters needed time together. Some of the time Paul took Dewey with him to his office at the church and other times the girls took Dewey when Paul's duty dictated it. Paul brought him on calls to parishioners and the people were growing openly fond of the happy little boy. One morning when Paul and Maddy were waiting for Gabrielle and Dewey out by the buggy, Paul told her how much he'd grown to love the boy and how glad and thankful he was that Gabrielle had talked him into adopting, that he couldn't love him any more if he was their own flesh and blood.

One sunny afternoon the sisters took Dewey down to the river to ride on the paddlewheel steamboat. From the time they walked the plank to get on, Dewey was bug-eyed astonished. They toured the boat as it headed down stream and then settled on a bench in the upper deck. Dewey gaped, overcome with this marvelous machine that plowed atop the water and with the noise and steam and shrieking whistle he didn't let go of Aunt Maddy's hand.

"Mother says you have a beau," Gabrielle said.

"Two beaus and counting." She laughed. "One for the city, a gentleman, one for the country, a cowboy, flip a coin."

"Are you serious?" Gabrielle asked.

"Mother wants me to choose Alan, a businessman who teaches economics at the school and who is studying to become a lawyer. He's sweet and smart and is three years older than us."

"And who is the other one?"

"Chip, the cowboy, works with his parents and brothers on the family ranch and is studying to be a veterinarian. He's rugged and kind and thinks I walk on water. When he smiles I feel all warm inside. He's our age."

"Do you love him?" Gabrielle asked as Dewey pointed out a gull swooping overhead.

"I don't know . . . sometimes . . . one then the other. With Mother and Father it sounded so easy; they met, fell in love and married. With you and Paul it sounded so easy. You met, fell in love, and married. When I think of marrying Alan or Chip I get goosebumps and I'm all confused."

"Maybe there's a third one out there, ever think of that? Maybe that's why you're confused."

"When did you know with Paul? Did you know right after you were married?"

"No . . . I still don't know."

"What? What do you mean? You're man and wife, you . . . well you know . . . you have relations, you must love him to do that."

"Mother told me once that she had to learn to love Father. Maybe that's what I'll have to do, maybe that's what you'll have to do."

"Is it fun?"

"Is what fun?"

"You know . . . in bed?"

"You're getting awfully nosy."

"Well, is it?"

"It depends who you're with. If you're with the one you truly love it's the most wonderful thing in the world."

In her mind Gabrielle flew back to the swimming hole and her memories of Daniel there in the wildflowers and grass.

"You were lucky, you didn't have to choose between two so that no matter who you did choose you'd break the other's heart."

"Yes . . . I was lucky."

Gabrielle agonized, if only she could tell her dear sister, tell her what it's like to break the heart of the one you truly love, what it's like to choose the one you don't love, but she knew she couldn't.

"I wish I could help you, Madd. You'll have to listen to your heart, try to find the one you truly love and maybe you'll get lucky also."

"They are both pressing hard to have relations," Maddy said as she glanced furtively into Gabrielle's eyes. "Each of them insinuates that that will show we love each other. I've listened to Mother so far, that the girl has to be the strong one to guard the gates to paradise. Isn't that quaint?" They both laughed.

"Guard them well," Gabrielle said.

The steamboat slid up alongside the wharf and whistled shrilly. Everyone was up and gathering their belongings and Gabrielle had been saved from lying to her sweet undamaged twin sister.

The six days were filled with a buggy ride to Mahtomedi, merry-go-rounds and picnics and steamboats, games on the lawn, filled with many happy memories until it was time for Maddy to board the Northern Pacific train going west. Paul and Dewey walked to the far end of the huge depot while the twins found a bench with time to spare before the train was called.

Maddy took hold of Gabrielle's hand and looked into her eyes.

"I have to tell you, Gabby, I don't feel as close as we've always been. There's something coming between us, something I can't put my finger on. Is that because we've grown up? Is that because you're married?"

"I don't know, Maddy, maybe it's because we've been apart so long."

"No, it's more than that. Its like you've shut a door between us that I can't open from my side. Only you can open it, only you have the key."

Maddy could see Paul and Dewey coming across the cavelike depot and she hurried.

"I miss my twin sister and I can't reach her. She ran off when we were going to school together and I never knew why. I laid awake nights trying to understand. You were always the only one I could talk with, honestly, never Daniel or Zack, not even Wart, and now I have no one."

"I know what you're feeling, Madd, and if there is something between us it's my fault. Please be patient. I promise you that one day I'll open that door, I promise you I'll give you the key."

The three of them gave Aunt Maddy hugs and kisses and wished her well as she climbed up into the train. They waited until the Northern Pacific pulled out of the station.

"Where is Auntie Maddy going?" Dewey asked.

"She's going out west toward the mountains, Dewey," Gabrielle said. "Someday we'll take you there."

Paul hoisted Dewey onto his shoulders and Gabrielle quickly wiped the tears from her face.

## TWENTY-TWO

IN THE HOT OPPRESSIVE HUMIDITY, Gabrielle longed for the cool exhilarating mountain air at home. She visited over the front yard fence with Myrna Agnew while Dewey, the smallest of the bunch, played in a sandbox with neighbor kids. It wasn't really visiting; Gabrielle couldn't get a word in edgewise as Myrna was known to carry on without taking a breath. They stood in the shadow of a large maple tree that gave them some mercy from the dripping heat. Gabrielle noticed Walt, the ice man, plodding along with his rawboned white horse and covered wooden wagon, working his way up Summit Avenue, bringing a block of very welcome ice for their iceboxes.

Walt was a short, solid man as friendly as a puppy. When he arrived at Myrna's he lifted a heavy iron weight from the wagon and set it on the street in front of the horse. With the horse's halter rope tied to the weight, Walt walked around to the back of the wagon. He had often informed his customers that the paltry weight wouldn't stop the big old horse if he wanted to run off, but it gave him the impression that he was tied and if he did try walking off he'd stumble over the dragging chunk of iron.

Neighbor kids, who were playing in the yards and along the boulevard, spotted the ice wagon and came running and cheering, hoping for a chunk of ice, much better than candy in the muggy atmosphere. Happily Walt used his large ice pick to chip off treats for the kids who circled the back of the wagon.

Myrna called. "Twenty pounds, Walt, please."

And then before Gabrielle could say a word, Myrna was jabbering again as the children ran off with their summer prize. Dewey, who had been playing with the smaller kids, tried to get

Gabrielle's attention. The women carried on as Walt went by with a twenty-pound block of ice that he held against the rubber cape on his back with a pair of large tongs.

"This weather is hard on the ice," he said.

"We'll take twenty pounds, too, Walt," Gabrielle said.

"Yes, ma'am."

Dewey pulled on Gabrielle's dress, pointing at the wagon.

"Can I get some ice, Mama?"

"Yes, yes, go on," Gabrielle said as Myrna got back into church gossip and hearsay.

Dewey ran to the wagon. The other kids had cleaned up all pieces of ice on the tailgate so Dewey scrambled up into the wagon and searched for shards the others had missed. The ice was stacked three rows wide, three blocks high, most of them weighing about forty pounds. There was an empty spot in the middle row where Walt had removed several blocks. Shoulder high to him there, Dewey looked for slivers between the hard, smooth blocks. He wiped away some of the sawdust and licked the refreshing ice.

The horse, that usually didn't move an inch, stomped forward a few feet to avoid the pestering flies. The wagon lurched slightly, the upper block began to slide. Dewey saw it and tried to hold it back. It was much too heavy for the five-year-old and it fell heavily into the notch between the blocks to the right and left. Dewey was knocked backward and fell under the ice. Following the law of gravity that gave no quarter to little boys, the block pinned him to the floor. With the ice on his chest he couldn't take a breath. He couldn't call out. The world stopped on top of him.

Walt came out of Myrna's house and stopped to visit with the women. It was only minutes. One of the younger neighbor kids, returned to the wagon hoping for another shard of ice. He climbed on the tailgate and immediately started shouting.

"Dewey's under the ice! Dewey's under the ice!"

Walt and Gabrielle sprinted, reaching the tailgate at the same instant, both quickly up into the wagon. They found Dewey under the clear cold ice like a mummy, his arms pinned to his sides, looking up at the ice that was crushing him. Gabrielle tried to get a grip on the ice but her hands kept slipping. Walt, with a loud animal-like howl, got his hands behind the block and with a mighty thrust, shoved it off the boy and out the back of the wagon where it shattered on the pavement.

Gabrielle had her boy in her arms. He wasn't breathing. Walt helped her lay him on the lawn and she quickly began blowing into his mouth.

"Come on, honey, come on! Breathe! Breathe!"

Walt took a hold of the boy's legs and bent them to his chest, compressing them hard with the weight of his compact body, shouting and growling and praying. Myrna ran for help. Then, after long, frantic minutes, Gabrielle gathered Dewey in her arms. She'd been mostly silent during their attempts to revive him, but now she screamed above the city din as people in the neighborhood gathered.

"No! You can't do this to him, he's just a little boy! Take me! Take me! You can't do this! What kind of a God are you? You take out your vengeance on a helpless child. Damn you, God, damn you!"

Dewey was dead.

The neighbor children stole away without a sound. People who had gathered drifted back into the neighborhood as if the world was kind.

"It's my fault," Walt kept repeating, as he kneeled in the grass and rocked back and forth. "I didn't hook the chain. The chain keeps the ice from sliding. I didn't hook it. It's my fault. I killed the boy. I didn't hook the chain."

Myrna helped Gabrielle pick up Dewey and stand. She paused by Walt who was beside himself with grief.

"It's my fault!" Walt shouted.

"No, it's not your fault," Gabrielle said to him in a quiet broken voice, "you had nothing to do with what happened, nothing to do with it."

Inside the house she held him in her lap while she sat on the sofa and wept, allowing her heart to pour out its unbearable sorrow. Myrna stood by helplessly, trying to think of something to do. She had sent word to Pastor Douglas at the church.

How ironic, Gabrielle thought. While the stifling heat oppressed the city, her boy was killed by ice. Was that God's practical joke, her angelic boy crushed by a block of ice cut out of a frozen winter lake? Grandfather Abraham was killed by ice. How cunning God could be, how devious. That block of ice stored in an icehouse in the dead of winter and covered in sawdust to wait like a bullet in a gun. She knew God could do anything. She and Daniel were damned. And those around her were damned as well. It took Paul and three neighbor men to pry Dewey out of her arms.

They say over a hundred mourners showed up for the funeral and burial, some people Paul and Gabrielle had never seen. Word had spread quickly around Saint Paul about the boy who was killed by the ice. Dozens milled through the overheated manse like lost sheep and enough food to feed half the city overburdened tables and laps. Mourners spoke in hushed tones and no one smiled. Friends tried to get Gabrielle to eat something.

"You have to keep up your strength."

*No she didn't. Her cherished boy was dead. She didn't need her strength, she didn't need to eat, she didn't need to breathe or her heart to beat.*

When the last of the faithful left them there were no words yet discovered to express the devastation and a great silent absence hung over the house, an inescapable horrific void. It was hard to breathe. Paul didn't preach for several weeks. Gabrielle showed up at some of her meetings and commitments but she found no enthusiasm for any of it. It all seemed so petty and trivial. She moved like a stick woman, a mannequin as she and Paul ghosted around the hollow house. They tried to talk with a delicate kindness but it always dissolved into pain. Word came from the ranch, Aunt Grace sent Gabrielle four hundred dollars as if she could read Gabrielle's mind. Words of sympathy came in the mail from Maddy and Zack, and long letters from Elizabeth and Jeremiah. And a short note from Wart that was so bittersweet it broke her heart.

Gabrielle and Paul crossed paths one morning in the kitchen, looking for something to eat. She sat at the table with a half-eaten bowl of oatmeal and strawberries when Paul came in.

"Can I get you some oatmeal?" Gabrielle asked, throwing a glance in his direction.

"No, no . . . I'll just have some coffee."

"There's no more ice in the icebox," she dared to say. "Things are spoiling."

It was as if they both realized their marriage was spoiling.

"You heard that Walt quit, said he'd never deliver again," Paul said.

"Yes . . . I heard."

"You know God has forgiven you, Gabrielle, it was an accident," Paul said softly. "God forgives whatever you're condemning yourself for, it could just as well have been me."

"But it wasn't you, it was me, I'm the one who's cursed, who's condemned."

"Don't talk that way, you're not cursed. Where'd you ever learn something like that?"

"When I was a young girl, from the Bible," she said with a sigh.

"Well that's plain nonsense."

"It's all nonsense."

"Have you lost your faith, Gabrielle?"

"Oh, nooooh, my faith is stronger than ever," she said with a wicked smile. "I believe in God like never before. I've seen His handiwork."

Paul lifted the coffee pot off the stove, poured a cup and set it on the table.

"You can't go on like this. I know how it hurts, oh God, I know, but we must go on, life goes on."

"Does it?"

"You know *I* forgive you don't you, you know that?"

"Then why can you no longer sleep in the same bed with me?" she whispered.

Paul didn't speak. Dewey's highchair stood mutely in its place by the table. Gabrielle made eye contact with Paul.

"How do you explain this to your congregation? *What* on earth do you tell them?"

"I tell them what I've always told them. God is a loving, forgiving Father. His grace is so wide and everlasting he can forgive us anything, he can *do* anything."

*"Anything? Anything?"* she pounded the table with a fist and

sent the oatmeal bowl crashing to the floor. "Oh, God, how I wish I could believe that. We should have renamed Dewey, we should have called him Lazarus," she said with bitterness. "Have Jesus lift the crushing ice off our little boy, have Him shout 'Lazarus, come out!'" she shouted. "'Dewey, come out! come out darling little boy!' and have Dewey climb out of that grave!"

She glared at Paul's helpless face as she walked from the kitchen.

Gabrielle carried on. She also carried a great stone in her belly. It wasn't a child she carried but the truth she'd kept from Paul. She tried to live normally, to get involved again in her many interests and causes but she was a skeleton walking. Her memories of Daniel's love sustained her. Drowning in the pounding waves of guilt, she promised each day that she would tell Paul the truth, all of it. And each night she'd berate herself for failing.

One evening they agreed to ride out to the cemetery and as they sat in the grass beside the grave, with the sun fading in the west, she took a deep breath and ripped the scab off the long festering wound. She looked into Paul's eyes.

"Paul, I have to go away."

Paul didn't speak for a moment. "I think you're right, I've thought you might go back to the ranch for a while, get your balance, heal, be with your family. I know I haven't helped you much."

"You don't understand. I have to go away for good, from here, from you. Go away and not come back."

"What on earth are you talking about? You'll feel better with a little more time. What do you mean 'not come back'? It's only normal that—"

"I love my brother."

"Of course you do. You need to be with your family, your brothers and sister. Your mother and father."

Gabrielle's words came one by one like great stones she had to roll uphill.

"I'm in love with my brother, with Daniel."

"What do you mean?"

"We're in love with each other, not a brother and sister, a man and a woman. We grew up together and then one day we realized we were in love."

"That can't be, it just can't be," Paul half whispered. Shock spread across his face like a shadow.

"Paul, I've been dishonest with you from the start and I can't do it any more. The day I met you I was in love with my brother."

She gulped for air, finding it almost impossible to speak the words.

"That doesn't matter, you can change that, you can agree to end this strange relationship, just get over it. Ask for God's forgiveness. . . ." Paul trailed off suddenly, hit with memories of Gabrielle's questions about God's forgiving love.

"We were lovers," Gabrielle lied.

"Wha . . . , what?"

"We were lovers."

"I can't believe what I'm hearing, this can't be true, you couldn't, it can't be true."

In the spur of the moment Gabrielle didn't know why she lied. Something in her wanted to cut it clean. Set Paul free.

Paul's face twisted with confusion and anger. He jumped to his feet and held his hands over his ears and walked in tight circles.

"Stop it! Stop it! I don't want to hear anymore, I don't want to know anymore, I can't bear anymore!"

Paul squatted on the lawn, looking over the small grave into Gabrielle's eyes, one hand over his mouth.

"I love Daniel as a man. I will always love him. I think of him the moment I awake in the morning and wonder how he is and he's the last one on my heart when I go to sleep. I love him and he loves me and we're trying to make it right with God for what we've done."

"This can't be true, it can't be. You've dragged me into your sin, you've contaminated everything between us."

"I know, I never should have married you, I know that was wrong, I didn't love you that way. I thought I could learn to love you, I was dishonest and I thought being your wife would make up for the terrible thing we had done, would reconcile Daniel and I with God."

"I love you!" Paul shouted. "I thought I knew you, you couldn't have done this, this sin, I can't believe it."

She told him all of it, how shocked and surprised they were

when they realized they were in love. How they had agonized about what to do. How they took different paths to somehow make it right. How she was damned and that's why God killed Dewey under the ice. How she was afraid Paul would be caught in this curse unknowingly and hurt again.

Paul sat in shock, unable to move or respond as he tried to comprehend what his young wife was telling him.

"I prayed every day, every night," she told him. "You know what I prayed? I prayed that God would somehow make it right. I'd tell Him I knew He could do it, that He could do anything, He could change the story, make it that Daniel was adopted. I'd hear the story of how our mother had a hard delivery with Daniel, he was so large. I'd hear old Doc Simpson telling about it. I'd pray God'd make me adopted, I was so different from Maddy, but we were twins, born a few minutes apart. How could God change that? As impossible as it was I believed God could somehow make it right so Daniel and I could be together like normal people."

Then Gabrielle was talked out, emotionally exhausted. She would take the things she needed to travel and leave town. She'd found a position with the Society that placed children out. In two days she'd leave on a train full of kids. He could tell the congregation whatever he wished: accuse her of adultery to get a divorce, tell them she went back to her family in Montana, tell them she went insane.

"I'm so sorry, Paul, so sorry. You're such a good man. I'll never deserve your forgiveness, I'd never ask for your forgiveness. I thought we might make it work with Dewey. I almost forgot I was damned and maybe the people around me are damned as well."

Paul wept beside the little grave, thoroughly confused and shocked, a man whose world just caved in on him. Gabrielle went to him and held him in her arms.

"I'm so sorry, Paul, so sorry. I'll be ashamed the rest of my life for hurting you so terribly. I didn't know that when you're damned the people around you get hurt."

In the buggy they wove their way back to the cold empty house on Summit Avenue where Paul thought his happy life would never end. Gabrielle slept on the old sofa in the living room and she could hear Paul pacing most of the night above her.

Gabrielle got selected by the Society to be one of the adults who escorted the children to their designated families in the West and then monitored the placements to see if the kids were happy in their new homes. On a train crammed with young children, she was on the way to South Dakota. When the train pulled out of the station, she saw Paul, standing there waving, tears washing down his face.

# TWENTY-THREE

BECAUSE OF HER PAST EXPERIENCE with the Society, Gabrielle was welcomed back and hired. How perplexing her life had become, how all at once it became enmeshed in shattered hopes and broken relationships and unforgiving death, how her life had been split apart and she'd lost Dewey and damaged Paul and had no success in banishing Daniel from her thoughts.

She journeyed to Halo, Wyoming, a small growing town on the high northern plains, guarded by majestic mountains to the north and west. Miles distant, the snow-covered peaks promised faithfully their clear cool waters to nourish the arid sun-parched brown, transforming it into bright lush green. The many snow-fed streams that started small quickly merged on their rush down the mountains' flanks until they became one, the Broken Knife River. The river cascaded out of the mountains miles northwest of town and gently flowed across the level prairie, a hundred feet wide and shoulder deep. The beginnings of Halo grew on the east side of the river along an oxbow curve where the current was moderate and predictable. In fact the only time the Broken Knife kicked up its heels was a week or two in early summer. The first pioneers to see the potential of irrigating the dry ground with the abundant water unfolded their tents and staked out their claims, believing they had found their western dream. One hundred and sixty acres homesteaded and when proved up an additional one-sixty, making a half-section to farm. They had few incidents and little contact with the Indians because the white face stayed out of the mountains, killed very few buffalo, and lived on trout and deer and elk. Gabrielle was impressed with this land; it reminded her of home. She thought Daniel would like it and she calculated how many miles lay between them.

Crossing the Broken Knife had been a problem ever since early settlers camped along its banks. Travelers following the Bozeman Trail had to go nearly twelve miles south to ford the Broken Knife or weave their way around many of the forks and marshlands to the north. The biggest sign of settlement and local pride was the community effort to build a bridge. They built it as an extension of Main Street and it put Halo on the map, a solid crossing of the Broken Knife. It not only saved people miles on the trail but it would also coax them to purchase supplies or consider settling in Halo as their western journey's long-sought destination.

Shortly after the bridge was built, folks began building and settling on the west side of the river as well. When Gabrielle arrived on the Union Pacific spur that ended at Halo, a mishmash that covered a dozen square blocks along Main Street with houses tapering off east and west into open country. Besides business enterprises and a school and church, Halo boasted a newspaper. A weekly. The Society's representative, Luella Larson, drove Gabrielle from the little brick depot to *The Halo Star* in a buggy. The newspaper office and print shop occupied the first floor of a two-story flat-roofed building. The Society provided the second story apartment for their local supervisor.

Luella, a thin well-dressed woman in her late forties, tied the horse and helped Gabrielle with her luggage. The stairs to the second floor was on the side of the gray clapboard building. With the trunk in tow, Gabrielle started up the stairs when a tall man wearing a black apron and an inky cap, burst through the front door.

"Ho, no, no! Let me do that," he shouted, stopping Gabrielle in her tracks.

"Oh, my, thank you," Gabrielle said.

"This is Mrs. Paul Douglas," Luella said to him, confusing Gabrielle for a moment.

"Gabrielle," Gabrielle corrected her.

"Hello, nice to meet you, I'm Ned," he said and he whipped the heavy trunk up the stairs as if it were weightless. He skipped down the stairs and started to take Gabrielle's bag and purse.

"Oh, thank you, I can take these," Gabrielle said.

"Welcome to Halo," he said, "you're news, just in time to make this week's edition. And if I'm ever making too much noise you just pound on the floor. I forget sometimes that there's someone living up there who might like to be sleeping at three in the morning, right Luella?"

"Right," Luella said with a touch of of experience in her voice.

"I work late a lot," he said.

"I sleep pretty sound," Gabrielle said, "thanks for the help with my luggage."

Luella led Gabrielle up the stairs and Ned ducked into the building.

At the top Luella opened the door and Gabrielle dragged her trunk into the apartment.

"He's a good man," Luella said, "but sometimes tiring. He gives our work a lot of coverage, thinks we're wonderful, loves the children we bring."

Luella insisted on sleeping on the cot, giving Gabrielle the featherbed, and they spent the evening discussing the work at Halo. Ned provided them with trout for their supper, then they walked through the town acquainting Gabrielle with places she'd have to know: the doctor's home and office, sheriff's office, minister's house next to the small white steepled church. She looked up the street and hurried past the church as if she could erase memory. A three-room school, dentist and barber, blacksmith, livery stable, dry goods and hardware, bakery, laundry and, sprinkled along the way, several saloons in the mix.

"I'd prefer to use a horse," Gabrielle said as she looked over some of the horses in the livery stable.

"Can't, not practical," Luella said, "you take children with you at times, you need the buggy, never know when you'll have to recover a child. There will be a horse at your disposal for the times you know you won't have to bring a child."

They passed folks along the street and many of them seemed to know Luella: men tipped their hats, women nodded, children chased and the horse and buggy traffic waxed and waned.

"Do we try to let people know we're coming?" Gabrielle asked.

"Sometimes, when you can, but you need the buggy to carry

things, like sometimes they'll give you a chicken or a duck or a bottle of milk. And don't forget to have your fishing pole along. You can bring supper home with you. You *do* know how to fish, don't you?"

"Yes, I know how," Gabrielle said. They walked in silence and watched a softly retreating sunset fade away behind the distant mountains.

Luella caught a stage going south the next afternoon and Gabrielle waved as the six horses found their pace. She turned toward town and gathered herself, an aching aloneness swooping down on her. She had seen one familiar name on the list and she planned on heading out to that ranch first thing in the morning. She hadn't mentioned it to Luella because Luella had circled six kids' names she thought needed contact first. Gabrielle spent the afternoon and evening settling in, but she couldn't forget that in the morning she'd ride out to find Billy Bottoms.

After breakfast at the bakery Gabrielle hitched the horse, Kemo, to the buggy, packed in her water and food and rain gear, and left town as the sun colored the eastern clouds. The Appleton farm lay to the southeast about eight miles according to the hand-sketched map Luella had given her. Gabrielle saw antelope, deer, elk, black bear, and several wolves. The incredible beauty of the country tempered her sorrow. What was Daniel doing with this day?

She crossed several streams and skirted marshland where beavers had damned waterways and turned them into ponds that over the years would become lush meadows. She waved when she passed other ranches and folks waved back as if they knew her. She could tell the age of these homesites by the number of buildings and how much ground was plowed and irrigated. Some had been there for a decade or more, others still living in tents. Dogs would run out toward her as if she were a threat.

After nearly three hours the Appleton farm appeared on a little rise, graying in the sun. House, horse shed, barn, and other outbuildings, mainly built with logs, some with rough-cut lumber. Several corrals, a garden with irrigation ditches, and cropland greening. A windmill stood above it all except for a grove of towering cottonwood that shaded the house and yard. She approached with a bittersweet ache in her chest. Would seeing Billy bring it all back, if they had adopted him would Billy have been there to protect Dewey? If they'd adopted Billy would Dewey even be there in the ice wagon? A cold sweat broke out on her forehead and her heart raced.

Gabrielle turned in the dirt road and stopped the horse in the yard. A large shaggy mutt came running, barking, followed by a small girl with curly sun-bleached hair. Gabrielle tied the horse and turned to greet the welcoming party. The dog came on and, recognizing someone he couldn't bluff, made friends quickly, but the girl stopped short and stared at the ground shyly. She wore a homemade flour-sack dress and went barefoot.

"Hello," Gabrielle said.

The child stood in one spot and twisted back and forth as if she were about to bolt. The dog continued to bark.

"That's Buster," the girl said, tugging at the dog that outweighed her.

"Is Billy here?" Gabrielle asked.

The girl pointed toward the barn and rolled her tongue.

Gabrielle headed for the outbuildings when a woman emerged from the front door of the low-slung log house. Short and stout, she wore a long gray work dress with stains and spills, large boots and a bright blue sun bonnet. Her smile punctuated her weathered face.

"Hello!" Gabrielle called. "I'm Mrs. Douglas from the orphan train."

"Oh, hello, hello, is everything all right?"

She hustled across the dusty yard. The women met and shook hands.

"Is everything all right?" the woman repeated.

"Oh, yes, fine, I'm just here on a routine visit to see how Billy's doing. Is he doing well?"

A sign of relief crossed the woman's face.

"He got throwed from the horse . . . but he's fine."

Mrs. Appleton led Gabrielle toward the barn, the dog and little girl following. Chickens scooted in front of them and they passed a corral where a large draught horse stood whipping flies with his tail.

"Charles. Oh Charles!" the woman called, "Yoo hoo!"

A tall man came out of the larger shed in bib overalls and a broken-down straw hat that made Gabrielle think of a scarecrow. He had a head full of shaggy black hair and he hadn't shaved recently. Gabrielle looked into his narrow face.

"Hello, I'm Mrs. Douglas from the orphan society. I've come to see how Billy is doing."

"Doin' just fine," the man said.

He wiped his forehead with a red bandanna and stood there as if that was the end of it.

"Where is Billy? I'd like to see him."

"Oh, he's irrigatin'," Mr. Appleton said and nodded to the west.

"Point the way and I'll hike out and find him."

"No need, he'll be in promptly, it's dinnertime," Mr. Appleton said. "You go in the house with the missus. Billy and I'll be along shortly. I'll grain your horse if you'd like."

"Thank you," Gabrielle said and she followed Mrs. Appleton to the house.


After the women had visited in the kitchen for half an hour while Mrs. Appleton laid out dinner, Mr. Appleton and Billy ambled into the kitchen and Gabrielle sprang out of her chair.

"Billy! Billy Bottoms!" she shouted, "I never thought I'd see you again. Do you remember me?"

"Yeah, sure I do, Mrs. Douglas, how are you?"

"I'm fine, I'm working for the Society now, I'm living in Halo."

"Is Mr. Douglas with you?" Billy asked.

Gabrielle's throat constricted and for a moment she couldn't speak. She feared this would happen if she saw Billy, that he would bring that slice of her life back on her plate.

"No," Gabrielle said, "he's not . . . ah, he's still serving his church in Saint Paul."

"Will he be coming out to Halo?" Billy asked.

"I don't know, Billy."

With Billy's question hanging in the summer air, Mrs. Appleton had them all sit at the table and Mr. Appleton said grace.

Gabrielle glanced at Billy and noticed an ugly colorful bruise on the side of his head and used it for a change of subject.

"What did you do to your head?" Gabrielle asked, examining the wound more carefully.

"I got thrown off the horse, right into a corral post," Billy answered quickly, with a little embarrassment in his voice.

"He sure took a dive," Mr. Appleton said and laughed.

"Part of growing up on the ranch," Gabrielle said, thankful for the reprieve. "I must have been thrown fifty times if once."

"Were you raised on a ranch, Mrs. Douglas?" Mrs. Appleton asked.

"Yes . . . up in Montana . . . hope to go back some day."

No matter how she tried to forget, the memories of Daniel and their life together kept intruding on her present moments.

"Amanda, would you get us some cool milk?" Mrs. Appleton asked.

The shy girl hopped down from her chair and hurried out the kitchen door.

"You've sure grown, Billy," Gabrielle said.

"He works like a man and eats like a man," Mr. Appleton said.

"I'm sorry I didn't have something fancy for you," Mrs. Appleton said, disparaging the fresh bread and potatoes and beans she'd served.

"Do you go fishing or hunting?" Gabrielle asked Billy, "or swimming?"

"Oh, sometimes," Billy said.

Gabrielle felt a tenseness at the table that she couldn't name but guessed it was probably this family feeling under examination.

Amanda burst into the kitchen.

"Skunk's in the chickens! Skunk's in the chickens!"

The Appleton family nearly knocked each other over stumbling out the door. Mr. Appleton grabbed the rifle he had hanging over the door. Gabrielle joined the riot. They shouted and pounded the walls of the long narrow chicken shed where chickens were attempting suicide with fright, exploding in every direction and squawking bloody murder. Buster, the Appleton's dog, was trying to corner the skunk and Billy had all he could do to hold him away from the battle field. The skunk streaked between Mr. Appleton's legs and scooted under the small granary.

"Don't get sprayed! Don't get sprayed!" Mr. Appleton shouted.

He grabbed a pitchfork and handed Gabrielle the rifle. Crouching, he shoved the pitchfork under the granary floor and rattled it around the best he could. Then, in a flash, the skunk broke for open country away from the barnyard. Without a thought Gabrielle cocked the rifle, swung it to her shoulder, aimed for a moment and squeezed off a shot. The skunk, with tail flagging high, exploded in a fluff of black and white fur and dropped in a heap far out in the short stubble field. The Appletons stood wide-eyed with a touch of awe at the long shot she made at a fleeing varmint.

"Holy moly, did you see that?" Billy was still struggling to hold Buster at bay.

"Mother Mary," Mrs. Appleton said as though she'd just seen a miracle.

Gabrielle looked the rifle over and then handed it back to Mr. Appleton.

"It shoots true," Gabrielle said.

"I'd guess you've done that before," Mr. Appleton said.

"Yes, a lucky shot," Gabrielle said.

"That was no lucky shot," the rancher said. "Go bury it deep, Billy, so Buster won't get into it and stink up the place."

They came back to a cold lunch, everyone jabbering about the high adventure that burst into their normal dinner hour thanks to a bold skunk.

"Sure like to thank you, Mrs. Douglas," Mr. Appleton said. "That was some shot, some shot. We've been after that thief for months."

"Got a chicken or two and a bucket full of eggs," Mrs. Appleton said.

Gabrielle spent more than another hour with them but she hadn't been able to get Billy alone. One or the other of the parents stuck to them like burdock as Billy showed her around the ranch. One of the sheds was a workshop where Mr. Appleton did his woodworking.

"Billy will be a good carpenter one of these days," Mr. Appleton said as he pointed out the many tools. "He catches on quick."

Mr. Appleton remained in the tool shed and the other four moved into the barn. In the center they had a thick rope attached to the ceiling hanging free to the dirt floor. Billy explained how they'd fill a wide net with hay and hoist it up to the loft. After the winter of '88 they stored as much hay as they could cram into the building for the stock.

Billy took hold of the rope and hand over hand, without using his legs or feet, climbed to the level of the loft. He paused there, showing off, and then continued climbing to the ceiling. Gabrielle clapped and whistled.

"He gives me a fright when he does that," Mrs. Appleton said. Billy hung there for a moment, some twenty-five feet above the floor, like a bat, and then came humming down the rope to the barn floor. He gave Amanda a wave and she climbed on his back. With her arms around his neck, up they went, hand over hand, until he delivered his chubby little sister to the loft. Billy demonstrated several other ways they swung and played on the rope, their own indoor playground, and Gabrielle wanted to try. She took hold of the rope and jumped off the floor, hanging with both hands. She managed to switch hand over hand four, five . . . times and dropped to the floor, laughing.

"You are really strong, Billy," Gabrielle said, "really strong."

"Am I really strong?" Amanda piped in.

"Yes, you are really strong, too, Amanda."

"Billy has to finish work and chores before he can play in the barn," Mrs. Appleton said.

"After working all day and chores how does he have the strength to climb the rope?" Gabrielle asked.

"I don't know," Mrs. Appleton said, genuinely perplexed.

As they toured the ranch, Gabrielle brought up the future possibility of adoption and Mrs. Appleton showed a genuine enthusiasm for that prospect though Gabrielle couldn't read Billy's thoughts on the matter. For a moment Mrs. Appleton went off to the outhouse and Billy finally asked the question that had been hanging in the air most of the visit.

"Did my mother ever come back from Duluth looking for me?" he asked.

"No, Billy, not that we know of, we haven't heard from her again," Gabrielle said.

"Why isn't Reverend Douglas with you?" Billy asked.

"Reverend Douglas and I are no longer together. It didn't work out."

"Are you living all alone now?" Billy asked.

"Yes, I'm alone, but I have all you wonderful children to see each day and get to know."

Billy turned silent, caught up in thought.

"Maybe someday I can live with you," Billy said.

When she left they all waved as she turned the buggy west, carrying the jar of raspberry jam and a half dozen eggs they'd given her. She pondered this first visit and concluded that she'd done well, though she believed she ought to visit with the child in private so the child could speak frankly. Billy's final words haunted her.

*Maybe someday I can live with you.*

She cut north for several miles and found the Peabody's spread, wanting to make as many visits as she could in a day. The Peabodys had taken a skinny eight-year-old girl, Matilda, who had a bright-eyed disposition. Both of the Peabodys were fat, very fat, and the thought passed through Gabrielle's head with a chuckle that this little hummingbird of a child would flap her wings off running errands for the two much-slower adults. But after spending an hour with them, and talking with Matilda alone, Gabrielle had a good feeling about them. She believed the Peabodys were a loving happy couple who laughed a lot, and Matilda was happy with them. They had lost two children in their journey west and they wanted to adopt Matilda as soon as possible. She already called them mother and father.

The setting sun painted a melancholy sky and she knew she had to fight off the haunting loneliness. Dewey's death hammered at the door of her heart and she pushed herself to go through the motions of living one step at a time. She'd catch herself talking with people and realizing she didn't know what she was talking about and asking pardon to faces that looked at her blankly.

She arrived in town as the sinking sun fired the sky with a brilliant afterglow. She cared for her horse at the livery stable and then ate at Aunt Sally's Cafe, two blocks from her apartment. As she filled out her first official daily report, she decided to leave out any references to the skunk and the "lucky shot."

The only thorn in the day was her memory of the time Daniel caught a baby skunk for her when she was six or seven and she raised it until one day it let her have it and no one would go near her and she couldn't go to school and she had to sleep in the barn for a week or more. Both Daniel and she had cried when they took the skunk far out into the forest and turned it loose.

All in all she felt satisfied that she could do this work, could carve out a good life for herself doing what she loved until she and Daniel could live together.

"I was hoping you weren't lost," Ned said as he approached her table.

"Oh, no . . . just trying to cover a lot of ground."

Ned stood there, tall, ink smudges on his face and forearms, his black apron hanging from his neck to his knees.

"I'll be setting late tonight," he said. "Just throw your pot at me if I keep you awake."

"What's news tonight?" Gabrielle asked.

"Almost had a drowning in the Broken Knife, one of the McCarthy boys. They said their dog saved the boy. Anything happening out your way today?"

Gabrielle thought about the "lucky shot" and the constant struggle against predators. She thought about a strong boy who could climb a rope like a veteran sailor and who hoped his mother would come back from Duluth looking for him. Gabrielle thought about the families carving a living out of this magnificent and demanding land. She thought about Matilda, given up by her heartbroken mother because she couldn't care for any more children. She thought about these orphans, so young, left in the lost-and-found of the world, hoping and praying to find a new family and a new life somewhere near Halo, Wyoming. And she thought about Mrs. Paul Douglas, trying to find a life here with a ragged hole in her heart.

"No . . . no news out my way today."

# TWENTY-FOUR

THEY SAY TWO OR THREE SATURDAYS slid by before Albert Kincaid succeeded in persuading Daniel to attend one of the fights. It was dark when they hiked past several head frames on a poorly lit road that snaked around the mines and slag piles. The Henderson warehouse loomed above them uphill in the shadows and there was little traffic by horseback or buggy in this part of town. But the closer they got the larger a company they found themselves in as miners materialized out of the landscape to enthusiastically observe the fisticuffs or maybe, in the emotion of the moment, to wager their hard-earned cash on outcomes. A few, feeling feisty in the devil-may-care atmosphere, might even be tempted to step up and do battle themselves.

It seemed to be common knowledge, at least among the miners, that the sheriff and deputies were paid to look the other way. But the miners still had the pretense of sneaking into the warehouse for this clandestine venture and it was true that many townspeople, if they heard about the fights and the gambling that went on so close to home, would be only mildly surprised or, at least, not shocked.

At the dark weatherbeaten door a fat man in a bowler hat, full beard, and a grubby three-piece suit checked them in as they filed in past a flickering one-wick lamp. The man held out a cigar box and in a graveled voice repeated to each of them as they passed,

"Two bits. Two bits."

They each dropped in a quarter and crossed a large dingy storeroom that was stacked with wood crates, rolls of heavy cable, and huge iron machinery parts. Kincaid walked ahead and their boots echoed hollow on the oil-stained wood floor. At the far wall they filed through a small wood door that opened into a large well-lit building. This warehouse was stacked with heavy rough-sawed lumber of every size imaginable and when Albert opened the door the rush of shouting voices jarred their senses.

At the center of the cavernous room there was a large circle painted on the worn wood floor. A hundred or more men stood four and five deep surrounding the designated ring, shouting and cheering. In the center two men were stripped to the waist and already fighting, a short quick Chinese and a solid slow white man. The spectators, all men, cheered for and encouraged the fighter they'd bet on. Kincaid shoved his way closer and Daniel stayed just behind him, tall enough to see over the top while Kincaid was shouting as if he knew one of the fighters.

"That's Moose McKenzie," Albert said as he pointed at the white man. "He'll win. Wish I had some money on him but the odds wouldn't be good—he wins a lot."

"They keep odds on them?" Daniel asked.

"Yeah, and the fighters try to work up to the big fights where they can make good money."

The fighters grabbed each other in a clench and the referee quickly separated them by poking them with a cane. The fight lasted another two or three minutes and then the Chinese, the lighter of the two, went down and couldn't get up.

"The Chink will fall back to the bottom now," Albert said.

"And then what?"

"You mean for the Chink?" Kincaid asked.

"Yeah."

"He'll have to start at the bottom and work his way up."

"How much does he make tonight?" Daniel asked.

"Nothing, unless he had some side bets."

"How much did Moose make?"

"I don't know what level he's at but he probably made seven or eight bucks. Good money."

The bets were paid while two other men peeled off their shirts and walked around the circle as new bets were made.

"You gonna bet?" Kincaid asked.

"No."

"Would you lend me four bits. This one's a sure bet."

Daniel fished in his pocket and came up with two quarters.

"Who are you betting on?"

"Bulldog Butler, he's a sleeper, I'll get good odds."

"How much will you win?" Daniel asked.

"I'll double my money."

"You mean you'll double *my* money."

Daniel swatted him on the back as he hurried off to make his bet.

Albert made some bets and was ahead for a while and he shouted loudly until a coughing jag shut him down. Daniel watched the men who fought, some almost playful, older, evenly matched, putting on a show while enjoying themselves. Some battled in dead earnest, fighting to cover their bets and make the money they'd risked. And then there were a few who were mean, angry, out to hurt their opponent, out for blood. He could see in their eyes, the excitement of testing their skill against another man. Some fought with confidence, some with fear, some with a killer instinct. He didn't like watching most of it, the punishment some were taking, the pain and bruises and blood. A few were knocked out, a few left wobbly on the floor, and those who stood over them in triumph, fighting for the money or for their sweetheart or for the personal glory.

He wondered if he could work up the anger and meanness to fight there. Who would he call up in his memory to motivate him to do battle? Ben Weebow? Ranski? Those he knew who mistreated their animals? Then he realized it would be God. The God who made him fall in love with Gabrielle. The God who condemned him for loving her. He could work up a wrath against God to fight a hundred men.

On the way home, Kincaid owed Daniel the four bits.

"A sure thing," Daniel said, and then he laughed.

"It would be a sure thing if you'd fight."

"I don't like to fight. I don't like to hurt people. My father taught me it was a sign of weakness."

"Weakness! The way you dropped Ranski was power, pure unadulterated power."

"That was self defense. It's weakness to join a fight, takes much more guts to not fight, to not give in to the temptation to get even, to answer a challenge, or to make money by hurting some poor guy."

"How about your girlfriend? You said you want to save up enough so you can go off together. You ain't gonna save much money working in the hole. Fight and make money so you can be with her, that'd be fighting for love, wouldn't it, wouldn't it?"

"Maybe . . . I don't know, I guess so."

"So think about it, just think about it. If I can talk you into it, you'll have to think of something that will bring out the anger in you, the rage. Can you do that?"

"Yeah."

Albert Kincaid was old enough to be Daniel's father but their warm and affable relationship didn't go that direction. It was more like older brother teaching and watching over younger brother. From the start Daniel felt a responsibility to use his youth and strength to stand by him in his daily struggle against miner's wheeze and the hard work. Albert taught Daniel all he knew about working and surviving underground and Daniel did enough work to keep them both employed. Daniel liked Albert right off and he sensed that Albert felt the same about him. He feared for Albert's future and kept after him to give up working underground.

Albert kept after Daniel to fight with the tenacity of a horse-fly, during work, after work, on the way to the mine, on the way home from the mine, Daniel managing relief from the onslaught only on Sundays when he'd spend the day with his horse, Buck, in the foothills.

"You could put away a hundred dollars if you worked your way up, a hundred dollars or more," Albert said as they loaded ore.

Albert was failing, his strength obviously leaking out of him day after day with Daniel doing what he could to cover for him. It was a challenge for both of them to get Albert to Saturday night, to get him through one more week of work still standing, still employed, still a miner.

Even at those times when Daniel was able to think of other

things, Albert would remind him of Gabrielle, pull her back into his present, start him again in that unending cycle of planning how they'd run away and live happily ever after. But Daniel read something else in Albert's voice, an unrelenting fear that he'd no longer provide for Sally, no longer provide for himself, an overwhelming anxiety that in the end they'd find themselves in the cold gnarled hand of hunger, begging warmth from another's stove, huddled together against the bitter Arctic blast of the unending winter to come.

"Maybe I'll give it a try," Daniel said as they ate lunch sitting on the back of the ore car in the wobbly light from their candles.

Preoccupied with something else, Albert didn't respond.

"Hey!" Daniel said and kicked Albert's shoe.

"What, what?"

"Maybe I'll give it a try," Daniel said.

"Give what a try?"

"Fighting. Getting rich on a sure thing."

"You mean it? You really will?" Albert slapped his hands together and shouted. "Son of a bitch, we'll be rich! Son of a bitch, we'll be rich! This Saturday? This Saturday?"

"Yeah, this Saturday, if I can still walk after a week in this dungeon," Daniel said.

"What's all the shoutin' 'bout?" a miner down the tunnel called.

"Daniel's fightin' Saturday," Albert said. "You can make some money, good money."

"He'll probably git killed," the man called back.

When they arrived at the warehouse Saturday night Albert showed Daniel the ropes of getting a chance to fight. Sam, a bald-headed barrel of a man in bib overalls and miner's jacket wrote Daniel's name on a tablet with a carpenter's pencil and looked him over.

"Kinda young, ain't ya?" he said. "These men can be deadly."

"He's a lot older than he looks," Kincaid said, "and twice as tough."

"Well, we'll see if we can work him in," the man said, "if not tonight maybe next week."

Several other men crowded Daniel and Albert out as they surrounded the man.

"Rockhammer!" Kincaid yelled, "Don't forget: Rockhammer."

They turned and pushed their way closer to the fighting.

"Sam was the top fighter here for nearly a year, made a pile of money, good money," Kincaid said.

Daniel thought about Jeremiah as he stood waiting in the crowd while the fights went on. Not Gabrielle, not the money, but he thought of his father. What would Jeremiah think of this? And suddenly he felt a deep loneliness for his father, wanted to feel that powerful handshake, that crushing hug, see that bear-like body standing against the world. He thought that if he got the chance to fight that night it would be confusing. His father taught him not to fight unless it was a fight against bullying or brutality or outright evil. But these men weren't evil and he didn't want to hit them.

About the time both of them gave up hope of Daniel fighting that night, Sam poked Daniel and told him to peel off his shirt. Albert ducked away to find a bet against this newcomer. Daniel pulled on the sweat-soaked mitts and shoved his way into the ring. An older bearded man with a torso like a tree trunk outweighed Daniel by twenty or more pounds. They faced off. With a mature confidence the man nodded at Daniel, smiled faintly and said, "Cooper."

Daniel, feeling marbles in his gut, nodded back and said, "Rockhammer."

"Now don't run away, lad," Cooper said.

The referee told them what they couldn't do, which wasn't much, and with a chopping motion of his hand shouted, "Fight!"

Albert had shoved his way to the front and yelled, "Give 'em a Ranski!"

Cooper was right handed and shuffled slowly to his right. Daniel circled with him, keeping his distance, ducking Cooper's faint jabs into the air. Then, losing patience, the man threw a wide haymaker that Daniel quickly sidestepped and retaliated with a solid shot to the ribs. Cooper's guard came down as he winced from the blow and Daniel's left hook caught him square in the jaw before he could recover. His knees buckled and he went down face first. The fight took one minute.

The crowd whooped it up and Daniel kneeled beside Cooper to see if he was all right. The man sat up, slowly shaking his head.

"What hit me?" he slurred.

"That was a Ranski," Kincaid said. "A God almighty Ranski."

Cooper broke his nose when his face hit the floor. They helped the bloody man up and Sam cleared the floor for the upcoming fight. It was a big one, Pork Chop Parker was up in the good money. Daniel pulled on his shirt and they watched Pork Chop beat a newcomer named Mike Madman Moss, who had worked his way up with a dozen wins. Daniel didn't want to watch any more and they headed home through the dimly lit streets.

"That only took you a minute," Albert said, elated with his winnings.

Albert had found two-to-one odds since Daniel was unknown and gave the appearance of a young man out of his element. Kincaid had saved beer money and bet the whole dollar. He got two back. Daniel had Kincaid bet a dollar for him and he won two. He earned two dollars and twenty-five cents for his winning fight. Kincaid headed home with winnings of a dollar seventy-five, subtracting the two-bits to get in, and Daniel, minus the two-bits, had winnings of four dollars. Kincaid had a bounce in his step and a new hope in his voice.

"Think of it, if I'd bet five dollars," Kincaid ventured and coughed. "I'd have ten dollars now, *ten* dollars."

"You first have to have the five," Daniel said and swatted his excited friend on the back.

"I can talk Sally out of it. She's got it. If she could see you fight she'd see. She's a smart lady, she'd see, you're a sure thing."

"Easy for you to say, there are some tough men here."

"Ya gonna fight next week?"

Their faces came to Daniel—Gabrielle, Zack, his father and mother.

"I don't like hittin' 'em, Albert, I just don't like it."

"They're lookin' for a fight, most of 'em like to fight, that's why they come here. You're just givin' them some sport . . . and a chance to make some money. Nobody's holdin' a gun on 'em."

"Yeah. I know, I know," Daniel said. "But you don't feel their flesh and bone on your knuckles."

"Ya gonna fight next week?"

"Yeah . . . yeah, a few more."

"I'll start working on Sally."

"First we got to get you through the week in the hole."

"I'm good, I'll sleep all day tomorrow."

When they split up Daniel looked out across the city and felt an open recurring wound, not from any blows from the fighting but from the pain of living without Gabrielle and his family.

On Wednesday they had a bad day in the mine. Albert couldn't stop coughing no matter what they tried. Daniel went down the tunnel and distracted the straw boss with questions in an attempt to cover for Albert and somehow they got through the day. On Saturday night Albert seemed better and they hiked to the warehouse to fight. They each carried their betting money, Sally had come up with four dollars, and they hoped no one much noticed Daniel's quick victory the previous Saturday. When Daniel signed up to fight, Sam, the man with the fighting list, didn't seem to recognize him. That was good and Albert worked the crowd to get the best odds he could work up, betting against the young blond miner.

Maybe Sam did remember Daniel because he called him into the ring for the fourth fight against a miner named Woody Winslow. Winslow reminded Daniel of a giant spider, dark-skinned, black hair, tall and thin, all arms and legs, hairless, permanently dirty face. Winslow danced left and right, flicking out his fists at Daniel as if he were catching flies. Daniel told himself to pay attention, this man was very fast. Daniel danced in a circular motion and Winslow's long reach tapped Daniel's gloves where he held them high in front of his head. Daniel told himself to be patient and the big spider lolled him into relaxing with the flick, flick, flick of his hands.

Then Winslow made a lightning thrust at Daniel's head that Daniel barely ducked. It came so fast it threw Daniel off balance and he missed his chance to retaliate. The spider danced, his long arms pointed, his hands flick, flick, flick. Daniel gathered himself, scolded himself for losing focus. Patience. The crowd roared as it enjoyed this good fight, choosing sides and shouting out late bets for any takers.

Daniel sensed it coming, flick, flick, and Winslow came fast for the head. Daniel blocked the first fist, ducked the split-second fist that followed, and sent his right hand hard against Winslow's rib cage. In a spontaneous reflex the spider dropped his guard and Daniel's left hook came like a locomotive out of a tunnel. The sound of the impact frightened Daniel. The spider collapsed in a tangle on the floor and the fight was over.

Miners surrounded Daniel with congratulatory banter and slaps on the back while he pushed his way through the crush to see if Winslow was all right. Several of Woody's friends had him sitting up, having revived him with cold water to the face. Daniel pulled on his shirt and jacket and Albert showed up jubilant with their winnings. Daniel told him he didn't want to watch any more and was headed home. As they pushed through toward the door, here and there they heard the name "Rockhammer."

Outside Albert said, "That ain't good, them remembering your name. We won't get such good odds any more."

"I didn't like it," Daniel said.

"You didn't like what?"

"The sound of my punch on his head."

"Yeah, I know, I know. Maybe this will make it sound sweeter."

Albert handed Daniel eleven dollars and seventy-five cents.

"When I come home with eight Sally will give me more. She'll see. What would happen if I had twenty-five to bet? Think of it."

"You think about taking care of yourself and getting better."

"Ya goin' ta fight next week?"

"I don't know. Maybe . . . maybe I just won't hit them in the head."

"We should be staying to watch the bigger fights so you can see some of the guys you might fight, see how they fight."

After watching him in these two fights, Kincaid realized what it was that Daniel had as a fighter. Daniel was fast, unnaturally fast. It was speed, Daniel's hands moved faster than the men's hands he fought. He was quicker. It was a gift that he didn't even know he possessed. He'd never been trained to fight, hadn't fought at all growing up, but his hands were too fast for the men he fought, it was incredible speed, blinding speed, almost freakish.

"You rest up good tomorrow, get lots of sleep," Daniel said. They went their separate ways.

Daniel headed home and he winced a little as he recalled the developing melodrama at the boardinghouse. He hoped Claire wouldn't be up. The rumor spreading through the boardinghouse was that Daniel was in love with Claire, Etta Anderson's daughter, and that he crossed Ranski for bothering her. She obviously did favor Daniel at the table, serving him with the platters of food ahead of the others. Ranski had moved out shortly after his attack in the alley and the more Daniel denied any romantic interest in Claire the worse it got. And lately Etta started letting him have the first bath after work. He hoped to slip in unnoticed and looked forward to Sunday, his day away from the mine.

When Daniel first came to Butte he found a sanctuary amid the gray choking hell, a breath of fresh air, an escape to the life he knew. He'd look forward to Sunday when he'd hike to the south end of the valley and Gillespie's livery stable where he boarded his horse, Buck. He'd saddle Buck and ride many of the trails that led into the foothills to the south. It felt so natural to have the horse under him and remember the feel and smell of horse and leather, a combination that couldn't be duplicated, putting the life in the mine and his growing despair behind him for a day. The only trouble was that Buck reminded him of Gabrielle and the ranch and his heart ached for an impossible life with her.

Gillespie's was a popular place, especially on Sundays, with the coming and going, shoeing and grooming, buying and selling, boarding and trading. The operation included several sheds and barns in various stages of sun-bleached and wind-worn, a dozen or more corrals of various sizes, a ring-shaped corral for breaking horses, many acres of pasture, and a two-story wood-framed house to the west that needed paint and shingles.

Daniel liked the quiet, slightly stooped man named Gillespie right off, the way he treated horses, the way he treated people fairly and honestly. With a slight limp in his right leg, he seemed to be worn down, as if the place was overwhelming him: fence that needed mending, piles of horse apples and straw everywhere, barn doors off their hinges, water tanks leaking.

"You run this operation all by yourself?" Daniel had asked the first time he brought Buck.

"No . . . no, it's me and my family. My girl Nettie does a lot, she's good with the horses."

With a trimmed black beard and a tooth or two missing he always had a chew of "tobaccy" under his lip.

"You have a big family?" Daniel had asked.

"No . . . just my wife and Nettie. But we make do."

"Is Nettie your only kid?"

"Yep, but she's a good worker."

"Is she around today?" Daniel had said as he threw his saddle on a saddle rack. "I'd like to tell her some things about Buck."

"No . . . she's off somewhere today . . . but I expect her anytime now."

"Can I help you with the feeding?" Daniel asked, seeing how much needed doing and people with boarded horses scrambling around the place.

"That'd be kind of you, I'm a little behind."

On several Sundays Daniel worked until dark, trying to "catch up" with the chores that needed to be done for thirty some horses. He found it an effective way to burn a day in the company of the things he'd grown up with—ranch life, the land and animals, and working outside in the rain and wind and sun. The Sundays went quickly and delivered him somewhat from the loneliness.

When Daniel left on foot each night he would glance back and he'd often see Gillespie come out on the porch of his house and hang a lantern. Then he would sit in a chair and gaze down the road as if he expected someone.

Daniel often helped Gillespie with some chore or two on the Sundays he hung around the stable. It seemed that Nettie was always off somewhere and he still hadn't met her. Of the many people who came and went on Sunday, he noticed a girl who introduced herself one day when they were both pitching hay to the horses. She was pretty. She told him she boarded a horse, lived on west side of town, and her name was Jennifer. Folks called her Jenny. Daniel couldn't help noticing the beauty of her. She was feminine, petite, but very good with her horse. He guessed she was eighteen or more. Her family didn't have any ground to keep a horse, living right in town, and she came to Gillespie's often. And she was usually there on Sunday and conspicuously saddled and ready to go when he was. They often made small talk when they bumped into each other doing their chores.

On the Sunday after Daniel's second fight, a gorgeous fall day, Daniel was about to ride out for a few hours when she rode up to him.

"Would it be all right if I rode along with you? I don't know many of the trails around here and I'd like to try some new ones."

"Sure, I'd like the company, won't have to be talkin' to my horse."

He figured she was lying, that she probably knew the foothills much better than he, growing up here and all, probably riding since she was very young. Daniel felt flattered that she asked him. He didn't know if he was imagining it but she reminded him in some subtle way of Gabrielle.

"Do you miss your ranch a lot?" she asked as she followed him across a meadow.

"Every day."

"I don't know how you can work in the mines when you could be there."

"You've sure got a good-looking horse," he said.

Daniel didn't want to talk about the ranch and he wished he'd never told her about it.

"Prince. He's ten, got him as a colt."

They began climbing, into the white pine and Douglas fir, going for long stretches without speaking, listening to the click of the horse's hooves on the rocky trail. By mid-afternoon they stopped and looked out over the valley, dominated by the mines, those huge abscesses scaring the earth and killing it. Neither of them spoke for a time.

"It's sad," she said.

He nodded.

"We better get back," he said and he turned Buck for Gillespie's, trying not to think of another six days underground.

"Have you ever met Nettie, Gillespie's daughter?" Daniel asked, letting Jennifer and Prince lead the way home.

"No, I never have. I don't think she stays around on Sundays."

"That's probably it," Daniel said. "I'm only here on Sunday."

When they'd cared for their horses they started walking for the hill and town. Daniel didn't know how he got into this and he didn't know what to expect.

"Would you like to stop at Molly's for some supper?"

Molly's was a tavern and restaurant of a sort and Daniel hadn't ever eaten there.

"I'm kinda grubby," Daniel said, about to retreat.

"You're fine. It's not fancy."

Daniel ate a delicious T-bone with baked potatoes and beans and homemade bread. He wondered what he was doing there, sitting in a cozy booth with candlelight and an excellent meal and a lovely young woman. Gabrielle came into his mind and his thoughts surprised him. Gabrielle wanted him to have a life, to be happy. Could he be happy without her?

As they were leaving Molly's a man he didn't recognize called to him, "When ya gonna fight again?"

Daniel waved at him and hurried out the door.

"Fight?" Jenny looked confused.

"Oh . . . just miner's slang from down the hole."

He walked with Jenny further into town and then they went their separate ways halfway up the hill where people were enjoying the warm Sunday evening. When he got back to the boardinghouse, Claire, in a bright red blouse he'd never seen, was waiting for him. She led him to the kitchen where she'd kept his supper warm. She sat across from him while he forced himself to eat the large ham and scalloped potato supper because he didn't want to hurt her feelings.

They talked until Daniel had to get to bed. He said good night and went down the hall in a daze. He couldn't help but notice; Claire was growing up, filling out, becoming a young woman who made a lovely red blouse come alive. And besides she had a heart of gold.

\* \* \*

Saturday night Albert and Daniel hiked to the warehouse in the dark. Daniel got listed and waited while the fights went on. Albert had brought some large sum to bet with and he wouldn't tell Daniel how much.

"It'd make you too nervous when you fought," Albert said, "you'd be thinkin' about the money instead of the fight."

Luck swung their way when the man who was supposed to fight Lodgepole Perringer didn't show. It was a "money" fight and Daniel was picked to fill in if he chose to. Kincaid didn't know if they should take the fight and expressed his foreboding.

"We better skip this one, Daniel, take a regular fight. Lodgepole is working his way into the good money, he's damn near seven foot and weighs around two fifty. You won't be able to reach his head."

"We can get better odds if I fight him, right?"

"Yeah, yeah, but what good is that if he beats you?"

"I'll take the fight."

They waited while other fights went on and word spread that a guy named Rockhammer would fight Lodgepole. With fear and trembling Albert spread his money around making bets. Lodgepole showed up and the fight was on. Daniel was impressed by the man's size, his huge face and hands. From the waist up his hard body was covered with hair and his eyes peered from under black bushy eyebrows and a full beard. As they circled, jabbing and throwing feigned punches, sizing each other up, Daniel could see that Lodgepole was big, very big, but slow.

Lodgepole shuffled left then right then left, waving his left-handed mitt in a beckoning motion, urging Daniel to come closer.

"C'mon, little fella, c'mon. Let's see what ya got."

Then quickly Lodgepole lunged. Daniel side-stepped the punch, throwing a hard shot to Lodgepole's gut. The huge man winced and, as with others of Daniel's victims, down came his guard. But a split second later when Daniel came with the hammer, Lodgepole's guard was still hanging high enough to block Daniel's blow and protect his head. The Ranski wouldn't work on this tower of a man. Daniel would have to find another way. They circled, Lodgepole threw wicked yet wild punches that Daniel knew could knock him down if they ever connected. The miners shouted and cheered and Daniel could sense that Lodgepole was wearing down, his beard and body dripping with sweat.

Then Daniel suddenly stopped, dropped his guard and pointed at Lodgepole's feet.

"Your boot!" he shouted. "Your boot!"

Lodgepole stopped, lowered his hands, and looked down at his feet. In a blink Daniel caught him with an uppercut and a left cross. The crowd of miners stood stunned and Lodgepole crashed to the floor as if Daniel had used an axe. It happened so quickly no one thought to shout timber. Daniel was the first to the fallen tree and several others helped the big man to sit up. He was conscious if a little confused as to where he was. Daniel felt bad the way he suckered Lodgepole but a fight was a fight. That old ruse was well within the fighting rules.

Albert collected over thirty dollars and with what he bet for Daniel and the twelve dollars Daniel got for fighting Lodgepole, Daniel was going home with forty-two.

"Lordy, lordy, he went down like you'd used a crosscut saw," Kincaid said.

"I didn't like hitting him," Daniel said as they walked home.

"Aw shucks, you only hit him twice."

"I know, I know, but it was a dirty trick."

"Listen, he was trying awfully hard to hit you. If he had I'd be pushing you home in a wheelbarrow. He wanted to fight and he was bigger than you so enjoy your winnings. Besides, that's the oldest trick in the books. You taught him something, made him a better fighter, made him a better person. He shoulda learned that trick in second grade."

One fall Sunday when there was a bite in the air, Gillespie's buildings and corrals appeared to be losing ground to the elements and the wear and tear of the horses. Daniel figured he'd put in a good day around the stable rather than go out on Buck. In one corral there were two poles eaten through by the horses. Daniel found the double edged axe and hiked out into the hills to the lodgepole stand. These trees made excellent fences with their long straight trunks and only scattered limbs at the high end.

Daniel picked out two that were dead, making them much lighter than sap-filled live trees. He took the axe to the first and had it down quickly. He walked beside it pruning branches and at about fifteen feet in length he cut off the top. He dragged it downhill to the corrals and went back for the other. When he was cutting the top off the second tree, something uphill caught his eye. Curious, he walked through the trees and found a large lichen-covered boulder partially protruding from the ground. Behind it stood a wooden cross. He kneeled in the pine-needle bedding and rubbed the accumulated pine needles and twigs off the cross. The board was weathered and splitting some but he could make out the carefully printed name.

"NETTIE"

He knelt beside the grave and was overcome. Nettie hadn't run off somewhere. Nettie was dead and gone. And it was too painful for Gillespie to face living without her, to admit she wasn't coming back. Oh, God, could Daniel ever tell Gillespie he knew? Or was it kindest to go along with the old man's delusion. Had he denied it for so long he believed it?

Daniel dragged the pole downhill and wondered how Nettie died. How old was she? And how did Gillespie account for her disappearance to neighbors? Daniel knew that one—must be the same story he told everyone, that she'll be home soon. As Daniel slid one of the poles into the notched posts, he gazed up the hill to the lodgepole stand and for a moment thought he heard Nettie's voice in the whine of the trees. It was as if she were calling to her father, telling him she would be home soon.

Daniel visited with Gillespie while he repaired hinges on the horse barn door but he didn't mention Nettie again, no more questions. His heart went out to Gillespie in his long lonely journey without someone who wanted him, without someone to cherish him. He wondered if he could go on living like Gillespie, under the pretense that Gabrielle would soon be coming home to him.

They say that Daniel threatened to quit. The fighting was wearing on him as he moved up to some of the more difficult matches.

But Kincaid kept at him, the winnings piling up. Then a challenge came from the far side of Butte, a man from those western mines, Olaf Swenson, known as "The Swede." Daniel refused at first but was persuaded by more than one miner. He warned Kincaid not to bet too much on this fight, he might not win. Kincaid wouldn't pay much attention and had weaseled ten dollars out of Sally. He had seventeen he'd won the previous week and together he had twenty-seven dollars. Without telling Daniel he bet it all. The odds were even. Each man had a winning reputation.

Daniel had stripped off his shirt, gotten the mitten-looking gloves on and was waiting when Swenson arrived. He looked to be six foot three and probably weighed two hundred and forty pounds. He wasn't fat. He was big, big hands, big head, big feet, big laugh, the man looked as formidable as a boulder. The referee gave them instructions of what they could do and what they couldn't and the miners crowded around the circle.

At the word "fight" the two men shuffled toward each other and then danced in a circle. Swenson stayed away from Daniel's reach, smiling and laughing in a way that unnerved Daniel for a moment. They circled. Daniel waited and that seemed to rattle Swenson. He stopped smiling. Cautiously the "Swede" moved in close enough to box with Daniel's mitts but not close enough to land one on his body. Suddenly Swenson's patience ran out and he threw his right, a wild haymaker. It left him off balance for a heartbeat. In that heartbeat Daniel blocked the punch while his right dealt a crushing blow to the ribs. Then Daniel's left came with the force of a sledgehammer and the fight was over as quickly as it started.

The Swede folded like a heron settling on a nest. Daniel knelt beside his opponent and helped him sit up. No blood. The man knew where he was, he'd be all right. But he wanted to know what hit him. Daniel pulled on his shirt and jacket and on the way home Kincaid counted the money that was a "Sure Thing."

And Daniel was a sure thing. He didn't fight every Saturday, but when he did they had to get their bets down fast. He won his next five fights and won a reputation. He would circle patiently until his opponent threw an off-balance or wild punch. Daniel was quick. He'd dodge or duck or block the punch with his left arm. With lightning speed he'd smash his right fist into the man's rib cage or stomach with such force the man dropped his guard for a split second. That's all Daniel needed. In an instant his left fist came out of the blur like a hammer. The man's legs buckled and he hit the floor, the fight was over.

Each Saturday, on the way home, Albert counted the money several times. His cough sounded worse every day and he pushed Daniel to fight. Like a squirrel in the fall he saved up his money for the day he could no longer work in the mine.

Daniel began to feel differently about fighting, think differently, and he knew he'd better get out of it before it changed him, before he felt exhilarated when he knocked a man flat, before the killer instinct emerged from somewhere deep inside of him. He didn't tell Albert but he had almost enjoyed knocking out the last man he fought. And he meant to hurt him.

# TWENTY-FIVE

GABRIELLE SETTLED INTO an industrious routine, visiting from one to three or more children a day in all directions out from Halo, as well as the few who lived in town. Months melted into the past and when she could see an end to the list of children first assigned her, word came from Chicago that another orphan train was forming, bringing nearly three dozen children as far as Halo.

In spite of her zealous and unremitting attack on her work she'd managed to make friends with those whom she'd cross paths on a daily basis. Ned, living below her with his newspaper, the *Halo Star,* had the energy and optimism of a friendly bear cub. Molly O'Hare, a slim, self-conscious woman a few years older than Gabrielle, worked at the grocery and dry goods store, lived alone in town, and bore a ghastly scar on the left side of her face, a token, Gabrielle learned, of a fiery Indian encounter when she was a young girl. Melancholy and helpful, Molly did whatever she could to hide the blemish, wearing her hair down to her shoulders and often using a scarf or bonnet. She'd never been married, loved kids, and helped Gabrielle whenever she could.

Ned had a wagon with two bench seats and he'd invited Gabrielle and Molly to go out in the country on Sunday to picnic and fish and explore. Ned didn't talk much about his past and diverted conversation whenever that subject got too close. One evening Ned invited Gabrielle into the newspaper office for coffee when she'd returned from work. As usual he was smudged with ink. She welcomed the opportunity to let Ned know where she was in life before he had any notions of romance. Ned was visibly relieved to find out that Gabrielle, now separated and divorced, loved a man who she hoped she'd soon be with for the rest of her life. This allowed their friendship to deepen.

Gabrielle had to coax Molly to go on the outing and with Ned's help they talked her into a reluctant acceptance. Gabrielle had already planned to turn Ned down if Molly backed out and it was as if they each played chaperone to the other two, that they were only safe as a threesome, that they all guarded their scars in a fragile balance.

With wagon and team, Ned crossed the bridge over the Broken Knife and headed down the west side of the river. Gabrielle and Molly sat in the second seat behind Ned as he urged on the horses. The girls got to laughing as they bounced high off the bench seats that were only attached to the wagon with springs. Gabrielle had promised herself she would live this day in the moment, partly for Molly's sake, not allowing the past or future to steal it from her. She prayed that somewhere Daniel would do the same.

They bounced for more than three miles, the gravelly road parallel to the Broken Knife. Waving and calling to the few folks and ranches they passed, they laughed as they outran the dogs. Ned turned the horses when they came to Lost Creek, a small stream that flowed out of the mountains to the west. Ned followed the creek for half an hour. When he reached a grove of huge cottonwood, he reined in the horses and jumped out of the wagon box.

"Here we are ladies, it's time to have fun," Ned said.

"I'm glad you didn't include that ride as fun," Gabrielle said and both of the girls climbed down with relief, still laughing.

They stood on the bank of the quiet creek and breathed in its cool clear beauty. Along its banks, willows drank from its life-sustaining moisture and the towering cottonwoods marched along its banks as sentinels, bringing their shade as a gift. Gabrielle could look east where they had come and trace the tree line down Lost Creek until it joined the Broken Knife. She could see houses and outbuildings of every size and shape scattered sparsely across the high prairie like brushstrokes on an artist's canvas. The mountains to the west were more than twenty miles away and the treeless prairie spread all the way to the foothills, then the vast forests growing up to the tree line, until lastly the rocky snow-covered peaks. The mountains on both sides cradled the endless prairie for as far as she could see.

The three of them stood silently for a moment as if they'd stumbled into Eden. Then Ned clapped his hands. "We're wasting daylight," and he turned for the wagon.

In minutes Ned had the horses hobbled, the women had jars of lemonade and potato salad wedged between rocks in the cool creek, and all of them snatched the willow poles from the wagon and were baiting their hooks with the worms they'd brought from town.

"If we don't catch any trout we can eat the worms," Ned had said on the way.

He pulled off his boots and waded into the creek that was more or less twenty feet wide and never more than three feet deep except in the pools. The girls followed his lead. Molly tied her dress up to the knees and Gabrielle wore britches. Before the girls made it into the creek, Ned had hooked a lovely rainbow trout.

"Holler when you have what you can eat for lunch," Ned called. "We'll catch what we want to bring home just before we leave."

In minutes the girls each had a trout and Ned built a small fire with good dry kindling shed by the cottonwoods. He fetched a large iron frying pan and tin eating utensils from a box in the wagon. Gabrielle cleaned their three trout and Molly laid out a table cloth and retrieved the lemonade and potato salad. When the fire was hot enough Ned melted a square of lard and fried the fish with a touch of salt and pepper.

"Only way you can eat them fresher is if you catch 'em with your teeth," Ned said.

Molly brought apple pie in her basket and a bar of chocolate.

"Have you fished much?" Ned asked Molly as they sat on the ground around their delicious picnic.

"When I was little," Molly said, "a long time ago."

Gabrielle sensed some pain in Molly's voice and broke in.

"Our ranch in Montana has a river running through it for five miles. We grew up fishing."

"Did you ever make flies?" Ned asked.

"All the time, when the trout wouldn't go for worms," Gabrielle said.

When they'd finished their pie, Ned told them to bring their tin plates and follow him. Wading upstream in the gentle current they found a gravel bar. They searched for agates in the shallow water and Ned showed them how to pan for gold with their plates. The women showed some excitement at the possibility of finding gold and the three of them spread out over the bar, searching. After a while Ned slowly edged closer to Gabrielle who was lost in the task. He scooped water his plate and heaved it at Gabrielle, soaking her. She screamed from the cold unexpected shock and jumped from her crouch. As she caught her breath she turned to face Ned, who stood knee deep and roared with laughter. Molly almost fell down, shaken and stumbling from Gabrielle's curdling scream.

"Why you dirty . . ." Gabrielle said, and with her hair plastered to her face she quickly scooped her plate in the river and shot back. In seconds they were in a full-bore water fight, drenching each other with no holds barred. Suddenly they stopped and looked at Molly, who was standing there laughing at the spectacle. Simultaneously they turned their guns on Molly and drenched her with about five fully loaded flings of their plates. As the battle tapered off and with their clothing soaked to the skin, they agreed there was nothing else to do but to swim. They found a deep pool formed where a large cottonwood trunk had fallen across the creek, creating a natural swimming hole, and they piled in and frolicked like kids.

The idyllic day flew away quickly. They explored the creek and surrounding ground on foot, drying their clothes without taking them off. The damp clothes felt good as the afternoon warmed. They found tepee rings on the open ground where Indians had camped not so long ago.

On the way back to the wagon they came upon a partial skeleton, the bleached ribcage of a human being. It lay partly buried under willow and cottonwood leaves a short distance from the creek. The three stood silently, each lost in thought.

"We must bury him," Molly finally said.

"It was probably a man by the size of the bones, most likely a white trapper or prospector," Ned said. "Probably caught in a blizzard or worse. The Indians wouldn't have left him out here like that."

"You're right," Gabrielle said. "Let's bury him."

They found a small depression away from the creek and Ned pulled the ribcage free. One of the ribs broke off and Ned carefully laid the bones in the hollow. Quietly and solemnly they carried rocks from the creek bank and covered the remains. When they finished it appeared to be a normal grave. They stood around it like relatives, no one knowing what to say. Ned nodded at Gabrielle.

"You want to say something?" Ned asked.

"Ha!" Gabrielle said. "You may want to give him a better chance than me."

"I will," Molly said.

Ned and Gabrielle glanced gratefully at Molly and waited.

"May his journey end now, Lord, may he find his family at last."

After pausing several minutes, Molly picked one lupine and laid the delicate dark blue flower on the grave.

At the wagon they went back to fishing. When they had nine fat trout, they loaded up the wagon, hitched up the horses and set out for town in totally dry clothes. Gabrielle hadn't thought about Daniel, Molly had forgotten to hide her scar, and Ned hadn't looked over his shoulder once.

The ride home was less raucous as Ned held the horses back some. When they crossed the bridge into town Ned stopped the horses as a handsome cowboy rode up on a beautiful sorrel gelding and tipped his black wide-brimmed hat to the ladies.

"Ned! Ned! You've been holding out on me," he said with a laugh. "Here you are out spending the day with two lovelies and I'm here with none."

Ned laughed. "Cole Copperman, you've never been with 'none' since you were fifteen years old."

"Are you going to introduce me?" Cole asked. "I know Molly

for sure, Molly," he said and tipped his hat to her. "But I don't know this lovely." He tipped his hat to Gabrielle.

"This is Mrs. Paul Douglas, our agent for the orphan train in Halo and surrounding territory. I've been showing her the country."

Cole brought his horse alongside the wagon and extended his hand to Gabrielle. She extended her hand.

"Mrs. Douglas, it's right nice to meet you. If I can ever be of service please don't hesitate to call on me."

He held Gabrielle's hand for a moment more.

"Ned, the next time you're taking these lovely women out into the wilds, I'll be glad to offer my protection."

"Thanks, Cole, we'll keep you in mind," Ned said.

"Good evening then," Cole said. He tipped his hat, spurred his horse, "Hah!" and the horseshoes pounded the rough-cut planks as he cantered over the bridge.

"Who was that?" Gabrielle asked as Ned drove the team for home.

"He's a cowboy who works for a big spread north of town," Ned said.

"He's been nice to me when he's at the store," Molly said. "He's always dressed fine."

Gabrielle worked fast and worked late, wanting to finish contacting the boys and girls first assigned her before the next bunch arrived from Saint Paul. She got her letter off to Grace as she had for months, the unopened envelope and letter inside that Grace would mail on to Elizabeth, keeping Gabrielle's location a mystery. Elizabeth would send her letters back to her daughter—a post office box in Saint Paul—and Carla, the owner of the deli she used to work for, would forward them on to Halo. Gabrielle cherished those letters from her mother and any news about the ranch that would include Daniel. Though they'd agreed to stay apart and hurt no one further with their curse, she feared that if Daniel knew where she was he would come for her.

\* \* \*

By the time the locomotive steamed to the edge of town, Gabrielle had visited all the children on her list and looked forward to the new thirty-one she would now be responsible for. Ned had printed the flyers and helped post them all over town. Though most of the children coming were spoken for, there would be six who did not have a permanent family yet, but all six would stay with various families temporarily. There had been eleven a few weeks ago, but Gabrielle rounded up good families for five.

Gabrielle approached the cars with a nervous mixture of happiness and worry. Children came pouring out, some silent, some fearful, some jabbering and running, playful. A stout woman in a black dress and a ruffled black hat followed the kids, looking the worse for wear. Mrs. Bowker would turn the children over to Gabrielle and ride back east when the train took on water and wood.

With Molly's help they got the kids and their baggage organized and accounted for. The children stood anxiously on the depot platform and the expectant families waited on the ground, guessing which child was theirs. A crowd of people from town had gathered in front of the platform to watch this happy drama unfold. Gabrielle stood on the gravel road just in front of the platform and faced her new charges. The gathered folks behind her were animated with anticipation, waiting on Gabrielle to end the suspense, some of these people having waited for this moment for months.

She welcomed the children to Halo, hoping they had a good trip, and then she proceeded to read off the matching names. As the children were called, one by one they stepped forward to the edge of the platform and were excitedly welcomed and helped down into their new life. Many of those called came to the edge with anxious smiles, people approved with oohs and aahs, and the process went smoothly. Gabrielle felt joy watching the children's faces and the faces of their new families. But when Gabrielle came to the end of her list and they were all matched up and accounted for there was one left over.

One chubby little girl stood there alone, waiting, and decidedly cross-eyed.

The people stirred uneasily. Gabrielle called the name of the family she'd lined up but they didn't respond. She was sure she'd seen them there earlier. She tried to find them in the crowd but couldn't. It was the thing Gabrielle dreaded most, her nightmare.

The girl's name, MARGARET, was pinned on her coat. Gabrielle always choked up to see little kids meet their new families. But when a kid was left standing, unwanted, Gabrielle had all she could do to keep from bawling. She didn't know what to do. People glanced around, couldn't look at the little girl, looked at the ground, shuffled their feet, started to slip away as if it were too painful. The forlorn look on Margaret's face was devastating.

Gabrielle called, "Margaret! Anyone here for Margaret?"

Gabrielle thought how tough this girl must be inside for all she's gone without—without parents that she remembers, without family, at times without food or shelter, without love, without friends, without being wanted. And there she stood, facing the other kids and parents, her heart breaking, again.

"Anyone?" Gabrielle called.

The world stood still, no one breathed.

"Here! We want her!" a man's voice in the back called.

The crowd parted and Mr. Pearson stepped forward. He climbed onto the platform and got down on one knee beside Margaret. He took her in his arms and hugged her.

"We want her," Mr. Pearson said. "We surely do."

People began to clap and cry and cheer. Pearson stood and picked up Margaret with one arm and her little carpet bag in the other and he carried her off the platform. Gabrielle could see Margaret's face over Mr. Pearson's shoulder. It was glowing.

Little Margaret went home with Mr. Pearson, and though she knew nothing about it, Gladys Pearson was profoundly proud of her husband. The Pearsons, Gladys and Jake, owned and ran a dry-goods store that also sold groceries. Molly worked for the Pearsons and lived upstairs over the store, the living quarters that Molly would share with Margaret. The Society's information on Margaret had no word about her age and those who had found her in the streets of Saint Paul guessed she was five.

The first night after all the excitement, Molly and Gladys tucked Margaret into her small feather bed. A while later when she was getting ready for bed Molly heard Margaret softly crying. Molly opened the bedroom door and stepped in with a kerosene lamp.

"Are you afraid of the dark?" Molly asked her.

"No."

"Why are you crying?"

"I finally found a home."

# TWENTY-SIX

THE TOWN WAS GETTING READY for the biggest event of the summer. The leaders of Halo had convinced the community that any town worth its salt and beans had a town hall. They'd pushed the idea for over three years and that summer the hall was under construction, thanks to contributions and volunteer labor. To celebrate this accomplishment they were holding a dance on a Saturday night when they had daylight until nearly ten o'clock.

The large floor of the building was completed in planed lumber, ideal for dancing, and several stud walls were framed as well. The event had been advertised for weeks, not only in town but across the countryside as well, north and south along the Broken Knife, inviting one and all to join in the celebration with lots of good food and dancing. The talk was they expected more than two hundred folks to show up.

Gabrielle and Molly went back and forth on whether they would attend the dance or not. When one chickened out the other would convince her it was the social event of the year. Gabrielle felt that with her work with all the families it was best to make an appearance at these types of events. No need to stay long. Just say hello and be available to anyone who might need to talk about their child. She finally convinced Molly with the suggestion that they'd stick together and take Margaret with them as an excuse if they felt trapped in some polite, uncomfortable situation. And there was Ned, putting in his two cents, persuading the ladies to attend.

The chairs and benches circling the dance floor quickly filled as people finished eating and the musicians began to play. Five of them with banjo, guitar, saxophone, fiddle, accordion, not to mention mouth organ. They set up at the north end of the town hall floor and couples quickly started to dance. The promoters were overwhelmed and pleased as nearly two hundred people piled into the new hall.

Gabrielle walked with Ned, wearing a dress-up skirt and blouse for the first time since coming to Halo. She felt comfortable in her boots and wide-brimmed hat. Ned wore an ironed shirt and pants with a rope tie and western hat. She wiped an ink smudge from his cheek as if he'd been spooning with his first love, *The Star*. He looked right handsome in his dress-up duds. Several of the orphan train families brought food to Gabrielle to contribute to the feast: bread, pie, cheese, cake. She and Ned had all they could do to carry it.

Molly and Margaret saved seats for them and Gabrielle visited with many of her adoptive families. She kept an eye out for the Appletons and Billy as she mingled with those feasting on the pig roast. Luckily a family from down river had contributed a buffalo or some of them would've gone without meat. It was a festive sight with everyone dressed in their best, including the children, and it seemed to matter not if their best meant merely freshly washed work clothes or expensive outfits from the mail-order catalog.

Molly and Margaret and Gabrielle sat on a bench alongside the dance floor where soon it was standing room only. Women twirled in their dresses and men stomped with their boots and the dance floor reverberated as if it were alive. Ned came out of the crowd, bowed, and asked Margaret if she'd like to dance. She glanced at Molly for a moment and Molly nodded. Ned took her hand and off they went into the current with Margaret doing her best. Gabrielle wanted to kiss Ned. He'd turned the "last-chosen" into the "first-chosen."

The music stopped for the moment when Cole Copperman came straight for them across the floor. He looked like a picture in a book, beautifully dressed, walking as if he owned Wyoming, with a smile as big as the moon.

Gabrielle held her breath. He nodded at her and tipped his hat to Molly.

"Molly, my girl, would you honor me with this dance?"

Molly was overcome for the moment. She swallowed.

"Yes, thank you . . . I don't know how real well . . ."

"Fiddle-faddle, any woman who looks as good as you doesn't have to know how."

He offered his hand. She took it and just as the music began he swept her into the dance. Gabrielle couldn't see Molly's face but she bet Molly's out-shone Margaret's. Gabrielle thought: There are some good people in this world.

Cole asked Gabrielle next and they danced three. He held her closely and she tried to keep some space between them. He turned out to be a cowboy who could dance.

"You're a wonderful dancer," Cole said as they waltzed.

"I had to be, my mother wouldn't let us off the ranch until we were. My brothers are naturals. They couldn't go play or hunt until they finished their dance lesson. I think Mother did it just so she could dance since my father doesn't much."

Ned danced with Gabrielle but Cole cut in, twice. Cole and the three girls sat resting and drinking root beer. Some of the men snuck out to their wagons and buggies to take a snort out of some hidden jug.

Dusk slid over the mountains, bonfires were lit, and little by little people headed for home, the children and old folks first. Gabrielle agreed to one more dance with Cole and he held her uncomfortably close and she began to think that this might have been a mistake.

"Will your husband be coming out soon?" Cole asked as they danced a slow two-step.

"My husband and I are no longer together."

"Oh . . . I'm sorry . . . then you're alone?"

"Yes."

They danced slowly and she thought of Daniel.

"I've got a buggy tonight," Cole said. "Would you like to take a ride down by the river? There's part of a moon up there."

"Oh, thank you, Cole, but Ned will see me home."

When that dance was over they waited by a bonfire as the music went on and the dancers thinned. Molly would walk a very tired Margaret home and Ned, when he joined them, would do the same with Gabrielle. They stood awkwardly waiting for Ned.

Molly left with Margaret leaving Gabrielle alone with Cole. What was she doing? Cole had been a complete gentleman. He believed she was an unattached woman, she ought to be flattered, but she wasn't flattered. She was damned and she hadn't warned him.

Ned showed up in a happy mood.

"Well then," Cole said, taking Gabrielle's arm, "thank you for a most enjoyable evening. I hope they build another town hall soon."

They all laughed. Cole turned and marched away into the shadows. Gabrielle and Ned walked along the almost deserted street.

"You been drinking?" she asked him.

"I just might have been." He stumbled slightly.

"I'm so glad you're here to protect me. You want to lean on me?"

Gabrielle took Ned's arm and she was bombarded with confusing ideas. Could she ever love another man the way she loves Daniel? Could she love a man like Cole Copperman? Sailing from the moon in the night sky the answer had been echoing for ten thousand years. "No!"


Gabrielle rode the buggy east of town planning to reach two ranches on a warm overcast day. It took Gabrielle more than a week to settle back into her routine now that the number of her orphan train kids had more than doubled. She figured she should save her visits to families in town for the days when they had bad weather. She'd received a letter from her mother by way of Saint Paul with news of the ranch but very little about Daniel. What mention there was of him she milked from the paper like drops of water to one dying of thirst. He was working in the mines in Butte and they didn't hear much from him. It wasn't much to go on.

She played mental games to block out his memory and their years growing up on the ranch. She was doing well the day before, without a thought of him when, coming up out of a little coulee, she spooked three cow elk. Instinctively she reached for her rifle and instantly was hunting with Daniel. From then on memories flooded into her consciousness and she couldn't rid her mind of them the rest of the day. The many times they hunted together, the times they'd practice shooting tin cans and how frustrated he'd be when she'd outshoot him.

She decided to get a rifle for her trips. From time to time she could provide some of these families with meat. She stopped at an intersection of two lightly used roads and checked her map. It occurred to her that if she cut south a mile she'd pass in front of the Appleton ranch and have a chance to see Billy. She turned the buggy and felt sorry she hadn't had a rifle. She could have made the Appletons a gift and made up for some of the food Billy consumed.

When she turned into the yard, Buster came bounding and barking. Mrs. Appleton and Amanda were in the garden. Gabrielle tied the horse and walked to meet them.

"Well, how nice to see you," Mrs. Appleton said, "what brings you out this way?"

"I'm making rounds, just going by and hoped I'd catch Billy."

"Oh, they're off in the woods cuttin' poles. Takes em' all day."

"I thought you might have another skunk problem."

They laughed.

"There's something else after our chickens, don't know what, but that's the way it is with chickens."

They visited for a few minutes until Gabrielle knew she had to keep going. Mrs. Appleton hustled for the house.

"I have something for you," she said and ducked into the house.

"Billy fell off the horse again," Amanda said, twisting shyly.

"Oh . . . that's too bad, was he hurt?"

"Yep."

Gabrielle untied the horse and got in the buggy. Mrs. Appleton came with a bunch of carrots and Gabrielle accepted them.

"They're real sweet, comes from the good water," Mrs. Appleton said.

"Thank you," Gabrielle said as she put them in the buggy box.

"Billy having any more trouble with the horse?"

"Oh, no, he never goes near the horses."

"Say hello to him and to Mr. Appleton from me."

"I surely will, I surely will."

Gabrielle drove the buggy out of the yard and headed north. Amanda waved and Buster ran with them for a quarter mile.

Gabrielle hurried out of the dry goods store with the rifle Jake Pearson loaned her in hand and almost bumped into Cole Copperman.

"Whoa, girl, where's the fire?"

"Oh . . . excuse me, I . . ."

"And with a rifle. Who are you after?"

"Cole, I didn't see you, sorry."

Cole looked like he just stepped out of a western fairy tale.

"Gabrielle, you can bump into me whenever you'd like."

"I'm trying to get out to one of my families and I'm running late."

"Why the rifle?"

"I spooked some elk yesterday and I'd like to give my people some good meat if it happens again."

"You're a lady who's hard to catch up with."

"It keeps me busy."

"Well, next week I'm taking the wagon to Ironwood. Would you like to go along? You can bring your rifle and there'll be a better chance of seeing game there than where you've been riding."

"Ironwood," Gabrielle said, catching her breath.

"Yes, we'll be back by supper."

Gabrielle stammered slightly.

"Thanks for the offer, but I can't take the time right now, I have a lot of ground to cover before the bad weather sets in."

"You ever been to Ironwood?"

"No, I've heard about it though."

"You can bring someone with you if you want, can ride horseback if you prefer."

"I'm sorry, Cole. Thank you kindly for the invitation."

"Very well, it would be nice to have you along. We'll do it some other time," Cole said with a smile. "Good-bye."

"Yes, some other time," Gabrielle said. "Good-bye."

She hurried down the boardwalk to her buggy, slid the rifle into a scabbard, and drove away. She didn't know why her heart was pounding and her breath short. Was it the "some other time" that she'd allowed to hang there between them. Or was it the "you're a lady who's hard to catch up with?" Had he been trying to catch up with her? In the future she'd be honest, straightforward, she'd make it crystal clear. She had a man she loved waiting for her somewhere in Montana Territory.

Gabrielle often spent evenings with Molly and Margaret and sometimes the Pearsons. They'd take turns cooking supper but most of the time it would end up potluck. Jake had fashioned an eye patch for Margaret that was becoming and seemed to help her do better with her vision. She couldn't wait for school to start and by playing around the store she had learned her numbers and made a few acquaintances and friends. Once, while in the store, Gabrielle overheard a young girl playing with Margaret.

"You're an orphan aren't you?" the girl asked.

"I was an orphan but I'm not anymore."

"I wish I could be a orphan," the little girl said.

"Why?"

"So I could ride on the train."

One evening, when Gabrielle had been invited to supper at the Pearson's, she found herself trapped. At the set table in the Pearson's two-story frame home sat Jake and Gladys, Molly, Margaret, and Cole Copperman with his ruggedly appealing smile. Literally speechless, Gabrielle nodded, finally said "Hello, Cole," and sat in the chair Cole held for her. Gabrielle tried to return Cole's smile and from the corner of her eyes flung daggers at Molly. Molly shrugged slightly as if pleading that she knew nothing about this. Luckily Gladys loved to talk and she kept the room from dropping into total silence.

"Have you had any luck with the rifle?" Cole asked Gabrielle.

"No, no . . . I haven't run into any game that are in range."

She wanted to use the rifle on Gladys, or Jake, or whomever put her in this pickle. Of course Cole would think she was behind the dinner party, that she'd instigated it. The dinner went on forever in Gabrielle's mind and she was answering Cole's unrelenting questions.

"And your family has a ranch in Montana?" Cole asked.

"Yes, Montana Territory."

"Cattle?" Cole asked.

"Yes. Herefords."

As if with a woman's intuition she was aware of the dilemma she'd gotten Gabrielle into, Gladys changed the subject.

"We sure are thankful for the work the Society does," Gladys said. "Families for all those homeless children." Gladys smiled at Margaret and ran her hand over Margaret's head. "It's a wonderful program. You must be proud of your work, Gabrielle."

Gabrielle smiled. "Yes, it gives me great satisfaction."

Finally the party was over. Margaret off to bed with Molly, and Jake offering to take Gabrielle home.

"I don't mind walking," Gabrielle said, "it's a beautiful night."

"I won't hear of it," Cole said. "There are a few ruffians in Halo, I hate to say. I have my buggy right out front."

"Well," Jake paused, "if that's all right with Gabrielle?"

"That'll be fine," Gabrielle said.

Cole and Gabrielle gave their thanks to the Pearsons and rode off. There were few people afoot and the town was quite dark. Cole took a long way around but Gabrielle didn't point that out. Cole reined in the horse and turned to Gabrielle. Quickly she opened the door on her side and climbed out. He hurried around the buggy and took her arm, walking her to the stairs to her living quarters. She went up one step, stopped and turned. On the step she was even with him, face to face.

"Thank you for the ride," she said.

"I enjoyed getting to know you," he said. "I've wanted to for some time."

"It was a lovely evening," she said.

He took her hand and pulled her close.

"Cole, I want to be honest with you, you are a good man. I am not what I seem. I'm in love with a man who loves me. He's in Montana and I can't be with him right now but one day soon we'll be together. I've given him my heart and soul. I'm not available for a romance and I can't share my heart with any other man."

Cole held onto her hand.

"But you're not together yet, you're not married?"

"No, but . . ."

"I'm a very persistent man. I don't give up easy."

"Please, Cole, I don't want to make this hard for both of us."

He put his hands around her waist.

"No, Cole, don't."

"One kiss," he said. "One kiss and I'll not bother you again. That's not asking much."

She paused. He held her close.

"One kiss and that's the end of it?" she asked.

"Yes," he said, "one kiss for what might have been."

"All right," she said, reluctantly.

He pulled her to him and kissed her tenderly, firmly, with an animal hunger and she realized she was closing her eyes.

Cole stepped back. "Good-night, Gabrielle."

"Good-night."

Cole waited until she reached the top of the stairs and then he drove away. She watched him disappear into the town's shadows and she carried her mixed emotions into her rooms. She felt relief. She felt guilty. She caught the odor of cigar on her lips.

# TWENTY-SEVEN

JEREMIAH AND ZACK built cross fence in an upper meadow when they noticed riders coming a mile below. On that blustery day, brilliant white puffy clouds sailed with the sun and the horsemen reminded Jeremiah of the Blackfeet Abraham used to tell about. Whoever they were he figured they'd stopped at the house and Elizabeth would send them on. It appeared to be four or more mounted men but at that distance it was too hard to tell. It would be a half hour before they reached Jeremiah and Zack and the Rockhammers kept after the fence.

They worked in silence, Zack in a sour mood after Jeremiah told him right out, as he was accustomed to do, that a post Zack set wasn't good enough. Jeremiah had a well-known reputation that a post he tamped was immovable, solid, as though it had grown there like a tree. Zack, in a huff, had gone back and taken his anger out on the post and then moved the horse and wagon up the line, putting a more-than-necessary distance between them. His arms ached from tamping and he knew he was in a foul mood. He realized that Jeremiah was grooming him to run the ranch one day, and he tried to remember that, until Gabrielle ran off and disappeared, he would never have been in line for this inheritance.

She always said she'd never leave. No matter how much Zack looked up to her, he found it hard to forgive her for running off and deserting all of them in the manner she had. He couldn't understand any of it. Sometimes the thought crossed his mind that she might still come back and become Rockhammer boss. He knew Jeremiah never gave up hope that Daniel would return one day and Zack would be "little brother" still. Zack loved Daniel so completely that he prayed he'd come home even if it meant he would be odd man out.

The family feared Zack would be odd man out as well when it came to romance and marriage and children of his own. If Zack didn't go forth and multiply, how would the Rockhammer family fare against the normal attritions of life in the remote mountains? Zack had several girlfriends during the years he finished the grades and became a full-time cattleman. The family was pulling so hard for him to find a sweetheart that they'd make a big event out of the least possible encounter. If Zack no more than tipped his hat to a girl or spoke to her in Buffalo Jump they'd spread the word and want to know who she was and where she lived and if he was going to court her. Any word of a girl his age appearing with a newly arriving family was immediately reported to Zack as if he should run and tackle her before the competition beat him to her.

Elizabeth thought Mary Teasel would be a worthy mate for Zack but after courting her for more than six months they had a falling out and Zack moped around the ranch for nearly a year. Elizabeth hoped the experience hadn't soured Zack so that he wouldn't try again and the family sensed his deep-seated loneliness. But his life on the ranch sustained him. He loved horses and the valley and the work of tending cattle and he hoped that one day, when Jeremiah was too old to do the work, he would be the boss of the Rockhammer. For that he believed he needed a wife and he was ready to begin looking again.

The riders, five of them, approached through the meadow single file, rocking to each horse's gait.

"We'll remember who we are, son," Jeremiah said as the riders came within earshot.

They pulled up a short distance from Jeremiah and stayed mounted. One was his long-time neighbor, Henry Weebow, and one his boy, Ben. There were three other men, city men with vests and watch fobs and felt hats that appeared totally out of place.

"Afternoon, Jeremiah," Henry called with a loud, friendly voice.

"Henry," Jeremiah said.

"I've brought someone to meet you," Henry said. "You got a minute?"

"I reckon. Step down, men, rest awhile," Jeremiah said.

They dismounted. When the two well-dressed men swung off their mounts, the third younger man hurried to help one of them. Henry and the two men walked to where Jeremiah had the wagon and he noticed that one of the city men had a limp. He also noticed that the Weebows were riding excellent horses with squeaky-new leather saddles to boot. Ben wore an animal fur vest, a large shiny belt buckle, and silver spurs that jingled when he walked. Henry wore the same old buckskin clothes and the indestructible stovepipe hat.

Jeremiah leaned the tamping bar against the wagon and removed his leather gloves.

"Henry, looks like you've been horse tradin'," Jeremiah said with a warm smile. "Where's yer faithful old mule?"

"I put the old fella out ta pasture," Henry said and chuckled.

"You're ridin' a mighty fine horse there," Zack said, running his eyes over the big gray gelding.

"Jeremiah," Henry said, "this is John David McIves."

Jeremiah reached out and shook his hand. "Pleased to meet you," Jeremiah said. "This is my boy, Zack."

Zack nodded.

"Likewise, I'm sure," McIves said. He had a strong handshake and an intelligent, clean-shaven face and his clothes didn't appear as though they'd just come six miles over the dusty road.

"And this is Randolph Plummer," Henry said, nodding at the other man. Jeremiah reached out and shook his soft, damp hand. The man had a pot belly and a short black beard and he appeared to be worn out, totally out of his element. His clothes were as fancy as McIves's but didn't wear as well on him. Zack felt sorry for Plummer's horse.

Jeremiah glanced at the man who stood a ways back, holding the reins of their horses. Wearing a long duster and a black wide-brimmed hat, he regarded Jeremiah without expression. Jeremiah walked over to him.

"And who are you?" Jeremiah said as they shook hands with a mutually powerful grip.

"Tanner, sir." He never blinked. "Miles Tanner."

The man's face carried no emotion, as if he'd lived this long without being touched by human wreckage and loss.

"Oh, that's my right-hand man," McIves said. "He travels with me, couldn't get along without him."

Zack sized them up, which one might cause trouble. He did this more often now with the atmosphere settling around the valley. Quietly he was nurturing a growing confidence with the guns. He knew what to expect from Ben Weebow.

Jeremiah walked back to the other men.

"Jeremiah . . . ah, might I call you Jeremiah?" McIves asked.

Jeremiah nodded.

"On the way up here Henry was telling me you have two beautiful daughters and that he had hoped that one day one of his boys might marry one of them."

"You don't say," Jeremiah said.

Zack had all he could do to keep from busting out laughing.

"There wasn't much chance for that," Zack said with a smirk that Ben saw.

"I'm afraid the girls are long gone," Jeremiah said, "except for Maddy comin' home now and then."

"That would be quite a holding, your ranch with Weebow's," McIves said.

"Jeremiah, Mr. McIves is a mining engineer," Henry said. "He's looked at my strike very carefully and he thinks I might have a bonanza!"

"That's right, Jeremiah," McIves said, "that quartz vein Henry's found will make him a rich man."

"Well . . . Henry, I'm happy for you," Jeremiah said and he stepped closer and patted Henry on the shoulder. "Real happy."

"Well, Mr. McIves and Mr. Plummer have offered me a partnership with them to develop the mine; they're sure it'll pay off big."

"Very promising," McIves said, "very promising."

"Well, you got to hand it to him, Henry never gave up on it," Jeremiah said.

"I have a large mining company," McIves said. "Consolidated

Mining Incorporated. We've developed mines in California, Butte, Nevada. We would like to help Henry develop his find."

"Well," Jeremiah said. "I'm glad Henry will do well. He's worked hard up there for a long time."

"We understand that the east face of the mountain is on your land, and we're going to need a road across there to work the mine."

"Well, I'm sure Henry's told you about our understanding on the matter," Jeremiah said. "Our family made a vow a long time ago not to tear up that mountain building a road. I've allowed Henry to come and go as he pleased with his horses and mules."

"We could buy an easement from you," Plummer said, removing his hat and wiping his brow with a sopping handkerchief. "Or we could lease the land and it would eventually revert back to you."

"You'll have to go up the other side," Jeremiah said.

"That would cost ten times more than accessing across your short piece of land," McIves said. "The cost would be prohibitive to make it a profitable venture."

"I told you," Ben said and waved a hand in the air, "he's hardheaded."

"Now, now, we'll have none of that," McIves said. "We're gentlemen here. Certainly we can find a compromise."

Jeremiah glanced at Tanner who appeared indifferent.

"There are other ways to do this," Plummer said. "We could buy your ranch."

"The Rockhammer isn't for sale," Zack said with insult in his voice, "not now, not ever."

"And who's going to run it when you give in, Jeremiah?" McIves asked.

"My boy Daniel will be comin' back any time now. He'll run the ranch."

"That'll be the day," Ben said, "he's working in some stinkin' mine down in Butte."

"Maybe he could work this mine so close to home," McIves said.

Zack felt the lead in his stomach, his father ignoring him in the chain of command. Was he afraid to name Zack as future ranch boss in front of these men? Would they laugh?

"Maybe the surveyor stakes aren't accurate," McIves said, his voice hardening.

"I've had the government survey and a private surveyor verify what my father staked out thirty some years ago," Jeremiah responded. "It's all properly registered and recorded."

"We could build that road with very little damage," McIves said.

They talked in circles, the conversation got less and less polite, the attitude tense and frustrating.

"We're wastin' our time with these boneheads," Ben said.

"You hush up, Ben," Henry said, pointing a finger at his boy. "You just shut your mouth."

Zack sidestepped slowly toward the wagon where his rifle laid in its scabbard. Tanner followed him with his eyes.

"Jeremiah, please think it over," McIves said. "There's many tons of gold up there but we need the road to bring it out. Please think about it. Often in a stalemate, if you look at it long enough, another way shows up. Maybe there's a way we haven't thought of yet. We can all benefit from this—"

"Please, Jeremiah," Henry said. "There's a lot of money in it for all of us, a lot of money."

"Don't go begging," Ben said. "We'll find a way."

They wound down and ended amiably with handshakes all around. They gathered their horses and Tanner helped McIves onto his mount.

"We'll talk again," McIves said, sitting on his horse. "Think it over, Jeremiah. Think it over."

They started across the meadow.

"Yeah, Rockhammer," Ben called back, "there's always another way!"

"Just keep movin', Ben!" Zack shouted.

They headed out single file, Tanner last to leave.

Jeremiah watched them go, growing smaller and smaller down the valley. He remembered how his father, Abraham, told him of his promise to the Blackfeet chief. They had been blessed as the chief promised. There would be no switchbacking road scaring the face of that awesome mountain.

"I'm glad you were in on this, Zack. Someday when you run the ranch, you'll have to stand up for Rockhammer's word, for Rockhammer's promise."

As they went back to work, *Someday when you run the ranch* was all Zack heard.

Martha passed away that spring. She was capable and purposeful until a few days before she died. Knowing she would soon lie next to Abraham in the eternal pasture of the Rockhammer kept her occupied. Zack would carry her out to sit on a porch chair, bundled in blankets and a bonnet. She would stare, with a deep penetrating thirst, as if to drink in while she still could the ample Montana landscape. Jeremiah and Zack dug her grave. Maddy came in from Bozeman and Daniel from Butte. Aunt Nellie journeyed all the way from Ohio for a visit. Skipper laid on the fresh grave with sad eyes, already missing the family member who put a pan of food out for him every night. Daniel said a few words and they paid their respects and mourned the loss of one more generation gone on the Rockhammer.

# TWENTY-EIGHT

GABRIELLE SAW THEM a mile away but it wasn't until they turned and came toward her that she recognized Billy and the Appletons in their wagon, rambling toward town. It had been more than two weeks since she'd missed Billy at their ranch and she was excited to see him, still harboring an unlikely dream that one day she and Daniel could adopt him. As the distance between them closed she remembered Amanda saying that "Billy fell off the horse again." They really didn't have a riding horse, only the draft horse for the wagon and plowing. It struck Gabrielle that those horses are generally pretty accommodating when it came to riding.

She slowed her horse and prepared to stop when Mr. Appleton gave a short wave and rumbled on by. Billy, in the seat next to Mr. Appleton, looked off across the land without acknowledging her. She turned quickly in her seat and waved, expecting them to stop, but they never slowed, never looked back, leaving her there in their dust. She was baffled. Was someone hurt? Were they racing to the doctor? Soon they were only a bump on the horizon. She started the horse and wondered if she should go out of her way and stop at the Appleton ranch. No, she had ground to cover, she would get an explanation in time. If they needed help in some kind of an emergency they would have stopped. It appeared as though Mrs. Appleton was about to look at her but she turned her head at the last moment, gazing off to the south.

After a fruitful day with two good visits under her belt she could see the outline of Halo on the horizon. The culminating joy of this calling was seeing these lost little kids finding homes at last. The days and weeks were flowing by and turning into years without Daniel, years washed away and gone, without the sound of his voice, without his strong protecting everlasting love. Without Daniel and her family, sometimes *she* felt like a lost little kid. Hungry and tired and dusty, she didn't notice the rider until he closed up behind her, startling her. He must have come out of a little draw she'd passed that harbored a small stand of aspen. She was upset with herself for not being more observant and alert in this open country. She recognized Cole Copperman as he pulled alongside the buggy.

"Gabrielle! Hello! What are you doing over here?"

She thought that should be her question since the ranch he worked was on the other side of town and eleven miles north.

"Working," she said, "checking up on my kids."

Gabrielle didn't stop and Cole kept pace.

"You must have them scattered all over the place," he said.

"Pretty far, but I get to see a lot of the country this way."

"Say," Cole said, "I'll bet you're good and hungry. How about supper at Victoria's? I'm buying, my contribution to the good work you're doing."

"No thank you, Cole."

"Hey, it's only supper."

"No thank you, Cole."

They came into town from the southeast.

"I warn you, I'm persistent," he said.

"You forgot to warn me that you don't keep your word."

"Ha!" Cole laughed.

Gabrielle turned the buggy for the livery stable and Cole rode down Main Street on his magnificent horse.

"Maybe next time," Cole called.

Gabrielle fed and groomed her horse and then walked home to the room above the *Halo Star*. Ned sat waiting on her top step like a pigeon. Lately it had become his habit to bring a fresh copy of his editorial for her approval and advice before he went to press. Growing up through long winters with books she had become a helpful editor.

"Come on in," she said and he followed her. She flopped on the horse hair sofa. "Well, give it here."

Smudged with ink, he handed her the sheet and sat beside the table, fidgety as usual.

"Any news today, an accident or such?" she asked.

"No, not that I know of. Why? You hear something?"

"I passed the Appletons today on the road and they rolled right by me without stopping, like their wagon was on fire."

"Nothing happened in town that I heard of," Ned said. "She ain't pregnant or anything."

"It's probably nothing," Gabrielle said, "but strange."

She started reading the editorial.

"You misspelled February again," she said. "Two 'r's."

"Dang!" he said.

The townspeople, as well as those who came from miles away, looked forward to Halo Days, a two-day fair featuring livestock and food and competition, celebrating Halo's anniversary though they couldn't completely agree on how many years ago the town had scratched out a beginning next to the Broken Knife River. It was the most festive time of the year and people traveled long distances from the country and other towns. Any decent space that was available for sleeping could be rented and many participants camped out with their wagons and tents. Competitions went on throughout the two days and spectators crowded the arenas where the contests took place. Bets were made, entry fees collected, and winner-take-all prevailed.

Draft horses dragging weighted sleds, bareback bucking horses, bulldogging, roping, marksmanship with rifle and pistol, bull riding, sheep shearing, and a greased pig were some of the favorites. People began arriving Friday afternoon and Gabrielle took advantage of the chance to mingle and visit with several of her kids and families. As dusk settled over the bustling scene, Gabrielle spotted Billy and the Appletons, setting up camp near the river with their wagon. She approached with an unnatural uneasiness after the incident on the road.

"Hello," she said, "glad to see you're here."

"Oh, hello," Mr. Appleton said, "we wouldn't miss this for anything."

"Hi, Billy, Amanda," Gabrielle said.

"Hello," Billy said, glancing shyly into her eyes.

"Billy's going to catch the pig," Amanda said.

"I've heard about that," Gabrielle said. She stroked her fingers through Billy's hair. "You going to do that?"

"Yeah, I'm gonna try." He was growing up, almost a young man.

"I'll expect some bacon," Gabrielle said.

"I'm gonna catch a chicken," Amanda said.

"Do they do that?" Gabrielle asked.

"Oh yes, they have a contest for children," Mrs. Appleton said. "You ever try to catch a chicken?"

"Yes, plenty of times," Gabrielle said. "I used to want to shoot 'em."

They were setting up a large tent in their wagon like the prairie schooners that had crossed that country a few years back.

"I'll look for you tomorrow. When is the greased pig event?" Gabrielle asked.

"Sunday afternoon," Billy said with enthusiasm.

"I'll let you get settled. Good-night," Gabrielle said.

She walked past the many campers back into town. Things seemed as normal as pie with the Appletons. It was as if she had been invisible on the road.

Saturday morning Ned caught Gabrielle as she hustled down her stairs, eager to join the throngs in town. A cloudless sky and balmy southwest wind greeted the fairgoers.

"Hey, I could use your help today," he said. "I'll never keep up with it."

"What can I do?"

"If you would cover some of the events that I can't get to, you know, who won, how much was the jackpot, if there were exciting finishes, anything out of the ordinary."

"I'd be glad to, sounds like fun," she said.

"Okay, find me later. Check in at the fair platform every hour and we'll divide up the events. You want some breakfast?"

"No . . . thanks, I'm going to find Molly. I hope she doesn't get stuck working at the store."

\* \* \*

Gabrielle's first assignment for the *Halo Star* was reporting on the draft horse pull. There were seven single-horse contestants and nine teams. The one-horse skids were the first to be pulled and after the first round four were left. When each had had a turn, the men piled several more boulders on the sled. The farmers walked beside the sleds with the reins in hand and challenged and encouraged their powerful animals. The horses' muscles bulged and the harness leather strained and the horses farted and snorted and seemed to be trying to win for their own reward.

Two of the horses inspired Gabrielle with their eagerness to please their owner and only one farmer used the whip. He didn't win. The one-horse pot was seven dollars and the two-team was nine. Gabrielle could sense which farmers loved their horses. Her homesickness for the ranch surfaced along with her memories of their horses and the stories of Grandpa Abraham and his horse saving the Blackfeet chief's son. She hurried through the dispersing spectators to get her report to Ned.

The day went quickly with its frenzy of activity. She helped Ned with two other events, bareback bucking horses and bull riding. The bull riding wasn't as exciting as advertised because the bulls weren't cooperating. The first two out of the shoot bucked several times and then trotted around in the corral like a carousel. The third bull brought down the house. When he was prodded out of the shoot he walked to the center of the corral and sat down with the cowboy still struggling to hold on.

The bull just sat there. The crowd hooted and cheered, the cowboy used his spurs, but the Longhorn just squatted. With some humiliation, the rider climbed off, took hold of the bull's halter, and tried to pull him into a standing position. The spectators were roaring with the fun of it. The cowboy shook his head and walked to the gate. A rancher, maybe the bull's owner, walked out with a tie rope to collect the animal. The bull jumped to his feet and charged the unsuspecting man who narrowly missed severe injury by jumping high onto the corral rails. The crowd gave the bull a standing ovation.

When most of the major contests for Saturday were over they held the chicken chase for the little kids. Amanda showed up as well as Margaret. Volunteers stood shoulder to shoulder around

the inside of the corral and twenty-one little kids, five years old
or less, gathered at one end. Two gunny sacks containing six
healthy chickens were set in the middle. The kids had to pay
an entrance fee of ten cents to participate but if they were the
first to capture a chicken they got all six plus the jackpot. At the
count of three, the birds were let loose and the world turned into
utter chaos.

The people watching—parents, siblings, relatives or just
plain spectators—were laughing so hard they were hardly able
to stand. Chickens were going every direction and kids were
diving and screaming and knocking each other down. Gabrielle
cheered for Amanda and Margaret and a few of her other kids
who were wholeheartedly in the fray. The escape artists were
airborne at times, running zig-zag, jumping over the kids' outstretched arms, and desperately trying to squeeze between the
volunteers' legs.

Finally, a stout girl got hold of a chicken's leg and amid an
onslaught of pecks, managed to grab the other leg while taking
a beating from the bird's wings. With a great flurry of feathers
and dust, with the chicken squawking bloody murder and bat-
tering the girl's head and face, the girl held the fowl upside down
between her legs and stumbled to the judge as if she had a load
in her pants. A cheer went up though the chase continued for a
time. Gabrielle didn't recognize the winner, who would receive
two dollars and ten cents plus the six chickens. That would de-
pend on whether or not they could catch them. At the request of
the official judge, everyone attempted to round up the other five.
Gabrielle felt the chicken chase might be one of the most enjoyable events at the fair and she wondered how Wart would have
done with all that help.

Gabrielle flopped on the boardwalk in front of Pearson's Dry
Goods enjoying a lemonade and a caramel apple. Someone sat
closely beside her and she didn't have to look.

"Hello, Gabrielle, having a good time?"

"Yes, Cole, I am. I just about died laughing at the chicken
chase."

"I missed that, darn. I love to watch those kids."

"Are you competing in some event?" she asked.

"Yeah, tomorrow," Cole said, "trying some roping. I'm done with the bulldogging, leave that to these younger bucks."

"Something you used to do?" she asked.

"Yeah, nearly killed myself."

"I think I'll try some roping," she said

"That's only for men."

"Why, are the men afraid of the competition?"

"Speaking of men, I'm confused," he said. "You told me you have a boyfriend off somewhere and yet I see you with Ned like sweethearts."

"No, Cole, like a brother."

The words caught in her throat. She felt flustered and she knew it showed on her face. "Ned is like a *brother*. I'm helping him with his newspaper, not that it's any of your concern."

"Well he sure is at your place a lot for a brother."

Gabrielle nailed him with her eyes. "Are you spying on me, Cole?"

"Just riding by."

Gabrielle stood and finished the glass of lemonade.

"How about a buggy ride tonight?" he asked.

"Why don't you try marksmanship tomorrow."

"Marksmanship?"

"Yes, or don't they let women do that either?"

Gabrielle slipped into the crowded store.

Sunday morning Halo Days was enjoying the largest turnout ever. Gabrielle and Ned covered different events before the noontime break when everyone paused to feast on the great variety of food. Gabrielle had witnessed the calf roping where Cole Copperman and his splendid horse took second place, out-dueled by a young cowboy from west of Iron Tree.

The crowd for the greased pig contest was four or five deep around the corral, plus a ring of volunteers shoulder to shoulder inside the corral to prevent the pig's escape. Fourteen boys twelve years old or younger gathered at one end and the spectators buzzed with gleeful anticipation. Three men had slathered the young fifty-pound pig with lard and were ready to turn it loose. Gabrielle, wedged in the crush near the middle of the corral, could see that Billy was smaller than half of the boys. Ned stood a couple of rows behind her but was tall enough to see. Gabrielle picked out the Appletons on the other side with Amanda sitting high on her father's shoulders. Gabrielle felt her heartbeat with the excitement of it all, pulling for Billy so deeply, knowing now much he needed to win at something. The judge raised his arm and shouted.

"Catch the pig!"

The men turned the pig loose. It ran toward the oncoming storm of howling boys, paused, and retreated as if shot out of a gun. When it reached the dead end of the corral it turned and momentarily faced the army of boys bearing down on it. It leaned like it was going left and cut to the right, dashing down the sideline where a boy had it blocked. He grabbed it, the pig screamed with an ear-piercing shriek, and the boy watched it slither quickly through his hands. The spectators roared. The pig ducked and dodged and swerved. It was faster than the boys and when they tried to grab it all they got was lard on the hoof.

Gabrielle's emotions rose and fell as Billy had a hold of the porker and then had a hold of nothing. The boys leaped and dove and tackled. They slid belly down and knocked each other over. Gabrielle cheered with the crowd and laughed as the boys shirts and faces became smeared with mud and grease. For moments, the pig stood at one end and the boys stood at the other, panting, a standoff. Gabrielle could hardly breathe when Billy got hold of the pig and headed for the winner's pen. She cheered and shouted and the pig squirmed free and hit the ground running. With exhaustion growing on both sides, one of the bigger boys had the pig in his arms and staggered toward the finish. Gabrielle held her breath until the pig kicked and squirmed and broke free.

The people were so involved she couldn't tell anymore if they were rooting for the boys or the pig. After several more flying tackles and sliding in the muck, Billy managed to get on top of the pig. With both arms he reached around its neck and grabbed its two front legs. Gabrielle's heart was in her throat as Billy struggled to stand and maintain his grip. As he staggered for the crate two boys tried to tackle him but he was so greasy they couldn't hold on long enough to bring him down. A roar went up when Billy dropped the pig in the little pen and the pig seemed the most relieved of all.

The crowd dispersed quickly, recovering from the nerve-racking entertainment. The Appletons were proud of Billy and after he got his three dollars and fifty cents, they were going to take the little pig to their wagon where they had a crate Mr. Appleton had nailed together. Gabrielle wanted to hug Billy but he was a greasy mess. Mr. Appleton had fashioned a rope around the pig and struggled to hang on to it.

"Come on," he said to their family, "let's get back to the wagon before he gets away."

"You go ahead with the pig," Gabrielle said, "and we'll get Billy cleaned up."

"No, Billy better come with us," Mr. Appleton said. The pig just about slithered out of his arms and he nearly lost it.

"My place is just down the street," Ned said, "we'll get him under the pump and bring him to the wagon squeaky clean."

"Billy, you come with us," Mr. Appleton said.

"He'll only be a minute," Mrs. Appleton said to her husband, squeezing his arm.

"Well . . . all right," Mr. Appleton said, struggling with the pig, "but you come right along, Billy, right along."

The Appletons hurried off through town with Billy's trophy and people clapped and cheered. Gabrielle had to get to the small hill north of town where the shooting contest would be held.

"Will you take care of Billy?" she asked Ned. "I've got to go by Pearson's and pick up my rifle and revolver."

"Yeah, I'll hurry," Ned said. "I don't want to miss the shooting."

"There's a shirt on the back of my door, brown," she said. "It'll fit Billy."

"Okay, c'mon, Billy, let's de-hog you," Ned said.

"I want to see Mrs. Douglas shoot," Billy said.

"We'll hurry."

Gabrielle cut through the crowded town and her emotions lapped up to the surface. The last time she competed with a gun was a thousand years ago on the ranch with Daniel. She smiled slightly remembering how upset he'd been when she outshot him.

\*   \*   \*

A large crowd lined the sides of the crude rifle range. Participants would shoot fifty paced yards into a gravel pit where a cottonwood log provided a place to pin their targets. The competition with rifles would be settled first and then, as a novelty, they'd hold the quick-draw contest. Gabrielle had picked up the rifle and revolver at the dry goods store along with cartridges and she had to run part of the way, knowing that once they started they may not let her participate. When she arrived the judges balked at allowing a woman to compete. Cole was among the men ready to shoot.

"I see you took my advice," Gabrielle said to Cole as the men in charge debated.

"Yes, I brought a rifle you might want to use," he said.

He offered her the latest Winchester but she held up the rifle she'd borrowed.

"Thank you, but Jake Pearson let me use his," she said.

In the end it was Cole who persuaded the judges to let her shoot. After all there was nothing in the rules that prevented women. It just was unheard of in Halo. It didn't seem to matter that women often had to use a rifle in their daily life for varmints, predators, game, and protection. Some of the participants grumbled but she put her dollar in the pot and assured them that she probably wouldn't last long.

Jake had told her that the rifle shot a hair to the right. The competition began as one by one the men toed the line and standing, they fired away. The spectators had to hold their applause until the judge signaled the result. Then friends and family and those who respected good marksmanship would clap and cheer. Out of eighteen shooters, nine, including Cole and Gabrielle, made it to the second round. The size of the paper target was reduced and the nine blazed away. The pressure mounted and the shooters were slowly whittled down to four, among them Cole and Gabrielle.

"Where'd you learn to shoot like that?" Cole asked as they waited for their next shot.

"My father," she considered. "No, my brother."

She tried to clear her mind but Daniel's face and voice came to her and cheered her on. While they paused to pin a playing card on the log for the last four, Ned found Gabrielle with the other surviving shooters.

"Ned," she said, "where's Billy? did you get him cleaned up?"

"Yeah, yeah," Ned said. "I have to talk to you."

"Billy wanted to watch this," she said.

"I have to talk to you," Ned said.

The judge called her, it was her shot. She pumped the cartridge into the chamber and moved up to the line. She paused, took aim and fired. The crowd waited. The judge beside the gravel pit went to the log, looked, and raised his hand. A hit! The people clapped and cheered, many of them now pulling for this audacious woman. She stepped back and found Ned.

"Gabrielle," Ned said and motioned for her to follow him away from the crowd.

She walked a few paces up the road.

"Hurry, Ned, I might only have one more shot."

"Gabrielle, someone has been whaling on that boy," he half whispered.

"What are you talking about?"

"Someone has been beating him!"

"What! What do you mean?" she asked.

"I got his shirt off, almost had to wrestle it from him. His back has a fresh ugly bruise, the mark of a willow cane or leather whip. And there's the mark of an older one that's healed."

"Are you sure, couldn't it be from a fall, an accident?" Gabrielle fished. "Are you *sure?*"

"I'm sure. I'm sure. I'm an expert when it comes to identifying bruises on the human body."

All at once Gabrielle remembered Amanda's words. "Billy fell off the horse again."

"Oh, God! Oh God! That poor boy. Where is he now?"

"With his family, I didn't know what to do, they were breaking camp and heading out."

"Do they know you saw Billy's bruise?"

"No, no. I didn't say anything. But Billy knows I saw it."

"We have to stop them," she said and she found one of the judges.

"I have to go, an emergency, sorry," she said.

"But you may have won," the man said, taken aback.

"Sorry!" she said and handed Ned the rifle. The two of them raced for the stable.

"I'll go with you," Ned said as they ran.

"No, no, see if you can find Marshal Birt. He was here today. Tell him about Billy and that I'll be out on the road after them!"

"Which way do you think they'll go?" Ned asked, puffing.

"I think they'll cut across country and hit Windsor Wagon Road. That'd be the quickest."

"If I don't find the marshal I'll come with the buggy."

"Try to find him, I want the law in on this."

They split up in the heart of town and Ned shouted as he ran down Maple toward the jail.

"Be careful, Gabrielle, be careful!"

She hardly noticed she had run carrying Jake's revolver. At the stable she saddled her horse swiftly and for only a moment considered bringing the Colt rifle with her. She trotted through town, still filled with people enjoying the last of the fair, but when she reached the outskirts she nudged the horse into a hard gallop. The Appletons had a half hour start on her and there were several ways they could go. If they suspected that Ned had discovered their terrible secret they might take some of the rougher out-of-the-way roads.

Her anger grew at Charles Appleton for his brutality against that helpless child. Her anger grew at herself that she hadn't seen the signs, hadn't seen the fear in Billy's eyes, eyes that were calling out to her, screaming for help. Billy falling off a horse that Mrs. Appleton said he never had anything to do with, the Appletons avoiding her when Billy had a bruise, Amanda trying to tell her in the little girl's quiet way. She urged the horse on, flying across the country, while memories of the ranch flew with her, Zack falling off the horse into the snow without waking up, racing with Daniel across the hayfield and Bandit riding with Daniel when the snow was deep. The horses hooves pounded the ground as she urged him to run, to run for Billy, to run for all the helpless and brutalized children.

She came to the split at Endless Creek and guessed they'd go left. She scanned the treeless prairie ahead and thought she saw them. Through a small dip she came back up and could see it was someone, a wagon . . . the Appletons! They didn't appear to be hurrying and she thought fast as to how she should handle the situation. She slowed the horse and tried to take all desperation out of her manner. She glanced behind her to see if there was any sign of the marshal or Ned. Nothing.

Billy saw her first and waved. She caught up with the team and Mr. Appleton pulled them to a stop.

"Well, well, what are you doing out here?" he asked and the family greeted her with surprised expressions.

"Hello, I'm sorry I didn't catch you before you left, I was in the shooting competition and lost track of time."

"What do you want?" Mr. Appleton asked.

"Did you win?" Billy asked.

"I don't know, they weren't finished," Gabrielle said, "but it's time for Billy's interview and I thought we could do it in the morning as long as he was in town."

"What interview?" Mrs. Appleton asked.

"It's the policy of the Society to interview the children once a year to see how things are going," Gabrielle said. "It's in the agreement all the parents sign, you signed. I'll have some routine questions for you also, you know, for instance: Is he going to school, is he learning a trade."

"Well we don't need an interview. Billy is doin' just fine," Mr. Appleton said.

"Oh, I can see that," Gabrielle said. Her horse puffed and impatiently clicked its shoes on the rocky road.

"I'm teaching him to be a rancher and farmer and a carpenter for God's sake. Why be bothering me with reports?"

"Because I have to do it as part of my job, it's required of me, I have to get Billy's interview."

"Well, you can do this interview business next week some time," Mr. Appleton said. "We have a lot of chores to catch up on and Billy needs to help."

"I'm sorry Mr. Appleton, but I have to insist. Billy can ride back to town with me and we'll have him back home sometime tomorrow."

"Insist? Insist! He's *our* boy. I'm raising him, and he's going home with us tonight," Mr. Appleton blustered. "We can't be letting things go to ruin to fill out some fancy papers."

Gabrielle slid off her horse, dropped the reins on the road and climbed up on the back wagon wheel.

"How's your pig doing, Billy?" she asked. "I didn't get a very good look at him."

She examined the pig in the homemade crate and moved her feet up on the spokes.

"He's a nice looking pig," she said. "What are you going to do with him?"

"I'm going to grow her up, she's a sow," Billy said. "Maybe breed her."

Gabrielle climbed quickly into the wagon, pushed Billy on his stomach over the heavy canvas tent roll, and pulled his shirt out of his pants. In the center of his back the ugly welts ran about sixteen inches, were deep and wide and left many colors under the boy's skin.

"Is *this* the way you're raising him?" Gabrielle asked fiercely.

"You get off this wagon!" Mr. Appleton shouted and he picked up the reins. "You get the hell off this wagon!"

By the time he got the wagon moving Gabrielle was on her horse. She pulled up alongside the accelerating wagon and shouted.

"Come on, Billy, jump!"

With a puzzled look on his face, Billy tried to stand in the bouncing and careening wagon.

"Come on, Billy, he can't hurt you anymore, jump!"

"Charles! Stop!" Mrs. Appleton shouted, bouncing on the seat and holding on to Amanda.

Billy looked as if he didn't know what to do. Gabrielle kept her horse close, running side by side with the wagon, as they charged pell-mell down the road.

"Jump, Billy. I've got you! Jump!"

Billy climbed onto the edge of the wagon box. Gabrielle held out her hand. Taking a deep breath the boy leaped onto the racing horse's withers and Gabrielle pulled him into the saddle in front of her.

When he realized what had happened Mr. Appleton slowed

the wagon and stopped. Gabrielle kept her distance, turning on the horse with Billy in her arms.

"You put our boy back in the wagon!" Mr. Appleton screamed, "or I'll get you good, Miss Fancy Pants."

"You go ahead. Come morning, Marshal Birt will be looking for you." If it weren't for little Amanda, Gabrielle would have given Appleton a vocal tongue-lashing. "If I ever hear you've hit Amanda we'll take her too."

"You can't do this," Mr. Appleton said, "he's our boy, parents are supposed to discipline their children, it's our God-given duty."

"He don't mean to," Mrs. Appleton said. "He just has a bad temper that gets the best of him sometimes."

"You shut up, woman!" Mr. Appleton shouted.

"Excuses! All excuses!" Gabrielle shouted as she turned the horse for town. "It's never right to beat a child. Never!"

"I'll get you, bitch, I'll get you," Mr. Appleton shouted. Gabrielle and Billy rode off toward the setting sun and she wrapped Billy in her arms. She kept repeating in Billy's ear.

"He'll never hurt you again."

# TWENTY-NINE

BILLY STAYED WITH GABRIELLE OVERNIGHT. Ned never found Marshal Birt and Gabrielle filled Ned in on what happened. Ned informed her that her last shot won the rifle competition and she had a jackpot to claim.

"Who won the quick-draw?" Gabrielle asked.

"Cole Copperman," Ned said. "Some folks figured he missed that last rifle shot on purpose to let the woman win. That didn't set too well with a few of them."

She found Marshal Birt in the morning and showed him the bruise on Billy as well as scars from the past. Jeroboam Birt had three children of his own and he volunteered to accompany Gabrielle when she went out to the Appletons. She would give them legal notice that they were no longer eligible to receive any children from the Society and she'd get Billy's personal things. They rode out mid-morning, the marshal on horseback and Gabrielle with the buggy. She left Billy with the Pearson's at the store and her heart ached knowing that Billy would be reassigned to another district far from the Appletons and far from her.

Marshal Birt was in a sour mood and he hoped Appleton wouldn't give him trouble. He wasn't sure about jurisdiction and what proof he had that Appleton actually administered the blows, though Billy stated clearly that he had. Though obvious to reason, the vigilante hanging that occurred four years ago still gnawed at him. The order of law broke down; no judge, no jury, no evidence. There were questions about whether the ruffian should've been run out of town instead of hung. They'd jumped Jeroboam, blindfolded him, and locked him in his own jail until it was over. Except for a few fistfights and trouble brought on by drunkenness, Halo was usually a quiet, family town.

When they rode into the Appleton yard and dismounted no one appeared from the buildings. The big dog ran to meet them and barked as if to fulfill his duty. They walked toward the house as Mrs. Appleton came out the door.

"Hello, Mrs. Douglas, I figer'd you'd be out. I'm so ashamed." She was crying.

"I'm sorry for you," Gabrielle said, "I hope you will see that it doesn't happen with Amanda."

"Where's your husband?" the marshal asked.

"He's back there somewhere," she said, waving at the out buildings. "Charles!" she called, "Charles!"

The marshal walked toward the barn.

"Does he ever hit you . . . or Amanda?" Gabrielle asked.

"No . . . not Amanda," Mrs. Appleton said. "He means well, he loves her."

Gabrielle turned and caught up to the marshal.

"Appleton! Marshal Birt here!" he shouted, "I have to talk to you!"

As they reached the barn, Appleton came out with a pitchfork in his hands. He glared at Gabrielle.

"You get off my property, you stinkin' witch!"

"Calm down, Appleton," the marshal said, "I'm thinking about putting you in jail."

"What for? That boy's my responsibility, and when he needs to be disciplined it's my job. You ever spank your children, Marshal?"

"You call that spanking?" Gabrielle yelled. "That's cruelty!"

"You get her off my land."

Gabrielle handed the marshal a folded document. The marshal handed it to Appleton. The rancher took it and stuffed it in his bib-overall pocket.

"She's trespassing," he shouted and raised the pitchfork in a threatening way.

Jeroboam Birt was a big heavy man, overweight, slow-moving, but before Gabrielle could blink the marshal snatched the pitchfork from Appleton, broke it over his knee, and with the wood handle, cracked it across Appleton's back with such force that the rancher grunted loudly and dropped to his knees. Gabrielle jumped with the unexpected surprise of it. While Appleton gasped to find his breath, the marshal stood rock still, gripping the oak handle. Appleton's posture looked as if he were praying, or beseeching mercy from the lawman. Appleton found his breath, wheezing, and he looked up at Birt.

"Hurts, don't it," the marshal said and he flipped the handle on the ground.

Appleton struggled to his feet.

"That paper says you can never have anything to do with Billy Bottoms and if you do you're goin' to jail. It says you can't ever have a child again from the Orphan Train Society and if you break any of these rules the Society will press charges. You understand?"

"Yeah," Appleton said, wincing with pain.

"We've come for Billy's things," Gabrielle said to Mrs. Appleton.

"I have them together at the house," Mrs. Appleton said, sniffling.

"Is that all?" the marshal asked, looking at Gabrielle.

"Not quite. We want Billy's pig," Gabrielle said.

"Whoa!" Appleton said. "That's our pig. Billy won it when he was our family."

"No he wasn't," Gabrielle said, "you gave him up as family when you beat him. He won that pig for himself in spite of your cruelty."

"You can't do this," Appleton said and narrowed his eyes at Gabrielle.

The marshal looked at Appleton. "Get the pig."

"Now wait a minute," Mr. Appleton said, "you can't—"

"Get the pig," Birt said as he stepped toward the oak handle.

They rode home, Marshal Birt on his horse and Gabrielle in the buggy with Billy's belongings next to her on the seat and Billy's pig in her lap.

It took over three weeks for the papers to come relocating Billy with a proven, loving family in, of all places, the Montana Territory. Gabrielle waved as the train chugged west away from Halo, wishing she was on the train with him. Her feelings for this child had grown far deeper and wider than she'd wanted, especially in the past three weeks when Billy stayed with her. She'd catch herself watching him out of the corner of her eye, picturing Dewey, and what he would have been like if the tragic accident had not happened. As the train disappeared over the horizon, leaving a drifting black cloud of smoke as the only evidence it'd been there, she couldn't avoid the thought that maybe in some convoluted way she'd damned Billy too. She prayed for Billy, for his safety and success, and hoped for a quirk of fate that might bring them together again.

Gabrielle found it difficult to get back in the routine of visiting families and children and her thoughts of Daniel and the ranch were sometimes overwhelming. Jake Pearson had given Billy eight dollars for the pig, more than it was worth, and Jake had softened the blow by telling Billy he'd keep the pig for a year or so and that Billy ought to come back and see him sometime.

She had almost not noticed that Charles Appleton had tied up his team and sat in the wagon only a short distance up the street from her apartment. When Gabrielle finally saw him he was glaring at her. It was not the first time. She walked the other direction, actually out of her way, to avoid him, and when she looked back he followed her with his stare. Another time she spotted him walking a ways behind her on a busy Saturday. At the next corner she turned amid the horses and wagons and people on foot, and he turned and followed. It angered her. She stopped, turned around and started back toward him. But in the bustle of the traffic he'd disappeared.

Ned had helped so much with Billy. Their friendship was a safety net for Gabrielle. They were back and forth between her apartment and the newspaper shop, she editing his writing, sharing meals, he covering for her when she was on the road all day and Society business needed attending.

One night they were eating late at her table, when she'd been gone all day, and Ned had cooked a stew.

". . . And he's always staring at me," she said, "following me until I get too close. Then he ducks away."

"You think he's doing it on purpose?" he asked.

"Yes, of course. I never used to see him—maybe once in a blue moon. Now it seems it's two or three times a week."

"You want me to say something to him?" Ned asked.

"What would you say? It's not my street, it's not my town. He's not breaking any law."

"Have you told Marshal Birt?"

"No . . . but Jeroboam might put the run on him," she said.

"How about Cole? He's mighty eager to please you."

"No, I don't want to be beholden to him for anything, I don't want him to know anything about my personal life."

"He after you lately?" Ned asked.

"Same old stuff: Would I like to go for a buggy ride along the river? Would I like to go out to the ranch for a picnic? Would I like to go to the Grand for supper?"

"That sounds good," Ned said. "I'd like to go to the Grand Hotel for supper."

"Yes, well, I think it would involve more than supper, or he would have supper served in an upstairs room."

They laughed. Then Gabrielle turned serious.

"When you told me about Billy's bruise, you said something like you were an expert when it came to identifying bruises on the human body. What did you mean?"

"Oh. I was just riled up . . . didn't mean nothin'."

"It sounded like more than that," she said and sensed he was hiding.

"Wasn't that big of Jake Pearson to buy Billy's pig?" Ned asked. "He's a real stand-up guy."

"Yes, we were all becoming attached to that little pig."

She lit two lamps and Ned stood and seemed ready to leave. He paused at the door.

"I lied about the bruises." He sat down. "I can trust you."

"Yes, but don't feel you have to—"

"No, I want to, I need to," he said. He took a deep breath as if he were about to jump off a cliff. "When I was a boy my father used to beat my mother." He paused, caught his breath. "They hid it from me but I'd hear them, I'd eavesdrop, I'd hide. My mother would have the bruises, she'd lie about them, how she got them, as if she were protecting my father, as if she was ashamed of what was happening to her. I hated him, I planned how I would kill him one day. I was growing up. I was afraid of him. He was big and he'd hit me a few times too.

"Then one day I got a crowbar. I hid it in my room. The next time he was beating her I got the piece of iron and went into the kitchen. He had a hold of her hair. I was behind him. With the noise of his rage and her screams he didn't hear me. In that moment my mother's eyes found me and they pleaded with me to help her. I wanted to see his face. I wanted to see the last thing going through his mind. I poked him in the back with the crowbar. As he turned around, still holding my mother by the hair, his face filled with surprise and he started to open his mouth. I only hit him once, on the left side of his skull. It sounded like a shovel hitting a ripe melon. He dropped to the kitchen floor, dead before he got there.

"My mother scraped up all the money she could, I packed a small carpet bag, and I told her I'd write when I could but the law would be watching the mail. I found rides west. I changed my name and I worked my way across the country. I was wanted for murder, still am. I figured there would be hundreds of men named Ned Smith and that's who I've been ever since. I learned how to run a press, worked at two newspapers, in Illinois and St. Louis before I found my way to Halo. I'm a fugitive. As I look back on it I'd probably got off with self-defense. I never saw my mother again. A close friend of hers sent me a letter in St. Louis telling me she was dead. She died with many scars. And that's why I recognized Billy's bruises."

Ned stopped. They sat in silence for a time. Gabrielle put her hand on Ned's shoulder.

"I'm sorry, Ned, so sorry. You deserve to be happy. They ought to give you a medal. Your poor mother."

"Twenty-six years."

"Twenty-six years! You've served your sentence, and then some."

"Do you think God forgives me?"

"Are you glad you did it?" she asked.

"Yes! I am glad."

"Then I don't know about God."

Gabrielle woke. She had had a long day and got to bed at dusk. Something woke her. She lay quietly, listening. Pitch dark. The town was quiet, it must have been after midnight. There! She heard it again. Something familiar. The creak in her outside stair. She held her breath. Who would be on her stairs at this time of the night? Not Ned.

She slid out of bed and tiptoed barefoot. As she moved through the kitchen she picked up her butcher knife. She stood silently. A dog barked down the street. A light wind ruffled the kitchen curtain. She paused. There, again. She heard it. On the stair. A cold sweat broke out on the back of her neck and forehead. She was afraid to open the door and afraid not to. She lifted the latch on the door and opened it slowly. The rusty hinges squeaked more loudly than she remembered. She stepped out on the landing and gazed down the stairway. It took a minute for her eyes to adjust to the darkness. Nothing! No one! She scanned what of the town she could see from there. She had a strange feeling that someone had been there, on the stairs, a presence, like the scent of an animal.

The next morning she woke Ned by banging on his living quarters door. She had a long trip that day, way south along the Broken Knife.

"So you weren't moving around last night?" Gabrielle asked as Ned, in his pajamas, wiped the sleep out of his eyes.

"No, you said good-night early and went up to bed," Ned said.

"And you didn't come up later?"

"Nope, I set a little type and then read for a while."

"Do you walk in your sleep?" she asked.

"Not that I know of." He laughed.

"I've got to get going. Maybe it was nothing," she said. "See you tonight."

"Bring me some news," he said.

"I'll try."

\* \* \*

A week later Gabrielle found herself riding out to the Wheelers' ranch north of town with sad news to deliver. It was the part of this work that she hated and she was well aware of it because her own sadness lingered so close to the surface and was so easily triggered. She'd visited the Wheelers twice since coming to Halo, the twin sisters who'd been placed there almost two years ago, Tina and Tilly, now eight, were likeable and energetic girls. They were thankful for their home with the Wheelers, who had no children of their own, but they longed for the day when they'd be reunited with their sick mother who remained behind in Chicago. Gabrielle imagined how difficult it must have been for the twins' mother to have to enroll them with the Orphan Train Society when she was no longer well enough to take care of them and wave good-bye as they went off on the train west. She wrote letters to them often and they had learned to write letters in return. For all of them it was a sustaining hope for the future that the mother would recover and be well enough to come west to be reunited with her girls. And now Gabrielle carried the message that slammed the door on that hope.

Gabrielle knew her sorrow had to do with Maddy and the distance that had come between them, once twin girls who kept nothing from the other, whose hearts beat with the same rhythm, who could finish the other's sentence before it was out of her mouth. She never could explain to Maddy why she abandoned the family and ranch. She never could explain why she'd run off and left her twin in the dark, giving up their bond of closeness, betraying their deep understanding of the other, shattering the intimacy they'd known since they were learning to walk. Gabrielle knew she'd hurt Maddy deeply, cut her out of her life, and left her confused and estranged.

As she rode into the yard Gabrielle felt the lead in her chest slide down into her stomach. She tied the horse and walked toward the many outbuildings that were a testimony to how long the Wheelers had been here and how well they were prospering.

Mrs. Wheeler came out a side door on the house.

"Mrs. Douglas! How nice to see you."

"Hello, but please call me Gabrielle."

"What a nice surprise," Mrs. Wheeler said, taking Gabrielle's hand, "the girls will be happy to see you."

"No." Gabrielle sucked in a breath. "No, I bring great sorrow."

Mrs. Wheeler dropped Gabrielle's hand.

"Oh, dear, oh, Lord, is it—"

"Yes, their mother's dead."

Mrs. Wheeler stepped back a pace and held her hands over her heart. "That poor woman. Won't never see her darlings again."

"Where are the girls?" Gabrielle asked.

"They're out in the garden, by the horse barn."

She pointed off to the east.

"Do you want to—" Gabrielle said.

"No . . . no, I think you better," Mrs. Wheeler said. "I don't think I can right now."

Gabrielle shaded her eyes with her hand and looked off toward the horse barn. She managed a slow deep breath. Then she told herself she could do this, that she was well-practiced in the art of bringing sorrow and sadness to those around her, that she could temper the blow with kindness and tenderness and love.

"Tina! Tilly!" Mrs. Wheeler called. "Girls!"

At first nothing moved. Then from around the horse barn came the twin girls, laughing, racing together straight into the awful news.

They arrived in a little cloud of dust.

"Look who's here," Mrs. Wheeler said.

"Hello, Tina," Gabrielle said, forcing a smile. "Hello, Tilly."

Tilly was the shy one, Tina the ringleader.

"Hello," the girls chorused, obviously delighted with the company. They were identical and only by their distinct personalities was Gabrielle able to tell them apart.

"Mrs. Douglas, ah . . . Gabrielle would like to talk with you," Mrs. Wheeler said. "I'll be in the house." She glanced at Gabrielle and turned for the house.

Gabrielle quickly surveyed the ranch and picked her ground, a wooden bench beside a large stock tank and windmill.

"Let's sit over here," she said and they followed her to the windmill. They settled on the peeled-log bench and watched Gabrielle's eyes for signs.

"Tina, you ever swim in the tank?" Gabrielle asked, her voice deserting her as she found a way to identify who was who.

"Yes, when it's really hot," Tina said. "Sometimes after dark."

"You two must have a lot of fun fooling people, your teacher, your friends, your boyfriends. You're the spittin' image of each other."

"Tina has a boyfriend," Tilly said.

"Don't neither."

"Do so."

"Don't neither."

"Tommy Brown, at school, you're always brightening up to him," Tilly said. "I see you."

"Did you ever think of fooling Tommy Brown, Tilly?" Gabrielle asked. "Like sitting with him at lunch or something. I couldn't do that with my twin sister, we didn't look anything alike."

"Sometimes our mother got us mixed up," Tina said. "She told us that when we were babies she'd paint one of my big toes and as we grew up she'd cut my hair real short."

Gabrielle gathered her strength.

"I'm here to tell you about your mother." She took hold of each of the girl's hands. "Your mother died, Tina, Tilly. Your mother passed away."

The girls sat stunned for a moment, looking quickly into each other's eyes. Gabrielle held their hands and found it hard to breathe.

"She's dead?" Tina asked.

"Yes, she died over three weeks ago," Gabrielle said.

Simultaneously they began to cry. Tina reached over and wrapped her arms around Tilly, comforting her.

Gabrielle let them sob and found herself fighting back tears like a good Rockhammer.

"Why did she die?"

"Her lungs gave out, she couldn't fight any longer."

"Where is Mother?" Tilly asked.

"She was buried in Chicago," Gabrielle said.

"She's in heaven with God," Tina said.

"Can we write Mother a letter?" Tilly asked.

"Yes, if you like," Gabrielle said.

"When I grow up I'm going to go to Chicago and find her grave," Tina said.

"Yes, that would be nice. Never forget how much your mother did for you, how hard it must have been for her to let you go to this good life, knowing how much she'd miss you. She loved you very much."

Gabrielle sat with the girls for some time, knowing she had to leave soon, that she'd be caught by the night and the darkness. She went with the girls into the house and included Mrs. Wheeler in their grieving. She turned down an offer to eat supper and stay over—she wanted to get back to town that night.

"I hope I'll see you soon," Gabrielle said while untying her horse. "When you get to town come see me," she told the twins and hugged each of them. Then she swung up on Prancer and turned for town.

"Greet Mr. Wheeler for me," she called as she nudged the horse into a smooth run.

"We will." Mrs. Wheeler said. Gabrielle saw her mouth the words "thank you."

The sun was flirting with the mountain peaks to the west. She'd have to ride an hour or more in the dark.

She pushed Prancer while they had daylight and she knew she'd have no moon. Several times she spooked game, hearing them bolting in the shadows or catching a glimpse ahead on the road. Relentlessly darkness took the land and she slowed to an even trot. She felt drained after bringing the sad news to the twins, knowing her own experience contributed to her pain and how much the twin girls reminded her of her childhood.

It took some minutes for Gabrielle to realize she was hearing an echo of her horse's hooves from somewhere behind her. She strained to hear. Was she imagining it? No, she wasn't. It was there, the occasional click of the iron shoe against a rock, the cadence of the horse's weight thudding against the ground. She pulled back to a slow walk. She listened. The horse behind her matched the slow walk. She prodded Prancer into a canter and the pursuing horse copied him step for step. She reined her horse to a stop. She listened. She held her breath. There wasn't a sound from behind her, only the night noises of critters: an owl, frogs, crickets.

"Hello there!" she called. "Who's there?"

Nothing. She nudged Prancer into a trot and continued into the darkness along the road. Was it gone? No, it was back, closer, matching her pace. She knew it would be dangerous to run for long, hard to see the margins of the narrow road, she could fall, break the horse's leg. She thought of stopping and moving quietly off the road a distance. The horse was closer. She pulled the rifle from its scabbard. Then she could see a faint light. She recognized Halo in the dark. She spurred Prancer and galloped across the fine wooden bridge that spanned The Broken Knife River, into the comfort and safety of town.

Gabrielle rode to the edge of town and turned her horse beside the first building. She stayed mounted and she waited to see who would come across the bridge out of the darkness.

No one ever did.

# THIRTY

CLAIRE WAITED AT THE ENTRANCE to the mine for over an hour with the letter in her sweating hand, dreading her role as messenger of woe. They wouldn't allow her on the lift and she didn't want Daniel to get the tragic news from some stranger. She had her own turmoil to deal with, her life tipped upside down. Her heart told her it was the beginning of the end. Etta had fallen in love and planned to sell the boardinghouse, marry, and move to California with her new husband. Now twenty-one, Claire hadn't been invited to go along. She had the knowledge and experience to run the boardinghouse but she didn't have the money to buy it. Her mother's husband-to-be didn't think the boardinghouse would be a good investment for them at such a distance and Claire suspected that the man was more interested in investments than he was in her mother. To think of leaving in the midst of it all was heartbreaking. In every way she'd tried to conceal her love for Daniel but she always knew he'd go back to the ranch.

Unsuspecting, Daniel shuffled out of the mine with a swarm of miners and the day's accumulated grime. Like a great black mouth the mine regurgitated its hodgepodge as they came above the grass, surprised that the sun was still bright in the sky or that they were yet alive. She ran to him amid the weary parade and delivered the deadly letter.

"Claire," was all he could manage and his expression slid from a surprised grin to quickly darkening worry. He stepped aside the flow of miners and tucked his lunch bucket under his arm. With sooty fingers he pulled the letter from the opened envelope.

"I hope you don't mind," she said. "I opened it because I guessed it was important news from your family."

"Thanks, Claire. I don't mind."

He read the short message.

*Father is dead. Come quickly.*

Daniel staggered slightly, stood unbalanced, staring at the five words on a piece of paper as if he couldn't believe them, understand them, as if these were words meant for someone else, words flying with the curvature of the earth, an arrow shaft to the heart.

"I'm so sorry, Daniel, so sorry."

She wrapped her arms around him tentatively and held him, for the moment she was the stronger of the two. He had a hard time breathing and he sucked great gulps of air. He dropped his lunch pail and held on to her as if she were the only sturdy tree in this wind storm.

"He was in good health," Daniel said, clinging to her, "still full of life, strong as an ox, he could work alongside me all day. He can't be dead, he can't be, there's some mistake, the devil's joke."

It crossed Daniel's mind like a distant flash of lightning. Did God have a hand in this, had God found him four hundred feet underground and settled accounts? If so, for how much did He hold them accountable, he and Gabrielle? What ransom would it cost them, how long must they pay?

Daniel and Claire stood holding each other as the worn out miners filed by, some wisecracking, some silently, some calling out encouragement to this man and woman who were standing in the oblivion of grief.

Daniel rode Buck hard all the way home, as if he got there quickly his father would still be alive when he arrived. He slept an hour or two at times, sometimes in shelter, sometimes in the wild, sometimes asleep and nearly falling off Buck more than once. He found food in the towns or from isolated ranches far off the beaten path and he often forgot to eat, nearly forgot to let Buck feed.

The family gathered around Daniel as their last hope, as if he could do the impossible and bring his father back, as if he had the miracle to turn back time. Elizabeth looked worn down, Maddy was inconsolable, and Zack wept openly. Wart took it as hard as if Jeremiah were his long lost father and in a way he was. They sent out word for Gabrielle but had heard nothing from her yet, still believing she was living in St. Paul. They buried Jeremiah beside Abraham and Martha and Alfred in the family plot on a small ridge above the river with a grand view of the Rockhammer Valley.

"How did it happen?" Daniel asked when the men had migrated to the porch so as not to further upset the women.

"I was riding back from the high meadow when I saw Father's horse just standing," Zack said.

"Yeah, I was on the other side of the river and I couldn't see Jeremiah anywhere," Wart said, "but his horse was just standing there, not grazing. Something didn't look right."

They had found a small Indian pony for Wart, an animal he could mount by himself, and they had a saddler fashion a rig that he could ride. After a few tentative tries Wart had been growing braver and braver, riding all over the ranch.

"It took me awhile to get over there," Wart said, "had to go back to the gravel bar. When I rode up to his horse I found him sprawled in the grass on his back. I tried to get him to open his eyes but he was dead. He still had his hat on, but he was dead. I remembered thinking that his hat shoulda come off. Then I saw that Dancer had a broken front leg."

"Father was dead," Zack said, "the horse must have stumbled and pitched him. When I pulled off his hat I could see he had an ugly blow on the side of his forehead."

"Yeah and his hat was on backward kinda, musta happened when he fell," Wart said.

"How long had he been dead?" Daniel asked.

"He'd been dead for several hours or so, as far as we could figure," Zack said. "He'd been gone since early breakfast."

"But he never galloped when he rode," Daniel said, "he always took it slow. A walking horse, even with a broken leg, can't pitch a rider far if at all. Not Dancer. He's as gentle as our milk cow."

"We put Dancer down," Zack said.

"Take me out there, where you found him," Daniel said.

"Right now?"

"Right now," Daniel said.

They saddled their horses and rode out, through the big meadow, along avalanche ridge, where Abraham died, along The River That Rolls Rocks, two miles or more into the valley. Dancer's body, eaten by coyote and ravens had become a sad skeletal reminder of the animal the family had enjoyed for years. They dismounted and Wart showed Daniel where he found Jeremiah's body. They stood there in silence as if they were at the grave, no one willing to break the prayerful mood. Then Daniel knelt and examined the horse's broken leg. He shook his head slowly without speaking.

"What's wrong?" Zack asked.

"Never seen a leg broken like that, don't see how he could have done it. Looks like he ran into something solid, like a rock or stump, but he'd have to be covering ground." He stood and waved his hand over the land. "Nothing around here like that."

Then he started walking in a larger and larger circle, his head down, his eyes riveted on the ground, searching. The other two followed Daniel's lead though they had no idea what they were looking for. Daniel circled further and further from the horse carcass.

To the north about twenty paces Daniel stopped and knelt. In a gravelly area where there were small springs bleeding out onto the ground there were small patches of clay. The Blackfeet had used it to make bowls and such. In the clay there was one clear print of a horseshoe, a horseshoe that Daniel had never seen, a horseshoe they'd never used on the Rockhammer Ranch's horses. Without a word, Daniel stood and kept searching in an ever widening circle. After close to an hour he called them in.

"Let's go," he said and they mounted and rode away without Dancer, the only one who could tell them what had happened.

That evening they gathered around the fireplace and talked.

"A few days after Jeremiah died, Henry Weebow came all the way to the house to tell me how sorry he was," Elizabeth said. "I asked him how he found out and he said word had gotten out. There were two men with him but they stayed out on the road. I'm sure that one of them was Henry's son, Ben."

"If I'd seen Ben Weebow on the place I'da run him off," Zack said.

"He told me that he'd seen Jeremiah in town," Elizabeth said, "and Jeremiah told him he could have an easement to build a road."

"Did he have anything in writing?" Daniel asked.

"No, he didn't," Elizabeth said, "and I've gone through everything on his desk."

"I don't believe him," Daniel said and the others agreed.

"He and Jeremiah were some of the first ones out here," Elizabeth said. "They had been friends way back in the early years. Maybe . . ."

"No way," Daniel said. "Grandfather Abraham made a promise to the Blackfeet and kept it all those years. Father told us about it many times and he kept that promise all his life. He'd never break it for Henry Weebow's road. And we're not going to break it either."

They all nodded as if they recognized that Daniel was now the head of the family, the ramrod of Rockhammer Ranch.

"You're damn right we're not," Zack said.

"Watch your language, Zack," Elizabeth said.

"Well, they're working on the mountain as if they knew they'd get the road." Zack said.

"Yeah, we can hear them dynamite sometimes," Wart said.

An oppressive gloom settled on the room. When it got late and they were all talked out, Daniel grabbed a heavy blanket. "I'm going out to the grave," he said.

"Want company?" Zack asked.

"No . . . thanks . . . I better go alone."

"I miss him too you know," Zack snapped the words. "I love him too."

"Don't take it personally, Little Brother, I have a lot to think through, I'll be awhile."

"I'm not *Little* Brother, I'm your brother. Wart is Little Brother. I'm taller than you and I weigh more so I'm not *Little* Brother."

"All right, Brother." Daniel smiled sadly and nodded. "I want to be alone with Father but you can come along if you want."

"No, no, you go ahead," Zack relented.

"You want to play checkers?" Wart asked Zack.

As they headed for the kitchen Wart spoke as if it were a badge of belonging. "Remember, I'm Little Brother."

They both laughed.

The night had turned dark with heavy clouds resting on the mountain peaks and ridges. Daniel walked the short distance from the house, stumbling several times on sagebrush and uneven ground. He found the graves, fenced to keep the cattle off them. The iron gate squeaked when he swung it open and he found the fresh earth heaped over Jeremiah's grave. At first he stood, his hat in his hand. Slowly, under cover of night, a male Rockhammer, against the family's acceptable behavior, gave his heart permission to allow his dam to burst. The sorrow stormed over his barricade as he sobbed and shouted and screamed in a torrent of grief and anger and guilt.

When he could weep no more he wrapped the blanket around him and sat beside the grave. He couldn't help but believe that in the scheme of things he had something to do with his father's death. That this was something between him and God. If he'd stayed on the ranch and worked alongside Jeremiah this wouldn't have happened. If he hadn't fallen in love with Gabrielle, he probably would have found his life here. And yet, in the teeth of this pain and inconsolable grief, he thought of her, wondered if she'd gotten word of this yet, if she'd come home, praying that she was well and safe and still carried her love for him.

He told Jeremiah the truth, all of it, asking for his forgiveness even if God would never forgive the two of them and their love for each other, the tenacious arms of love. He sat huddled beside the grave until dawn peeked over the mountains to the east. He stood stiffly and carried the blanket back to the house where his mother waited for him with worry in her face.

Elizabeth got Daniel current on some developments on the ranch. Wart had taken Jeremiah's death very hard. A few days before he had been alone with Elizabeth at the house and shared some shocking news with her. She told Daniel that before Wart joined the Rockhammer family he had been wanted by the law. Wart felt sure that the law back in the Dakotas thought he had murdered somebody. He had told Jeremiah the truth and, now that Jeremiah was gone, Wart wanted the family to know the story. They decided to wait until Daniel was home, so this very night, before Daniel left for Butte in the morning, Wart wanted to get his story off his chest. Daniel found himself mildly amused and looked forward to it. Everyone loved Wart's storytelling and this ought to be a good one.

The other urgent matter Elizabeth spoke to Daniel about was the possibility of adding yet another person to the Rockhammer family. Elizabeth had seen a church member in town and he had told her that they were expecting to adopt a child; indeed, the child—an older boy—was training west at this time. His wife had suddenly taken ill and he wasn't sure if they could claim him when he got off the train. Elizabeth learned the boy was fourteen and had recently lived with a farm family. She and Jeremiah had been seriously considering giving this young man a home at the Rockhammer but now, with Jeremiah's mysterious death, it was either the craziest idea or the smartest. Daniel figured they could use all the help they could get and it crossed his mind that there was strength in numbers.

"When does he arrive?" Daniel asked.

"Likely tomorrow," Elizabeth said.

"I'll go to Butte and wind up my affairs there," he said. "I'll be back in a week or two."

"You're coming home?"

"Yes, Mother, I'm coming home. Don't worry, we'll be all right."

"Yes, maybe we'll be all right, but how do I go on living without him at my side, the heartbeat of my life, without my dearest friend?"

"We learn to carry on," Daniel said, hugging her, "like Rockhammers."

He held her tightly and for the first time noticed a frailty in her that distressed him, this strong woman who had given him life and raised him up through all those difficult years and against all odds on the Rockhammer.

"And I worry about you, wasting those years in Butte. I couldn't understand, your brother and sisters couldn't understand. Every time I'd see you or hear from you I'd pray you were telling us you had found the love of a woman. Where is your heart, Daniel? Have you buried it in those godforsaken mines or on this distant isolated ranch? Is there no one for you to love and share your life with?"

He wanted to tell her everything he'd just confessed to Jeremiah but he couldn't. He knew he never could.

Wrapping up this conversation with his mother, he asked, "What is the young boy's name, the one coming to the ranch?"

"Billy," Elizabeth said. "Billy Bottoms."

# THIRTY-ONE

*Wart's Story*

BACK WHEN THEY WERE DRIFTING, Wart and Stella, the elephant, were utterly lost, crossing hot, dry, breath-sucking ground without overtaking a road or sighting a homestead in any direction. The arid land looked like tombstones for some prehistoric beasts, twisted and carved by a thousand saltwater seas. It appeared to Wart as if God and the devil had a rock fight and the devil won.

Wart could see forest-covered hills miles off on the horizon but in this sunburnt land all they found was sagebrush, cactus, and scattered native grass turned into sun-cured hay. They had gone without water days on end and while Stella fed on the skimpy grass Wart broke open cactus with rocks like he'd heard tell about and sucked the moist sometimes bitter inner meat. Since coming on this barren land they hadn't hidden much during daylight hours although if they found shade under some jutting rock ledge they'd pause for a few hours during the hottest part of the day. Traveling at night had become too dangerous.

Step by dusty step fear hatched and grew in Wart as he wondered where he could ever bring Stella into safe harbor. Who would take her? Who would keep her and care for her? What would become of her? Starvation? He could imagine ravens and hawks and coyote picking clean her body. What had he got them into? Then as a partial answer to his prayers they stumbled on a creek that ran full of water. Stella helped Wart down and they both drank until they could hold no more. Petrified of water, Wart would not go near the refreshing flow so Stella, as if sensing Wart's dilemma, sprayed him as if he were on fire, both of them shouting sounds of happiness and joy, enjoying the soaking in this scorching inferno. Wart decided to follow the creek until they found their way out of that geologic cemetery and reached the forgiving forest on the far distant hills.

They'd only traveled an hour down the creek when they climbed out of a steep ravine and found themselves on a wide level plateau covered with burnt grass and completely treeless. Like a beautiful remnant of lush prairie that had somehow escaped the ravages of the local rock war, it rose somewhat higher than the adjoining land and was surrounded by sharp rock ledges. As Wart scanned this surprising discovery, guessing it to be several hundred acres, he saw what appeared to be a covered wagon way to the north edge. With some excitement he threw caution aside and urged Stella to hurry. As they closed the distance Wart could see two people coming toward them from the wagon, waving what appeared to be a white dish towel. Wart thought their mannerisms were those of wounded soldiers surrendering to the enemy across the field of battle, giving up the fight.

When they were within a few hundred yards, the two people, a man and a woman, stopped abruptly and quit waving the white towel. Wart and Stella kept coming until they could see the fright on the weather-hardened faces of the two.

"Hello, hello, we're glad to see you," Wart said in his graveled voice as Stella helped him down.

The couple, appearing as though they'd been in a shipwreck, stood utterly dumbfounded. Under his wind-beaten, wide-brimmed hat the middle-aged man's salt and pepper beard looked like a scalded hedgehog. He used a carved pine crutch as he hobbled on his right leg. The woman stared wide-eyed out of her battered bonnet and hardened sun-baked face, her long gray dress trail-worn and frazzled above beaten leather boots.

"I'm Wart and this is my friend, Stella. We're on our way west and we're bald-faced lost."

The man tipped his dusty hat and observed the strange little man and elephant as if he couldn't believe his eyes. He shook his head and glanced at his wife. By his expression you couldn't tell which of the two, elephant or dwarf, amazed him most. Finally he gathered his wits.

"I'm Frank Hobbs and this is my wife, Tilly. Where on earth did you come by an elephant?"

"I bought him from a circus back in Dakota and we're looking for a place to settle. Are you settling here?"

"Heavens to Betsy no," Hobbs said, gaining his equilibrium. "We're just trying to get through this hell hole, don't know how we got tangled in here in the first place."

"You listened to that know-it-all back in Nebraska," Tilly said.

"It's like a maze," Frank said, swinging an arm out over the landscape.

"That jackass couldn't find his way out of the outhouse," Tilly said, shaking her head, "and Frank here listened to him, a short-cut, save us three weeks. Huh!"

Ignoring Tilly, Frank carried on.

"Ya keep on ending up back where ya started from. Never saw such a place. We lost a horse, broken leg, and our boy has gone to buy one."

Tilly stood gaping at Stella. "Is he dangerous?" she asked.

"Stella is a she, a lovely little girl, wouldn't you say? She's as sweet and kind and loving as you'll ever find in any human. And smart, she's awfully smart."

Wart stroked her trunk and she bowed her head to the amazement of the Hobbs. Wart thought they looked too old to be traveling by wagon across country, or was it that they appeared too fragile, maybe a couple taking their last stab at life. Tilly stood tall and thin, her face gaunt, framed in her floppy gray bonnet and her hands callused and gnarled. She appeared to be a woman who smiled easily but at present found it hard.

"Is there a road through here, are we near a town?" Wart asked.

"No, no road as such," Frank said, wearing his leather suspenders over his smudged and frayed long-sleeved undershirt despite the temperature.

"How in tarnation did you get this far with a wagon?"

"We just picked our way. We think there's a town a ways north of here, that's the way our boy went looking. Should be a town called Sandstone. The boy took our map with him. We expect him anytime now."

"When did you last eat?" Tilly asked.

"Oh, yes, what's the matter with me?" Frank murmured. "It must have been the elephant to make me forget my manners."

"Or the dwarf," Wart said and laughed.

They all laughed. Frank waved his arm.

"Come on over to our camp and have something to eat?"

"That would be real neighborly, thank you," Wart said.

They turned and walked through the dry yellow grass and the summer blue sky. Tilly still wore amazement on her face and walked a bit behind the elephant.

"A circus! Land sakes, that's wonderful," Tilly said as her face relaxed into a smile. "I saw a circus once back home, elephants and all. How on earth did you get here?"

"We don't rightly know, we're hoping someone can point out a road or a town or a ranch."

"Well, Wally will be back soon," Frank said, "and he'll be able to steer you in the right direction."

"How old is your boy?"

"Wally? . . . ah, he's twenty-three, turned twenty-three a week 'fore we left," Frank said. "Good with horses."

At the wagon they fed Wart until he could eat no more. The main course was a stringy rabbit and oatmeal. They had a good camp, a good supply of sagebrush stacked by their fire circle, a spring with fresh cold water nearby, a toilet pit a ways off the ledge, and they bedded down in the wagon. Their remaining wagon horse seemed to be doing well on the sunburnt grass. Their boy, Wally, had taken their saddle horse in his search for help. Stella grazed nearby while Wart sat in the shade under the wagon, visiting with Frank and Tilly.

"Did you hurt yourself when you lost the horse?" Wart asked.

"Oh, no, did it crossing a rocky hollow, wagon started slipping and about to capsize. I jumped off and tried to hold her upright and get her over the rock. The team panicked some and they let the wagon pull them back, the jolt knocked me into the rocks. Wally got 'em straightened out and drove 'em over the hump, kept the wheel from goin' over my legs. It's my hip that's bunged up."

"Did you break it?" Wart asked.

"Mighta . . . mighty sore . . . seems to be gettin' a little better."

\* \* \*

Wart was dozing when it hit him like a bugle's fanfare.

*Wait a minute! Wait a minute! This isn't a breakdown, this is a settlement, this is a homestead!*

The condition of their camp had been shouting at him!

"How long has Wally been gone?" Wart asked.

"Oh . . . we don't rightly know, we've kinda lost count. Lost our calendar in a river crossing a ways back but Tilly's been keeping track. How long's it been, Tilly?"

Tilly tucked up her long dress a bit and knelt beside the wagon tongue. There were notches carved in the worn wood. Tilly counted.

"Best as we can tell he's been gone thirty-seven days," she said, "give or take a few."

"Thirty-seven days!" Wart nearly gagged with shock. "Mother Mary! Shouldn't you be out lookin' for him?"

"Can't," Frank said. "Told him we'd wait right here till he showed up. Besides, can't move the wagon without another horse. All we can do is wait. Wally's a good boy. He'll be coming any day now . . . any day now."

"Thirty-seven days!" Wart said as he looked into the wagon. "How is your food holdin' out?"

"We're stretchin' it best we can," Tilly said, recounting the notches on the wagon tongue.

Wart felt guilty for eating their rationed supply after waiting here for their boy for over a month.

Tilly sat on the one chair they had beside the fire ring. Wart was amazed at their calm, stuck out there God only knows where, eating up their food supply without a team to pull them back the way they'd come or at least to some form of civilization.

"Don't you think you ought to go lookin' for your boy before you starve?"

"You know, I was surprised at the game out here," Frank said. "Wouldn't guess there was a scrawny Jack rabbit within ten miles, but there is and we've been eatin' fairly often. I've my .30 caliber Winchester and plenty of ammunition. We've et antelope, deer, and a young bear that tasted just like pork."

Wart paused for a time, thinking. Tilly and Frank appeared to him as folks who could be eaten and swallowed by this land.

"Frank, I don't want to stick my nose where it don't belong, but maybe the three of us could go find your boy together and get your wagon on its way again. Something mighta happened to Wally, maybe he can't come back for some reason, broke a leg or something."

Wart didn't want to name it but he knew in this land Wally could well be long dead.

"We talked about doin' that but we didn't want to split up any further," Frank said. "Wally knows where we is. We don't know where he is. If I go lookin' fer Wally then Tilly won't know where I is and Wally won't know where I is and Tilly don't know where Wally is and it'd just git worse and worse."

"But you can't stay here much longer. Winter's comin' and the cold and the wind will drive you off this flat and you'll run out of food. Maybe the three of us could go lookin' for Sandstone or whatever town is out there."

"Wally's a good boy," Tilly said, "he'll be here soon. He'd never let us down."

"Did he have much money with him?"

"Yes, sir, enough to buy a good horse and some supplies," Frank said.

Wart didn't want to worry them with his well-developed cynicism, but maybe Wally saw a way out, to take the money and their saddle horse and just ride away.

"You get along good with Wally?"

"What do you mean?" Frank asked.

"Oh, you know, some youngsters forget their responsibilities and just wander off, follow a whim, lose track of time."

"Don't have to worry about Wally," Tilly said, "He's as reliable as the sun."

Wart and Stella stayed another night, trying to convince the Hobbses to go look for Wally who was as reliable as the sun. And then, when they awoke the next morning, like waking from a dream, they understood the pickle they were in. They covered the wagon with sage brush they chopped in the ravine, packed their belongings tightly under the folded canvas, and loaded what food and clothing they could on their remaining horse and on Stella. With his bad hip Frank had to ride the horse and Tilly and Wart rode Stella. Off they went, down into the tangled rock and carved landscape. a strange caravan slowly heading north, the lost searching for the lost. Most of the day atop Stella, Tilly beamed her bright joyful smile across the land like a young girl whose wildest wish had come true.

They pushed on all day, sometimes having to backtrack when they found their way into a dead-end canyon, going in circles and recognizing ground they'd covered an hour ago, quickly getting their hopes up when they'd cross a trail until they realized it was a game trail. They found drinkable water only once, a spring running out of a red rock outcrop as though it were bleeding. Just when their spirits were lowest and the sun was sinking on the horizon, they came out of the tortured rock into prairie grassland and cottonwood trees. For the first time all day they could see some distance and with a renewed hope their pace quickened. Shortly before dark they cut across a road—not a game trail but a double track made by wagon wheels.

Wart convinced them to pull far off the road for the night since they had no way of knowing what they were getting into. The night air cooled and they sat around a small fire drinking coffee and eating cornmeal mush with hard biscuits. Wart felt it was a good time to level with the Hobbs. He told them he was wanted by the law for grand larceny, how he'd stolen Stella from the circus, and that he should separate himself from them when they run into people, that he and Stella would stay out of sight until they found out where their boy was.

The Hobbs couldn't believe Wart could be wanted by the law and offered to help him in any way they could. Tilly clung to an optimistic outlook about the whereabouts of Wally and she wanted to sleep on Stella to get off the ground because she was terrified of rattlers and usually slept in the wagon. Stella helped her into a small cottonwood where she propped herself in a clutch of branches in a way in which she could sleep. They fell to sleep quickly, the men on the ground in bedrolls, like a bizarre bunch of highway men: a man on a crutch, a woman sleeping in a tree, and a dwarf snuggled against an elephant, as though lurking beside the road for unsuspecting victims.

Morning came quickly and they were on the road at dawn.

Wart and Stella allowed them to go ahead out of sight with the understanding that Tilly and Frank would come back and tell them what they'd found. As the day came on so did the sparse local population and Wart led Stella far off the road. Only a few used the road, on horseback, in a wagon, one buggy. Nearly an hour later Tilly found them out of sight moving parallel to the road.

They had talked to a rancher who informed them they were about four miles from town. Sandstone. No, the man hadn't seen Wally. Wart told Tilly that he and Stella would come on across country until they were a mile or more from town. He'd find a good spot to hide Stella in the gravelly hardscrabble foothills that rose to the west where it was unlikely anyone would be trying to farm. Tilly hurried off to catch up with Frank.

They say that Frank and Tilly paused on a rise looking down on the dusty little town of Sandstone. Frank rode on their draft horse and she walked beside him and they both held their breath in anticipation of finding their boy. The road ran down the hill and right through the middle of the town, about a dozen blocks of crude and rugged buildings constructed out of log and sawed lumber. The town squatted on nearly level ground in a small basin at the edge of a large valley that ran off to the north, surrounded by rocky foothills and snow-covered mountains.

They searched up and down the main street asking people if they'd seen Wally. They had no luck until one man suggested they try the livery stable. They didn't find Wally there but they found their saddle horse in a corral. It took some time to find the man who ran the livery but when they did they were shocked and confused.

"That's our horse," Frank told the man.

"That's our horse," Tilly repeated, "had him eleven years, our boy broke him, I've got a scar on my leg he gave me."

"I don't know about that," the skinny fidgety man said. "All I know is one night he belongs to some stranger who wants me to keep him here overnight, that one there too," the livery man pointed at another draft horse they'd never seen, "and the next morning they've arrested the fellow and locked him up for stealing horses, say the horses belonged to the Jarco brothers and I'm supposed to keep them here as evidence until the judge comes through."

"That's our boy, those are our horses," Frank said.

"Where do they have the boy locked up?" Tilly asked.

"Down behind the Chinese laundry and cafe. Ain't much of a jail."

They hurried the three blocks and found a man sitting on the porch of a square one-story building that had a sign above the door. JAIL. Several chickens pecked around on the porch and the man in his tipped-back chair dozed in the warming sun.

"Excuse me," Frank said in a loud voice.

The man bolted upright and almost fell off the porch. Tilly held on to the horse's lead rope as if they were about to lose them all.

"Just catching a nap," the man said, recovering his balance and hoisting up his pants a bit. He wore a black mustache and had a friendly face with large puppy-dog eyes and looked to be in his thirties.

"What can I do for you?" he asked with a smile.

"Are you the sheriff?" Frank asked, bracing himself with his crutch and holding his rifle under one arm.

"Nope, ain't got no sheriff. I's the deputy."

"How can you be a deputy if there ain't no sheriff?" Frank asked.

"I's a deputy for the U.S. Marshall."

"Can we see him?"

"Not unless you've got awful good eyes," the man said, laughing and slapping his thigh. "He's in Rainbow today, don't know when he'll show up."

"Can we see the man you've locked up?" Tilly asked.

"You his kin or something?"

"I'm his pa, this is his ma."

"Oh, sorry to hear that," the deputy said.

"Why're you sorry that we're his folks?" Tilly asked.

"'Cause that young fella's goin' ta hang."

His words were an unexpected punch to the stomach. Both of the Hobbs lost their breath. Tilly recovered first.

"Oh no, you can't hang our boy, he ain't done nothing wrong, he's good boy, a good boy."

"They caught 'im stealin' horses," the deputy said. "The judge'll hang 'im fer sure. He don't cotton to no horse thieves."

"Can we see him, talk to him?" Frank asked.

The deputy lifted his sweat-stained hat and scratched his head.

"Well, I guess it won't do no harm." He nodded at Frank who still carried his Winchester under one arm. "You'll have to leave that out here."

The deputy led them through a small office and opened a heavy wood door. The town of Sandstone had two iron cells. One had a drunk man sleepin' it off. The other had Wally Hobbs, their son. When he saw them he jumped off the narrow cot and grabbed a hold of the bars.

"Ma! Pa! I knew you'd come! I'm in trouble."

They say that Frank and Tilly Hobbs talked with their boy Wally for most of an hour. They could hardly believe Wally's story though they knew it was true. When they told him about the dwarf with the elephant he looked at them as if they had sunstroke, as if they'd been drinking bad water.

"An elephant! A real live elephant? How could anyone have an elephant in this country?" Wally said, looking into his parent's eyes with a raised eyebrow and an incredulous expression. "Are you going crazy? Did the heat fry your brains?"

"Quiet, quiet," his mother hushed him, glancing out the open door to the office where the deputy sat. "We can't let anyone know about him, he's wanted by the law."

"Well I can see why you don't want anyone to know about it, they'd think you'd been bit by a rabid dog."

Then Wally told them his story. He had ridden all day the morning he left their camp. He'd found a road and several folks pointed the way to Sandstone. In town he hurried in his search for a good draft horse and by the time the sun set he'd found one and tried to dicker the price down some but they were short of horses in Sandstone and he had to pay more than he wanted. A big gray powerful gelding, close to the size and weight of their horse, he figured they would pull together and make a good team.

He took the big gray and his saddle horse to the livery stable and paid one dollar to board them overnight. All of a sudden hunger swooped down on him with the darkness and by inquiring he had been directed to a saloon that served man-sized meals. He had plenty of cash left and felt proud of the good horse he'd found. He couldn't wait to show the horse to his parents and receive their nod of approval.

He had no idea what day it was but the saloon was doing a brisk business. Wally found an empty table off to the back and pulled up a chair. A player piano competed with the jumble of voices and laughter and the air hung thick with smoke. The wood floor was covered with sawdust and two couples danced in spite of the noise. A real attractive gal brought him a glass of beer and he didn't have the courage to tell her he didn't drink alcohol. He ate a one-pound beefsteak with all the trimmings and enjoyed the music and watching all the people.

A short man in a black wide-brimmed hat and a trimmed graying beard asked if he could sit at Wally's table. Not a whole lot older than Wally he had the sharp facial features of a ferret and he wore a weathered buckskin vest. Wally welcomed the company and invited him to sit. When he had settled comfortably the man lit a pipe and pulled out a deck of cards. They shook hands and exchanged names though Wally didn't catch the man's, something like Jarno or Jarco. He asked Wally what brought him to Sandstone and by the time Wally finished his story two other men had settled at the table like pigeons home to roost. One of them was the brother of the guy with the buckskin vest and they started to play poker. Wally watched with fascination, never having played the game. They were laughing and talking and having a good time. After awhile, when he showed signs of leaving, they asked Wally if he played poker and when he told them he never had they invited him to give it a try, just a friendly little game.

Shucks, they'd help him and they'd keep the limit low. They convinced him that it was easy and he'd catch on quickly. And besides, he could make a little money and quit anytime he wanted. What the hell, he had no place to go. Play cards with these friendly men, then find a place to sleep. He could head out in the morning with the new horse that he couldn't wait to show his parents.

At first he won. It was easy, it was fun. He pulled out his leather pouch and took out a few more coins, then bills. He bet and took chances and they slowly upped the ante. He won a seven-dollar pot and they complimented him and told him he was a natural-born poker player. They bought him sasparilla, delivered by the pretty woman with a short red dress. The pots grew and his pouch shrunk until he found himself needing to call on a large pot or lose most of his money.

He had three jacks, sure to take the pot, but he had no more money to call. They told him he could use his horse in the betting. He hesitated. He was sure to get it right back with three jacks, wasn't he? The short ferret-like man with the gray beard shoved a tablet and pencil across the table to Wally without a word. Then he folded his arms and waited. Wally scratched out a bill of sale for his horse and he had a bill of sale for the horse he just bought. Reluctantly Wally laid the bills of sale in the pot and called the only man left in the hand. The man in the buckskin vest calmly laid down four sevens. Wally lost his breath as if someone punched him in the stomach. He stared at the four sevens while he laid his three worthless Jacks on the worn oak table.

"Tough luck, kid," the man said as he pulled the money and bills-of-sale to him.

The other men offered their condolences and shook their heads and slapped him gently on the back as if young men lost their family's dream here all the time or if they had known what the outcome would be all along.

"I'll buy them back, my family is waiting for me."

"Sure, kid, but these horses will be goin' down the road. We're a little short of horses in these parts."

Wally sensed he'd been cheated but he didn't know how. They dealt the cards so fast right off the pile and the way they shuffled they couldn't know where each card was, could they?

As the bunch in the saloon, now joined by the deputy, walked through the darkening town to the livery stable to identify the two horses the Jarco brothers now owned, Wally pleaded with them, told them again how his parents were stranded out in the rock, that he'd work it off, please, he had to have his horses. His pleas fell on deaf ears. He felt like he was walking to the gallows.

Then, when the horses had been satisfactorily identified, the Jarco brothers led them off into the dark unforgiving night. But they weren't alone. Behind them in the shadows lurked a desperate young man, Wally Hobbs, as reliable as the sun, a good boy who was about to become a horse thief.

From a safe distance Wally followed the Jarco brothers and the horses. He could hear them talking and laughing until they reached a place a short distance from town. Wally could make out a log cabin, a small shack and lean-to, and a small pole corral where they put the horses. The brothers ducked into the cabin and a flickering light came on briefly. The last Wally heard from them was laughing that cut like a razor, laughing at the hick who didn't know a deck of cards from a cowpie.

He waited a good hour after the last light went out in the cabin. He crept up to the lean-to and found his saddle. He quietly saddled his horse and tied a lead rope on the draft horse's halter. The hinges on the corral gate squeaked slightly when he slowly swung it open, thankful there was no dog. He left the gate open and walked the horses a good distance from the cabin. Then he swung up into the saddle and headed out of town, cautiously in the dark, hoping the horse could see better than he. He was overcome by a strong rush of satisfaction. Here he was after all, on the road back to his folks, bringing a good sturdy horse for their journey west, away from the nightmare Sandstone had become.

He never would understand how the three men and the deputy got ahead of him in the dead of night. But they knew the lay of that land and he'd been an easy prey. He couldn't see their guns when they stopped him, but for an instant he was sorely tempted to spur his horse and run for it, into the night, into the darkness, into what was left for him of hope.

They tied his hands behind him for the ride back to town and he gave up on explaining and pleading halfway there. They stabled the two stolen horses at the livery and then locked him up to wait for the circuit judge. The squat rustic building had two iron cells and the one cell had a modest traffic of drunks and ruffians and homeless drifters but the other cell had become the permanent address of Wally Hobbs though he got no mail and had no visitors.

The days dragged by with no sign of the judge or the marshall. Wally begged them to send someone out to find his family and tell them where he was and what happened, that they would have more money. He tried to bribe men when they were in the other cell overnight but he could only promise them money and he didn't even know how to direct them to the wagon. He told them there was gold in the wagon, he promised an outlandish reward, but he found no takers in Sandstone.

Rumors drifted in the summer air as to how close the circuit judge was holding court and as the days trudged by Wally Hobbs changed. He became a trapped animal that plotted day and night how he would escape and how he'd skin alive that rat-faced little poker player and shove four sevens up his ass.

And that's where Frank and Tilly found their boy, in jail, waiting for the judge so Wally could get properly and legally hanged for stealing his own horses. The one wisp of hope they found in it all was that the US marshall had returned from Rainbow and it turned out that he despised the Jarco boys and had been wanting to hang them for a long time but he could never nail them with enough evidence or catch them in the act and he knew they did most of their dirty work a long way from Sandstone.

The marshall, Matt Berry, appeared as though he'd been carved out of rock, well over six foot, two hundred pounds, and though naturally gregarious was personally dedicated to bringing law to the west. The marshall wore his strength like clean clothes and never ventured anywhere without his heavy long-barreled .45 Colt revolver. A Sandstone joke was that Marshall Berry never went to the outhouse without his pistol.

As far as Wally's case went, the marshall was real suspicious with the Jarco boys involved, figured they outright cheated this farm boy out of his horses with a deck of cards. But he said the witnesses, even his own deputy, were clear on the matter if somewhat reluctant and he couldn't do anything about that. It would be up to the judge whose reputation with horse thieves was deadly. The marshall had to leave the next day for Twilight, a day's ride from Sandstone, with bile in his throat to have missed nailing the Jarco brothers again.

When Frank and Tilly had collected all the information Wally could give them, and picked up some fresh food at the grocery, they met Wart and Stella in the woods and led them more than a mile back into a thicket of scrub pine and aspen where they settled and ate and expressed their feelings. Frank's anger, Tilly's fear and worry, and Wart's scheming to get Wally out of jail. Late in the afternoon Wart rallied the Hobbses and prepared to leave for town.

"We can't ever be seen together," Wart said. "You lay low here, rest up. I'll go into town and get your boy and your horses back."

"How you goin' to do that?" Frank asked, with skepticism coloring his face and doubt clogging his voice.

"The same way those cheatin' skunks got him," Wart said.

Wart left the Hobbses and their horse with Stella, hidden where a magpie couldn't find them and he hiked for town. He'd get there just about in time for a big beefsteak dinner.

Wart ran his plan through his head all the way to town, realizing he would have to do a clever bit of acting while frightened out of his wits. Once in town he tried to stay in the background shadows and alleys while he familiarized himself with the buildings, making sure he had the right saloon and ignoring the many looks and staring he was used to. Then, after lurking between two buildings while he calmed his breathing, he marched around the corner and pushed through the swinging bar doors he could just about walk under. He blustered in as if he were the Flying Young Dwarf on the Trapeze and sat at a table set for eating. While he ate he kept an eye on the card tables, disappointed that not many men were playing.

When he finished he moved across the saloon and sat at one of the larger round tables. Through the smoke and noise, the men who were playing cast secretive glances at him as if they didn't

want him to catch them staring. A few gawked across the tables
with baffled expressions without realizing they were staring. Remembering why he was there, Wart smiled back when he caught
their eye. One tall man Wart would bet was a farmer sat at his
table and struck up a conversation. Wart waited for the swindle
to begin and felt puzzled when it didn't. Then he heard someone
at another table say loudly, "You Jarco boys'll never change!"
and the three men at that table laughed. Jarco boys. The man at
the livery told Tilly that those were the names of the men who
owned the Hobbses' horses.

Wart excused himself from the kindly farmer who was simply
resting from his hard day's work with a mug of beer and some
peanuts. Wart was encouraged, the saloon was filling. Wart
skirted the card tables, with other spectators, and watched the
gaming. The players tried to ignore him. Then at the table where
the Jarco brothers were gambling, he stood behind a man and
studied what was in his hand. He could barely see over the man's
shoulder and he rose up on tiptoe.

"Would you like to play?" asked a short man with a sharp narrow face and a worn buckskin vest. It was the man the Hobbs's
boy had described to his parents. Bull's-eye!

"Oh, thanks, but I don't know how, never played."

"Well it's pretty simple, sit down, sit down," the man said as
he pulled out a chair for Wart. "We're just having a friendly little
game. We'll learn ya, won't we boys?"

The assembled men nodded and chorused their welcome.

"All you need is a few dollars and a little luck," the man with
the pointy nose said.

Wart climbed into the wide chair and reached in his pocket.
He pulled out a leather pouch with a drawstring and set it on the
table. It made a thud as if it were heavy.

"Do you have a little luck?" the man asked.

"Look at me," Wart said, and he swung his stubby arms to the
left and to the right. "What do you think?"

They hesitated for a moment, not sure how to react, and then
Wart's broad smile and robust laugh ignited theirs and they
roared with the humor and irony of it, this harmless freakish
creature who'd certainly run out of luck and Wart wanted the

man to remember him. He looked him in the eye while the others stared unabashedly. A bald bartender with a huge belly brought a high stool and helped Wart sit on it, bringing him comfortably level with the table top, right where he had to be to shuffle and deal.

"Thank you," Wart said, "you gentlemen are about to associate with a real living breathing dwarf. It isn't catching, I assure you. My parents were normal folks just like you and I'm not interested in your daughters, just passing through."

They all laughed uncomfortably and somewhat ill at ease.

*Put them at ease. Bring down their guard. Let them feel in control.*

The poker lesson started quietly, things on the up and up and Wart won and lost. They let him deal in turn and he purposely made a mess of things when he shuffled. Wart learned from table conversation that the Jarco brother in charge was Wilbur though they also called him Jark. His younger brother was August. About a half hour into the game Wart asked the players, "What do you mean by 'no limit'?"

"That means you can raise the bet for as much as you want," August said.

"You mean a man could walk in here and bet twenty-five dollars?" Wart asked with a touch of awe in his voice.

"Yup," Wilbur said, "but it can only be what you have on you right now, not something you'll pay up tomorrow."

"Oh, well, Wilbur, it could be something close at hand," August said, "like if you wanted to bet your saddle that's right out on the street."

"Or your horse?" Wart asked as he dealt a round.

"Yeah, whatever the horse is worth," Wilbur said.

The game continued another hour until Wart had nearly cleaned all three of them out. He noticed Marshall Berry had settled at a table and was eating supper. Perfect, unless the lawman recognized Wart from a wanted bill. He had to take his chances. This was the killer pot. Wart was dealing. He had let a card in his hand slip for an instant, enough for August next to him to see. It was a seven. Wart was sure they'd signal that information around the table and hoped he'd dealt Wilbur what looked like an unbeatable hand.

Wart raised Wilbur twenty-nine dollars. Wilbur acted as if he had a good hand, an unbeatable hand, beaming with confidence, but he was out of money. It was a big pot that grew gradually with everyone contributing until one by one they were burned out, all except the Jarco brother and Wart. Men from other tables had gathered around to watch this strange little man dueling with the local card shark. Marshall Berry sauntered over to watch.

"We have a twenty dollar limit," Wilbur said.

"Nooooo!" the spectators chorused, enjoying the hole the stranger had the Jarco brothers in. "No limit! No limit!"

Wilbur tried to borrow money from the men surrounding the table but no one offered. Wart sensed Jarco wasn't the kind of man who had friends. His brother had gone belly up twenty minutes ago.

"Well, how about my horse, just down the street, he's worth twenty at least," Wilbur said, sweating and squirming in his chair. "Ain't that right Marshall, them is my horses."

"They're held by the court until the judge gets here." Marshall Berry said. "I suppose you can gamble with them if you're sure they'll be yours. You got papers on 'em?"

"Yup, right here!"

He patted his vest pocket and held his five cards tightly over his head. He couldn't give up on this pot that was nearly eighty dollars.

"Two horses," Wart said, holding up two stubby fingers.

"That's robbery, you only raised me twenty-nine dollars."

"Make your bet or fold," Wart said. "You mentioned more than one horse, so I say two horses."

Wilbur turned to the Marshall.

"Can we do that, Marshall, it'll only take a few minutes?"

"If this man will allow you the time," Berry said and he glanced at Wart.

"For a reasonable amount of time, say twenty minutes," Wart said.

Wilbur shouted at August, "Go git 'em, God dammit! Go git 'em!"

In record time August led the two horses into the saloon, the saddle horse saddled. Marshall Berry had moved over to stand at the bar, seeming to enjoy the Jarco's dilemma. Other men were coming in from the street as word spread.

"Do you have the bill of sale for each of them?" Wart asked.

"Yes, right here!" he shouted, fumbling for the folded papers in his vest pocket.

"Sign them and place them in the pot so there's no misunderstanding," Wart said.

"All right, you little monkey's ass."

Wilbur signed them with an air of disgust.

"There now, dammit, I call! I call!"

Everyone in the saloon crowded the table. Wilbur had one card showing, a King. He turned over his cards with a flare and slammed them on the table. A full house, kings and nines. Wart held his breath, he'd done good so far.

"What do you think of that, you ugly little freak?" Wilbur snarled with an angry curl twisting his lip.

"I think I have two horses," Wart said with a wide smile growing across his face, "and about sixty more dollars."

Wart had the one card showing, a seven. He fanned his cards on the worn wood table with a flurry. He hadn't lost his touch from the circus.

The men watching cheered and groaned. Wilbur and August gasped and then Wilbur stood up and banged his fist on the table.

"He cheated! You all saw it, he cheated!"

The four sevens laid there with a nine. Four of a kind.

Wart pulled the money to him and stashed it in his leather pouch. He tucked the bills of sale into his pocket and several of the men watching the game helped him lead the horses over to the livery. He would leave them there until morning. Then he went with the Marshall to the jail and he woke Wally. Wart made his mark on each bill of sale and sold them to Wally for a dollar.

"Now, Marshall, those horses legally belong to this young man, Wally Hobbs, they're his property, is that right?"

"Yep, all legal according to the law," the Marshall said.

"Then how can he be in jail for stealing his own horses?"

"Don't seem right. I'll ponder it tonight."

"One more thing, Marshall. If you and your deputy was to be hiding in the weeds down the hill from the livery later tonight, you might do a little business. Those Jarco fellas are plenty mad about them horses."

"That came to mind. I let word out that I was going up river a few miles yet tonight and wouldn't be back for a day or two. But what I'd like to know is who are you, what's your name?"

"Mercy. Mercy Possible."

"You a friend of the Hobbses?"

"No, I just met them along the road and I like to play cards."

"Why did you give 'em the horses?"

"They're of little use to me." Wart stood and patted the top of his head. "Gettin' on and off is a problem."

The Marshall smiled. "Yeah, see what you mean. Still. It was real decent of you."

They shook hands and the Marshall cocked an eye at Wart.

"Have you been around this way before?"

"No . . . never been this far west before." Wart tried to hold a smile on his face. "Why do you ask?"

"Oh . . . there's something about you that seems familiar."

Wart hurried down the road. He didn't look back.

The next morning Wart and Stella turned southwest to skirt cross country around the badlands after saying good-bye to the Hobbs. The Hobbs family was headed back to their wagon with a good team and their saddle horse and Wally still couldn't get over the elephant. They'd be coming back through Sandstone on their way west, hearing that the circuit judge had arrived. And, best of all, hearing that the Jarco brothers were in jail waiting to be hanged for stealing horses.

Wart and Stella cut southwest happy to leave Sandstone far behind. They headed southwest because they told everyone in Sandstone they were heading northwest. Wart wondered if Marshall Berry would all of a sudden remember where he'd seen him before, probably on some wanted poster with his likeness on it. There couldn't be many dwarfs roaming around the West, could there? They hiked south for three days, at times being turned back by rock outcrops and buttes and by avoiding the few ranches scattered far and wide on the horizons.

An unspoken agony grew in Wart's gut and he anguished over what he was to do with his beloved companion. In all his days, however many they were, Wart had never been loved as he was these days of journey. He tried to keep the worry off his face because it seemed that Stella could sense his moods so quickly and accurately. As he rode on he would sing loudly in an attempt at a cover but he feared Stella saw through it easily. The creek took a serpentine course through a deep cut in the land until, even with Wart on top, they were below the horizon as if marching in a trench.

Stella and Wart slipped through a narrow passage in a ravine, following the creek upstream, and suddenly came face-to-face with George Randolph III. The three of them were so startled at seeing each other they didn't speak for a scary silence in which each of them was contemplating flight. In the end it was this rough-looking, earthy man who found his voice first.

"Who in hell are you?" he asked, backing away from Stella.

"I'm Wart and this is my elephant, Stella. We're lost."

"I would guess so."

The man wore a black derby, a worn out buckskin vest over his gray long-sleeved shirt, and pants that looked as though he'd crawled from Illinois. He had a gap in his front teeth and his face looked like burnt leather.

"How in hell did you get out here with an elephant?" He lifted his hat and scratched his head, still completely dumbfounded. His thin white hair stuck out in all directions and his face was hidden by something resembling a nest.

"We've just been wandering. Actually we're runnin' from the law."

"The law?"

"The law," Wart said. "We're on the lam."

"Well, you're safe from the law out here but not from the Army."

"The Army?" Wart squinted.

"Yep, they're protecting land that belongs to the injuns, keepin' prospectors and the like out."

Stella helped Wart reach the ground and she kept an eye on the man. He had a spartan camp with a small tarp hanging loosely over the entrance to a small cave. A roll of bedding was spread and he had a fire ring in front of the cave. A half worn out shovel and pick leaned against the rock wall along with two shallow metal pans and there were several cans of food and the man's belongings stashed in the cave.

"Any white folks go into them hills they's likely to come out without their hair. The injuns say them hills is sacred. They was given them by the government a few years back. We're on their land right now and they don't cotton to us being here."

"What are you doing here?" Wart asked.

The man held out his hand. "I'm George Randolph III." They shook hands. "You're a little bugger, ain't ya."

"What are you doing here?"

"You won't tell anyone?"

"How could I do that, I have no idea where I am."

"Well then, I's panning for gold."

"I've heard about that, you find gold in the river," Wart said.

"And in the gravel around old river beds."

Stella lumbered over and drank from the creek.

"Be careful, Stella, you might swallow some gold," Wart called. "Are you panning here in this stream?"

"No, up a mile where another creek joins this one."

"Why don't you camp up there?"

"Not safe, the Army prowlin' around, and injuns. I stay out of sight here and move back and forth in the dark. I pan during daylight and then wait till dark to hightail it back here."

"Have you found any yet?"

George Randolph III showed Wart a big gap-tooth smile and said "That's something you never ask a man so he don't have to lie. Now, are you hungry, son?"

"You don't have to call me son, I'm probably older than you, and yes, I'm real hungry."

George opened a can of peaches, handed it to Wart along with a dirty fork that he wiped off on his pants. Wart wolfed the peaches and offered some to Stella. She shook her head and

Wart knew it was because he had gone the longest without food. Wart and George sat in the shade of the cave and Stella settled close to the creek.

"How did you end up out here?" Wart asked.

"I worked for the post office in Hillsboro, Ohio, for over twenty-seven years. Then the bank where I kept my life's savings went belly up and I lost every cent. We all knew where the money went but no one could do anything about it, legal that is.

"What did you do?"

"I thought about it, could've killed the little toad. But I'd always wanted to go out west, read about it, heard about it, and I decided this was my only chance. If we was broke we might as well be broke in the West. If we got to start over, why not start over in the West? My wife wouldn't hear of it and went off to Pennsylvania to live with her sister. I headed west, did odd jobs, hooked up with folks in wagons, snuck on a train or two. The law was after me, too, so I watched my back."

"Why was the law after you?"

"Before I left town I burned the som-bitch swindler's house to the ground."

He slapped Wart on the back and laughed with his toothy smile.

"I have to find a place for Stella, we can't be just drifting. They're bound to find us sooner or later. Where could I find someone to take care of an elephant and protect her and treat her well? They live a long time, you know."

"Ya don't say," Randolph said and screwed up his face as if he were thinking.

"I think there are men out there who would do her harm, abuse her, even want to shoot her for sport," Wart said softly as if he feared Stella would hear.

"By golly, I think I know someone."

"You *do*?"

"Injuns."

"Indians? Why would they take care of her?"

"I've had some dealings with a few of 'em. Never tell anyone but I brought 'em a repeating rifle, something they hold in high esteem. The Army would hang me if they caught me. The injuns blindfolded me and put me on a horse and took me to a special place in them hills.

"They wanted more rifles and I told 'em I'd get some more, hoping to get their permission to pan. They'd killed three or more miners they'd caught on their ground.

"While I was riding out of the hills they showed me a place where there were bones of a huge animal cemented right in the rock. The ribs and skull and backbone clearly showed and the injuns seemed to think that those animals lived in their world before and would come back if they kept the white man away, if they kept the hills sacred. The injuns believed that their good times would return, and the great animals would defeat the white man and drive them out and their life would be the way it was before. Well guess what?"

"What?" Wart took the bait.

"Them som-bitchin' bones looked exactly like some kinda elephant!"

"An elephant?"

"Just as real as that one lying right there."

Randolph tossed a small stone on Stella's back and they all laughed.

George Randolph III convinced the Indians to go with him to see the sacred animal with Wart. He had trekked into the rough little town of Deadwood and quietly traded three nuggets for a rifle that had somehow been smuggled through the Army's ban. At the agreed time a small band rode out at dusk to witness the living, breathing creature they couldn't believe was there. Wart and Stella were waiting nervously, Wart starting to feel remorse for bringing her to this hostile land, when almost in the dark they could see the Indians coming into the clearing single file.

Each in turn beheld this huge, living, breathing animal from out of their legends and song, then quietly slid off his horse and knelt on the ground in speechless awe.

Under the cover of darkness, the dumbfounded Indians smuggled Stella and Wart deep into the thickly forested hills. There they treated her with great honor. For many days Wart taught those who would be her caretakers what she understood and the many things she could do. Children loved to ride on her and play with her in the pools along the river and run screaming and laughing after Stella would hose them down with her trunk.

Then one night, when there was no moon, they took Wart and Stella deep into a huge cave and lit a large fire. The Indians sang and danced and their shadows danced on the walls and Stella danced with them. One of the Indian holy men who could speak a little English told Wart that no whiteface had ever seen the cave and lived to tell about it.

After a few days Wart knew it was time to be on his way. The Indians thanked him profusely and gave him directions on the way to walk where he would be safe. They filled his pack with food and the time came to say good-bye to Stella. The Indians gathered to say good-bye to the strange little man who had brought them hope and joy. They backed off and gave Stella and Wart that moment alone.

Stella wrapped Wart in her trunk and held him skyward, above her head. Then with a great roar she trumpeted out a sound he'd never heard before, high pitched, a wailing of sorrow that echoed off the rock cliffs carried out over the hills and into the sky, an outcry of love that shook like thunder. She slowly let him down and he could see the tears streaming from her eyes. He kissed her on her cheek.

"I love you, sweetheart, I'll never forget you, thank you for saving my life."

He'd dreaded this moment for a long time and felt thankful that she'd have a happy home for as long as she lived. He picked up his pack, nodded at the Indians that circled him, turned abruptly, and walked away. Stella called one more time but Wart didn't turn around, he couldn't, or he might have decided to stay there the rest of his life. Several braves trailed him, making sure he got clear of the hills and on a safe road.

Wart never looked back.

\* \* \*

They say that George Randolph III managed to smuggle two more repeating rifles to the injuns. One night in a wayward saloon, he heard there'd been a gold strike up in Helena and he gave up encroaching on injun land even though they looked the other way with his panning. He told a few fellow travelers about the dwarf and elephant as he headed north but figured no one believed him.

# THIRTY-TWO

THE JOURNEY TO BUTTE seemed longer than usual, leaving the ranch and family behind. Daniel could have taken the stagecoach for part of the trip, slept on the way, but he could travel faster by taking familiar shortcuts over the foothills. There he would cross ravines, work around cut banks, ride through narrow passes a buggy or wagon could never negotiate, and shorten the distance overland by several hours.

Arriving in Butte he went straight to the boardinghouse. Etta wasn't there but he found Claire in the kitchen, working on the evening meal.

"You're back," she said, about to hug him but restrained the impulse.

"Yes, only for a day or two. I'm moving back to the ranch."

With sadness in her voice she said, "I always thought you would."

"What's happening with the house?"

"My mother found a buyer. The new owners, a married couple, want me to stay on and help them run the place. Mother thinks I should. They'll even pay me more than I'm making now."

"That's good, Claire, you sure have the know-how, but do you *want* to keep on here?"

"I don't know. It's decent work. Mother and her new husband are soon leaving for California."

"Would you like to go with them?"

"Mother thought I'd be better off here, where I know people."

"I've got to say good-bye to some friends, but I'll be using my room a few more nights."

"We owe you money back, you've paid till the end of the month."

"Keep it. Consider it a wage for taking care of me so well."

Daniel walked to the door and turned.

"I'll miss you Claire."

"I'll miss you," she said, shyly looking at the floor.

Daniel went out to his horse and rode away.

At the door to Kincaid's weather-beaten little house, Sally was glad to see him and whispered that Albert was in a bad way. Daniel found Kincaid in bed and the old miner claimed to be doing just fine.

"Good to see you," Kincaid said, "I wondered what happened to ya. Lotsa the boys askin' about ya, they wants ta know when you're gonna fight the Greek. You goin' ta fight some more?"

"No . . . my father died, I'm going back to the ranch."

"Oh tah hell, I'm sure sorry to hear that, Daniel, real sorry. How'd he go?"

"A horse accident. Runs in the family. He got thrown, rode a horse for more than fifty years."

"I guess the mine ain't the only one out tah get us. I'm sure damn sorry, Daniel."

"Thank you."

"Glad you're goin' back ta the ranch, escapin' the devil's damned playground 'fore he drags you into hell."

"Are you going to get yourself over to the hospital?"

Kincaid coughed and spit a stream of phlegm into a coffee can.

"Too late for that. I'm a goner. I kept sayin' it wouldn't get me, I'd be one a the lucky ones and every day ya lie ta yourself and then ya tell yerself you'll quit come spring or next summer and Sally beggin' me till her voice is bloody raw. Nope, I'm a goner and I ain't leavin' Sally enough to bury me."

They both fell silent.

"Sure wish you'd fight one more. We'll never know if you coulda beat the Greek. We coulda made some good money, it's a sure thing."

"I've heard that before." Daniel laughed, then Kincaid

chuckled. "I wish you'd get to a hospital, but you always were a stubborn jackass."

"You take care of yourself," Kincaid said, finding it hard to breathe. "Come by this way sometime. I'll miss you."

"I don't know if I'll be back. I want to thank you for your friendship. You saved my life down that hole in the dark."

"And whenever I remember working with you in the tunnel I see you loading the car with *my* share o' the load as well as your own, doing the work of two men, working the hammer for your turn and then for mine."

Kincaid's voice broke and he covered his emotion with a round of coughing. Daniel had to escape before he broke down. He stood and gripped Kincaid's hand. Then he turned quickly and left the small room. Sally had stepped outside. Daniel took a roll of bills from his pocket and slipped it into the bread box. Then he found Sally with despair in her eyes.

"He won't see spring," she said.

"I know . . . I know."

"Come back and see us. Ye've been a good friend. I'd a bet you'd a beat the Greek, easy money."

"Thanks, Sally, you've both been good friends."

"God bless ye Daniel Rockhammer, He's looking' down on ye with lovin' eyes."

As Daniel rode away he didn't know about that, about "God's loving eyes." He knew he'd never see his friend again. It never occurred to him that he was negotiating with God. He wiped the tears from his face with the back of his hand.

Daniel found Gillespie graining horses along one of the large corrals. He swung off Buck and wrapped a rein around a hitching post.

"My father was killed by a horse, I'm going back to the ranch."

"Oh . . ." Gillespie said as he tipped his hat back and scratched his head. "Sorry to hear that, it's a damn shame. How'd it happen?"

"It seems he was thrown."

Gillespie dumped the remaining oats into a feed box and set

the pail on the ground. He shuffled to the barn and settled on the bench along the south wall. Daniel felt the old man was inviting him and he ambled over and sat beside him. Neither spoke for several minutes as a magpie squawked from the feed box, competing with the horses.

"Things like that happen fast," Gillespie said, slowly shaking his head. "Your father was a good man. I never had the pleasure of meeting him, but I see him reflected in you. You're both damn good men."

"You're right about him," Daniel said, believing that in God's eyes he was far from a good man. "You plan to keep this outfit going?"

"Yeah, lots of kind folks pitch in around here, keep things in order."

"And there's always Nettie," Daniel dared to say.

"You got a lady friend back home?"

"Yes, somewhere back there."

"You be careful what lass you settle down with, be mighty careful," Gillespie said.

"Why didn't you ever marry again after your wife died?"

"My wife didn't die . . ." Gillespie paused, as if he were remembering. "She ran off with some slicker when Nettie was ten. It was just Nettie and me then, she's a very happy girl, loves our life here, finished the grades, can ride anything with four legs."

Neither spoke for several minutes. Gillespie spit a wad.

"You found the grave didn't you?" Gillespie asked.

"Yes. I came on it by accident, I'm sorry if—"

"It's all right. 'Bout time someone knows. Sometimes I catch myself thinking she's just out there in the stable, or in town gettin' groceries and I'm always talkin' to her and she don't grow no older through the years."

They sat without speaking as the wind picked up and Gillespie spit onto a dried up pile of horse apples.

"Nettie was working a green sorrel mare," Gillespie said. "I watched her from the barn. She was a wonder with the horses. That mare had only been here a few days. She had it in a halter with a lead rope. It suddenly reared and kicked her in the head. It warn't three seconds, dead before I could get to her. She was only sixteen and never got the chance to say good-bye." He shook his head slowly. "But I s'pose you know about that now with your father."

Daniel searched for some word to offer on the altar of this man's heartrending grief but he could find none.

"No man or woman yet has conceived the language, no one has found the words deep enough to speak of it," Daniel whispered.

"I had to tell myself she'd be back," Gillespie said, "or I'd go insane. Sometimes I think I am insane."

"I know what you mean. God give you peace."

As Daniel rode away he felt a strange longing to remain in Butte beside these friends who had become a part of his life.

Daniel caught Jenny in her backyard whaling the dust and dirt out of rugs that were draped over the clotheslines. She offered her sorrow and surprise over the news about Daniel's father and her heart skipped a beat when he told her he was leaving Butte and returning to the ranch. He dismounted and she dropped the rug beater and embraced him with some urgency.

Neither spoke for a time as the denizens of Butte bustled by seemingly ignoring this couple clinging to one another.

"I knew this day was coming," Jenny said.

"They need me on the ranch."

"Will she be there, your sweetheart?"

"No . . . we can't be together there."

"Then where can you be together?"

"Nowhere, nowhere we've found yet, someday . . . but not yet. Not yet."

"If I found my way to Rockhammer Ranch some day would I be welcome?"

"Of course. I have a good-looking brother. Take care of Gillespie when you can. Nettie isn't coming back, she never left. She died some ten years ago."

"Oh, no . . . that poor man. Why does he go on pretending, why does he carry on so long?"

"Because he might go crazy if he didn't keep her alive in his head and heart."

Daniel suddenly realized that he and Gillespie were brothers in matters of the heart.

"Should I say anything, that I know?" Jenny asked.

"No, but ask about Nettie once in a while so he thinks you believe it. He'll tell you when he can. The grave is uphill to the south just along the edge of the lodgepoles. I found it when I cut a couple poles awhile ago."

"I have a new boyfriend."

"Good. Good for you. He's a very lucky boy." Daniel meant it.

"Nothing permanent, just until you become available," she winked, "just until you and your girl are no longer in love."

"That time will never come, Jenny. We will love each other until the end of time."

He swung up onto his horse and looked down into her bright sunny face.

"Take your fella out to Gillespie's, put him to work."

"I intend to, I'll put flowers on the grave."

"That's good, put some there for me."

Daniel turned Buck and held him a moment more.

"It's a good thing you wore your ranch clothes. Mother's probably watching out the window and she'd horsewhip me if I had anything to do with a miner."

"Sounds like a wise woman. I hope your new boyfriend doesn't work in the mines."

"He's a teacher."

"Good! You're a great girl, Jennifer. Be well, be happy."

She looked up at him, shielding her eyes from the sun.

"Good-bye, Daniel, I hope you and your sweetheart will find a place where you can be together."

Daniel tipped his hat and rode away.

The following morning, after a sound sleep, the first in many nights, Daniel ate his last breakfast at the house and said good-bye to the miners he'd come to know. Claire served him plenty of helpings for a long journey. She no longer cared if it was obvious to the other boarders. By the time the miners were off to the mine, Daniel had Buck loaded and ready to go. He swung up into the saddle. Claire stood on the stoop in her apron, trying to hold back the tears. Daniel looked down at her.

"Good-bye, Claire, thanks for all your good food and care, you've been more than kind."

"Good-bye, Daniel, go with God." She caught a sob.

"Say good-bye to your mother for me please."

She couldn't hold it back any longer and she cried. She stood with her chin on her chest, knotting her fingers, and her body shook with the sobbing. Daniel waited, searching to find the words that would give comfort in this pool of sorrow. Then it came to him in a heartbeat, as if someone else were speaking the words.

"Claire, would you like to come with me?"

She looked up, wiping the tears from her face with her apron.

"What do you mean?" she asked with surprise.

"I mean come with me to the ranch. My mother is getting on in years and the work is too much for her. I'm offering you a job—cooking, keeping up the kitchen and house, working in the garden, doing the laundry, work, a job."

"Oh . . . I don't know . . . you mean go with you right now?"

"Yes, yes, right now. Compared to Butte you'll think you've gone to heaven at Rockhammer Ranch."

"I'd have to ask my mother, I just can't up and go."

"Why not? Isn't that what she's doing to you?"

"But . . . what about . . . I can't—"

"Grab your personal things, the things you need, I'll be back in an hour with another horse. We want to leave with as much daylight as we can find. Hurry!"

Before Claire could answer Daniel turned Buck and trotted down the street. Claire stood for a moment, transfixed. Then she hurried into the house to gather her things. She caught herself humming, singing, twirling. She had a new job, a new life, and she was going to Rockhammer Ranch with Daniel. When her small sack was all packed, she realized she didn't have much and she realized she had the whole world.

# THIRTY-THREE

DANIEL RETURNED to the boardinghouse leading a bay filly that had a smooth gait and a good disposition. From spending so much time at Gillespie's Daniel knew the horse was well broke and that Jenny had ridden her often. She had a flowing blonde mane and tail, her name was Sugar, and Claire loved her immediately. They tied on what little Claire was bringing and left town in a hurry. Claire found some split-skirt-riding britches of her mother's that fit so she could ride a western saddle.

When they climbed to the final ridge above Butte, Daniel paused and gave the horses a blow. He gazed back over the smoking valley and gave a great sigh of relief that he was leaving it all behind, praying that his time there would account for something in the eyes of God against the unforgivable sin—as Gabrielle always referred to it. He wished Kincaid, Gillespie, and Jenny well, thankful he could rescue Claire from its choking and dead-end grip. With a final glance Daniel turned Buck and they headed north as that tortured land fell out of sight behind them.

He led the way across breathtaking open land, miles of sagebrush meadows, weaving through aspen groves and forests of Douglas fir while always on the far horizon to one side or the other the sheltering majestic mountains cradling snow throughout the summer. All afternoon they saw less then a dozen buildings and crossed only a few roads. They raced against the coming darkness and Claire, who hadn't much experience on a saddle horse, hung on for dear life. The little filly kept up with Buck and they rode into the coming dusk far enough to reach Wilson's stage depot, on a main road, where they were fortunate to find a night's lodging and good food.

By lamplight Claire watched Daniel unsaddle and feed and bed down the horses. She wanted to learn all she could about taking care of Sugar and she hoped she could buy the filly when she'd earned enough money. She and her mother hadn't had a horse since her father died and her father had always believed caring for a horse was a man's job. She had a feather bed all to herself in a small room and she insisted on paying the one dollar. Daniel had a bed in a bunkhouse and it seemed they were the last to eat in a rustic log room in front of a fireplace.

"Well, have you been able to catch your breath?" Daniel asked, sitting across the small table from her.

"No, I feel like some princess in a fairy tale who got swooped out of the forest and carried off to the enchanted castle."

"How are your bones? I can see you're mighty sore."

"Yeah, my whole body is sore. I think that was the longest ride I've ever ridden in a saddle."

"How do you like Sugar? She looks real smooth."

"Oh, she's very smooth, I love her."

Claire wanted to ask him if she could buy the filly but felt it was too presumptuous on the first day of her employment. She would wait for a better time, hoping they wouldn't sell the beautiful horse the moment they got there.

"Well the ride'll be tough but you'll believe you're in an enchanted land when we reach the ranch."

When they finished eating, the proprietor, a heavy-set woman in high-laced leather boots, men's britches, and a Mexican hat, came to their table.

"You folks get enough to fill the belly?"

"Yes, more than enough," Daniel said.

"You know you folks ought to take the stage in the morning. There'll be room and it would be a whole lot more comfortable. Why this poor dear can hardly walk."

She patted Claire on the shoulder.

"Would you like to do that, Claire?" Daniel asked.

"No, no, I'm fine," Claire said. "Just a little stiff."

"You could sit back and better enjoy the ride," the woman said.

Claire thought taking the stagecoach would be a good idea but she didn't want to give up on Sugar.

"I don't want to scare you, but there's been several road agent robberies in the past few weeks."

"Thanks for the warning, but we'll be fine," Daniel said.

The woman threw another chunk of wood on the fire and left the room, no sale.

"Will we run into any road agents?" Claire asked.

"No. They'll be out on the main roads, not in the back country we're crossing."

After a short night's sleep and a hearty breakfast, Claire and Daniel rode off ahead of the sun. Daniel had figured they were more likely to be stopped by road agents on the main road than through the more rugged back country. They forded creeks where there were no bridges, climbed steep grades where a stage or wagon couldn't negotiate. Claire found it hard to visit with Daniel as she was always trying to catch up.

"I've never seen such spectacular country, and the animals!" she shouted. "It's magnificent, and to think I spent my life in Butte."

Daniel felt his heart open to the bright shining world and the crisp mountain air scented with pine. At moments like that Gabrielle rode beside him and he could hear her laughter and remember her suntanned face and the glory of her as she became one with the horse and one with the land. How could it be wrong, how could it be evil that he loved her so deeply, so completely, so helplessly?

They spooked a small herd of elk in the morning and a black bear later in the day. Ravens scolded with their wild haunted calls, tracking them, awakening their isolation. Marmots whistled from lava rock burrows, magpies chattered over territorial rights, and bluebirds splattered color over the dry yellow prairie grass. When they stopped briefly at noon a porcupine tried to join their picnic.

Every bone in Claire's body ached, every muscle felt sore and her fanny pounded the saddle relentlessly until she would have gladly gotten off and walked.

Toward evening Daniel gazed at the sky as they crossed a large meadow where there was no visible trail.

"How do you keep from getting lost?" Claire asked. "We haven't seen a building or a road or a sign for hours."

"Oh, sometimes I do," he answered and immediately remembered his ride to Bozeman to find Gabrielle. How he ached until he thought he'd break. It was different now, after these years, the pain. He loved her more deeply and longed for her as constantly as his heart beat. He thought of her incessantly during his waking hours and she was the last thing on his mind when he fell asleep. Where was she? Was she safe? Was she happy? Would he see her sometime soon? Did she still love him? He knew she did, surer of her love than he was that the sun would rise.

"It's amazing," Claire said as she pulled up beside Daniel on Sugar, "I don't know how you do it."

"You'll be able to do it after you've been at the ranch for a while."

"That's hard to believe. I'd get lost sometimes finding my way around Butte."

Daniel couldn't help noticing how pretty Claire looked mounted on the filly, her blonde hair flowing from under her bonnet and circling her becoming face. Actually she wasn't really riding but rather clinging to the saddle pommel with one hand and the reins with the other while her feet were in and out of the stirrups.

"Looks like it'll be clear tonight," Daniel said as he gazed at the sky, "we'll have to sleep out."

"Sleep out?"

"Yep, for a few hours. We can't reach Sawbuck Station tonight."

"What about . . . what . . . about the animals?"

"They won't bother us. We'll go a little further and find a good tree. We're doing good. We can make Buffalo Jump by tomorrow night."

*Tomorrow night! Ye gads!*

Claire thought they were closer than that. She bit her tongue, didn't want to complain. If Sugar could do it she would do it too.

Half a moon hung in the western sky, giving them some night vision. Daniel found a good tree, a huge spruce with fanlike branches, spreading only a few feet off the ground, and a deep bed of needles circling the trunk. They hobbled the horses and ate dried beef, biscuits, and apples. Daniel made a small fire and they sat beside it as the night's chill prowled silently around them.

"How are you doing?" Daniel asked.

"Good, fine, surprised."

"It must be overwhelming, having just jumped on a horse and ridden away from your life on an hour's notice. But try not to worry, please. If it doesn't work out I promise you can always go back. I'll take you back."

"Oh, no, the ranch sounds wonderful, I'm glad you asked me. I needed to get away from the boardinghouse and from Butte. Just the country we've seen today has been amazing. And I love Sugar, all though right now I think both she and I are worn out."

"You two are doing right well. Buck and I are worn down too. We're travelin' many miles here, many miles, and I've been pushing it."

Daniel poked the fire a bit and Claire edged closer to him.

"Claire, I have something to tell you that I hope you'll keep to yourself, something I don't want my family to know."

"All right," she said, wondering if it had anything to do with her, momentarily confused about her feelings for Daniel. Was the horse a love gift?

"I'm telling you this so you'll better understand me and my family."

"All right," she said, about to lean her head on his shoulder.

"I have a woman I love, Claire, and she loves me, but we can't tell anyone for now."

Claire edged away from him.

"Is she married?"

"No, she's not. Why did you ask that?"

"Because you act like a married man."

"I do?"

"Yes, you do."

She thought of the many times at the house when she left her heart open to him, when she heard how he protected her from Ranski, when he enjoyed the food she favored him with and the times they talked. Even her mother could see there was something there between them and she warned Claire not to get involved with a miner. Yet in all that time he never made an advance, never wooed her, never touched her, until he invited her to go home with him to the Rockhammer.

"I guess I feel like I'm married, given my heart and soul, but I didn't realize it showed."

"You've always treated me as if you were in love with someone else, as if you were married."

"I hope I never gave you the impression that—"

"No, as much as I wanted your attention it was all my hopes and dreams. You were a perfect gentleman."

"Well I'm telling you now because more than one at the ranch will assume that we are sweethearts. They'll understand that's not the case after a while. In the meantime I'm asking you to keep my secret, to tell no one that I do have a lover, especially my mother who worries that I have no woman in my life."

"Oh, I promise, you've been so kind to me, I'd never tell."

"You have been a good friend, Claire. If I didn't love another I would surely come knocking on your door."

"Oh . . . Daniel," she said shyly and ducked her head. "You're just trying to make a girl feel good."

The fire burned out and Daniel checked the horses. Then they crawled onto the bed of needles, under the great comforting tree, and into their bedrolls.

"I feel like a wrapped Christmas present under here," Claire said and laughed.

"I wonder how old this tree is and I try to imagine all the Christmases it has seen," Daniel said. "I hope you sleep well."

"Good-night," Claire said and she squirmed closer to Daniel.

Daniel dropped off quickly but she heard noises from the night and she couldn't sleep. After a while Claire needed to relieve herself but she was too afraid to leave Daniel's side. The battle went on between her aching bladder and her fear of what was lurking out there in the night. She couldn't ask Daniel to go with her and she didn't dare go alone.

"Daniel, are you awake?" she whispered.

He didn't answer and finally the pain told her she could hold it no longer. She dragged her aching body free of her bedroll and crawled out from under the sheltering branches. She stood. At first she couldn't recognize a thing until her eyes became accustomed to the faint moonlight. Suddenly an immense black monster with huge horns rose up close enough to touch. Towering over her it snorted with a terrifying unearthly sound. She could feel its warm breath. For a second she stood frozen, breathless. Then she panicked.

"Daniel! Daniel! Help!" she shrieked as she dove back under the branches like a burrowing prairie dog with its tail on fire.

Daniel crawled out from under the branches just in time to see the big black bull moose stomping off as if his territory had been violated by some strange screaming unknown creature. Daniel stood and enjoyed a good belly laugh.

"Come on out, your caller has left without you."

"I'm not coming out until daylight."

"You scared the daylights out of a moose, a big bull moose."

"Well, he scared the daylights out of me so we're even."

That wasn't all. As they settled down in their bedrolls and Daniel again fell fast to sleep, Claire realized she didn't have to empty her bladder any longer. She hoped her underwear would dry by morning.

After another long, hard day's ride they reached Buffalo Jump before dark. Claire could hardly walk and Daniel asked her if she'd like him to line up a buggy for the last leg of the journey. On the one hand she hoped Daniel would insist on the buggy, but on the other she wanted to arrive at the ranch on Sugar like an experienced mountain girl. She told him she'd be fine and he didn't insist. After they cared for the horses, with Claire asking unending questions, he gently walked her around town in the coming dusk to stretch her aching muscles and to acquaint her with the closest civilization to the ranch.

Daniel felt proud of her because he knew how much she must hurt after the rugged miles they'd traveled, and she'd done it without knowing how to ride and without complaint. He knew the family would question her spirit and toughness and he felt he had chosen well. They ate at Victoria's Restaurant and Saloon and stayed at the two-story Grand Hotel, the best accommodations in town. Claire wanted to pay for her room but Daniel insisted, convincing her that she was already in the employ of the ranch and the ranch paid all bills at the Grand Hotel.

They met distant neighbors as well as townsfolk and Daniel introduced Claire as a new employee of the Rockhammer Ranch. She wondered what would happen with Sugar at the ranch. Would they keep her? Would they sell her? She hoped they'd let her buy Sugar with money she'd earn over time. And that brought her to her wages. They'd never talked about how much she would make working at The Rockhammer? But she had much less anxiety about it when they said good-night, about to retire to their rooms. Daniel handed her several folded bills, said it was for the past three days and a little in advance. Said everyone needed to have a little money. In the lamplight of her room she unfolded the bills. She caught her breath as she counted out fifty well worn dollars. With what she scraped up when she left Butte she had nearly seventy dollars. She wasn't used to generosity.

With a growing excitement Daniel woke Claire early and they were soon on the road. Claire insisted she saddle Sugar and with Daniel's instruction she pulled the cinch tight and got the filly to take the bit. When she climbed on and her fanny hit the saddle it felt as though she had settled on rock.

Along the road Daniel reminisced about the many things they'd encountered on their trips to town, and closer to the ranch, the things they'd experienced on their travels to school. Maddy's pool, Skipper losing his tail to the grizzly, the spot where Jeremiah came upon Wart and brought him home, the times they drove cattle they'd sold to town or the days they drove a good bull back to the herd. And in the family stories how Grandfather Abraham used the road before it was a road and the Blackfeet were burning down his cabins.

By the time they reached the arch and gate to ride through the gorge, Claire's excitement matched Daniel's. He stopped under the large carved sign hanging high above the road.

--ROCKHAMMER RANCH--

"Welcome to the Rockhammer," Daniel said, with a big smile.
"Thank you," Claire said and she felt a shiver down her back.

Daniel turned Buck and they trotted the horses through the shadows of the gorge out into the glory of a blazing sunset that lit up the mountain ridges and peaks like a great bonfire.

"Here's your enchanted land," Daniel said and he was surprised by a sob.

Touched with this familiar magnificent country, he was overcome with emotion. He turned his face from Claire, found tears in his eyes, knowing this land wasn't enchanted for him and Gabrielle. The prince was forbidden by God to ever ride off with the princess at Rockhammer Ranch.

The family took to Claire like battle-weary soldiers on the front line welcoming reinforcements. Jeremiah's death still hung over the ranch like storm clouds and Claire was like a fresh gust of wind blowing away the darkness. They all weren't at the house until supper and Daniel's return along with the surprise of Claire gave a festive mood to the table. They all went out of their way to make her feel at home and Elizabeth prayed that Daniel and Claire might turn out to be sweethearts.

In the weeks during which Claire settled in, Elizabeth waited anxiously to hear from Gabrielle. It took three weeks, they knew, for a letter to get to St. Paul. They still didn't know if she had heard about her father's death. So many unanswered questions. Elizabeth wished her family was all together. She thanked heaven for Claire, a beautiful and sweet girl who was so competent, already helping Elizabeth run the house efficiently.

Under the shadow of Jeremiah's death, Daniel worked with the herd like a man possessed, with Zack right there in his shadow. And newcomer Billy Bottoms joined his new family on the Rockhammer and within days took to his new life with joy and zeal. He wouldn't talk much about his past. He just wanted to follow these capable young ranchers around and soak up the ranching life. Zack was only five or six years older than him and Zack took him under his wing. The past few years had been congenial to the cattle and they figured they were running nearly two hundred pairs. Billy and Wart worked wherever they could do the most good and Claire was tireless, a gem in the house and out.

She couldn't get over Wart and whenever there was some time she'd wheedle a circus story out of him, which he embellished to greater lengths each time he told it. They were becoming fast friends and she would bake tarts and cookies that were Wart's favorites, and he would get her reading books and talking about them in the evening when chores were done. Sometimes Zack and Billy would join them.

Zack had hung around the kitchen before in search of sweets but he was no longer looking for sugar. Elizabeth's heart sang. She thought highly of Claire as a warm, kind, intelligent young woman who would make someone a marvelous wife. Elizabeth hoped for one grandchild at least, and with Daniel and Gabrielle unmarried and Maddy away teaching school still trying to decide if it is Alan or Chip, it would be up to Zack.

# THIRTY-FOUR

DANIEL AND ELIZABETH received a formal letter from Consolidated Mining Incorporated of Denver, Colorado. In it they were invited to meet at the Grand Hotel in Buffalo Jump, three weeks hence, for dinner and a discussion about the land in which they and Henry Weebow had a common interest. Mr. John David McIves and Randolph Plummer would be present. The letter cautioned the Rockhammers not to talk about Consolidated's interest in the "project" but to keep referring to it as "old Henry Weebow's diggin's," a topic of local gossip for years. The letter stated that Consolidated Mining would look forward to seeing them on the appointed date and was signed by John David McIves.

Daniel and the whole family swung back and forth on whether they ought to meet with Consolidated or not.

"They'll have a slick lawyer or two," Wart said as the family sat at the supper table. "They'll lie through their teeth."

"Grandfather Abraham made a promise to the Blackfeet years ago," Daniel said, "long before Weebow had homesteaded that ground. Father made the same vow as Abraham and I feel obliged to do the same, to honor their word, to honor ours."

"Those are the same high rollers who showed up a few years ago," Zack said. "Henry Weebow and Ben brought them out. Henry said these hard rock geologists were telling him that he might have a significant find, even a bonanza."

"That's what they all say," Wart said.

"In Butte," Claire said, "it seemed you heard about a swindle every day."

"What do they want?" Billy asked.

Daniel explained to Billy. "They want to build a switchback

road on our side of the ridge, carve up the high side of the mountain for half a mile or more."

"Jeremiah made an agreement with Henry Weebow, the agreement Henry had with Abraham, that Henry could cross our land by foot or with mules as often as he wanted," Elizabeth said, "but neither Abraham nor Jeremiah ever gave permission to build the switch-back road."

"But now," Zack broke in, "but now that it looks like the mine might produce, he wants to break the agreement. And now, to top that, he claims that a few weeks before he died, Jeremiah, had agreed to let them build the road."

They discussed it most of the evening and then agreed with Daniel's opinion. He thought it would be to their advantage to imitate the Trojan Horse, to hear what the Consolidated people had to say, to see what they were up to. He wanted to know if they were planning any legal action against the Rockhammer's claims and if they were recorded properly. But most of all, he wanted to check the shoes on the horses they rode to see if any matched the shoe print he found on the ground where Jeremiah died.

The thing that haunted Daniel, as well as the rest of them, was that Tanner, or whoever did the killing, was still there in the aspen grove, watching, while they found Jeremiah and carried him away to the house. The killer would have had to remain hidden in the trees until dark and then sneak away through the gorge and gone. It tormented Zack the most. He was there and didn't think to post a well-armed guard in the gorge, to chain the gate that night when the murdering skunk rode through. But Daniel and the others reminded Zack that at first they believed it had been an accident so there was no reason to post a guard or chain the gate.

Every day, when the necessary work was done, Daniel would find himself combing the aspen grove for any human sign that the assassin hid there before and after he struck down Jeremiah. He had found several piles of horse apples in an area that no horse would have been loose to graze or ridden in trees that dense. He found the bark rubbed off a tree at about the height you'd tie a horse. He found what he believed was human scats and a small corner of paper that looked like a wrapper for chewing tobacco. He would look for the tell-tale bulge in Tanner's lower lip.

And so Billy made a trip to town to get supplies and to send their reply. The Rockhammers would sit at a table with John David McIves, old Henry Weebow, and a Blackfeet warrior about a promise made. The Blackfeet had vanished from this land but the promise remained. That first American believed that the mountain had a soul.

The miners and Weebows had obviously come from the Weebow diggin's when they came into town and tied their horses at the livery. The Rockhammers were waiting at the Grand Hotel and, after formal greetings all around, they settled in the dining room and began the leisurely meal. Henry and Ben Weebow, John David McIves, Randolph Plummer, and Tanner, McIves's ever-present guardian. Tanner didn't sit at the table but stood off near the lobby door like a cigar-store Indian. Daniel, Elizabeth, Zack, and Billy came from the Rockhammer. Daniel wished Gabrielle sat there with her spirit and toughness.

"We're here today," McIves said, "to help Henry develop his find, his dream, which could be quite substantial. He and his boys have worked hard for many years but now they have run into a logistical problem to recover the ore. Working together today I'm sure we can arrive at an agreement that pleases everyone involved."

A waitress began serving heaping plates of pork and beef and homegrown vegetables.

"I was so sorry to hear of your husband's tragic accident," John David McIves said to Elizabeth, sitting directly across the table from her.

Elizabeth had aged in the past few years, and Jeremiah's death had seemed to accelerate the process, but she was still a handsome and dignified woman who could hold her own with the likes of McIves.

"Thank you, the ranch isn't the same without him."

"I know what you mean," McIves said. "I lost my wife three years ago. Maybe it would be good for you to get away from the isolation of the ranch for a time, move into Helena or Bozeman where you could enjoy the bustling society and culture."

"Mother loves her life on the ranch," Zack said with a light snarl in his voice.

"You have a very large operation on the Rockhammer," Randolph Plummer said. "We figured six thousand four hundred and seventy-three acres."

"Have you been checking our claims at the land office?" Daniel asked as he looked across the table at Plummer.

"It's just a routine procedure," McIves said. "We wouldn't want to waste time dealing with land that wasn't legally owned and recorded."

"Jeremiah was very thorough about that," Elizabeth said.

"So we've seen," Plummer said, with a fork full of apple pie in his mouth, "but there's always something, something overlooked."

Elizabeth made brief eye contact with Daniel.

"Daniel," McIves said, "are you aware that your father gave his verbal permission to Henry a short time before he died?"

"I find that hard to believe," Daniel said, "when he had promised his whole life never to give such permission. It was in his blood, Rockhammer blood. And if he had done such a thing he would have surely told my mother about it."

"Yes, but we've learned that people change their minds," Plummer said, "especially when they grow old."

"Henry would have to have it in writing, in any case, and notarized," Elizabeth said.

"So, you don't plan to honor your father's request?" McIves asked.

"Only if it can be proven that he gave Henry that permission," Daniel said and Elizabeth nodded.

The discussion continued in a congenial manner and when a waitress brought coffee all around, Zack whispered in Daniel's ear, "Keep an eye on Tanner," and he slipped into the kitchen and out the back door. He ran behind the hotel, turned at the corner, and sprinted three blocks to the livery. Daniel's plan was to have Zack get a good look at the shoes on the three horses the Consolidated men rode without them seeing Zack doing it. Daniel had already noticed a very subtle bulge in Tanner's lower lip. It was almost time to find the marshal.

Zack went from horse to horse, lifting their feet and looking for the unique horseshoe design they found near the spot where Jeremiah died. On the second horse, a tall gray gelding Tanner rode, Zack found matching shoes. Zack checked the third horse and the mules the Weebows rode but found only the common local variety on those animals. With the deadly evidence he ran back to the hotel and paused at the back door, catching his breath. He wished he'd brought his .45 Colt pistol as the anger boiled through his body. He wanted to walk in and shoot Tanner between the eyes, then quickly the other four. Instead he had to keep his composure and go in and sit with those murdering maggots.

"Well then," McIves was saying, "Henry would like to purchase an easement, a small tract of land for a very generous amount. After the agreed on number of years the land would revert back to the Rockhammer."

"There's no easement or lease or rent that will allow a switch-back road on the side of that mountain," Daniel said.

"All right, all right, let's get over this. We have enough faith in Henry's find that we're willing to buy your ranch, lock, stock and barrel."

"The Rockhammer is not for sale," Elizabeth beat Daniel to the draw.

"Five thousand dollars!" Plummer said.

"You haven't enough to buy the Rockhammer," Daniel said.

"No quibbling. Ten thousand," McIves said.

Zack came back through the kitchen, sat down, and discreetly handed his mother, Elizabeth, a folded note. She was still nodding her head no at McIves as she read the scribbled message.

*They killed Father.*

Elizabeth felt the rage overwhelm her heart and she wanted to lash out at this imposter sitting across the table from her with Jeremiah's blood on his hands. But she held course. The plan was to give no hint that they were on to these treacherous murdering bastards. They still had to prove it and if the Consolidated men knew the Rockhammers were sniffing along their trail they could hide or destroy what evidence had been carelessly left to be discovered.

From her lap Elizabeth passed the note to Daniel. He paused, following the conversation at the table. Then he glanced down into his lap, read the note. He knew it was fortunate that Gabrielle wasn't with them. She would have shot Tanner where he stood and marched the other four off to jail.

"Gentlemen, we have a long ride," Daniel said as he stood. "We've covered the necessary ground."

He wanted to give McIves the Ranski, lay him out on the hotel dining table, but more so he wanted Tanner. Both parties left the hotel quickly and the Rockhammers gathered where the buggy and horses were tied. They didn't speak but one could see the steel resolve in their eyes.

Zack pulled his rifle from his scabbard and checked to see if there was a round in the breech. Daniel took him by the arm.

"Not now," Daniel said. "Not yet."

They were fortunate to catch Marshal Tom Taylor in town before they left for home. They told him their story of Jeremiah's death and their suspicions and their evidence and their conviction that Jeremiah was murdered. Tom had been far off at the time Jeremiah died and he never saw the body though he did see the strange break of the horse's leg. The marshal didn't think they had enough evidence to take them to court but he said he'd see what he could find on Consolidated Mining.

Daniel and the family were extremely disappointed by the marshal's lack of enthusiasm though they knew he was a good man. They carried their heavy hearts home, Zack driving the buggy with Elizabeth, and it was as if each of them knew that they would find their personal way to avenge Jeremiah. Daniel knew it was best Gabrielle wasn't among them for now. He felt they wouldn't be able to prevent her from taking the law into her own hands. They all agreed that they wouldn't tell Gabrielle about the evidence for the time being. Selfishly, Daniel thought it would be a sure way to bring her home.

# THIRTY-FIVE

GABRIELLE STABLED HER HORSE QUICKLY, cutting corners but making sure Prancer had grain and water. She dragged herself through the poorly-lit streets and stumbled up her stairs, exhausted. She'd covered over eleven miles that day and made two visits: one young boy adjusting well to his new surroundings and family, and a very unsettled and homesick girl. At the top of the stairs, she slipped in the door in the pitch dark, closed the door behind her and felt her way toward the lamp. A split-second too late, and without time for her natural instincts of survival to kick in, she realized she wasn't alone.

With a powerful thrust he pulled a gunny sack over her head and jerked it down over her hips. She gasped in shocked surprise. The sack was a tight fit, her arms pinned to her sides, helpless. He must have been standing there in the dark where she almost touched him. With a grunt he threw her on the bed, strong, powerful, on her like a bear, sitting on her legs. She tried to kick but he was dead weight. She raised her head off the mattress and screamed. Instantly he shut her mouth with an iron-fisted punch to the head. She flopped back onto the bed, dazed, stunned. She couldn't breathe, grain dust filled her nostrils, her lungs. The world turned utterly dark. Blood ran into one eye, she felt dizzy, her head throbbed and she couldn't understand what was happening to her.

He fumbled to unbuckle her belt, ripped open the front of her overalls, breathing heavily. He started pulling her britches over her hips. Then he got off her and one by one pulled off her boots. She felt as if she were suffocating, no air, no light, fear choking in her throat. He started pulling down her overalls again and then quit. For a moment she couldn't feel him. A deafening silence. Where did he go? Then a solitary thump followed by a deep guttural sound, and he plopped on her like a great dead carp, his head hitting hers with a whack. He lay there without moving, as if he were the one in the sack, his head pressing against her face, heavy, silent.

"Gabrielle! Gabrielle!" someone called.

That voice, who was there? What was happening in this black, terrifying chaos?

"Daniel! Oh, Daniel, help me," she called.

She began to cry, sobbing into the burlap that was jammed against her mouth. The heavy weight on top of her made it difficult to breathe.

"Gabrielle!" It was Ned's voice. "Gabrielle!"

Then the heavy body rolled off of her and hit the floor with a thud. She could breathe! She could turn her head.

"Ned! Ned! I'm here on the bed," she called with a croaking voice.

Ned found a lamp and lit it.

"Oh, my God," he said.

He sat on the bed beside Gabrielle and with fumbling hands worked the gunny-sack along her body and over her head.

"Oh, Ned, thank God." She was crying. "I couldn't breathe, I couldn't see, I thought I'd die."

"You're safe now, you're safe now," he said while wrapping his arms around her and holding her tightly.

"Who is it? My God, who is it?" she asked with dread while regarding the man on the floor face down.

Ned rolled the body over and they gazed down at Cole Copperman, a look of great surprise frozen on his face.

"Well I'll be a son-of-a-bitch," Ned said. "Whew!"

"Cole? Cole? I . . . I thought it was Charles Appleton," she said.

"I swear, I never would have thought," Ned said.

"Is he out?" she asked.

Ned knelt and held his face close to Cole's. He paused. Then he got up and sat in a chair.

"Is he out?" she asked again.

"He's dead."

"Dead?"

"Yeah, dead as a doornail. He won't ever bother you again."

Ned covered the nattily dressed body with a blanket.

"What on earth did you hit him with?"

"My four pounder, the hammer I use setting type. I heard something up here, like a scream, but it was kind of muffled and for a second I hesitated. But then I figured I'd better come up and see if you were all right. I grabbed the first thing I laid my hands on. When I got up here I couldn't make anything out for a moment it was so blasted dark in here. Then I could see his form and I knew it wasn't you. Cole heard me, turned toward me. In that second or two I figured he wasn't supposed to be here so I conked him. Only hit him once, side a his head. He dropped like I'd shot the bastard. Wish I could have hit him a few more times."

Somewhat wobbly, Gabrielle moved away from the body to a chair by the table. She coughed and began to gag.

"Quick, hand me the dishpan, I'm going to throw up."

Ned grabbed the pan and got it to her just in time as she let go into the pan. Ned steadied the pan and waited. She heaved several times and then it was dry. Ned placed the pan on the table and handed her a dishtowel. She wiped her mouth and winced. In the lamplight she glanced in the dresser mirror and saw she was swollen, bloody, and bruised.

"Damn, he really messed up your face."

She touched her cheek gently, sore, stinging. He fetched a glass of water which she drank lustily. She held the washcloth to the side of her face and looked away from the mirror.

"When he was on you, you yelled for Daniel."

"I did? I don't remember."

"I thought you were shouting at *him*, that *he* was Daniel."

"No . . . Daniel is my brother."

"How long did Cole have hold of you before I got here?" Ned asked.

"I don't know . . . can't remember . . . seems like a long time."

"I never heard you come home, what time did you get in?"

"Well . . . I don't . . . I can't remember."

"Do you remember where you were yesterday?"

"Ah . . . no . . . what day is this?" She couldn't get her bearings.

"Tuesday. The paper comes out tomorrow," Ned said.

"I can't remember . . . where was I today? What's wrong with me?"

"You've been cold-cocked, knocked silly. You ever get conked out before?"

"Once, I fell off the barn roof when I was eight. Couldn't remember anything for a while. My brothers and sister thought it was funny."

"Well that's what's goin' on now. What's my name?"

"Well, I surely know your name."

"What's my name?

"Ah . . . Ned."

"What's your brother's name?"

"Daniel . . . did I call him?"

"Yep."

"That's strange . . . I mean I can remember my brother's name but I can't remember what I did today."

"You come on now down to my place and get some rest and I'll go find Marshal Birt. I saw him yesterday and he said he'd be around for a few days. Probably sleepin' in the jail. And we better get Doc to look at your face."

Ned helped her down the stairs and tucked her in his bed.

"You rest now. I'll hurry."

"Would he have killed me?" she asked looking into Ned's eyes.

"Maybe not. Looks like he was making sure you didn't recognize him."


Gabrielle startled when Ned came through the door of his apartment. It was daylight. She'd been asleep.

"How are you doing?" he asked.

"I must have dropped off . . . I was asleep." She sat up.

"The marshal is up in your place with Wendy Stockwell, his deputy. They'll get Cole out of here. Then we'll get Doc over to have a look at you. How's your head?"

She touched her swollen face. "Sore."

Ned swept a stack of old newspapers off a chair, pulled the chair close to the bed and sat.

"Ned, I want to thank you for saving my life." Her throat filled and tears ran freely across her cheeks. "How can I ever thank you?"

"Gosh, Gabrielle, I'm so damn glad I heard you." His voice broke. "I had dozed off in my clothes, like usual, when something woke me, a muffled shout, a strange noise I'd never heard. I lifted my head and cupped my ear and held my breath for a moment, listening. Everything was quiet and I thought it was nothing. I wanted to stay in my warm blankets and go back to sleep."

"But you didn't," she said. "You didn't! That's the moment you saved me, those few seconds of decision. What made you get up and climb the stairs? Why didn't you stay in your warm bed and go back to sleep?"

"I don't know, but I'll tell you this. If I'd stayed in my warm bed and gone back to sleep and found in the morning he'd had his way with you, that you'd been killed, I wouldn't be able to live with myself. I would not be able to live with myself! In that moment, when I decided to see what the noise was, those few seconds changed our lives completely, yours, mine, Cole's. When I sneaked up the stairs with the hammer I remember telling myself how foolish that was, that I was hearing things, and I decided I'd never mention to you how I was sneaking around the building that night."

"Oh, God." Tears washed freely over her cheeks. "I was a blink from death."

"I'm damn glad . . ." Ned fought back his tears. "I'm damn glad I was there to stop his clock. Damn glad."

"I'm damn glad, too," she said, catching a sob.

Gabrielle looked into his eyes.

"Ned, I want to ask you something, something very personal."

He nodded.

"Do you mind? If you do I don't need—"

"No, go ahead, it's all right." he said.

"Do you believe in God, I mean really really believe?"

Ned regarded her and gazed at the calender on the wall.

"I do, yes . . . I do," he said.

"Do you believe God forgives us when we ask for his forgiveness? When we break His law, when we do something that we know is wrong, sinful?"

He paused. "Yes, I believe he will forgive us."

"Will you ask for His forgiveness for killing a man?"

Ned cocked his head and looked at his hands, creased with black ink. He sighed.

"Yes, I will ask for His forgiveness," he whispered.

"Are you sorry for what you did?"

Ned sighed. "Sorry? No, I'm sure not sorry, I'm glad I was there to stop him."

"Then it won't work. You might as well forget about asking for forgiveness. When you ask for forgiveness you have to be terribly sorry for what you did. Otherwise it won't work."

"I'm glad I killed that slime bag."

"I've never told this to anyone. A long time ago I broke God's law, I knew what I did was wrong, I knew it was a terrible sin. I asked Him for His forgiveness. I ask Him for His forgiveness a hundred times a day, year after year, as many times as there are stars. But here's the catch: I don't receive His forgiveness if I'm not sorry for what I did, awfully sorry. And what I did is the most wonderful thing that has ever happened to me. I could never be sorry for doing it, never. So I've been damned since then and I damn the people who are closest to me, like you. You're not the first good person I've damned."

"Listen, girl, what happened here last night with Cole had nothing to do with you being damned. This was the act of a man evil had invaded, a man who happened to pick you out of the blue. It has nothing to do with your past or what it is you have between you and God. So get that out of your head. My part in it is my doing, my choice, because of something that happened to me long before I ever knew you. Do you ever think that you may have it wrong, that your theology is tangled, that God hasn't damned you after all?"

"Oh, I'm damned all right. I've tried to live a good life but when I begin to believe otherwise, that maybe God has forgiven me, along comes an ice wagon or a Cole Copperman."

"Well, I'm glad I could save you from this brutal, evil man. I suspect I'll have to move on again, but I'll be all right."

"Oh, no, Ned, don't leave. You're happy here and it's been so long. Surely they will have forgotten. You don't have to put much in the paper do you?"

"No, a small news item on the front page, giving credit to the marshal, as much as possible, but there are lawmen out there with handbills on me, papers on someone who got away with murder and they're like bulldogs, they never let go. They lie awake at night thinking, plotting."

"I wish you'd stay. I suppose the Orphan Train Society might not want me to continue at this post, want to move me to another town if there's much negative publicity. I seem to be stirring up a lot of dust."

They heard a strange noise and looked out the side window. The marshal and deputy were dragging Cole Copperman down the stairs, each with one leg, and Cole's head bouncing on every step, thud, thud, thud.

# THIRTY-SIX

DANIEL WAS SPLITTING WOOD on the chopping block for the insatiable stoves when he saw a figure on horseback coming up the road. The rider was too far away to recognize and he kept working, enjoying this task that Jeremiah had taught him when he was very young. From time to time he rested and watched the visitor who was slowly coming on. Squinting, he held his hand against the sun. There was a familiarity in the way the rider sat on the horse. He turned back to the log on the chopping block and was about to swing the axe when it hit him. Gabrielle! No longer at a trot, the horse came charging. He dropped the axe and ran toward her, his heart pounding like the hooves of the horse. She slid off the horse before it had completely stopped and they embraced with unbridled joy, swirling, and swinging in a circle.

"I knew you'd come, I knew it," he said.

"I started as soon as I got word of Father's death."

"I feared I'd never see you again."

"I prayed you'd be here," she said. "How is Mother?"

"She'll be happy to see you. She's completely lost without him."

"We better let go, someone could be watching," she said.

"Just a brother greeting his long lost sister."

Reluctantly they parted and walked toward the buildings while donning their masks for the world of make-believe. Elizabeth came out on the porch and Gabrielle ran to her. Daniel led Gabrielle's horse to the corral and allowed them this time together. They wept aloud and clung together and howled out over the land. When they'd emptied the reservoir of grief they'd stored, that would certainly fill again, they sat on the porch and one by one the family showed up. Zack, Wart, Aunt Grace, and Daniel introduced Claire to Gabrielle. Then Billy Bottoms came across the yard and stood just off the porch. When Gabrielle saw him she lost a breath and sprung off the wood bench.

"Billy? Are my eyes deceiving me? Billy Bottoms! What are you doing here?"

She hugged him fiercely and he stood astonished.

"Mrs. Douglas! What are *you* doing here?"

Everyone laughed and hooted and grasped the happiness so fragile at Rockhammer Ranch. Billy told Gabrielle his adventures since she last saw him and she kept shaking her head in disbelief. Gabrielle went out to the grave with Elizabeth and they were gone most of an hour. Gabrielle prayed silently that she and Daniel hadn't brought their sin and punishment down on Jeremiah. Had they damned him too? She came close to telling her mother the truth but knew what damage it would do to her and the family.

When the family was gathered around the supper table, and after Elizabeth had persuaded Claire to sit with them and to quit waiting on them out of habit, Elizabeth said that Gabrielle's arrival was God-sent. Daniel and Gabrielle exchanged a glance.

"It's time to round up the herd and get the babies branded and make little steers out of little bulls," Elizabeth said. "I was just planning to hire some help, but now, with Gabrielle here I think we can do it ourselves." She smiled at Gabrielle. "Can you still rope a bucking calf?"

"Yes, it hasn't been that long ago," Gabrielle said. "We can teach Billy."

When supper was over Claire served some strong coffee and Gabrielle's family told her every shred of fact about what they knew of Jeremiah's death. Gabrielle's nostrils flared like a horse, and she had to stomp around the room as they brought her up-to-date on the Weebows and their unfortunate entanglement in the affairs of the Rockhammer.

A few days later they would be executing the roundup, each of them having an assignment—even Claire—and a fresh excitement brightened the mood. Gabrielle and Daniel would be mounted and cutting out the calves and roping, Zack and Billy would wrestle the roped calves and hold them down long enough to brand. Zack would castrate the little bulls and Wart would keep the fire going and the branding irons hot. Claire would work the gate and soon discover how quick the calves were, chasing back to mom. Aunt Grace would stand outside the corral and keep count. Elizabeth, acting as straw boss, would oversee the operation and bring fresh water and food as needed.

Daniel snuck out around midnight and Gabrielle was there ahead of him.

"I couldn't have gone another minute," she said as they crawled under the blanket he'd brought.

"*You* couldn't! I almost grabbed you at the dinner table and took you in my arms and told them all, everything, out with it, so I could breathe again, so I could quit holding my breath."

"O God, you feel so good," she said. "Are you really here in my arms?"

"Yes, I'm here, and I don't ever want to let you go."

"Are you going to stay on the ranch?" she said as they held each other.

"Yes, I'm not leaving again. Please stay, for now. Stay here with me. We can do it. It won't be as bad as being hundreds of miles apart, we could see each other and work together, please."

"I'll try," she said, "I'll try, but we have to be careful. We were always so close, you have to tease me and roughhouse with me."

"I know, I know," he said.

"And you have to treat me as your kid sister, banter with me and compete with me and try to act as we did before, even though we've grown up. We'll have to act our parts perfectly."

"It'll be hard, we'll be walking a thin line, afraid to slip and fall on one side or the other," he said.

"We'll have to be careful being together like this, we can't meet every night, I can't tell Maddy I'm going to the outhouse so often, she'll get suspicious, but she'll be going back to school soon and then I'll be alone in that room."

They talked and held each other until it was time to get back in the house.

"No matter how hard," he said, "we'll have each other, we'll be together, I won't have to wonder where you are and if you're safe and if you still love me."

"You live in my heart as long as I'm alive," she said.

With some relief and much hope they kissed goodnight and Gabrielle hurried into the night. He'd follow in a while. They had to be careful, never both be seen moving around in the middle of the night.

It was the kind of day that may be remembered with aching nostalgia. Perfect, like a day out of a fairy tale. A friendly sun with a soft westerly breeze and ravens and magpies sailing around and calling from the cottonwoods. Snow-covered peaks surrounded them and the greening of early summer was almost blinding. The day before it took most of the daylight to move the herd down from the middle pasture. They were all mounted, except Wart who stayed back with Elizabeth. They could hear the Herefords complaining in the large corral all through the night. The next morning they assembled under a crystal-clear blue sky for the long day's work ahead. Gabrielle and Daniel were mounted and showed no fatigue from their lack of sleep. They were together and yet far apart and the earth in all its glory baptized all of them with beauty, beauty so bright they had to duck their eyes.

They took their places and started the work ahead with whoops, whistles, and shouts. The crew went after the little Herefords like rustlers, shouting and laughing and cussing and joking, The calves leaped over one another to escape these villainous human beings, called to one another as warnings, and bleated for their moms. They ran north and back south, dodging east and bolting west, trying to hide behind their mothers while the mothers bellowed and the calves bawled. They hurtled wide-eyed, digging in their heels against the pull of the rope, sprinting and swooping and cutting like a jailbreak from an insane asylum.

Billy got kicked more than once as well as Zack. Zack sprang to Claire's rescue when several calves jammed against the gate and she couldn't open it. Wart fell into fresh manure and cussed words none of them had ever heard. Gabrielle roped Daniel and pulled him off his horse to everyone's amusement, so he dowsed her with water from the jug. Just like they did when they were kids. Billy and Claire and Wart all did excellent jobs and by the end of the day were old hands. Aunt Grace refused to talk all day, making her count by penciling marks in her tablet. The crew had handled and branded eighty-three calves, meaning they'd only lost seven to the wolves, mountain lions, or sickness.

At the end of the day, they sat on the porch, filled with a bone-weary but satisfying tiredness. Zack and Claire were holding hands and acting goofy. Daniel kept stealing glances and sharing smiles with Gabrielle, Wart fended off requests for a story—he was just too dang tired. Billy, Elizabeth, and Aunt Grace had already retired. And when the night couldn't get any softer, from off toward the Weebow's side of the mountain came a distinct rumbling—a reminder that evil lurked just over the horizon.

# THIRTY-SEVEN

DANIEL NEVER SAW HIM COMING. The man just stood there beside the bell looking out over the river. Daniel had been grooming his horse after a long ride into the valley checking cross fences. Daniel slipped through the corral poles and walked cautiously toward the stranger, checking him for weapons and seeing only a walking stick. He quickly realized this was none of the Weebow bunch. The man moved slowly with a crippled step and Daniel saw that he was an Indian.

"Hello!" Daniel called as he closed the distance between them.

The man waved his hand across his chest and Daniel found himself doing the same. Daniel could see that he was very old, skin and bone, under a dirty ragged Canada blanket. Under the blanket he wore tattered clothing, some buckskin, some store-bought. A twisted scar across his face took out one eye and in his leather purselike mouth several teeth were missing. His thinning gray hair was pulled back and tied behind his head. He looked like a man who had stood against the catastrophes of life and lost.

"Hello, welcome," Daniel said as they stood in front of the house facing each other. "Welcome to our home."

The Indian nodded and looked over at the river.

"By what name is the river known?"

"We call it The River That Rolls Rocks."

"Mmmm." He nodded.

"I think the Blackfeet named it before white face was here," Daniel said.

"Mmmm." The Indian turned back and gazed into Daniel's face. "What is your name?"

"Daniel. Daniel Rockhammer, I live in this valley with my family. My grandfather lived here with the Blackfeet."

"Mmmm. What was grandfather's name?"

"Abraham, Abraham Rockhammer."

"Was grandfather a white face?"

"Yes . . . my grandfather Abraham was white face."

"I want to find one called Stone Face. Did you know him?" the Indian asked.

Daniel could see the man was tired, propping himself up on his walking stick.

"Let's sit on the porch, I'm tiring," Daniel said.

The man shuffled to the porch as if his lame body was remembering a lifetime of wounds. In his stooped condition Daniel figured he wasn't much over five feet. They settled on the porch benches facing each other.

"Did you know one called Stone Face?"

In his head Daniel scanned the stories Jeremiah told so often around the fire and he thought Stone Face might have been a name the Blackfeet called Abraham but he wasn't sure.

"That might have been the Indian name for my grandfather Abraham. But I'm not certain. Did your people know him?"

"Mmmm. I know him many winters ago, maybe he has gone to other world."

"You *knew* my grandfather!"

"When I was a boy."

"Are you sure . . . how did you know him?"

"He pulled me from the river, right over there." He pointed to the river bank in front of the house.

*"You're* the boy he saved?"

"I am the one, I am that boy."

"Oh, Lord, my father told us the story many times, as his father told him. This is incredible, it's hard to believe, to actually meet you."

"The river wanted to eat me. Stone Face and his horse beat the river. He dragged me across like a fish."

Daniel stood abruptly and shouted at the open front door.

"Gabrielle! Mother! Claire! Everyone, come quickly!"

Daniel sat back on the bench and turned to the old man.

"What's your name?" Daniel asked with excitement in his voice.

"I am Swims With Rocks."

"Have you come a long way?"

"Yes . . . a long way."

"Where are you going?" Daniel said.

"I'm going home, to be with my family, to be with my people."

Elizabeth came out on the porch, followed by Wart, and then Claire. They stood in awe of this strange old man who had come out of nowhere. Daniel smiled and felt goosebumps on the back of his neck.

"Mother, this is Swims with Rocks. He is the boy that grandfather Abraham saved from the river. He's on his way home."

The Rockhammer family did everything they could for Swims With Rocks but it wasn't much. They invited him to stay with them and rest up. Though he accepted some food, he refused to take any with him. Daniel offered him a horse for his journey though he feared the old man wasn't strong enough to ride. He was anxious to be on his way and they could think of nothing more to keep him there—to all of them he was a world-renowned celebrity. He was that and more to Daniel who felt a strong emotional tie to this man who was at the very middle of a family legend. Before he left, Swims With Rocks showed Daniel and the others a knife Abraham had given him. Worn down to half its original width, it had faint initials still showing "AR" carved in the bone handle.

The whole family stood out by the bell as Swims With Rocks said good-bye. He was determined to continue further into the valley despite Daniel's and the others' warnings.

"There's nothing up there but our cattle, no place to sleep, no shelter, no place to get food, you have to go back and around."

"I will go the way of my people," said Swims With Rocks.

"Well you can't go that way," Daniel pointed northwest up the valley, "the ridges are too steep, there's no pass, no way through."

"I know a way," the Indian said and pointed up the valley. "That is the way to my people."

He confused Daniel. Could there be a pass up there that they'd never found in all these years? That the Blackfeet knew and never revealed to them? The frail old man withstood their concerned persuasion and shuffled off, ill-prepared and going the wrong way. Daniel tried to visualize so many years ago, a small Blackfeet boy fishing along the River That Rolls Rocks.

# THIRTY-EIGHT

THEY SAY A DOOR was never locked at Rockhammer Ranch. Many doors had no lock, only a latch. It would have made no difference that night if the doors had been locked.

On that unsuspecting evening a chilly breeze carried the serenade of the night creatures to the house: insects, frogs, an occasional owl. Daniel and Billy sat in the dining room with Elizabeth, looking over the books and making plans for the coming days. Zack and Claire were out on the porch, spooning under a waning moon, and Aunt Grace, who was out at the ranch recovering slowly from a touch of pneumonia, was bundled under a quilt in the rocking chair.

In the kitchen Gabrielle ate what was left of the huckleberry pie while Wart, who had hauled wood for the big fireplace and lit a fire, sat on the wood box reading a book. Gabrielle and Daniel planned to meet at midnight and she found time dragging until they'd be together.

A hawk was mentioned in Wart's book and he looked up and told the family how earlier in the day he saw a beauty of a large red-tail hawk floating lazily high above the river. Wart followed the flight of the cunning predator, still excited by the uncounted animals they observed on the ranch.

"That beauty will clean up a lot of gophers," Zack said.

"Wart," Elizabeth winked to the others," why don't you train that bird to snag a chicken for you."

"That isn't funny," Wart said.

"Yes, Wart, why do you do that?" Claire asked. "You go crazy for a few minutes."

A chorus of voices joined, the many whose curiosity had been put off for the last time with "it's a long story."

With a grand sigh Wart settled on the woodbox.

"Yes, I would love to know," Grace said.

It felt like Wart was seriously considering revealing his nagging secret. Breath was suspended, glances exchanged, nobody moved. Wart finally spoke.

"Well I ended up in a orphanage for homeless boys. No one knew where I came from. We never had any parents, we were too poor."

Everyone laughed, even Wart. He smiled at Elizabeth.

"That's where you got your name, right?" Zack asked.

"Yeah, from that stinking headmaster. He said there weren't any papers on me. Every Monday they'd get together in the chapel, there were about a hundred kids. The headmaster figured I needed a name 'cause I told him something different every time he asked. I could tell he didn't like me. You can always tell if someone don't like you. He marched me up in front of all the kids and gave me a name.

"'Son, you are going to be known as a wart on the ass of God.' Wart! All the boys laughed and hollered and clapped: 'Wart, Wart, Wart!' It was funny but I figured this wasn't a kind place. And besides, they didn't know how old I was and every time they asked me I told them a different age.

"My name became popular for good or bad and they couldn't figure me out. Some kids were kind but others made fun of me and chased me around when we had free time in the afternoon. They made fun of me a lot and pulled pranks that I got blamed for. Sometimes a stray stone came my way or a dirty word. The orphanage had a cow, a pig, and a large flock of wild chickens roosting around an old weather-beaten chicken coop.

"One hot summer afternoon I could tell the big, older boys were bored. They were dangerous when they were plotting and it didn't take them long to find a target. I outran them for a while but they cornered me in one of the old ramshackle buildings. A skinny guy named LeRoy led the gang and I thought I was headed for the water trough. LeRoy liked to see me in the water. He was laughing and hollering with a mean look on his face and promising a good show for anyone who showed up out behind the old barnyard.

"They hauled me past the water tank and I made it out to the chicken coop. The headmaster didn't like it when they tossed me in the tank. I'd be dripping all over the next class. But the boys had something new that stirred them all up. Some dirty old rope. I wondered what they were going to do with the rope. I figured it wouldn't be fun at all. A bunch of boys got down on their hands and knees and tied me to an old chicken coop frame half buried in the hard packed ground. They tied me good.

"The chickens hardly noticed us but then a bossy rooster worked his way up onto my pants and started pecking like he was starving. The boys were howling and chickens were coming from every direction and the pecks were starting to hurt. Lots of pecks all over me. The boys opened my shirt and tossed more feed over me. It really hurt and I told them to stop and I could see the bloody pokes on my skin and I was trying not to cry. I was trying to protect my eyes. The little boys were slinking away first until it was only LeRoy and a handful of the bigger boys left. They untied me and took me to the woman we called nurse. She weren't no nurse. I run away the next day."

With Wart's last word the room went profoundly silent. No one moved, no one could find a word, but slowly each of them told Wart how sorry they were and how glad they were that he was here, forever, at the Rockhammer. But with the story out of the bag, Wart never had the urge to chase chickens again.

They came silently, swiftly, materialized out of the darkness like a nightmare. There were five of them, guns in hand. Ben and Rufus Weebow barged in the front, shoving Zack and Claire into the dining room ahead of them. Shocked, Elizabeth, Billy, and Daniel jumped up from the table with the impulse to fight.

"Sit down, Rockhammer!" Ben said. "Sit down! This is just a friendly neighborly visit."

Roscoe Camp, a no-account Daniel had seen in town from time to time, came from the kitchen, pushing Gabrielle with his pistol and grabbing Wart who realized too late what was happening.

"Hey!" Gabrielle said, "keep your grubby hands off me!"

"Look what I found," Roscoe called to the others, holding Wart off the floor by his belt. "A little freak!"

Aunt Grace, thinking the men wouldn't hurt her, stood up to defend Wart, but Frank Moss shoved her.

Billy ignored trouble and he quickly caught Aunt Grace and helped her back into her rocker.

One by one they settled into chairs around the table.

Moss, a grubby ruffian with a wide black Mexican hat, had been a familiar character loitering around Buffalo Jump over the past summer. Twice Daniel had hired him to load a wagon.

"You throwing in with this bunch, Frank?" Daniel asked.

"Ben Weebow!" Elizabeth hollered. "You take these men and get out of here right now. Jeremiah and your father were friends for forty years." She shook a finger at him. "You should be ashamed."

"Sit down and hold your water, grandma!" Roscoe said, pointing his pistol at her. The pistol shook slightly in his hand and his voice had a tremor. Daniel figured he was new at this, maybe a weak link.

The fifth man came from the front and when Daniel recognized him he knew they were in serious trouble. It was Tanner, the henchman for the big mining executive from Denver. He didn't speak, just stood at the edge of the room in a black full-length duster and wide-brimmed hat pulled snug to his eyebrows. He carried a large coil of rope in one arm and wasn't armed as far as Daniel could see. Because none of them made any attempt to hide their identity, he realized that they planned to kill them, the whole family.

"We didn't count on a midget," Roscoe said and laughed.

Tanner looked at Ben and nodded.

"That's enough, Camp," Ben said. "All right, everyone sit down. Sit down and shut up!"

The family sat on the edge of the chairs and exchanged furtive glances, colored with shock and alarm. Daniel tried to hold the fort emotionally and discover a way out of this.

"The big boys will take the mine away from you, Ben, after you've taken care of us," Daniel said as if offering a neighbor a cup of sugar or loaning him a tool.

"Just do what we tell you and no one gets hurt," Ben said.

"This all of them?" Tanner asked without emotion.

"All but one daughter," Ben said, "but she's out of the state teaching school somewhere. We don't have to worry about her."

"Where do you keep the money?" Rufus asked.

Daniel felt a flicker of hope. But if that's what they want—money—they sure wouldn't go about it like this.

"It's in the desk drawer in the living room," Daniel said.

Rufus went to the desk and found the cash. Frank took a .50 caliber buffalo gun off the wall.

"Always wanted one these," he said.

"Put it back!" Tanner punctuated the words. "There can't be anything missing people would notice. We take nothing, leave no evidence that anyone had been here."

"Does your father know what you're doing?" Daniel asked Ben.

"The old man's time is up," Ben said. "We're not gonna let you keep us from our fortune because of two old men and some stinking promises to some drunk Indians."

"Ben Weebow, did you kill Jeremiah?" Elizabeth asked. "Did you kill my husband?"

Roscoe Camp smiled.

"He got thrown from a horse is the way I heard it," Ben said. "He never was much of a horseman."

"You son-of-a-bitch!" Daniel said. "You're afraid to fight fair and square. How about it, right now, you and me, if I win you all just ride off, no one's hurt, or do you just pick on old men."

Daniel hoped he could bait him into a fight.

"You always were a bully, Ben," Gabrielle said. "even on the playground. Always afraid to take on someone your size. Your father should have drowned you the day you were born."

Ben stepped over and slapped Gabrielle hard across the face. Daniel stood quickly as Rufus hit him on the head with his pistol, sending him back into his chair.

"And you always had a big mouth," Ben said to Gabrielle.

Zack stood. "Try that with me!"

Roscoe shoved Zack back in the chair and put the barrel of his gun on Zack's head. He looked at Wart who stood in a chair.

"Who in the hell is this pipsqueak, or what is it?"

"Put it in the oven," Frank said.

"I give you fair warning, men," Wart said. "I am a powerful wizard and I can cast a spell on you that will kill you, a curse that will follow you to the grave."

Daniel held his smile within himself while he nodded at Wart.

"You'll be covered with boils and you'll go blind and your testicles will shrivel up and fall off and—"

"Shut up, you little monkey," Ben said, "or I'll cast a spell on you with lead." He turned his revolver on Wart.

Tanner barked. "Enough! We're wasting time with this horseshit." He nodded at Daniel. "Take him first."

Roscoe and Rufus shoved Daniel down the hall to the big bedroom and made him lie down on the bed, face first. They had a spool of new rope and they hog-tied him. Bound his hands behind his back, tied his ankles together, and then folded his legs up his back and tied them to his wrists. Then they tipped him on his side. He was helpless.

"Don't go anywhere," Rufus said and laughed.

"You always were a chicken shit, Rufus," Daniel said.

"Well who's tied like a hog about to be roasted and who's going to be rich?" Rufus asked.

"You won't be rich for long," Daniel said. "You'll never get away with this, everyone from here to Buffalo Jump will know it was you."

"They'll never prove it, they'll never prove it," Rufus said. "We ain't leavin' a clue. Tanner can make it look like an accident. Someone left the screen off the fireplace and when a few coals popped out on the floor everyone was sleepin'. By the time they woke up it was too late, just a terrible accident."

"Tanner and his bunch will kill you, both of you, you'll be a threat to them, and you'll end up with nothing."

"The hell you say," Rufus said. "They's givin' us five thousand dollars! Five thousand dollars, each of us. We'll just keep working at the mine as if nothing happened. If it gets too hot for us here Tanner says he'll get us good jobs in Nevada or California."

"Have you got the money yet?" Daniel asked.

"We'll get it tomorrow, when we's at the mine," Roscoe said.

Tanner called from the dining room. "C'mon, c'mon, get it done!"

"Maybe I'll take a little piece of your sister before I leave," Rufus said. "She always turned my crank."

He whacked Daniel across the shoulder.

"Go to hell!" Daniel said.

"Oh, no, you're the one going to hell," Rufus said and he walked back into the dinning room.

They took them one by one and hog-tied them on their beds.

"Take the old dame, Camp," Ben said. "She ain't part of the family but she's in the same boat."

"Why we tying them on the beds?" Camp asked.

"Just do it!"

Tanner snapped his words, observing coldly from the living room where a fire dwindled in the large fireplace.

Roscoe Camp dragged Grace into her bedroom and roughly shoved her onto the bed. Rufus grabbed Claire, who was trembling with fear and trying to be brave.

"I'll take this one," Rufus said. "They ought to find what's left a them in bed all normal like."

He hugged Claire from behind and fondled her breasts through her blouse as he lifted her from her chair.

"Don't you touch her, you filthy maggot!" Zack shouted.

"What are you going to do about it?" Rufus asked as he caressed the back of Claire's neck.

Zack jumped out of his chair and managed one step toward Rufus when Ben hit him with the butt of his revolver. Zack dropped to his knees.

"Stop it!" Gabrielle shouted, "stop it!"

Zack slumped on the floor beside his chair. Blood oozed from the back of his head. He looked up at Rufus who held Claire with his arms around her waist. Zack spoke slowly with a firm voice that belied his predicament.

"You better kill me, Rufus, you better kill me right now, because if I get out of this I'll find you and I'll tear your heart out with my bare hands."

"Oh, little brother, you won't be doing anything with your bare hands," Rufus said, "but I will." He laughed.

"Let her go," Ben said, "we haven't got—"

"Damnit, Ben! it won't take long," Rufus said. He glared at his big brother. "I just want a little fun."

"Be quick about it," Tanner said, "we're here too long."

Rufus carried Claire down the hall and into a bedroom.

While they tied up a groggy Zack, the last one, they could hear Claire fighting against the big, strong Weebow boy. Then they could tell he had her tied and had his way with her.

When they had them all snugly tied in their beds the house went silent and Daniel, struggling against the ropes, wondered how much time they had. Gabrielle was down the hall from him and he called her.

"Gabrielle, can you hear me?"

"Yes, oh yes, Daniel, don't give up, don't ever give up on us."

Then suddenly they could hear the intruders moving around the house, shouting at each other, breaking glass, slamming doors.

Daniel called to Wart who was tied down on a bed stand.

"Wart! Can you hear me? Can you get loose?"

Daniel hoped Wart had one more circus trick in his bag.

"I'm trying," Wart shouted. "I'm trying."

"We haven't much time."

They could hear Grace gagging, struggling to breathe.

"I'm with you, Daniel!" Gabrielle shouted. "I'm right there with you."

Daniel didn't answer. He listened. And then he knew. He could smell the smoke, hear the fire. The devil had come.

They say that the killers saturated the house with fire, kerosene and lamp oil torches that would conjure a fire that burns completely leaving no trace. The flames licked up the dry wood building like a hungry dragon, its tongue racing up walls and swallowing shingles, its torrid heat sucking moisture out of anything close and blowing out windows. The family shouted to one another, some closer to the inferno than others, but no matter how much they shouted they couldn't break free. The Weebows and the two ruffians had done their work well, their knots could not be loosened. Nothing living could stay alive long in that roaring hell.

Standing outside a safe distance the killers paused to admire their handiwork, a tremendous torch that lit up the valley, shooting sparks and carrying light debris high into the sky. Then they scrambled off on foot into the aspen grove where they'd tied their horses and galloped away into the night, hoping to be seen by no human eye.

Daniel, with a Herculean straining of every muscle in his body, managed to tip over the edge of the bed onto the floor. The choking smoke made it nearly impossible to see or breathe. He could hear voices shouting, calling for help, amid the roar of the predatory fire, but like a big overturned turtle he laid on his side on the floor, helpless.

"Gabrielle! Gabrielle!" he cried. They were damned after all.

Then the family shouted no longer while the cracking and splintering of the fire increased to a howl and each of them contemplated their own death.

They say Daniel thought he was dreaming, certain it was a vision, that he was dying and witnessing angelic beings from another world. He blinked his eyes several times and bit his tongue. Out of the overpowering heat and swirling smoke he saw Swims With Rocks crawling toward him with a knife in hand. The old Indian quickly cut Daniel free.

"In the other rooms, go, go!" Daniel shouted and waved toward the other bedrooms.

Swims With Rocks crawled up the hall and Daniel found Gabrielle by chance or destiny. He untied her quickly.

"Get out! Go, go!" he shouted.

"No, not until the others."

They crawled together, freeing those they found. Billy, Claire, Wart.

"Out through the kitchen!" Daniel shouted at each of them.

When Daniel had counted heads and sent Gabrielle out ahead of him, he found Swims With Rocks prone on the dining room floor. Daniel draped him over his back and crawled out into the yard.

"Is everyone out?" Daniel shouted to the scattered family.

"No!" Elizabeth shouted. "Grace went back in for something."

Daniel raced to the kitchen door and stopped as Grace, clutching a leather purse, stumbled out and fell into his arms.

Gathered in front of the house near the bell, they stood silently in the waning glow of the fire, singed and smudge-faced and ragged, watching their home disappear in the mystery of fire. The original cabin Abraham built, used now as a woodshed beside the kitchen, gone. The first addition Abraham and Martha built alone against the wilderness, doubling the size of the home where Alfred and Nellie and Jeremiah were born, gone. The wing to the north built out of sawed wood and shingles, all gone. Elizabeth's large living room with the grand fireplace, up in smoke. Bits of blackened coals and sailing flakes of gray ash—could this really be all that remained of the house?

Daniel hugged Swims With Rocks and expressed the deep gratitude they all felt for his miraculous appearance. One by one each of them embraced the old man and expressed their undying gratitude. Daniel reminded him that he had saved Abraham's cabin from burning a long time ago and only now had that first cabin burned down.

"How did you know we were burning?" Daniel asked him.

"Great Spirit quest by river where Stone Face rescued me. I saw the fire in the sky. It told me to come."

Daniel told him that surely whatever else had happened to him through his life, he was meant to come back and save Abraham's family, to repay that debt. The Indian nodded. Daniel wanted to ring the bell all through the night, to send word across the valley that evil was loose, but he didn't want to alert the Weebows that the Rockhammers were very much alive and on their trail.

When the house was all but gone, they eventually stumbled and coughed as they made their way to the bunkhouse. There they settled and made do with what they had. As the shock wore off they began hugging and making vows and promises of reprisal. Daniel and Gabrielle had their rifles hanging in their scabbards on the wall and there were two .45 Colts in a wood drawer with several boxes of ammunition. All their other guns were in the fire. There was enough bedding and bunks for everyone to lie down and try to sleep.

Wart and Swims With Rocks slept side by side on a bed of straw in a corner of the bunkhouse, under horse blankets. It was midnight.

Claire allowed Zack to hold her as they slept and she sobbed intermittently all through the night.

At dawn they were up and making plans. Elizabeth, Claire, and Wart would stay at the ranch, doing what they could to make things livable. Elizabeth made it clear to all of them that what happened to Claire would be sealed in the family's sacred vault never to be mentioned to another living soul. Zack spoke through his clenched teeth. "Amen! Rufus won't live long enough to tell the devil."

Gabrielle would outfit the buggy, make it as comfortable as possible for Grace with horse blankets and whatever. Gabrielle would drive the buggy with her saddle horse trailing. She'd have her rifle at her side. Daniel, Zack, and Billy would ride their strongest horses and shepherd the buggy to town. Daniel had his rifle and the other two wore the pistols. If they got to the Y without any sign of the Weebows—who would be trying to act normal as if nothing out of the ordinary had happened—Daniel would race ahead into town and hopefully locate Tom Taylor, the US marshal, or at least his deputy, Chester Lyme. Though they tried to convince him to stay, Swims With Rocks was adamant that he say good-bye and continue on his journey home.

As they galloped out of the gorge and pushed their horses for town, Daniel felt a smile dawning on his face and in his heart. The Weebows, in all their evil planning, hadn't figured on one little Indian boy who got rescued from The River That Rolls Rocks and came back to settle accounts.

# THIRTY-NINE

THEY REACHED BUFFALO JUMP at dusk on lathered horses. Daniel had raced ahead and with a stroke of good luck found Tom Taylor, the US marshal, in town, usually long distances away tracking some horse thief or worse. The Rockhammers settled in the hotel and made plans with the marshal. Tom Taylor was a solidly built man in his forties who wore a bushy graying mustache that matched the color of his big tireless gelding. Tom and his horse had the reputation that they could track the devil all the way to hell. Tom lived in Red Water with his wife and two kids and though he was warm and friendly when off duty, you didn't want to get on his wrong side. But when Tom was out on the trail the local residents were still isolated from any semblance of law and order.

Finding the doctor was a different matter; his wife thought he was off somewhere delivering a baby but hadn't seen him in two days. She helped Gabrielle get Grace into bed in the doctor's house. Gabrielle feared that Aunt Grace wouldn't recover from one of her coughing spasms or from the turmoil she'd gone through in the past terrible hours. The anger in Gabrielle had metamorphosed into hatred and rage and she wanted to go with the men to exact a just punishment. She and Daniel were able to embrace and kiss with an anxious desperation while they tended to the horses in the dark. Aching for Daniel, Gabrielle rested on a cot next to Grace's bed.

The marshal had four men with him the morning they were ready to leave town for the Weebow mine—Daniel, Zack, Billy, and deputy Chester Lyme. They were well armed as they gathered on horseback in front of the jail. Daniel thought Chester looked

343

like a miner from Butte, thin as a rail and slightly stooped. Single and not yet thirty, Chester wore a big .45 revolver and a big disarming smile whether he was watching a hanging or helping a lady getting out of her wagon on a muddy street. Marshal Taylor trusted Chester in any kind of showdown. Better still, Chester was fast out of the holster.

Gabrielle ran from Doc Benson's house and caught the men before they left. Zack circled on his horse, aching to keep his promise to Rufus Weebow. She came to Daniel and took hold of one of his reins. She looked up at him with an expression he'd never seen, a terrible sadness mixed with an unquenchable rage.

"I want to go with you!" she shouted.

"No, this is no place for a woman," Daniel said, "you could get hurt or killed."

"And when did you become bulletproof?" she asked, angry at being left out when she could outshoot most of them.

"Can you kill a man?" Daniel asked her.

Gabrielle met his eyes and without blinking said, "Yes!"

"Tell her, Tom," Daniel hollered to the marshal.

"He's right, Gabrielle," the marshal said, "you can do more right here. That woman needs your help."

The horses milled impatiently.

Gabrielle spoke softly to Daniel as he leaned down to her.

"Come back to me, my love, come back to me."

Daniel nodded, Gabrielle let go of his rein, and the marshal nudged his horse. They trotted out of town to make this little corner of the world safer from the evil that had taken root in the valley.

After pushing their horses for hours, the posse arrived at the trail to the mine and rode the weary mounts halfway up. They tied their horses in an aspen grove and cautiously hoofed it the rest of the way. The marshal laid out his plan as they climbed. He wanted to walk into the camp with Chester as though nothing had happened, a routine visit when the marshal and deputy were in the area, the kind of thing Marshal Taylor did do from time to time. It could be days or weeks before anyone discovered the mayhem on the isolated Rockhammer Ranch so they could easily pretend they didn't know yet. After all, there was no traffic on Rockhammer's dead-end road except those doing business with the ranch.

The marshal wanted to find out how many there were at the mine. Daniel, Zack, and Billy had to stay out of sight. If any of the Weebows saw them they'd know the jig was up. Daniel and the other two would surround the camp and cut off anyone trying to flee down the mountain. The marshal wanted to get the jump on them, disarm them, and bring them to town where they could be tried and hanged.

When the three were ready to spread out, Zack to the left, Billy to the right, Daniel in the middle, Daniel grabbed Zack's arm.

"Keep your head down, I promised your mother I'd bring you home alive."

"I promised Rufus I'd bring him home dead," Zack said.

As Marshal Taylor and Deputy Lyme approached the mine they could hear voices. They passed three mules and three saddled horses tied in the trees beside the trail quietly swatting flies. A short distance further the trail opened out onto a wide manmade plateau, about a hundred feet across. Blasted out of a majestic granite outcrop, a rock wall thirty feet straight up, the entrance to the mine had been carved out wide enough for ore cars. The rock and gravel they continued to haul out of the tunnel fanned out from the mine entrance and added to the tons of rock that were slowly burying the neighboring lodgepole trees.

The marshal and the deputy stopped a few paces onto the gravel-packed yard and quickly surveyed the layout. There were two tents on their left, one larger with a stovepipe, the cook tent. A stack of split wood stood behind the tent with a chopping block and axe. Several barrels stood just outside the tunnel and a variety of tools leaned against the granite wall. Several tons of milky quartz was piled on their right, maybe the rock that held the gold. A crude wood table and two benches sat near the entrance with a fire ring of rocks and an iron grill propped over the rock. A rifle leaned against the wall just inside the tunnel.

"Hello, anybody here?" the marshal yelled.

The voices went silent. Tom and Chester edged forward a bit and stopped about thirty feet from the tunnel. The only movement was a magpie scolding from the wood table. Then a strange rattling echoed hollowly from the tunnel and Frank Moss came pushing a wheelbarrow half full of rocks. On seeing the marshal he stopped in his tracks and stood holding the wheelbarrow as if he'd been caught with his hand in the cash drawer.

"Hello, Frank," Tom said, "working hard?"

"Whatta ya want?" Frank asked with a quiver in his voice.

"Oh, nothing, just passing through. Ben around?"

Frank set the wheelbarrow down. "He ain't here."

The marshal almost went for his revolver when a flap on the large tent flipped open and out popped Rufus.

"Hey, Tom, what're you up to?" Rufus asked real friendly like.

"On our way over to Red Water," the marshal said, "thought we'd stop and see how the mine's comin'."

Rufus had a revolver in his belt and the marshal could see another rifle leaning on a water barrel by the tunnel. Frank nervously pushed the wheelbarrow to the edge and dumped it.

"Is your brother around?" Tom asked Rufus.

"Don't know, I've been sleepin' . . . never can keep track of 'im. Is he in the shaft, Frank?" Rufus asked.

"He ain't here," Frank said nervously and he turned to go back into the tunnel.

"Say, could I take a look," the marshal said. "I haven't seen the tunnel for a couple years."

Frank looked over to Rufus as if waiting for instructions.

"Hell, yes, you can look," Rufus said, "you're not carting off any gold." Rufus laughed and the marshal forced himself to laugh with him. Chester smiled his usual poker-hand smile.

With the empty wheelbarrow Frank entered the tunnel and the marshal followed. Chester stayed where he stood and kept a nonchalant eye on Rufus. Chester knew Rufus well and he wouldn't let his guard slip an inch. He figured he could beat Rufus if Rufus went for the .44 pistol in his belt because he could free his Colt from his holster a second or two quicker. Chester believed Rufus needed killing and he'd gladly be the one to do it. He knew in his heart that Rufus was the one who raped Ellie Jorgenson over a year ago and got away with it. This was Chester's chance to even the score. He hoped Rufus would try it.

Daniel found himself crawling slowly toward the mine and holding his breath. He could see the mules and horses, half asleep in the sunshine, but he couldn't see the marshal or Chester Lyme. What were they doing? He thought how close they had come to dying. He and Gabrielle would have died together and no one would ever have known of their love. He couldn't help but wonder if they'd brought all this down on the family. How everything would have been so different if they hadn't loved each other, if they'd been strong enough to give each other up. Daniel crawled inches closer, praying he'd have his chance at Ben Weebow.

The marshal followed Frank into the dark tunnel. One lantern hung partway in but Tom couldn't see much of the side wall. He felt his way with one hand along the cool wet rock and at times his hand would make out small hollows off the main tunnel. He kept stumbling in the dark. He could hear Frank ahead and then the wheelbarrow stopped squeaking. The lawman could see another lantern ahead and he came into a wide cavern-like room. A pile of loose rock sat to one side and in the middle an open shaft dropped straight down. The marshal leaned over and looked. Pitch black, he couldn't see the bottom.

"How far down does she go?" Tom asked.

"Forty-two feet," Frank said as he quickly loaded the wheelbarrow.

"Is Ben back in here somewhere?" the marshal asked.

Frank didn't answer. He tossed one more rock in the wheelbarrow and rolled it away.

With only one lantern lit, and with his pistol drawn, the marshal searched quickly. Another narrower unlit tunnel angled off to the left and he could hear water dripping.

"Anyone down there?" he asked.

He picked up a heavy rock and dropped it down the shaft. It took a four count to hit bottom. After one more quick glance around he holstered his gun and hurried outside to join Chester. Frank dumped his load and went back into the mine.

"You spot anyone?" Chester whispered.

"No, how about you?"

"Just Rufus, he's in the big tent. I didn't think I could tell him to stay in sight. He'd know we're onto 'em. And where is Tanner? That murdering bastard is here somewhere."

"I'm sure Ben is here too," the marshal said, "I can feel him."

"And don't forget that weasel Camp. He's here somewhere. Should we call 'em out?" Chester asked, "or nab Rufus and Frank one at a time?"

"No. Let's hold off a bit. If Ben and Tanner are here they know this ain't no social call."

The marshal turned and gazed at the imposing granite wall and the mine entrance they had carved out of it. He was impressed with what the Weebows had accomplished and he lost concentration for a moment.

Then, a blink of the eye in the shadowed tunnel!

In a split second, Chester, on the right, dove for the rock pile as the marshal, on the left, dove for the wood stack. The rifle shots blazed from the mine in a deadly concentration. From behind the quartz pile Chester was able to put four quick shots into the big tent as he pulled himself into a crouch. The marshal, still exposed to fire from the tunnel, crawled slowly behind the stacked wood. He'd been hit.

"Tom! You all right?" Chester shouted.

"That sonbitch put one in my leg . . . stomach . . ."

The marshal made it to the cover of the firewood and collapsed. Chester peeked over the rock pile at the mine entrance. He could see no one, but in the chaos of that lightning-quick fight he sensed that someone darted from the mine.

"Hold on, Tom," Chester shouted. "I'll be right there."

When Billy heard the gunfire he stood up from behind the rocks where he'd been waiting, catching Frank scrambling down the talus slope. When Frank saw Billy with gun in hand Frank threw his rifle down and wet his pants.

"Don't shoo . . . shoo . . . shoot. I didn't light . . . light no fires!"

"You lying skunk, get your ass over to them mules."

Billy marched him to the mules and with a lariat tied him to a lodgepole as snugly as a biting pine beetle.

"If you make a sound I'll come back and castrate you."

Billy crouched as he crept cautiously toward the mine yard, wondering where the other men were and who did the shooting.

When the first shot roared out of the tunnel like a cannon, Zack was downhill from Rufus when Rufus came over the side, his pistol in hand. Zack had found a narrow trail that led to their latrine, two logs laid above a pit where a man could sit. There were lodgepole pines scattered across the mine's talus slope that looked like they were caught in a slow-motion avalanche. Zack ducked behind one of the trees and watched as Rufus headed down the latrine path. It didn't appear as though he was fleeing but rather looking for a better spot to join the fight.

With his pistol in hand he kept looking up to the edge of the plateau. When Rufus was twenty feet away, Zack stepped out from behind the pine with his rifle held waist high. For a moment Rufus didn't see Zack as other shots echoed from the mine yard. When he saw Zack he froze, stupefied. His jaw dropped, his eyes widened. His pistol was in his hand at his side.

"Please do something foolish, you pus-sucking maggot," Zack said evenly. "Oh, please try it."

"How the hell—" Rufus said as he dropped his revolver. It fell clackety-clack down the mountain, bouncing off rocks like Rufus's last hope.

"How the hell did we get away? Is that what your deranged and perverted brain would like to know?" Zack taunted. "It was one of those old men Ben was talking about that cut us free. I think Ben called him a drunken Indian."

"What are you talkin' about?"

Zack kept the rifle leveled at Rufus.

"I'm here to honor my father."

"Honest ta God, I didn't have nothin' to do with your father's . . . accident, that was all Tanner."

"I'm here to honor my father by keeping my promise to you."

"To me?"

"Yeah, to you. Father taught me to always keep my word no matter who I had given it."

Zack moved several steps closer and Rufus slowly held a hand up chest high open toward Zack as if it would stop a bullet.

"You do remember my promise don't you?" Zack asked.

"I don't know what you're talkin' about, Rockhammer, but you can't just shoot me down. Marshal Taylor and Lyme is up there. They have to take me into jail."

Rufus's eyes darted, the eyes of a cornered weasel.

"I told you you'd better kill me because if you didn't I'd find you and tear your heart out. Remember? You said you had that covered."

"C'mon, Zack, I didn't want to hurt your family, Christ, I've known you all my life, we went to school together, Tanner made us do it, honest to God."

"That's where you're goin', Rufus, honest to God."

Zack stepped back a few feet where the ground was somewhat level and he laid the rifle down.

"What are you doin'?" Rufus asked, with a puzzled expression on his face.

"Just you and me," Zack said. "You were always older than me and bigger than me and since this is our last fight I want it to be fair."

Cautiously they stepped close enough to touch, dueling with their fists like puppeteers. Then Rufus stepped back and with cunning quickness, pulled a knife. Zack, quick as Daniel, kicked him in the crotch, a crushing blow with his heavy leather boot. Rufus went down as if he'd been shot, howling like a ruptured dog. The knife fell harmlessly between the rocks and Zack stepped back a few feet and waited.

"You like to ambush old men and rape helpless women, huh? I'll make you two more promises," Zack said. "Number one: you aren't ever going to do that again. Number two: you're not going to jail."

Zack knew they'd need him at the mine, so he didn't have much time. He pulled his leather gloves tight while Rufus, who outweighed him by thirty pounds, got his bearings and stood. Rufus came at him swinging wildly and Zack managed to block the first barrage.

"This is for Jeremiah!" Zack shouted as he caught Rufus with a solid fist to the nose.

"This is for Claire!" he shouted and nailed Rufus again with a shot to the jaw. Rufus managed to land a right cross swinging wildly. They struggled like wild animals, grunting and panting. Zack gathered himself and cleared his head. He broke his grip and pushed Rufus back, leaving just enough space between them for his wicked right-handed uppercut. Rufus staggered and stumbled, knock-kneed, trying to find his balance.

Zack went a little crazy then, punching with both hands, dealing a frenzy of punishment from the left and right. Rufus went down, propped in a sitting position in the talus, but Zack kept punching, again and again until he could no longer throw a punch. When Zack was finally exhausted, Rufus was all but dead. Zack doubled over with his hands on his knees, struggling to catch his breath, hardly able to stand. Then, when he had gathered himself, he hoisted Rufus over his shoulder and carried him to the latrine. He paused for a minute.

"Rufus Weebow, you're a vile and putrid stain on the face of the human race that needs to be cut out. Go to hell!"

He heaved him into the pit and Rufus landed in the shit. Zack didn't know it yet that his right hand was broken but he did know that Rufus Weebow was dead.

# FORTY

DANIEL HEARD THE FIRST SHOTS and came quickly up through the trees near the trail. Four more shots told him the fight was on. He could see the marshal prone behind the woodpile and Chester was working on the marshal's leg. Daniel circled to where he could get to the two without being in the line of fire. He crouched into the lee of the chopped wood and saw that Chester had the marshal's belt snugged tightly around his thigh and his pants were smeared with blood.

"Who shot Tom?" Daniel asked.

"I don't know, the shots came from the mine." Chester said.

"They hit you more than once?" Daniel asked the marshal.

"Yeah, they took a little skin off my belly but I had some to spare there." The marshal laughed quietly while wincing with pain.

Daniel could see Tom's blood-soaked vest and pasty pale face and he figured they better get this done quickly and get Tom down the mountain.

Billy came into the clearing on the right and knelt behind the pile of quartz.

"I got Frank!" Billy told them. "Hog tied him to a tree."

"Good work, young man," the marshal congratulated Billy.

Zack scrambled up the slope on the left and settled beside the three.

"Did they hit you bad, Tom?" Zack asked, assessing the marshal's wounds.

"No, I'll live. You seen any of them?"

"Yeah," Zack said. "Rufus. He's in the latrine where I tossed him, don't have to worry about him."

"Did you kill him?" Daniel asked.

"I suspect I did," Zack said, "he couldn't breathe too good. He landed head first."

The three men regarded Zack with an expression just shy of laughter.

Billy shook his head. "I wish I coulda seen it."

"After the shootin' started did you see anyone headin' down the mountain?" Chester asked Zack.

"No, just Rufus," Zack said. "Did you see anyone leaving?"

"I don't know, I'm not sure," Chester said "but that most likely leaves three ah them up here."

Chester cupped his hands to his mouth and shouted.

"We know you're in there, Ben, Tanner, there's no way out! Come out and you'll get a fair trial."

They all paused and listened. There was no response from the mine.

"All right," Chester said. "Load up."

All of them checked their weapons and made sure they were fully loaded.

"Let's concentrate our fire at the tunnel entrance," the marshal said. "We might get lucky with a ricochet."

Chester nodded and all of them, including Billy, opened fire on the tunnel. Even the marshal had moved to a position where he could contribute his firepower and for several minutes the sounds of war had come to the serenity of the mountain. When their guns were empty and the gun barrels hot, the mask of tranquility returned as though nothing had happened. Chirping birds, a light wind, and a fair-weather sky.

Daniel realized the Weebow gang could hold out in the mine for days and they had to get the marshal to a doctor before he bled to death.

"Has anyone looked in the tents?" Daniel asked.

"No," Chester said.

"Hold on a minute," Daniel said.

He scrambled around behind the woodpile and slipped into the large tent. He came out quickly.

"Any guns?" Chester called.

"Just bunks, stove, food!" Daniel shouted.

He ducked into the small tent. A minute went by, two, then Daniel emerged.

"Any weapons or ammunition?" Chester called.

"No, but there's a box of dynamite!" Daniel answered. "that ought to drive the polecats out of their den."

"You know how to use that stuff?" Chester asked.

"Yeah, I do," Daniel said.

"He worked in the mines in Butte," Zack said.

"Give me a minute," Daniel said.

With three sticks of dynamite he slipped around the mine yard to the high outcrop wall. With his back flat against the granite he slid over to the edge of the tunnel. He waved an arm at the men watching from the far side of the plateau, warning them to take cover, and with two sticks in his belt, he scratched a match on his belt buckle and lit the fuse. He stepped quickly out in front of the tunnel and threw it underhanded far into the silent shadows. Then he dashed to the edge of the mine yard and ducked over the side.

The mine and the woods stood soundless. The earth stopped turning, the world held its breath. The men flattened themselves against the rock floor. Then the air sucked in like it was about to sneeze and the tunnel exploded!

Like a gigantic cannon the mine hurled a thunderous volley of gravel and smoke and dust with a concussion that shook the ground. The men felt the pellets hitting their hats and backs like hail but the cannon only hurled a few large rocks.

The men watched as the smoke and dust settled and they could see the entrance again.

Chester cupped his hands to his mouth and shouted.

"Ben! Tanner! Camp! There's no way out! Come out now or we'll blow you to smithereens. You kinda forgot about your dynamite."

As they reloaded they saw someone coming out of the tunnel.

"Don't shoot! Don't shoot!" Roscoe Camp called, limping with his hands in the air. He had no weapon visible.

"Keep comin', slow, slow," Chester called.

When Roscoe made it to the woodpile they pulled him down.

"Keep an eye on the tunnel," Chester said.

"Where's Ben?" Daniel asked Camp.

"What?"

"Where's Tanner and Ben?" Chester asked again.

"What, I can't hear you," Camp said.

"He's plum deaf, the dynamite," Daniel said and he stuck his mouth on Roscoe's ear. "Where's Ben?"

"He's in the mine," Camp said. "I didn't light no fire, it was Ben, he done it."

"What's Ben doin'?" Chester shouted, up to Roscoe's ear.

"He's back by the air hole but he can't get out through it."

"Does he have a gun?" Daniel shouted.

"Yeah, his rifle, but he's out of ammunition," Camp said.

"You sure about that?" Chester shouted.

"Yeah, he's out."

Daniel locked eyes with Chester.

"Can we trust him?" Chester asked.

"Only one way to find out," Daniel said. He pulled out his knife and held it against Roscoe Camp's throat. "If Ben fires one bullet, cut his throat."

Daniel shouted it so Roscoe could hear.

"He's empty, I swear," Camp said.

"They're not only liars, but they're chicken-shit too," Zack said. "He'd rat on his mother, he's telling the truth."

"You cover the tunnel," Daniel said to all of them, "I'm going to flush him out."

Daniel handed the knife to Zack. "Hold this on him."

Daniel reloaded his revolver, left the two sticks of dynamite with the men, and scrambled over to the large tent where he fetched a fresh lantern. Then he stayed far to the left of the tunnel until he was at its edge. He paused, caught his breath. After a moment he scratched a match off his belt buckle and lit the lantern. When he drew his Colt from its holster he turned and nodded at the other men who watched with nervous trigger fingers at the far side of the clearing. Then Daniel headed into the mine.

He moved cautiously, one hand holding his pistol, the other holding the lantern head high. He hadn't gone far before he felt his mouth go dry and his breathing quicken, the old terror gripping him. He tried to calm himself. The dynamite had left a scattering of loose rock on the tunnel floor causing him to stumble at times. The thought of tons of rock above him that could trap him like a rat, the tons of rock that could bury him in a tomb put a tremor in his hands and the lantern's light bounced along the wall. The tunnel seemed to be closing in on him and he felt paralyzed. He fought his childhood terror and inched his way deeper into the mine.

*There's plenty of light, it'll be all right.*

The interior was irregular and crude with crevices and hollows along the sides that appeared to be small tunnels flaring off in other directions. A cold sweat broke out on his forehead and he remembered the last time he came out of the mine in Butte, swearing he'd never step in a mine again. He paused. Far ahead he could see another light. He spooked several times, thinking Ben was lunging out at him from the shadows.

"Come on out, Ben, you're all alone now, there's no way out!"

His voice echoed slightly down the tunnel. Moving slowly, he never thought to look above. In an instant a large boulder of granite dropped from a ledge. It had given a slight warning before Ben could push it free. Daniel didn't have time to think. On the way to the floor he could only hold onto one, the pistol or the light. His instincts decided for him, he dropped the weapon. The boulder missed its mark by inches while Daniel rolled away and scrambled to his feet. Ben dropped on him like thunder, as if the tunnel had caved in, slamming Daniel's head against the rock wall and knocking the lantern out of his hand. It shattered on the rock floor and burned brightly as the oil spread. In the shadows, Daniel couldn't spot his revolver and he had no time to search. The two of them faced off in a boxer's stance, waiting for the first one to join the battle. Daniel felt strangled by the age-old panic that choked him. Ben was bigger than Daniel, meaner, and Daniel tried to concentrate on the immediate danger.

"I'm goin' ta kill you, Rockhammer, the way we killed your father."

"You're not dealing with an old man now, you cowardly son-of-a-bitch. You're dealing with me."

Daniel crowded Ben further into the mine. The lantern fire was burning itself out on the floor, the tunnel growing darker quickly.

"I was dealing with you when I killed your dog." He laughed.

"I knew you killed her. I should have drowned you in the school well."

"Yeah, and after I kill you I'm outta here free. Tanner has work for me in Colorado."

Out of the dark Ben lunged, swinging wildly. Daniel danced back and avoided the attack but the tunnel was nearly pitch black and he felt his throat and chest constricting, he could hardly breathe. He could see a flickering light far down the tunnel but his fear of the darkness outweighed his fear of Ben.

*So dark, so dark, I can't get out, I'll never get out.*

Daniel forced himself to press toward Ben and the distant lantern. At times he couldn't see Ben at all. It was as if Daniel was desperately fighting his way to the light, not fighting Ben, just that Ben was blocking his way. Step by step Daniel pushed and they exchanged glancing blows that did little harm. To fight off the terror he thought of Gabrielle and he reminded himself that Ben tried to kill her, was trying still, and Gabrielle's face shined through, diminishing the terror and fear of being underground. Catching his breath, he turned his full attention to fighting Ben.

"The only way you're getting out of here, you murdering bastard, is in the belly of a vulture. You killed my father! You killed my father!" Daniel finally went berserk, wildly swinging his fists in front of him and hoping to unnerve Ben.

Daniel kept crowding him, forcing him back toward the light. He could see Ben only in silhouette and the darkness made it hard to judge how close Ben was. Daniel could hear Kincaid's voice urging him on as he had in the Butte mine.

*Don't drop them so fast. It's easy money!*

Daniel trembled, still finding it hard to breathe with the tons of granite hanging over his head. All at once, welling up within him, he found the anger and rage and the promise that he would hold Ben Weebow accountable. Finally, just as Daniel hoped, Ben came with a haymaker. Daniel blocked it and stepped in close with the old one two. The Ranski!

The blows knocked Ben to his knees, but he was a powerful man, still in the fight. As Ben found his footing on wobbly legs and loose gravel, Daniel jammed his head into Ben's chest and drove him backward, backpedaling along the tunnel toward the light until Ben suddenly disappeared. Daniel froze, tipped, and caught himself just short of the shaft. With an animal cry, Ben Weebow fell into the darkness. It took three or four counts for Ben to hit bottom. It sounded like a ripe pumpkin.

For a moment, they were at the schoolyard and Ben was in the well again. And this time no one was going to fish him out and give him dry clothes.

# FORTY-ONE

AT THE DOCTOR'S HOUSE Gabrielle cared for Grace the best she could but her heart was up on the mountain with Daniel and the men. She couldn't help but shudder at the thought of all of them burning to their death, and the two of them, damned after all to the fire.

"Gabrielle! Gabrielle!" scrawny old Obediah Rice shouted as he came puffing up to the doctor's porch.

Gabrielle came out quickly, hoping it was word that the doctor had returned or the posse.

"Yes, Obediah, what is it? what is it?"

The lanky man had trouble catching his breath.

"The mi . . . mining man, the one wh . . . who was with the Weebows."

Obediah sucked air and held on to the porch railing.

"What? What about him?" Gabrielle shouted.

"Down at the livery, gettin' a big fast horse!"

"Does he know about the fire, that the Rockhammers are alive?"

"Don't know, but he's in a hurry."

Gabrielle called to the doctor's wife to watch Grace, and she grabbed her Winchester. She sprinted down the road, past the blacksmith and barber shop, and turned at the corner past the Silver Dollar Saloon. She cut between buildings and came out on Main Street in front of Black's Dry Goods & Feed and Clark's Hardware. She spooked two tied horses as she dashed past Victoria's Bar and Restaurant and she could see the livery stable ahead. Was she too late?

With more than a block to go she spotted Tanner, mounted, and heading east out of town. She didn't have time to saddle and ride, there were no good horses within easy reach and Tanner was getting away. She raced across the road to the lumberyard and climbed onto an open stack of rough cut four-by-fours. She stepped up them like stairs and reached a wood wall about shoulder high. She had the elevation she needed and she could still see Tanner, bouncing rhythmically at a fast trot, growing smaller by the second.

She pumped a shell into the breach and steadied the rifle barrel on the fence. There were only a few townsfolk on the road: two men on horseback coming, a lady in a buggy going, a woman off the road walking a milk cow, three boys with willow fishing poles climbing a fence. Tanner passed a man in a wagon, leaving a clear opening. Gabrielle's heart pounded and her lungs heaved as she tried to steady the Winchester. Tanner was almost to the dip in the road where, from her point of view, he would drop out of sight and be gone, free, into the unending mountain wilderness. She'd have one shot.

She took a deep breath, let it out slowly, and lined up the shot. She refused to acknowledge that it was hopelessly long. She slid her finger on the trigger. Tanner rose and fell with the rhythm of the horse, up and down, up and down. She took a small breath, held it, squeezed. The Winchester barked and slammed against her shoulder. She had released the bullet on its ordained journey.

The .30 caliber lead bullet, launched by an explosion of .55 grains of 207 Powers gunpowder, was on its way through the sunlit blue-bonnet air, on its destined passage to stop the murderous attempt to wipe the Rockhammers from this splendid land. It flew like light into darkness, a bullet cast for judgment day, a bullet tapered and polished to run honest and true, a bullet to bring about a reckoning, to turn back treachery and bring justice and peace to the land, a bullet sent for Jeremiah and Grace and all those who had been crippled and damaged and destroyed by the bearers of evil.

They say that the few who saw the shot thought it was impossible. To that they all agreed. A moving target at that distance on a bright windy day. They heard the report of the rifle and looked up. Some heard and saw the shot from the lumberyard. Tanner sat on the horse as it moved with a smooth gait, up and down, up and down, and then the wrath of God crashed into his brain stem and he flopped onto the road like a sack of oats and never moved.

Gabrielle walked from the lumberyard to the body that now had a handful of townsfolk gaping at it. The hand holding the rifle trembled and her throat clogged with emotion. When she arrived Tanner was lying on his back looking up at the sky. He'd never heard the shot. She glanced at the small group who seemed dumbstruck. Several were familiar faces.

"This man is wanted by Marshal Taylor for murder," Gabrielle said, her voice clogged with emotion. "The marshal is out hunting down his bunch right now."

Fear and sorrow and shock swirled within her and threatened to break out in tears. She steeled herself and reminded herself how Tanner stood there coolly in their home while Rufus raped Claire and the men tied them up to burn. She looked down at Tanner.

"Just another skunk." She jabbed his shoulder with her boot. "Just another stinking skunk."

She turned and walked back toward town. She shivered and suddenly felt cold and tired. She hoped the men had returned, desperate to see Daniel and know what had happened at the Weebow mine. As she walked through town reports of what happened preceded her.

Three different men paced the shot, from the lumberyard to the body. Their consensus put it at four hundred and thirty-one feet.

When Gabrielle got back to Aunt Grace, in bed in the doctor's house, Grace struggled to breathe and came in and out of consciousness. She'd been in the smoke too long. The doctor's wife had done what she could but she didn't know where her husband was or when he'd be back. Gabrielle sat beside the bed and wiped Grace's face with a damp cloth but her coughing grew worse and at times it seemed as if she'd choke to death. Then, in the afternoon, Grace rallied.

"My purse, dear," Grace said, motioning to the bed table.

Gabrielle handed her the leather purse she had rescued from the blaze and wondered what could be so valuable that Grace would risk her life to save it. Propped up in the bed Grace turned her head toward Gabrielle. She labored to breathe.

"Give me your hand, dear," Grace said.

Gabrielle reached over and Grace took her hand.

"I haven't got long and I don't want to go without telling you the truth," Grace said. "To finally tell you the truth."

"Please don't tire yourself, you're going to be—"

"Hush, dear, and listen, please listen."

Grace gagged and coughed up a sinister mass of yellow phlegm into a towel.

"When I was very young I got pregnant with a nice young man. I was terrified, I really don't know how it happened, a crazy moment of romance, one encounter, but I just couldn't have a baby, an illegitimate child. I had plans, I knew who I wanted to marry, someone who was going to make something of himself, a man who would be important and wealthy."

She paused and hacked a deep guttural cough.

"My family struggled when I was growing up. We survived years of poverty. Then my father got in with some men who speculated with land and quickly we were one of the wealthy. Getting pregnant was a foolish, reckless mistake that threatened my dream. I'd picked out the man I wanted, the rich and rising Randall Armstrong from a well-known Montana family."

This was alarming news to Gabrielle. Aunt Grace had had a child out of wedlock. "Uncle Randall was a wonderful man," Gabrielle said. "Even after he became governor, we were always impressed that you'd both come way up here to see mom."

"And you," Grace said.

"What?" Gabrielle asked,

"You. I came to see you."

"Me? What do you mean?"

Grace was clearly struggling but Gabrielle was now glued to every word.

"When I realized I was pregnant I didn't know where to turn. I was suffocating with panic, I saw no way out. Then I turned to your mother, Elizabeth. I wrote her and she answered. The letters took nearly a month. I made up all the excuses and sto-ries necessary at home and traveled to Rockhammer Ranch. No one gave it a second thought since we'd been so close before Elizabeth's marriage and my sweetheart was off in the Army for another year."

Grace coughed and her chest heaved as if it would expel chunks of lung.

"I prayed the rough roads and the bumping, jolting stage-coach would make me miscarry. The ranch became my refuge, my sanctuary. You see, your mother was pregnant too. I stayed on the ranch for nearly five months and we found out we were ex-pecting close to the same time. Turned out to be just thirty-one hours apart."

Grace squeezed Gabrielle's hand.

"Elizabeth isn't your mother, sweetheart, *I am.*"

Gabrielle sat stunned, shocked, as if her ears hadn't just heard what they just heard. Her heart pounded. She sat like she was nailed to the chair, frozen, gasping for air like her Aunt Grace, no . . . like her *mother.*

"I've loved you from the moment I saw you. Old Doc Simpson made out the birth certificate for twin girls. Besides Elizabeth and Jeremiah, who loved you dearly, no one else knew. It broke my heart the day I rode off and left you behind. Randall and I could never have children. That was my excuse for coming to see you children so often. I had to be careful how I held you, how I looked at you. Can you ever forgive me, dear? I traded you in for an adventure-filled life, for my selfish storybook dreams."

Gabrielle pulled her hand back and held her head between both hands. She struggled to find her voice.

"*You* are my mother?" She said it like a five year old.

"Yes, sweetheart, I'm your mother."

Gabrielle held her head in her hands as if she feared it would explode or go flying out the window.

"You're telling me Daniel isn't my brother, my blood brother?"

"That's right."

"And I'm not his sister!"

"Yes, you're not his sister."

"Daniel isn't my brother!" she stood quickly and shouted.

"Oh dear God, I can't believe it! Daniel isn't my brother. I love him, I've always loved him."

"Of course you do, he's—"

"No, no, I don't love him like a brother, I love him like a husband, the love of my life. I've loved him all these years, and he's loved me, and we believed we were damned, that God would punish us for our love, that's why we've lived apart for so long, I've missed him every day of my life."

"Oh, Gabrielle, can you ever forgive me?"

Gabrielle began to laugh. She looked into Grace's eyes.

"Are you glad you didn't raise me or are you sorry?"

Grace paused in thought.

"Yes, yes, in the end I'm glad, I'm so glad. I gave you a marvelous life, watched you grow up and knew you were happy. And marrying Randall was the best thing I ever did, bless his soul."

"Then," Gabrielle said as she bent down and hugged Grace, "I forgive you."

Grace began crying and fought to catch her breath. She pulled a folded paper from her leather purse and handed it to Gabrielle.

"You may need this some day."

Gabrielle unfolded it and looked at her birth certificate, no twins listed, just her name in old Doc Simpson's flowing cursive. It all began to sink in.

*She was not Daniel's sister. She was not Daniel's sister.*

"I knew you'd have a wonderful life on the Rockhammer. I wanted to tell you so many times, when you came to me for help in Bozeman, when you were living in Wyoming so alone, when Jeremiah was killed, but there were always other people who could've been hurt. I tell you now because there's no one left it could hurt. Only Elizabeth knows, and me. And I won't be here much longer."

"Who is my father?"

"He died in an encounter with the Crow. He was in the cavalry, unmarried, no children. So, my dear, it'll be up to you who you tell."

It struck Gabrielle with a lightening bolt of wonder. Only two people now knew the truth. Her and Elizabeth! She had an unquenchable longing to make it three.

Grace slipped off into unconsciousness without another word. Gabrielle sat beside her marinating in wonder and finding it impossible to remain still. Up to the window, out to the porch, back to the bedside, bursting to tell the world, to shout at people going by in the street, feeling she would fly apart with excitement yet knowing there was only one she could tell first. She was a stick of dynamite with its fuse lit, afraid she would burst if she didn't race to Daniel and bring him a new life.

The miracle overwhelmed her like the brilliant golden sun rising in her heart at the dawn of creation. She knew she couldn't leave Grace, not until the doctor returned, but she felt she'd explode with the incredible shining treasure she held in her heart. She would have to keep it and bear it and protect it alone until she found Daniel and they opened the impossible together, finding that the world had suddenly turned upside down.

They say Gabrielle rushed to greet the men when they rode into town and dismounted in front of the jail. When she didn't find Daniel among them her stomach turned to stone and Zack was quick to console her with the word that Daniel headed back to the ranch to be with Elizabeth and anxious to check on the herd and to start putting things back in order. Her feelings swirled like a tempest when she heard the story of the fight and saw Marshall Taylor carried into another room in the doctor's house. The men questioned her excitedly when they heard about Tanner, sure that he had gotten away, and they cheered and applauded her impossible shot that she knew would be stretched into miles by winter.

She wanted her turn at Rufus and felt cheated when she heard she wouldn't get it. She felt relief when she heard about the bully's return to the well, finally. Zack came back to town to let Doc Benson bind up his broken hand, that, now that the fight was over, hurt plenty. Frank Moss and Roscoe Camp were tossed into the jail until a circuit judge could hang them legally.

Doc Benson didn't show up as hoped, probably helping with a hard delivery, and Grace slipped into a deep coma. Gabrielle was torn, knowing she couldn't leave her mother, the mother she'd just discovered, and feeling her heart pounding with her desperate longing to find Daniel and change his world. Mrs. Benson, the doctor's wife, assured Gabrielle that she'd care for Grace, but Gabrielle couldn't force herself to walk away. If only Doc Benson would return he might know of something else to do. Gabrielle measured the time with heartbeats.

At the Rockhammer, Wart hollered at Elizabeth and then quickly ducked into the bunkhouse. Elizabeth, who was raking through the ashes in search of something of value, looked up with surprise. There sat Henry Weebow, on an old mule, stooped in the saddle, gazing at the burnt-out shell. They hadn't seen him coming.

Billy, in a back corral, picked up a rifle. Elizabeth skirted the wreckage and walked out to where Henry stopped on the road. He wore his tell-tale black stovepipe hat, a little tipped and covered with dust. When Elizabeth reached him he wouldn't lift his eyes. She thought he was about to fall off the mule.

"What can I do for you, Henry?" she asked.

"I come to apologize . . . to . . . I'm so sorry." He started crying.

"Are you all right, Henry? That's a long ride."

"I must a done something awful wrong with 'em . . . awful wrong."

"Would you like some water, Henry?"

"I had to come . . . and look you in the eye." He raised his eyes from the ground and looked at her. They were eye to eye for some silent moments. She felt no revenge, only compassion, for this destroyed and lost fellow human being.

"You get down now, Henry, and have a drink and some food."

"Thank you kindly, Elizabeth, Jeremiah and I were neighbors for almost fifty years and I've known you for thirty."

"Please, Henry, get down for a spell."

"Thank you but I have work to do at the mine."

"At the mine . . ."

Henry kicked the mule and headed down the road.

Billy came forward, still with a rifle in his hands.

"You won't need that, Billy," she said. "What could that old man possibly do at the mine?"

\*   \*   \*

The next day they heard the distant thunder on the perfectly cloudless summer day. The mine? Only later did Daniel put it together. Henry Weebow had dragged Rufus's body, what there was left of it after the scavenger birds and animals, to the shaft and pushed it in. He set charges along the wall of the shaft, lit the long fuses, and joined his boys at the bottom where the dynamite caved uncounted tons of granite and gold speckled quartzes down on their heads. Almost a month later Elizabeth was notified that Henry Weebow had deeded his property, several sections, to the Rockhammers for one dollar. The Rockhammer had almost doubled in size.

Grace died quietly before the sunset. After a long sleepless night, Gabrielle waited until first light, saddled her horse, and left town in a gallop. Stunned, she was flying on this whirlwind of emotion that lifted her, carried her like Pegasus, his hooves never touching the ground. She bore something she couldn't comprehend, something overwhelming, something conceived in mystery and joy and miracle, as if in her saddlebags she carried a reprieve from God!

As she approached the gap she could hear the river, roaring on this summer day from the high mountain snow. Under the archway and onto the Rockhammer, she felt like she could explode with this miracle if she didn't share it with Daniel soon. Up the road a mile to the house, or the shell of the house, hooting and calling until Wart appeared amid the wreckage.

"Where's Daniel?" she shouted, slowing her lathered horse and turning him in circles.

"He's over the river in the lower meadow!" Wart yelled. "What's up?"

"I have to find him," she shouted and kicked her horse into a run.

She followed the river, thundering past the high little ridge where Jeremiah and Martha and Abraham slept. The River That Rolls Rocks was living up to its name. Only a few feet higher, you still couldn't cross for fear of the horse breaking a leg or its rider falling into the turmoil. The places where they cross most of the year were useless today. The cottonwood bridge was up another mile or more.

When she scanned the sprawling meadow on the other side, she spotted Daniel on his horse. She cut down close to the river and waved and shouted but Daniel didn't see her. He was riding across the meadow and seldom looked back. She wasn't thinking, just moving. Then she grabbed her rifle, the weapon she took along when they'd headed for town to do battle with the Weebows. She pulled her horse to a stop, pulled the rifle out of its scabbard and fired a shot that startled her horse. She watched Daniel. He kept riding away from her. She pumped in another shell and fired. When the sound reached him Daniel turned and saw her. He waved.

Daniel rode to the river and tried to understand what Gabrielle was shouting but he couldn't hear over the roar of the water. They rode parallel to each other along the shore looking for a place to cross. Gabrielle waved frantically, pointing at him and hugging herself. Then she realized where they were, not far from the swimming hole. It was a deep pool where a bedrock outcrop blocked the river's flow momentarily and the swirling water for centuries had carved this place for kids to play. Gabrielle rode up on the rocky ridge, vaulted off her horse and pulled off her boots. Daniel recognized her intent and pulled up in the willows on the far side. He pulled off his boots and watched Gabrielle stand on the edge of the ridge, hesitate for a moment, and jump, making the whistling call of the red-tail hawk. Daniel charged into the water as Gabrielle came up, shouting. They ran in the water, tripping, falling, Daniel wondering what had happened.

"You're not my brother!" Gabrielle shouted and gasped. "You're not my brother!"

They splashed through the calmer water behind the pool. Gabrielle fell. She got up and tripped and slogged, shouting.

"I'm not your sister! I'm not your sister!"

Daniel hurtled over the water, falling and plowing forward, shouting.

"What are you talking about?"

They grabbed each other like they were drowning and kissed until they were about to suffocate.

"We have to be careful, they'll see us," Daniel said.

"It doesn't matter, let them see us, let the whole world see us."

"What are you saying?" Daniel asked.

"You're not my brother! You're not my brother." She kissed his lips, his face, his forehead.

"That can't be, you were born with Maddy."

"No, no, Aunt Grace is my mother! I'm not your sister!" she shouted breathlessly.

"Oh, God, how can that be? Are you sure? Are you sure?"

"Yes! Yes! I love you and I always knew somewhere deep inside that it was a good thing, a wonderful thing, a sweet beautiful thing."

They held each other as they stumbled onto the shore. They knelt in the grass facing each other, not far from where they first told each other of their secret love. They held the other by the shoulders and looked into each other's eyes.

"After all that time . . . ," Daniel trailed off. "It can't be true."

"Grace died last night but before she did she told me. She had my birth certificate. Old Doc Simpson did that for Elizabeth and Grace. Grace wasn't married."

"Do you know what this means? Do you realize what this means?" Daniel shouted, shaking her gently by the shoulders. "It means that God answered your prayers! All the times you prayed on bloody knees He answered you. All the sleepless nights you pleaded to Him, He answered you. All the days of your life you begged Him to make it right. Now He answered you. All the months and years when you did His work, asking for a miracle, He answered you."

They held each other without speaking, on their knees. They kissed, tenderly, sweetly, holding on, holding on. Daniel looked into her eyes.

"Promise me you'll never leave Rockhammer again," Gabrielle said.

"Promise me you'll never leave *me* again," Daniel said.

"I promise you!"

"I promise you!"

"I promise you!"

"I promise you!"

They laughed. Then Gabrielle frowned.

"Do you know what else this means?" Gabrielle almost whispered.

"What?" Daniel asked.

"It means that nothing is impossible for God!"

They sat back on their heels, overcome with joy.

"When these mountains have been leveled, our love will still be," Gabrielle said. "When the last star falls from the sky, our love will still be."

Their love echoed across the valley and out over the mountains, like a Blackfeet chant, two people who had faced the windstorms of the heart and won.